CRUEL KING

K.M. SCOTT

CRUEL KING

Ava

The King boys have been the center of my life for as long as I remember. Theo has been my best friend since I was four, and our families are as close as can be.

Except Matthias. The oldest King son never failed to look miserable whenever I was around, and every word out of his mouth to me was cruel.

Until a snowstorm trapped us in his house, and we shared two perfect days together.

That was five years ago. Now his father's dying, and he's back at the estate and more vicious than ever, as if our time together meant nothing to him.

I should hate him. I should be able to forget him now that I have a chance to be happy with someone else.

There's just one problem. I can't stop thinking about the man who stole my heart one snowy night all those years ago.

Matthias

She thinks I don't remember our time together. She's wrong. I've never forgotten.

Not when I moved to a different continent. Not when I didn't hear from her for five years. Not even though I've tried my damnedest to forget her.

I want to hate her. I should. But I can't. All I can do is look on with jealousy as Ava finds happiness with another man.

What do you do when the one person standing in the way of your happiness is your own brother?

2023 Copper Key Media, LLC

Copyright © 2023 Copper Key Media LLC

ISBN: 978-1-955335-52-2

Published in the United States

AUTHOR'S NOTE

If you read Frozen Heart in the Falling For The Enemy
Charity Anthology, please note that much has been
added to that here in Cruel King. I kept my word count
down for the anthology so I didn't monopolize too much
of the space out of respect for my fellow authors in that
project. As a result, I had to edit out some of the story.
All that was cut has been returned in this book.

CRUEL KING PLAYLIST

Until I Found You (Piano Version)-Stephen Sanchez
Somewhere Only We Know-Keane
I'm Not The Only One-Sam Smith
Against All Odds-Phil Collins
My Mistake (Was To Love You)-Diana Ross &
Marvin Gaye
Maybe I'm A Fool-Eddie Money
At Last-Etta James
Without You-Harry Nilsson

CHAPTER ONE

va

NEARLY OUT OF BREATH, I STOP BEHIND A TREE AS Theo yells from across the lawn, "I know you're here somewhere, little Ava. Come out, come out, wherever you are!"

He still calls me that nickname his older brother gave me when I was no more than five years old, even though I'm nineteen now. I think he uses it to poke fun at him, although he's rarely around to hear him say it these days.

"It's cold out here," Theo complains as he gets closer to where I hide. "Just give up so we can go inside already."

I silently answer his plea. Never! I'll never give up. We've been playing this game all our lives, the two of us on the lawn of the King estate, his family's home and my

1

father's employer's property, no matter the season or the weather. It's our own private version of hide and go seek.

Theo's been my best friend for so long I can't remember a time when he and I weren't running around on this grass. When he came to the house for me this morning, I didn't hesitate to join him, even though it's freezing cold out today like it has been every day of this week since Christmas. It didn't matter, though. He called, and I said yes to our little game.

"Ava, I'm serious," he says as he keeps moving toward the tree concealing me. "All you have to do is give up and I'll win. Then we can go inside and get something hot in us."

Coming from any other guy my age, that would sound sexy or perverted, but not from Theo. He simply hates winter and wants to go into the house, but he's too competitive to let me win. I've always joked that he must have been stolen by the Kings from some other family who lived in someplace warm because he hates the cold more than anyone I've ever known.

I stay silent, knowing he'll find me soon. Closing my eyes, I listen to the wind blowing across the grounds, happy to be shielded by this enormous maple tree's trunk. The air smells crisp, like right before a snowstorm shows up. It freezes the inside of my nose when I take a deep breath in, but unlike Theo, I love this weather.

Sensing something behind me, I open my eyes and turn around to see him smiling at me. He grabs me and pulls me to him in a bear hug. "Gotcha!"

My cheek brushes against his black ski jacket as he holds me tightly to him and brags about his win. "That makes nearly two hundred this year to your measly fifty or so."

I push him away, shaking my head at his incorrect calculations. "No way. I caught you at least one hundred times this year, so forget that fifty nonsense."

He smiles in that way that reminds me of a pirate. "I think you're crazy. We didn't even play for two months this summer when I was away. That makes your claim of a hundred virtually impossible, Ava."

"Oh, the two months when you were lounging on the beach looking for the future Mrs. Theo King?" I tease, rolling my eyes as I remember him telling me about all the girls he met when he was away on vacation this past summer.

Theo pushes his fingertips against my shoulder and laughs. "No way. You're the future Mrs. Theo King, so those girls meant nothing."

Since I was eight and he was ten, he's claimed that we're going to get married when we're older and live here on the King estate in the big house together. I've never believed that for a second. I don't think he actually believes it either.

"Have you been taking charm lessons from that brother of yours? Don't you know it's not nice to mention other women to your future wife?" I joke before I set off running toward my house.

Behind me, he calls out, "You're going the wrong way. Come up to the house, and we'll warm up!"

I look back and shake my head. "Not today. Until next time, that's at least one hundred wins for me!"

He smiles and rolls his eyes. "Little Ava doesn't know

how to count. Come up when you're finished at your house. I'll have Eleanor make you her world-famous hot cocoa."

As much as the thought of that sounds great, I can't join him at the big house. My father warned me the weather might get nasty this morning, so he doesn't want me too far from home. The main house on the King estate is nearly half a mile away from our house, and knowing my father, he'd definitely think that was too far today.

I slow down to a walk and look back to make sure Theo isn't going to sneak up on me. That would be typical of him. He's such a joker. I see he's nowhere to be found, so I turn back around to head home.

My father's been nothing short of overprotective since my mother died last year. She was fine for the holidays, but then in January, something changed. She started to feel worn down, but she assumed she had the flu and figured all she had to do was rest for a few days. Those few days turned into weeks, and when she finally went to the doctor to figure out what the problem could be, it was too late. Leukemia. I never knew anything about it before that day, and then two weeks later, she was gone, and that word filled my mind day and night.

It was worse for my father, though. My brother and I lost a mother, but he lost the love of his life. Ever since then, he's been different. He worries about me twenty-four hours a day. When I wanted to go away to school, he begged me to wait a year. I think he worries if I go away he may never see me again.

Well, except to my Aunt Jessie's. That's the only

place in the world away from this estate that he seems to be okay with me visiting for more than a day or so. Maybe it's because she's my mother's sister. Or maybe it's because she lives in New Hampshire away from anything and everything that could possibly hurt me.

Other than wild animals since her house is in the middle of nowhere.

By the time I get back to our house, he's waiting for me at the front door, staring out through the glass with a look of pure worry in his eyes. As I step inside, he says, "It's freezing cold out there. Why were you out so long?"

Sliding my coat off my shoulders, I shake my head at his nervous hen routine. "Because Theo wanted to play the game. I wasn't gone that long, Dad. It's not bad out."

"It's freezing," he says as he closes the front door and follows me into the living room.

My brother Andrew sits playing some game on his PlayStation like always. Twenty-years-old and he spends more time sitting on the couch with those stupid games than he does with his girlfriend. Today it's the same one he's been trying to master since Christmas morning, a downhill skiing game.

"Still wiping out on the slopes, Drew?" I ask as he leans left and then right before angrily tossing the controller onto the table in front of him as his character careens over the side of a snowy cliff.

He groans in frustration before sitting back against the couch. "I'll get it. It's just going to take a little time. I'll try again when I get back from Tanya's."

When he stands to walk out, I say to both him and my father, "It smells like snow out there. I think we're going to get a storm today. About time since it feels weird having Christmas break with grass and no snow."

"Did you hear that on the news?" my brother asks with a sneer. "Weathermen always say it's going to be the storm of the century, and then we get a couple inches, if we're lucky."

I shrug and look at my father, expecting him to say something to my brother as he grabs his coat off the rack near the stairs and gets ready to leave. "I don't know if it's going to be the storm of the century, but I bet we get some today or tomorrow."

My father watches without offering a word of warning to my brother as he gets his keys off the table near the door and waves goodbye. "I'll be at Tanya's. I'll probably grab dinner there too."

"Have a good time!" my father happily says before turning back to look at me. "Are you staying in today? You should if it's going to be snowy out."

My mouth drops open, less in shock than frustration at how differently he treats me compared to my brother. "So I need to stay in, but Andrew can just go driving around the countryside with snow coming?"

Without a hint of guilt or irony, he says as he turns to walk upstairs, "Your brother is different."

What he means is he's not me and he's not a female. I could tilt at that windmill and argue with my father that his sexism is completely unfair to me, but the last time I did, he looked like I was breaking his heart.

"I'm driving Mr. King to the city today. I need to get ready since we're leaving in twenty minutes."

As he hits the first stair, I say, "Cutting it a little close, don't you think?"

My father lowers his head so he can see me as I sit on the couch. Laughing, he answers, "It's not like there's much to do, honey. I'm a man. We're ready as soon as we dress in the morning. All I have to do is put on my coat and make sure I have my gloves."

"Don't forget your hat. It's cold out there, Dad," I say, mildly mocking him and his overprotectiveness.

But he doesn't pick up on my sarcasm and simply nods. "Yes, yes. That's right. It is cold, so I'll need my warm woolen hat for the trip today."

So much for being understood by your own family.

Ten minutes later, my father walks into the living room wearing his best gray wool coat and the dark gray wool hat my mother bought him right before she got sick. He rarely wears it, oddly enough. Maybe it's too hard to see it and not think of her. Or maybe he thinks if he never wears it that he doesn't have to accept she's actually gone.

"You look very handsome, Dad. You and Mr. King are going to make quite the couple of studs walking around Manhattan today," I tease.

My father strikes a model pose and runs his hand through his thinning brown hair.. "Thank you. Now promise me you'll stay home in case the weather gets bad."

Screwing my face into an expression of disbelief, I say, "No have a good time, Ava? That's what Andrew got."

"Your brother is your brother, and you are you. Completely different situations."

I have nothing to say to that. I guess I could point out how wrong it is that he treats me like this, but ever since my mother died, I've had a difficult time not being the daughter I know he needs me to be. So I take the inequality between my brother and me, accepting it so my father doesn't have to worry.

"No problem, Dad. I have no plans to go anywhere today. All my friends are off on skiing vacations."

He frowns and quickly says, "You know, I told you that you could go with them. I'm not a complete ogre."

I nod, knowing he did offer to pay for the trip if I wanted to go. "It's okay. I'm just not into skiing like everyone else who was going. I'm fine here. Maybe I'll play Drew's downhill game and see if I can do better than he did."

That makes my father chuckle. "Just don't tell him. He'll be crushed that the first time you touched that controller you mastered the game."

Always worried about everyone. That's my father.

"I won't. If I conquer the imaginary PlayStation mountain, I'll keep my win to myself."

He looks around the room for a moment, so I say, "Check your pockets. Your gloves are probably in them."

Shaking his head, my father says, "No, I have my gloves. I was just looking for the thank you note for Mr. King for that beautiful necklace he gave you for Christmas."

I point toward the fireplace mantel. "Right there on the end. Please tell him I love it."

He turns to take the card and smiles back at me as he walks toward the front door. "I will. You know he thinks of you like the daughter he never had, so he likes to buy you something special for Christmas."

With a nod, I smile and follow him. "I know, Dad. Mr. King is a very nice man to all of us."

My father turns around right before he opens the door and hugs me to him. "Remember to stay inside, especially if it starts snowing," he quietly says in my ear.

I lean back and shake my head. "I will, but you know, Dad, I'm not made of sugar. I won't melt if I get wet."

That gets me an eye roll before he kisses me goodbye. "I swear you'll understand when you have kids someday. I used to tell your mother you had enough sass to light up the whole island of Manhattan."

His mention of my mother for the first time today makes me smile. "And she used to tell you that you had the sweetest daughter in the world."

That makes him stop as he reaches to open the door, and when he turns back toward me, he cradles my cheeks in his rough hands. "You remind me of her, you know that?"

I cover his hands with mine and sigh. "I know. That's a good thing. Sweet and sassy, just like my mother."

He smiles, but in his eyes I see the hint of tears beginning to form. "Sweet and sassy," he repeats in a faraway voice.

"Have a good time, Dad."

Nodding, he sighs and releases my face from his gentle hold. "It's work, so I'm not sure anyone will be having a good time. I'll see you tonight, honey."

I watch him walk out the door and down the stairs toward the road that connects our house with the main house on the King estate. The sky is that milky white color it always turns right before it begins to snow and the wind has stopped, making the estate look calm and peaceful, like a scene from an old-fashioned Christmas card.

As I look out, I see the first snowflakes start to fall. Maybe I was right about smelling snow.

CHAPTER TWO

*M*atthias

THE FOOTBALL GAME IS DROWNED OUT BY MY brothers shooting a game of pool, so I aim the remote across the room to turn the volume up. In typical ball-busting fashion, Theo intentionally stands in front of me so it doesn't work. Asshole.

"What did you do that for? I'm trying to watch this, but you guys are noisy as fuck."

My younger brother I'm closest to rolls his eyes at me. "You watched that game when it was on the first time. Did you actually DVR it too?"

He acts like I've committed some kind of crime. "Yeah, so get the hell out of the way so I can hear it too."

Since he can't stop himself from getting on my nerves, it seems, he shifts his body left and right so I can't turn up the sound on the TV. Jesus. And my father can't figure out why I wish I was an only child sometimes.

"Quit trying to watch some game you already saw and shoot some pool like a normal fucking person, Matthias," Theo says as he grabs a pool cue from off the rack.

I look over at my youngest brother and see he's not playing either. "Bother Ronan. I'm trying to do something. He's just texting that damn girlfriend of his again."

Theo turns to look and nudges Marius standing next to him. "He's so fucking whipped. Again with that girlfriend."

Our brother Marius, who just turned twenty last month and is probably the most jaded out of all of us after his girlfriend broke up with him right before Christmas, shakes his head in disgust. "Run away from any woman who needs to keep you on that short a leash, Ronan. Don't make the mistake I did. To think of all the nights I wasted trying to figure out what Maia wanted. Fuck that."

Ronan throws him a dirty look and then turns to face me. "Why do you have to be such a dick? What about me talking to Kate is such a problem that you have to get them busting my ass?"

I roll my eyes at him and his whining. "Love is a waste of time, Ronan. Accept that fact and your life will be much easier. Trust me."

As he types out a text to reply to whatever that girlfriend of his said, he snaps, "Says the person who's never loved anyone. What the fuck would you know about the subject anyway?"

Out of the corner of my eye, I see my second youngest brother Kellen smirk. As if he knows a goddamned thing about love at the ripe old age of nineteen.

"Fine. Let yourself be pussy whipped. What do I care?" I say as I grab my sketch pad and a pencil.

Since I'm not going to get to see this damn game, it seems, I might as well amuse myself doing something I enjoy. I've shot enough games of pool for a lifetime, and I'm not in the mood for foosball, so doodling it is.

Theo breaks and sinks a few balls to start his game with Marius, but I know how this will end. Like every other game of pool played in this house with him, Marius will end up kicking his ass. He may be a jaded fuck who hates the idea of love even more than I do, but he's a hell of a pool player.

My father strolls into the game room and looks around like he's trying to find something. Or maybe somebody, except everyone who lives in this house is now here with his arrival. Well, not the staff, but he wouldn't come up here looking for any of them.

"You boys look like you're enjoying yourselves," he says with a chuckle. "Why isn't anyone doing anything with Ronan?"

The baby of the family, he's the favorite of our father. Marius and Kellen look at one another and then at Ronan before rolling their eyes.

"He's busy with his woman," Marius says with a healthy dose of disgust in his voice.

My father looks over at the sofa where his youngest sits engrossed in his phone and then turns to look at me.

"Ah, to be young again. Oh well. Get ready. You need to come to the city with me today."

Instantly, dread fills every inch of me at the mere suggestion that I need to go to the city with him, which means he wants me to help him with something regarding the family business. "What for?" I ask, already knowing the answer and hating it.

He gives me a look of pure disappointment that morphs into a glare he thinks I deserve because I don't care about learning anything about King Industries. "Because I want you to. It's about time you start learning the business you'll one day take over when I'm gone."

When he's gone. As if his demise is imminent. Maximilian King is all of fifty-five. Why does he act like he's about to leave this earth any day now?

I know the answer to that without thinking too much about that question. Since my mother died, he's been sure his own mortality is about to become all too obvious long before he thought it ever would. Losing your wife when she's only forty-five will do that to a man.

As sympathetic as I am, that doesn't mean I'm interested in getting involved in anything having to do with King Industries. I'm the oldest son, so it's expected, but I'm not happy about it and want to put off that eventual inevitability as long as possible.

"I'm not really into it today, Dad. Some other time."

I turn my focus back to my sketchbook, but that vague answer isn't good enough for him. "No. Today it is. We're leaving in a few minutes, and I expect you to be sitting next to me in that car when it leaves this house, Matthias."

Great. Now I have to think up a lie on the fly so I

don't get roped into his business trip to the city on what's supposed to be a vacation week. This is why he's going to die earlier than he wants. The man never takes more than one day off at a time. I can't remember the last time he took a vacation. Probably the year before my mother died, and that was seven years ago.

Mustering a cough, I pretend to be too sick to go with him. "Really, Dad, I wish I could, but I'm feeling like shit today. I think I might be coming down with something. You don't want me spreading it to everyone at King Industries headquarters, do you?"

My father levels his gaze full of disbelief on me and stares into my eyes, as if he thinks he's going to find the truth somewhere in them. He's on the wrong path there, for sure. As the oldest, I've had to master the art of looking like something I'm not so I haven't gotten stuck doing a million and a half things he thinks would be perfect for his firstborn. Faking a little sickness is nothing for me.

"You should be in bed then," he says in his best attempt at being sympathetic, even though he likely doesn't believe I'm anything close to sick.

I choke out another half-hearted effort at coughing and nod. "Yeah, I think you're right. Maybe I should spend the day in bed."

He twists his face into a grimace and turns toward my brothers still shooting pool. "Would any of you like to take a trip into the city? You won't have to spend all of it at my office, of course."

How nice for my younger brothers that they aren't expected to keep their noses to the grindstone when they go into Manhattan. That chore is exclusively for me.

Everyone but Ronan jumps at the chance to get away from the house for a day in the city. As they hurry out of the room to get ready, my father turns to his youngest and smiles.

"So what do you have planned today, son?" he asks in a tone sweeter than anything I've ever been able to get from him.

"Just hanging out with Kate when she gets back from exchanging some sweater her grandmother bought her," he answers, momentarily ignoring his phone.

My brother may be whipped by that girlfriend of his, but he's not stupid. He knows ignoring his brothers for a text is fine, but to stay on our father's good side, he should at least pretend like he cares what he says.

Not that it's really necessary. As the baby of the family, Ronan could set the house on fire and stand outside watching it burn with the damn matches in his hand and my father would still fawn all over him. Such is the life of the youngest in the King family.

The oldest, however, doesn't get that kind of treatment. I'm expected to excel at everything. In school, I needed to be on the Dean's List every semester, or I heard about it. And no lounging around texting some girl for hours on end. Oh, no. Not for the firstborn son of Maximilian King. That's not the way the heir to the King fortune should act.

Not that I've ever been the type to be whipped by a woman.

"Okay. Be sure to tell Kate I hope she and her family had a lovely holiday. Will her family be joining her for the party?"

Ronan smiles. "They wouldn't miss it. Her father said he's looking forward to meeting you finally."

My father nods solemnly, like he's judging the weight of my brother's statement. "It's about time. You and Kate have been dating since the spring. By rights, we all should have met by now. It's okay, though. The King holiday party will be the perfect setting for all of us to get to know one another."

He sails out of the room on that note, likely eager to round up his three sons interested in traveling into the city today so he can leave when he planned. Ronan returns to being fixated on his phone, and all I can do is shake my head at him.

"How exactly does she get shopping done when she's constantly texting you?" I ask, not really expecting an answer.

My brother doesn't say anything in response to that, so I turn my attention to the football game I'll finally be able to watch now that the other three Kings are gone. I don't always wish I was an only child, but on days like today, it would be nice.

Then again, if I was the only offspring for my father to focus on, there's no way I would have been able to beg off today's trip to the office to start learning the ins and outs of his business. Maybe it's a good idea I'm one of five instead of the only one.

"She's standing in lines most of the time," Ronan says, belatedly answering my question I posed a few minutes ago.

I shrug, accepting that could be true. She still texts him way too much. Who has that much to say to anyone?

"Can you believe he wants me to go into the family

business already? I'm barely twenty-three, for God's sake. I just graduated from college in the spring."

My brother stands from the couch and walks over toward me on his way out of the room. "I'm thinking you should consider yourself lucky he let you go this long. None of us like it, but it's pretty much all our futures."

"I doubt it. You guys get to be whatever you want in life. All I get to be is the heir apparent," I grumble, thinking that maybe being Ronan is the best thing any of us could wish for.

He nods like he understands, but he doesn't. I'd kill to be the youngest. It's definitely got to be better than being the oldest son.

"Well, Kate finally checked out and has a new sweater she likes and she thinks won't hurt her grandmother's feelings, so I'm off. You hanging out here all day, or are you going out too?"

I look at him, and all I can think is he's lost. What seventeen-year-old knows anything about his girlfriend's sweater choice or if it's going to upset her grandmother?

"I don't know yet. I was thinking of going up to a friend's cabin, but that didn't pan out."

Ronan nods and flashes me a smile before he heads toward the hallway. "Well, have a good time whatever you do. See you later!"

Alone, I watch the game for a few minutes, but I notice when I look out the window some snowflakes are beginning to fall. Maybe I will spend the day in bed.

CHAPTER THREE

va

A HALF HOUR OF TRYING TO MASTER MY BROTHER'S skiing game leaves me feeling nothing short of frustrated. I don't usually play video games, so maybe that's why I was so terrible at it, but now that I've tried it, I think I can safely say I'm much better at skiing in real life than I am on the PlayStation.

Tossing the controller onto the couch, I search for something to watch on TV. Everything is holiday movies. I've seen so many of them in the past month that I think I hate them all.

It's not like there's a huge variety of storylines. The classics focus on people finding their way to being good in the nick of time right before Christmas, and the newer ones are sappy things invariably about a woman happily living her life in the big city but having to return to her small-town roots for some tragic or not-so-tragic reason to help her family do something like run the Christmas tree farm or the bakery. Of course, she ends up falling for some small-town local yokel who wears too much flannel and isn't anywhere as successful as she is back in the big city. The tree farm or bakery ends up being a huge hit that makes them lots of money, and everyone lives happily ever after in Small Town, USA.

I stare mindlessly at the TV as I think about giving up everything for some guy in bad flannel. Nope. I wouldn't even give up my life and a career for someone who had millions and never owned a stitch of anything flannel.

My phone vibrates across the top of the coffee table, and I see it's my friend Eden. She hates her name, so it comes up on my contact list as E since she insisted I not use her actual name.

"Hey, what's up?"

"Nothing. I'm bored to tears here at my grandmother's for the annual Christmas holiday visit. I swear my mother hates me. First she tags me with a terrible name, and then she ships me off to her mother's every December. What's next? Signing me up for military school?"

I try to stifle my chuckle, but I'm unsuccessful. "I think it's a little late for that, isn't it? We already graduated."

"Then it will be something worse, I'm sure."

"Your name isn't terrible either. I think it's beautiful."

Eden huffs her disgust at that comment. "Says the girl who actually has a beautiful name. If I have to hear one more guy say they want to explore my Garden of Eden, I'm going to lose it."

I shouldn't laugh, but when she gets like this, there's not much else to do. "Maybe the guys will grow out of that."

She ignores my attempt to be supportive and continues complaining. "My mother has one daughter and four sons, and it's the daughter who gets the short end of the stick all the time. None of my brothers are forced to do this grandmother thing. Just me."

I know the answer to that unspoken question of why she has to visit and her brothers don't. "That's because your grandmother doesn't like your brothers. They're like four tornadoes whenever they show up anywhere. Maybe you should try busting up the place like they do. She might end these visits."

That finally makes Eden laugh. "No kidding. You'd think they'd have some self-control by this point, but I think they're worse now that they're older, not better. I don't think I have the heart to go tearing up my grandmother's house, though. She's too sweet. I just wish I was back home so I could be hanging out with you and everyone else. Since I can't, tell me everything that's going on. I'm living vicariously through you, Ava, so don't let me down."

Everything that's going on is absolutely nothing. She called the wrong person if she wants to someone to spill the tea. I don't have any to spill.

"Sorry, but I've got nothing. I'm stuck at home since there's going to be a snowstorm today. I might walk up to the main house and see if Theo's around in a little while. I'm sure my father would be okay with that."

"Christ, Ava. Your father is worse than my mother. You're nineteen, for God's sake. He's making you stay home because it might snow?"

Eden knows full well how protective my father's gotten since my mother died. That doesn't stop her from pointing it out, though.

"You know him," I meekly answer, having no other comment about my father's behavior. "Sorry. All I have is the possibility Theo might be around. Maybe call me later after I see him. He usually has some juicy stories."

My friend hums and then says, "I'd rather hear something juicy about that brother of his. I heard through the grapevine right before I left that he and his girlfriend broke up. Am I to understand that Marius King is back on the market? Because if he is, sign this girl up!"

Her interest in Theo's younger brother surprises me. "How did I not know you liked Marius? I thought you were into that guy you met at drama camp over the summer. What was his name? Cooper? Copper?"

"Cooper, and no, he's ancient history. As for Marius, you know my weakness for the dark and brooding guys, and that King brother is working those in spades. You have to find out from Theo if he's still single."

Just because I feel like teasing her, I joke, "What are you going to do about it all the way down there in Virginia? By the time you get back right after New Year's, he'll be hooked up with someone else. You're not the only woman who loves broody guys."

I can hear her frustration seep through the phone as I toy with her. "First of all, it's not nice to torture me like that. And second of all, what do you know about the broody guy syndrome that afflicts me and millions of other women? You never go for those guys. All you ever like are those eggheads you insist on dating, which by the way, seems like a poor use of your prime dating years, if you ask me. They always turn out to be tools. Come to the dark side with the brooding guys. Trust me. You'll never go back."

I laugh out loud at her assessment of my dating life. She's not wrong. My exes haven't been great. I don't know about the brooding guys, though. Theo's older brother Matthias always seems to be brooding, and he's nothing short of miserable, as far as I can tell. As for Marius, he's definitely got that dark thing going, but I've never seen him as anything but Theo's younger brother.

Not that he has to worry since Eden is just one of many girls I know who'd give their left arm to be with him.

"I'll be sure to get the scoop on what's going on with Marius if I go up to see Theo later. Anything particular you want to know?"

Eden lets out a purely wicked chuckle. "I like what I already know about him. Gorgeous, brooding, and from what his ex-girlfriend used to say, he's got what any woman wants."

"Money?" I joke.

"Well, there's that, but I was referring to what's between his legs. Maia used to brag that she walked funny after a night with Marius King. Now that they're history, I think I'd like to see if she was telling the truth."

Typical Eden. Out of all of my friends, she's the most sex-crazed of them all.

"Well, I don't know about that, but I'll find out if he's single. When do you get back?" I ask.

"Second week of January," she says in a sad voice. "They don't even have snow down here, Ava. What the hell kind of Christmas holiday doesn't have snow?"

"We don't have any either, so you aren't missing anything. I think we're going to get some today, though. Maybe it will stick around until you get back."

"I hope so. It's not Christmas without snow. Ugh, I think my grandmother is calling for me. She probably wants to go for another walk in the beautiful sunshine. This is agony, Ava. Pure agony! Call me as soon as you find out about Marius. I need something to keep my spirits up while I'm down here all snowless and full of sun."

That shouldn't make me laugh, but it does. Only Eden would find sunny days miserable.

"I will. I promise to get all the details."

"Thanks! Okay, I'm off to wherever my grandmother needs to go now. Remember, call as soon as you find out. I want something to fantasize about until I get back home."

"Will do. Talk to you later, Eden!"

The call ends with her explaining to her grandmother in the background that she'll be ready in a minute, and as I set my phone back down on the table, I think about her with Marius. She might be his type. Eden's got beautiful black hair and green eyes that never fail to make guys fall for her. She's also got a great body, something I suspect he'd like.

Maybe they'd make a good couple. That's, of course, if he's still available in a few weeks. She's not the only one who's been waiting for the Marius and Maia show to end.

Lost in thought about them as a possible pairing, my eyelids slowly droop closed, but barely a few seconds pass before I hear something like a crack. My eyes fly open, and I see the TV screen black and no lights on in the house. Damnit! Why would the power go out today? My father said he had the repairman fix that problem that was making the electricity shut off during the summer. Something about overloading the breaker, I think.

I reach for my phone on the table and see I have less than ten percent left on my charge. Terrific. Even worse, with no power, the heat won't be able to turn on. I'll be freezing in no time.

There's only one choice. I'll have to go up to the main house.

Not that I have a problem with that. The King estate has a gorgeous home belonging to Mr. King, and he's always telling me I can come up and swim in the pool and check out the game room any time I like. Theo's probably hanging out, so at least I won't be alone.

Throwing on my winter coat and gloves, I look out the window and see there's an inch of snow on the ground. I could drive up to the main house since it's almost half a mile away from here, but I promised my father I wouldn't use the car.

So it's the shoe leather express for me. Not a problem. It's not like I haven't walked farther in much more than an inch of snow.

About a quarter of a mile to the house, the snow begins to come down so hard I can barely see five feet in front of me. So much for this not being a problem. My feet get wet since I chose not to switch out my shoes for my winter boots, and my hair is drenched from all the snow landing on it.

A hat would have been a good idea. At least my hands are warm because of my new leather gloves my Aunt Jessie sent me for Christmas. I'll have to be sure to tell her how much they came in handy today.

I press on, trudging through the snow that has to be at least three or four inches deep by the time I'm more than halfway there. I've never seen snow fall this fast in all my life. I've lived nineteen years on this estate, and never once have I experienced anything like this.

And then the wind starts blowing, and I swear it feels like someone is slapping my cheeks over and over. My skin burns, and I imagine my entire face is bright red. My mascara is probably running down my face, frozen black tracks of makeup to make me look like some kind of ghoulish blizzard monster.

I lower my head so my chin is plastered to my chest and push on as the wind and the snow combine to make me feel like I'm going to freeze to death on this walk. If I had broken my word to my father and driven up to the house, I'd already be there by now, nice and warm and toasty with Eleanor in the kitchen by that huge fireplace they have.

It's all I can do to keep my eyes focused on the ground a few inches ahead of me as I slowly make my way up the final quarter mile hill that leads to the King mansion. I stuff my hands in my pockets since my brand-new gloves that worked so well a few minutes ago now feel like frozen things stuck to my fingers. It's like someone has set a sopping wet, ice-cold towel on my head, so I shake to get some of the snow off. It lands inside my jacket, sending chills down my back and making me even colder than before.

Through the blinding snow, I see the gray stone façade of the King house ahead and breathe a sigh of relief. If it's within view, I can make it there. I'll just be a soaked and frozen mess when I arrive.

Eleanor will take care of me, though. The head housekeeper, she lives in the main house's servant quarters built when they called staff servants. A kind lady I think must be in her late fifties, at least, she's known me since I was a little girl when she came to work for the Kings and my father would bring me to work with him. She always had lollipops hidden in her apron she'd give me before making me promise I wouldn't ruin my dinner by eating them first.

Snow cakes to my eyelashes, but I lift my head into the blizzard winds to see the house just feet away. Thank God! I don't know if I could have walked even a few steps more without collapsing.

I knock on the back door near the kitchen and hope Eleanor is nearby so I won't have to wait very long. I could simply walk in since Mr. King has told me time and time again I'm welcome whenever I want to come up here, but I don't want to create a snowy mess she'll have to clean up.

Her round face appears in one of the windowpanes, and her eyes open as wide as saucers when she realizes it's me. Flinging the door open, she grabs my arm and tugs me inside, bringing a blast of snow in with me.

"Oh, my word! What are you doing out in this

snowstorm, Ava?" she asks as she guides me into the heart of the kitchen. "Come right over here and we'll get those clothes off you before you catch cold. Did you walk all the way up from your house?"

The soothing heat from the fireplace begins to melt the snow clinging to me, making a puddle on the hardwood floor they put in a few years ago before Mrs. King passed away. I look down and frown, hating that I'm making the very mess I wanted to avoid.

"I'm sorry, Eleanor. There's melted snow all over the place now."

She slides my gloves off my hands and then eases my coat off me before pointing toward the chair closest to the fireplace on the other side of the kitchen. "Don't worry about that. God made mops for just that problem. Now sit down and warm up. You need to get out of those soaking wet clothes, though, but first, let me get you a robe. Sit down and relax. You must be frozen solid, you poor thing."

I can't help but smile at her mention of God making mops to clean up snow puddles. She really is a wonderfully sweet person, but sometimes she says things that make me want to laugh.

As I take a seat and feel the heat from the fire against my ice-cold skin, I begin to thaw out while I imagine God finishing with his creation of the universe and on the seventh day turning to one of his angels and whipping up a mop.

Beside me, Eleanor sets my gloves and jacket on a rack she's brought out so they can begin to dry. "How would you like a nice mug of hot chocolate? You loved it when you were a little girl. You, Theo, and Marius would come in from playing outside or building a snowman, and I remember your little face lighting up whenever I said I'd make you three some of my hot chocolate. You aren't too grown up for that now, are you?"

I look up into her pale blue eyes and see sincerity like I used to find in my mother's eyes. Eleanor's face is fuller, and her cheeks tend to be rosy all year round, but in some ways, she reminds me of my mother with her dark hair and sweet disposition.

"Definitely not too grown up for your hot chocolate, Eleanor, but I don't want you to go out of your way. I just had to come up here because the power went off in the carriage house, and I didn't want to freeze to death with no heat."

That news makes her expression fill with horror. "You aren't making me do anything, and you were right to come up here if your house has no electricity. What was that electrician doing at your house for a full week this past summer if only a few months later you don't have power on the one day you absolutely need it?"

I rub my hands together in front of the fire as I shake my head. "I was thinking the same thing. I hope my father gives him an earful when he calls him later."

Eleanor nods and points at me when she says, "If he doesn't, Mr. King will. When he finds out you were home without any heat, he's going to be furious. There will be hell to pay there. For me too if I don't get you straightened out, so let me go get that robe so you can get out of those wet clothes. Hang on. I'll be right back."

I smile as she hurries away. I wouldn't leave this chair in front of this roaring fire if someone paid me. I haven't been this cozy in weeks.

She returns less than a minute later with a fluffy white robe that looks brand new. Handing it to me, she says, "Take those clothes off and wear this."

I do as she orders but as I do, I ask, "This isn't new, is it? I don't want to put you out in any way."

Eleanor screws her face into a grimace. "First of all, you could never put me out in any way, Ava Sutton. I've known you since you were just a little slip of a girl, and you've never been anything but the most polite creature that walked God's green earth. Even more importantly, if Mr. King saw you sitting here in wet clothes and thought I didn't do anything to help you, he'd reprimand me so bad I might have to find another job. So if you want me to not have to go job hunting right after Christmas, you'll give me those soaking wet clothes and relax in this robe."

After handing her my wet jeans, socks, and sweater, I wrap the white robe around me and luxuriate in how wonderful it feels against my skin. It's heated from being in front of the fire for the past few minutes, so it's like a blanket of warmth around me.

"You didn't take off your bra and panties. They must be soaked too, aren't they?" she asks as she stands in front of me waiting for the rest of my clothes.

Sheepishly, I turn away and take them off too, stuffing them inside my jeans when I give them to her. "I didn't know if you wanted everything," I quietly say as I sit down.

"No one wants to sit in wet underwear," she says with a giggle. "Now let me go handle these, but first, the milk is ready for your hot chocolate."

She scurries across the kitchen with my wet clothes in her arms to create that delicious treat. It's the hot milk that makes it better than most people's hot cocoa, and when she returns with a giant mug filled to the brim, I happily take it. With a big inhale, I bring the sweet scent of the chocolate and milk into my nose. She knows I don't like the whipped cream Theo and his brothers always wanted on theirs, so mine is simply the best hot chocolate I've ever tasted.

"Thank you, Eleanor. I can't tell you how good this is going to feel," I say as I wrap both my hands around the mug and lift it to my lips.

As always, her creation is nothing short of heavenly. Standing beside me, she smiles when I hum my utter delight at how good it tastes. "Mmmm...you make the best hot chocolate in the world. Thank you."

She waves away my compliment but beams an even bigger smile after I finish. "Oh, stop. I'm going to go take care of your clothes. You sit and warm yourself in front of the fire here. I'll be back soon. None of the boys are here, unfortunately. Well, Matthias is, but he hasn't come downstairs at all today."

Alone, I revel in the feel of the warmth and the taste of the chocolate as it hits my tastebuds. I don't know how she does it, but even steaming hot, her cocoa never burns my tongue. I close my eyes and remember how Theo used to like so many marshmallows in his that you couldn't even see the hot chocolate anymore. It was just a mug of sugary white goo.

I hear footsteps and turn to say something to Eleanor about how Theo used to love those marshmallows, but instead of her I see his older brother walk into the kitchen and stop dead at the sight of me. Matthias King. The most miserable of the King sons, at least when it comes to me. I have no idea what I ever did to make him hate me, but he never fails to look utterly disgusted any time he lays his eyes on me.

"What are you doing here?" he grunts out in a tone full of revulsion, like I'm some unwanted creature someone should have chased out of the house by now.

"The electricity went out in my house, so we didn't have any heat," I explain, giving him a smile he doesn't deserve that's mostly for Eleanor's wonderful hot chocolate.

"So you came here?" he asks, his words practically dripping with disgust.

Just then, Eleanor walks back into the kitchen with a mop and gives me a look that tells me she sees how much he doesn't want me here. "Matthias, I just made hot chocolate. Would you like a cup? I remember when you were little and you loved it with lots of whipped cream."

Her voice sounds so hopeful as she kindly offers to make him a treat, but all she gets in return are an angry expression and gruff response. "No. How long is she going to be here?"

I open my mouth to say I'll be here as long as I need to be and if he has a problem with that, he should talk to his father, who tells me every time he sees me that I'm welcome in his home. However, Eleanor answers him first, saving him from a snappy comment he deserves and more.

"She has no heat down at the carriage house. We can't send her back to a house with no heat."

Why she thinks appealing to his sense of decency is going to work is beyond me. She knows Matthias as well as anyone in this house. She's seen how mean he is. She's especially seen how cruel he is whenever I'm around. Eleanor should know better than to think he'd be kind just because there's a chance I'd freeze to death down at my own house.

He gives her a blank stare and then turns to give me a sneer before heading over to the refrigerator on the far wall. She and I watch as he reaches in and gets a bottle of soda before spinning on his heel and marching out without another word to either one of us.

When I'm sure he's out of earshot, I look over at her and shake my head as she begins to clean up the melted snow on the floor. "Why does he hate me so much? I swear I don't think I've ever done anything to him. I'm best friends with Theo. You'd think that would make him at least be nice to me, but it never fails. Whenever he sees me, he's as nasty as he can be."

"I know," she says like she feels bad for me.

"His father is always so nice to me. He bought me a diamond tennis bracelet for graduation last year, and you should see the gold necklace he bought me for Christmas this year. Marius, Kellen, and Ronan are always nice whenever they see me too. But Matthias hates me, and I have no idea why."

Eleanor sighs and says, "I don't understand either. You two have so much in common. You'd think he'd be pleasant, at least."

She turns to focus on something she needs to do as I try to think of a single thing Matthias King and I share in common. Other than the fact that we've both lost our mothers, there's not one thing he and I have alike. He's a rude ass. He's cruel and insensitive, which makes him downright ugly to be around.

Of course, he's not ugly. You'd think that meanness in him would show on the outside of his body, but it doesn't. He's gorgeous, and he knows it. Tall and muscular with nearly black hair cut short, dark brown eyes, and a perfectly straight nose, he looks like a model you see in magazines. Like his other brothers with their chiseled cheekbones and jaws, he's striking to the point that it's hard not to look at him.

Not that I have that problem since he's a dick to me, but I know other people think he's stunning with a perfect mouth that begs to be kissed. Too bad it's always turned down in a scowl when it comes to me.

He reminds me of a soldier. Or a tyrant, in my case. I've never seen him smile at me, but on occasion I've seen him when other people are around and he smiles at them, and it's like he can light up a room when he does.

So it's got to be some problem with me since whenever I'm around, he's as cold as ice. I can't be bothered to figure out what his issue is, though.

CHAPTER FOUR

*M*atthias

I LISTEN AS MY FRIEND CAM TALKS ABOUT SOME PARTY he's got a hard on to go to tonight as I stretch my legs down the length of my bed. "You know there's going to be a ton of hot girls there too, so why not go?" he asks, a rhetorical question since he's already so fucking pumped up about it.

"Sounds good, but I'm pretty beat after the last couple nights," I say half-heartedly, not really interested in going out at all after seeing Ava down in the kitchen.

"What else do you have to do?"

"Nothing, I guess," I say as I stare up at my bedroom ceiling. "There's someone at my house right now. What time are you leaving later?"

The phone goes silent for a long moment before he

asks, "What? Who? Your brothers? Aren't they usually at the house?"

"No, not them. A girl. Ava. She's the daughter of my father's estate manager," I say as I close my eyes and think about what she looked like sitting in front of the fireplace in just a robe. "She's down in the kitchen where she belongs since she's the fucking help."

Cam's instantly interested in my houseguest. "Oh yeah? Is she hot, at least? Or are you stuck with some ugly chick in your house?"

I sigh as I try to think of a way to describe Ava. "Yeah, I guess she's not bad."

"As hot as Andi?"

The memory of the last time I saw my ex-girlfriend flashes through my mind, and I can't help but admit Ava's hotter than Andi. I don't want to tell Cam that, though.

"Andi's in a league of her own. You know that, man."

"Hell, yeah, I know it! You should have stayed with her. The guy she's with tells anyone who'll fucking listen how good she is."

Laughing at the idea of being with her now, I shake my head. "That was college. I grew out of her."

"So are you coming to the party or not, shithead?"

I shrug at the thought of going anywhere. "I don't know. I'll call you later if I feel like going. I might change my mind."

"You should. It's the holidays, the perfect time to party hard before we all have to get back to the grind next year," Cam says, giving me his best sales pitch.

The idea of my father's grind and how he wants me to somehow become a carbon copy of him fills me with dread. I don't want that for my life, but it's looking like my time avoiding the inevitable is nearly up.

"If I feel like it, I'll call you. Talk to you later."

He starts to say something about some girl he thinks I should meet, but a noise out in the hallway gets my attention. "Yeah, tell me later, okay?"

Tossing the phone on my bed, I walk out of my room to find out what's going on. I see nothing, though. Curious what it could be, I head toward the kitchen.

As I pass the game room, I catch a glimpse of someone out of the corner of my eye. I thought Ronan went to see his girlfriend. My other brothers can't be back already. They just left a little more than an hour ago. I doubt they're even in the city yet.

I turn my head and see it's not any of them. It's Ava lounging around up here like she owns the place. Walking in, I stop next to the sofa where she's sitting in that white robe from before.

"Comfy? Maybe you'd like a few pillows or a throw? How about some bonbons?"

When she turns to face me, I see the hurt in her eyes from my words, but it doesn't take long before that morphs into anger. She looks like she's going to cry either way.

Standing from the sofa, she puts her hands on her hips and glares up at me. In her bare feet, she's dwarfed by me, but I get no sense she's afraid of me, even though I'm nearly a foot taller than her and twice her size.

"Why are you like this with me?" she asks, her voice full of hurt even as her brown eyes stare up at me with nothing but hatred in them.

"I'm not anything with you. This is how I always act

when somebody just shows up at my house and makes themselves at home."

Ava shakes her head. "It's your father's house, not yours, and he's told me more times than I can count that I'm welcome here whenever I want. He wouldn't want anyone to be stuck in a house with no heat. That's the only reason I came up here. Trust me. I want nothing more than to be as far away from you as possible."

As I turn to walk out of the room, I mumble, "Then, by all means, do that."

Since I have no need to walk down to the kitchen again, I make my way back to my room. Behind me, I hear footsteps, so I turn around to see Ava following me and practically glaring daggers at me.

"Are you lost? What do you want?" I ask, knowing how fucking terrible I sound right now. "I'd think after all the times you've been here that you'd know your way to the door."

She stops and stares up at me in silence, but I'm sure she's going to cry at any moment. Great. Just what I need today. Some sobbing girl disturbing my vacation.

But instead, she pokes her finger in the air toward me and snaps, "What have I ever done to you to make you hate me like this? I'm best friends with your brother, the one you're closest to. I'd think that would at least show you I'm not some horrible person you have to be like this with."

"Well, Theo's not here, so you can leave whenever you're ready. Now would be a good time."

I've never understood how my brother could be best friends with this person. Who the hell is friends with girls? You either want to sleep with them or you don't.

I'm guessing he decided he doesn't want to sleep with Ava, but for the life of me, I don't understand why.

I stare down at her wondering where she gets her bravery from. Most people her size wouldn't dare to ask me questions like she is.

Dark eyes fix on my face, like she's trying to find the answer to that question she asked in my expression. That's not where it is, little Ava.

She really is beautiful. I can't figure out why Theo hasn't made a move on her after all these years they've been hanging out. Then again, he does like blondes, and Ava has light brown hair. She's also far less submissive than he generally likes his women. I can see that by the way she stabbed her finger at me a few seconds ago.

This one definitely has a backbone.

"Are you going to answer me?" she asks, tearing me out of my thoughts about how nice her mouth is.

I shrug and turn to keep walking toward my room. "No."

Her footsteps behind me tell me she's not going to take that as an answer, though.

CHAPTER FIVE

va

A MIXTURE OF HURT AND ANGER COURSES THROUGH me as I see him walk away without even being decent enough to answer me. I'm not done with him yet, though, so if he thinks just telling me no and leaving is going to end this, he's crazy.

I'm going to find out right now what I've done to make Matthias King so nasty to me.

"Don't walk away from me. I asked you a valid question. Why do you hate me so much?"

He finally stops and slowly turns around to look at me. I should be intimidated. He's huge, and when he takes a step toward me, it's like he's some terrible overlord looming over me.

Matthias shrugs, clearly minimizing my question. "Hate would require me to feel something for you. I feel nothing for or about you. Maybe you're just oversensitive."

Rage explodes inside my brain. How is it someone so stunning can be so cruel to a person who's never done a single thing to him?

"Oh, that's right. Turn to the dick handbook and go with a classic. I'm the one who has the problem, not you. Right?"

His dark eyes stare into mine as if he's hoping he can scare me off. When I don't budge, he shrugs again in that infuriating way that tells me he's amused at how upset I am.

"You said it, not me."

God, he's insufferable!

I take a big step toward him so barely a foot of space separates us. Jabbing my finger into his muscular chest, I tilt my head up and give him exactly what he deserves. "Don't be a coward, Matthias. You obviously have some issue with me. Anyone with eyes can see it. So what is it?"

After rolling his eyes, he answers, "I have no problem with you, other than the fact that you're a guest here who's currently berating someone who actually lives here."

"God, you are so rude! You know my house has no heat, and still you act like I'm some unwanted intruder, an interloper into your exclusive society where, of course, I don't belong because I'm the daughter of the help. Isn't that your real problem with me, Matthias?"

My emotions threaten to unspool inside me at any moment as I wait for his response. He doesn't even give me the courtesy of looking me in the eye, like I'm not good enough to respect that much.

When he finally turns to face me, his stare is so full of pure hatred that I instinctively step back from him, afraid what he may do. He's never been violent with me before, but we've never been alone like this before either.

We glare at one another for a long moment before he leans down and positions his face directly in front of mine. He's so close I could kiss those perfect lips of his, if I wanted to, which I definitely don't. I might want to smack his face, though. That he deserves.

And then he opens that beautiful mouth and out come the harshest words he's ever said to me. "If you know you don't belong, why do you keep coming here?"

Each cruel syllable feels like a sharp slap to my face. I step back as tears begin to fill my eyes and look away, not willing to give this person the right to see me cry. Yes, I'm the daughter of the man his father pays to run his estate. I'm the child of the help, and to someone like Matthias who was born with a silver spoon in his mouth, I'm not even worthy of kindness.

With the first tear, I run away. He doesn't get to see how much his words hurt me.

I hurry down to the kitchen where Eleanor stands at the sink washing vegetables. My clothes aren't dry yet, but I grab them off the rack anyway. I won't stay in this house not a minute longer.

"What are you doing?" she asks, but I shake my head, unable to answer.

I slip my damp jeans on, hating how cold they feel against my skin even after sitting in front of the fire for all this time. But I don't care if I have to walk home in soaking wet clothes. I won't stay here anymore.

"What happened? You're crying, Ava. Are you hurt?" Eleanor asks as she hurriedly dries her hands on a dishcloth and rushes over to me.

"I'm fine," I say, lying.

I'm anything but fine after talking to that son of a bitch. At least now I know what his problem with me is. I never did anything to him, unless you count being born into a lower class.

He hates me because I'm the help.

"Why are you leaving? The heat isn't back on in your house, and it's practically a blizzard out there now. There has to be a foot of snow on the ground, and more is coming down every minute. You can't leave in this weather."

I grab my bra and shirt and turn away from Eleanor as I get dressed in the still wet clothes. "I won't say here. I don't belong. Matthias made that perfectly clear."

Behind me, she lets out an audible sigh. "Oh, honey. Don't pay him any attention. Mr. King wouldn't want you to go back out in this storm and return to an ice-cold house."

I shake my head as the tears return. Not wanting her to see, I lower my head and stare into the fire. "It doesn't matter. I don't belong here. I don't need to give him another chance to make me feel unwelcome. I'll go back to where I belong."

At the touch of her hand on my arm, I can't stop myself from crying. "Oh, Ava. Please don't go. You could get hurt out there. Stay here with me, and I'll make you something to eat. We can talk, and I can make you more hot chocolate. You don't have to go."

She means well, but what does it matter if one of the help tells the daughter of the help it's okay? Eleanor and I are in the same boat here on the King estate. We're not members of the family, so we're not wanted, unless we can do something for them. At least she can, so she's welcome.

All I am is the daughter of Mr. King's estate manager. I serve no purpose at all here.

"No, I have to leave. Matthias made it clear I don't belong here. Thank you for everything. I'm going to go. Don't worry about me. It's only a little ways down the road to my house, so I'll be fine."

As I put on my coat and hurry toward the back door, she says, "Ava, please! I'll never be able to forgive myself if you get stuck out there. Stay!"

It's no use. I can't stay here. She may not be able to forgive herself if I'm found dead out in the snow, but the person who has the most right to be here out of all of us wouldn't lose a moment's sleep over it.

I'm just the help.

When I throw open the door to walk outside, the icy wind hits my face, instantly making my cheeks burn. The last thing I want to do right now is go out in this weather, but I have no choice, so I lower my head and slam the door behind me.

It's so much worse than it was an hour ago when I arrived. The snow covers halfway up my shins, burying my feet and much of my calves. I've never wished I was wearing boots more than at this moment.

Big, fat snowflakes fall onto the top of my head,

soaking my hair for the second time today. You'd think all the rage I have inside me right now would make me hot, but just a few steps in this blizzard and I'm freezing.

None of that matters. I don't have a choice. I don't belong at the King house, so back to my cold house it is. I need to call my father and tell him the repair guy needs to come out again. He'll be unhappy since it's the holidays and that electrician will charge double or triple time, but we can't live without heat.

I slip my hand into my pocket to fish out my phone. I barely have five percent left on the charge, so I need to do this quickly. I move my hand to press the number one to speed dial him, but a blast of wind hits me, and I drop my phone in the snow. It falls into a snowbank in front of me, probably ruined from the cold and moisture.

Can this day get any worse?

When I bend down to search for it, I can't find my phone anywhere. It couldn't have gone far. It fell straight down, so where is it?

I take a few steps to see if it slid away, but my foot hits something hard. I instinctively lift it to see if it's okay and lose my balance almost immediately, falling into the snowbank along with my phone.

The snow covers my skin, making me colder than I thought possible. I quickly feel around for my phone, but I can't find it. Then when I try to stand up, my foot hits that same metal object it did before, and I fall headfirst into the snow.

CHAPTER SIX

$\mathcal{M}$atthias

I SLAM MY DOOR, DISGUSTED THAT PRACTICALLY anyone can just walk in and make themselves comfortable in my house. She has her own goddamned house to sit and watch TV in. Let her go back there. I don't care if it's cold. Wear a sweater and a hat. She'll be fine.

Collapsing onto the bed, I glance over at the Playboy magazine next to me. I'd love to jerk off now. Talk about needing a release. But I'm too pissed after dealing with Ava.

Why can't she just stay in her world and leave me to mine? I blame Theo for this. He encourages her to come up and hang out all the time. My father's no better. Always telling her she's welcome. No, she isn't. It's better if she just stays away down in that little carriage house my father lets her family stay in.

I pinch the bridge of my nose to fend off a headache that's forming right behind my eyes. Fucking Ava Sutton. When I see my brother later, I'm going to tell him he needs to stop bringing her around here. If he wants to hang out with her, let him go somewhere else.

A blood curdling scream pierces the silence, echoing throughout the house. I'd know that sound anywhere. It's Eleanor. She probably dropped something again. I think my father needs to consider the fact that she's too old to be doing this job anymore.

Knowing he'll be up one side of me and down the other if I don't go at least ask her if she's okay, I hurry down to the kitchen and hope she isn't lying dead in the middle of the floor. There's no way he won't somehow find a way to blame me for that.

When I run into the room, she's standing at the door staring out in horror. "Ava! She fell in the snow as she was walking back to her house. We have to get her!"

Instantly, I fling open the door and run out into the fucking blizzard I didn't realize had dumped a foot of snow in the past few hours. What the hell was she thinking walking out in this?

Every flake that hits my bare arms stings, but I can't think about that right now. Ava lies on the ground with her head in the snow about twenty feet down the sidewalk, so I hurry over to her and scoop her up into my arms.

"I don't want to go back into that house," she complains.

Lowering my head, I can barely see as the snow

blinds me. I follow my tracks back to the house where Eleanor waits at the door. I step inside and she throws a blanket over Ava as she searches for any sign she's still alive.

"Is she okay?"

I nod as Ava looks over at her and smiles. "She's nearly frozen solid, but she's okay, I think."

Eleanor breathes a sigh of relief and kisses her rosy cheek. "I'm going to make you a cup of hot tea and some soup. Let me get that wet coat off you."

I wait for her to say she's going to make me something since I just ran out into a blizzard wearing only sweatpants and a T-shirt, but she ignores me and hurries over to the stove. Nice that I don't matter. I only live here.

"Bring it to my room. That's where she'll be," I say as I begin walking toward the hallway.

A look of surprise crosses Eleanor's face for a moment before she simply nods and says, "Okay. Would you like me to make you anything, Matthias?"

I shake my head and keep walking. "No. I'm fine."

Before I make it to the stairs, Ava says, "You can put me down. I can walk."

Her tone is sharp, like she wants to slap me to punctuate her sentence. I look down and nod my understanding, even though I have no intention of putting her down.

"Obviously not or you wouldn't have been face down in a snowbank a minute ago."

As I climb the stairs to the second floor, she rolls her eyes. "I tripped over that metal frog lawn ornament someone should have put away when winter came."

Just before we get to my room, she begins to squirm in my arms. "I don't need to be carried like a baby, you know."

I stop and look down at her glaring up at me. "No, you need to be carried like someone who tripped over a frog and fell face first in the snow."

She feels as light as a feather in my arms. I never realized how small she is compared to me. And she smells incredible, like flowers. Still, this tiny thing is full of anger for me.

I guess I have that coming, even though I saved her life.

"Seriously, Matthias, you can put me down. I'll just go hang out with Eleanor in the kitchen where I belong. You know, where the help hangs out?"

As much as I know I should just do as she wants since it's clear she's still furious with me, I shake my head and continue walking toward my room. "You'll stay with me. Clearly, you can't be trusted to go walking around on your own."

I see her dark eyes get big at that comment and force myself not to smile. She really is so easy to upset. Just a few well-chosen words and she's ready to fight like she's got an army behind her backing her up.

"Don't talk to me like I'm some kind of stupid child. Now put me down."

She squirms even more this time, but I hold her tightly against my body to keep her from moving. "Stop trying to get away. You're going to hurt yourself if I drop you."

Finally, after a few seconds of fighting me, she gives

up. With a heavy sigh, she stops wriggling in my hold, but I swear she looks like she's going to cry again.

What's the problem now?

"Even when you're trying to do something nice, you're mean. You know that?" she says with tears in her eyes.

I smile and reach down to grab the doorknob. "It's my gift."

"Sounds like a curse you're going to want to get something done about, if you ask me."

The thought of throwing her over my shoulder and carrying her into my bedroom that way flashes through my brain, and for a few moments, I actually consider it. She'd probably fight me the whole way to the bed that way too, though.

There's no winning with this person.

"Gift. Curse. Whatever it is, I like to think it's part of my charm," I say as I push the door closed with my back.

Ava's mouth drops open in shock. "Charm? This is charm? I don't think you know the meaning of that word, Matthias."

Always wanting to fight.

"Are you this way with Theo? Is that what makes him want to hang out with you all the time?" I ask as I make my way toward my bed.

That gets me a pout. "No, I'm not because he's sweet and he doesn't deserve to have me be like this toward him, which by the way, you totally deserve after what you said to me before."

She certainly is feisty. She's also delusional if she thinks my brother is sweet. He may act that way around her, but I doubt anyone else in the world would say Theo King is anything close to sweet.

"Yeah, sweet. Keep thinking that. Just don't be surprised when he makes a move on you that is anything but sweet, little Ava."

"Don't call me that! You don't get to use that nickname after how rotten you were," she snaps.

She really is full of piss and vinegar. Not that I don't deserve it. I know I do. It doesn't matter that I have my reasons for not wanting her around.

When I stop at the foot of my bed, she looks around like she's surprised. "Why did you bring me up here to your room?" she asks, her tone suddenly not as sharp as a second ago.

I don't answer her, preferring to keep the truth to myself. At least for now.

CHAPTER SEVEN

va

HE GENTLY SETS ME DOWN ON HIS BED AND CROUCHES in front of me to take off my shoes. More than a little confused about what's happening right now since less than a half hour ago he made it more than clear I wasn't welcome anywhere near him, I stare down as he carefully unties my right sneaker and then moves to the left one.

Even bent over like this, he's still so much bigger than me. I watch as his hands with their long fingers tenderly remove my shoe before moving to the other one, all the while avoiding my gaze as he stares down at the floor.

When he begins to take off my left shoe, I cry out in agony as a jolt of pain shoots through my ankle. He doesn't stop, and when he takes off my sock, I see my ankle is already swollen.

"Oh, God. Did I break it?"

He softly touches it a few times before looking up at me. Shaking his head, he says, "I don't think so. Just a deep bruise. We'll put some ice on it, and you'll be okay. You'll just have to stay off it today, at least."

I stare down at him in utter confusion. "Stay off it? You mean right here?"

Matthias nods like of course the answer is yes. "Yeah. Eleanor will bring you that soup and some hot tea. That way you won't make it worse."

Still unsure what he means or who replaced the cruel son of a bitch he's always been with this person, I ask, "Will you be here too?"

That makes him smile, and I swear it's like his face lights up, making him even more gorgeous than usual. "It is my room, so yes, I'll be here."

"With me," I say, needing to make that clear since none of this is making sense.

He shrugs before nodding. "Yes."

"The person you just recently told to go because she wasn't wanted here."

Matthias winces like my description of what he said to me not an hour ago right down the hall bothers him. "I think if you stay off it today you might find it's not too bad. I know ice is the last thing you're going to want on you after what happened outside, so we'll wait for that until you're all warmed up again."

I don't understand anything that's happening, but I can't disagree with wanting to stay warm inside the house. That he is being so nice right now makes me wonder, but I think this might fall under the category of not looking a gift horse in the mouth, so I swallow all the other questions I have and just watch as he stands up again and smiles.

"Okay, legs up on the bed."

As I lean against the mattress to steady myself, I feel something under the covers. Once my feet are up and Matthias carefully positions a couple pillows under my left foot so it's raised, I root around under the blanket and sheet to find a magazine.

I pull it out to look at it and read the title in big letters. PLAYBOY. Glancing up at him, I say, "So it's going to be us hanging out here and your nudie magazine?"

His cheeks turn a slight pink color like he's blushing, and I swear I've never seen anyone look so uncomfortable. Enjoying that after all he's said to me today, I begin to thumb through the pages. Lots of beautiful women with enormous butts and huge boobs. Typical man.

Looking up from a picture of a blond woman with the teeny-tiniest waist and giant hips, I see him staring at me. "You definitely have a type. That's for sure."

He gives me an odd look, like he doesn't understand what I mean, so I spin the magazine around to show him the image. "A type. Big boobs. Tiny waist. Bubble butt."

Matthias grimaces and shakes his head like the blond woman disgusts him, which I know can't be true since she's gorgeous, even if she is misshapen. "Those are just the women they choose. Not my decision."

"Why do you have a magazine anyway? It's the twenty-first century. You can find naked women and more all over the Internet."

A sly smile lifts the corners of his beautiful mouth. "You'd know a lot about that?"

I roll my eyes at his attempt to shame me. "I don't live in a cave, Matthias. Everyone knows about that."

He doesn't respond but points his finger at my pants. "They need to come off."

"What?"

I understand the words coming out of his mouth. I just don't understand how I'm going to remove my pants with him standing right there.

"You're going to make my bed all waterlogged. You need to take your pants off."

Staring up at him in horror, I shake my head. Nope. I can't take my clothes off with him standing right here in front of me.

"What? Now you're suddenly shy? A minute ago, you were looking at a naked woman and grilling me about my type."

I swallow hard, still unwilling to do as he insists. "I wasn't grilling, and it's not shyness. I just don't feel comfortable undressing in front of you."

He smiles and exhales a heavy sigh. "Fine. I'll turn around since I need those pants off so my bed doesn't turn into a lake from your soaked clothes."

Just then, Eleanor knocks at the door and Matthias yells, "Come in!"

She opens the door and immediately looks at me sitting on his bed. I see by the expression on her face she's surprised. That makes two of us. I simply shrug and give her a smile she returns with a big grin of her own.

In one hand, she holds the tray with my bowl of soup and cup of tea, and in the other, she grasps the white robe I had on before. As she sets the tray down on the dresser on the other side of the room, she says, "I figured you'd need something to wear since your clothes must be drenched. Get into this robe, and I'll take your wet clothes down to the laundry."

When she turns around, I still haven't moved since Matthias remains in the room. The two of us turn to look at him, as if to give him the clue none of what needs to happen is going to until he moves.

Finally, he holds his hands up in front of him like he's surrendering and steps back into his bathroom. "Okay, I'm going. Let me know when it's all clear for me to come out."

I wait until he closes the bathroom door before I pull the covers up over me and strip out of my wet clothes. He's right about soaking his bed. If I had stayed any longer in those clothes, neither he nor I would be able to sit here for a while as we wait for it to dry out.

Eleanor hands me the super soft robe in exchange for my shirt and pants, but instead of being willing to let me keep my bra and panties, she shakes her head and points at me as I clutch the covers up around my neck. In that motherly way she has, she says, "Everything, missy. It's no good only drying half your clothes."

As I remove my bra and panties and stick my hand out from the covers to give them to her, I say, "The socks are on the floor where he left them."

She gives me an odd look and then smiles. I want to explain I didn't ask him to help me and he did it all on his own, but I simply shrug and get to work putting that robe on.

When she crouches down to pick up my socks off the

floor, she says, "Now try to get some chicken soup and tea into you. That'll warm you up."

Matthias comes out of the bathroom when he hears her close his bedroom door. "So you can do as you're told. Just not with me."

Confused, I shake my head. "What does that mean?"

He points at me and smirks. "The robe. She told you to get undressed, and you listened. I told you the same thing, and you wouldn't do it."

Embarrassed, although I don't know why, I quickly move to shift the conversation from me to him. Lifting up the magazine, I ask, "I'm still wondering why you choose to go old school with your naked women."

As he hands me the cup of tea from over on the dresser, he says, "Because my father watches our every move. My brothers may like explaining themselves when it comes to that, but I don't."

It seems like a rational explanation, so I don't continue that conversation. Sipping my tea, I look around his room and admire it. The light blue painted walls and dark wood furniture all seem very masculine.

Very him.

"Your room is nice."

And as if he becomes someone else, he gives me a snide look and says, "I'm glad it gets your seal of approval."

Instantly, my feelings are hurt by his comment. "Why do you have to be like that? I was giving you a compliment."

Turning away, he avoids my gaze I'm sure is full of unhappiness and says in a low voice, "I'm sorry. You're right."

When he turns to face me again, he gives me a smile I think is genuine. That and the apology make me feel like whatever happened to make us go off track there for a few seconds is over.

"I just want to say that I can respect you having a type when it comes to your naked women in magazines, but that type of body isn't realistic. Just speaking on behalf of females around the world who have normal bodies."

That makes him smile even bigger. As he sits in the chair a few feet away over near the window, he says, "Normal bodies? I'm not sure those women in that magazine would agree they don't have normal bodies, Ava."

I'm struck by how my name sounds coming out of his mouth. His voice is sexy and deep, like speaking my name pleases him.

But I can't focus on that because he's practically challenging me to explain how the women in this magazine aren't anywhere close to normal. I'm not even sure they're real. I know at least parts of them aren't.

Holding up the magazine, I look over the top of it and point at the blond woman's oddly tiny waist. "See this right here? Not normal. Where are her organs? How do you fit all those feet of intestines in that tiny space? I'm guessing if this isn't completely airbrushed, she's had some work done."

Matthias laughs out loud at the beginning of my dissertation about what may be his dream woman. "Well, I guess now that you mention it, she does have a really small waist. But you can't have a much bigger waist yourself. I carried you upstairs, and I can tell you you're as light as air."

With a roll of my eyes, I say, "Trust me. My waist isn't this small. They'd have to remove some of my ribs to get it this size. And look at that butt. For God's sake, how does she stand up with that thing?"

He leans in to look at the naked blond's ass and nods. "My guess is she doesn't do a lot of standing."

A second eye roll I couldn't stop if I wanted to is followed by me shaking my head. "She's a person, Matthias. She has to stand up and walk around at some point. I bet she had implants to make it that big."

"You're not a fan of implants?" he asks, like they're something I should be a cheerleader for.

I don't have to think about that question for even a second. "No, I'm not. I think people are fine just as they are."

Folding his arms across his chest, he asks, "So you don't think people should try to improve themselves with exercise or anything like that?"

It's clear where he's going with this. I've been playing sports all my life, except for this past year I took off between high school and college. I'm sure he's seen me leave my house dressed in my uniform in the past few years.

"I'm not saying that. I'm saying nobody gets a butt like this from working out. It's not normal. You know, Coach told us that if we start to do stuff like this to our bodies that we better be prepared to keep up the maintenance for the rest of our lives. If Blondie here doesn't do that, she should expect some serious droopage to happen by the time she's in her forties."

For a few moments, he doesn't say anything but simply nods his head. "I'll have to keep that in mind."

I toss the magazine onto the bed and sit back against the pillows. "You're not taking this seriously, I guess."

With a faux look of surprise, he says, "Oh, but I am. Droopage. Forties. Sounds pretty bad. I suspect she'll have to go in for a tune up before then, though."

"Whatever. All I'm saying is normal people don't look like this. Then again, since these magazines have a particular purpose, you aren't exactly looking for a normal woman."

Matthias stands and walks over toward where I'm lying on his bed. Looking down at me, he smiles and shakes his head. "I'm not sure what to say to that. Let's just say that if I didn't have those to look at, I'd focus on someone real and close by."

I open my mouth, but not a word comes out. Did he mean if he was playing with himself that he'd be thinking about me? The choices are very few on this estate. The only females here on a regular basis are Eleanor and me, and I'm not thinking he's fantasizing about the housekeeper.

All I can do is look up at him in shock as the realization that he meant me fills my head. Those dark eyes of his stare down at me with an intensity I've never noticed in them before, and then he walks away, leaving me wondering what's going on.

As his bedroom door closes, I'm left with one thought I don't understand.

Matthias King fantasizes about me?

CHAPTER EIGHT

*M*atthias

I slip on my coat, hat, and gloves and walk outside after nearly confessing to Ava that I've been thinking about her and not those airbrushed models in Playboy for years. I need to get away from her before I make a mistake I know I shouldn't.

It's just that she looks so good lying there in that white robe on my bed that if I didn't walk out at that moment, I would have kissed her. And I wouldn't have wanted to stop at kissing either.

Jesus Christ, I need to forget even thinking that. I know better. Ava Sutton is not someone I can have. She's not even someone I should think about having.

The wind has died down from before, so at least I can see ten feet in front of me. I scan the area around the back door and judge that there has to be at least a foot to a foot and a half of snow on the ground already, and it's still coming down.

The head groundskeeper, a man named Jonesy who's worked for my father since before I was born, stands with a shovel in his hand at the end of the sidewalk leading to the road that winds around the estate. Looking around like he can't imagine how he's going to get rid of all of this snow, he turns his head left and right and then sighs in premature defeat.

Taking a step out from under the alcove near the back door, I wave at him. "Hey, want some help?"

He lifts his head to focus on me and pushes his red and blue New York Giants hat up his forehead. "Matthias?"

The tone of his voice tells me he doesn't understand the offer. I guess I shouldn't be surprised. I've never once shoveled snow here. Also, the few times I've spoken to Jonesy have been surface conversations at best about things like the weather and if I should move my car when he's cutting the grass.

I walk toward him and nod as I stop a few feet away. "Yeah, it's me. Just thought I'd come out and see if you could use some help."

He slowly nods, almost as if he still can't believe I'm standing out here with him. "Sure."

The King estate head groundskeeper has to be almost as old as my father, but the difference between them is Jonesy's weathered face tells anyone who looks at him that he's tough enough to handle winters like we get here. Not that my father couldn't, I guess, but he's got enough money that he barely has to deal with the weather at any time of the year.

Jonesy pushes his shovel toward me as he explains, "I've got another one in the shed. I'll get it and we can get rid of this snow in no time."

I grab the handle as the reality that I've never shoveled snow in my life occurs to me. Maybe I'm more like my father than I like to think.

With a smile that pushes up his ruddy cheeks until they meet his eyes, the groundskeeper points toward the shed. "I'll be right back. If you want, you can wait until I get my shovel."

I suspect Jonesy knows I've never shoveled a flake of snow in my twenty-three years too, so I wave off his offer. "It's okay. I got this. Just join in when you get back."

He eyes me suspiciously but continues to smile as he turns to walk through the path of footsteps he left when he walked over here from the shed earlier. I get it. I've never been known as the friendly King boy. Hell, I've never even been known as the sort of nice King. If anything, all anyone has ever thought of me is I'm the King son who says little, but when I actually speak, it's usually something cruel that comes out of my mouth.

None of that would be a lie. That doesn't mean I can't be nice sometimes.

I jam the shovel into the foot of snow currently freezing my legs and feet and toss it off to the side. It's a light snow, thankfully, so it practically blows away in the wind as I dump it onto the area next to the sidewalk.

So this is shoveling. It's not that bad. Then again, I've only been out here doing it for about two minutes. I'm thinking it's going to suck if I'm out here an hour from now still trying to clear off this sidewalk.

Glancing up at the door, I see the security camara and have to smile at the idea of my father watching this. He'd probably stand there with his mouth hanging open in utter shock if he saw me out here.

"You know, this is as bad as the storm we had in ninety-three. We had one in ninety-two too, but I think this one is more like ninety-three. I swear to God I shoveled a ton of snow that year. An actual ton!" Jonesy says as he joins me at the end of the sidewalk and digs his shovel into the snow at his feet.

I don't bother to mention those snowstorms occurred before I was born. He knows that, I'm sure, and I doubt he was telling me about them because he thought I knew firsthand about either one.

Thankful he's bothering to make conversation while we shovel since left in silence I'm going to think about Ava upstairs in my bedroom, I ask him to tell me about the last time we had a huge snowstorm because I can't remember for the life of me ever seeing this much snow.

Jonesy stops his work for a moment or two to think and nods when he remembers the storm that answers my question. "Right after you were born, I'm guessing. You're around twenty-two now, aren't you?"

I toss a shovel full of snow onto the pile I've begun creating and nod at his incorrect guess. "Close. Twenty-three."

"Then yeah, it would be that storm. I remember that one because your mother wasn't here because she was at the hospital having your brother Theo. January. No February. Those storms are always so much worse than these."

Curious why he thinks that, I push my shovel over

the concrete sidewalk in my attempt to find a better way to clear the path. It makes snow go everywhere all over where I just shoveled, though.

"Why are storms worse?"

He takes a big breath of ice-cold air into his nose, and all I can think is he just froze both nostrils by doing that. Nudging his Giants hat further off his face and revealing his big forehead with tons of lines, he stops working for a moment to answer me.

"Because there's no chance for a quick warm up so some of it melts. February storms are the worst. You know if you got all that snow even a month later it would melt pretty quickly, but in February and January, there's nothing but frigid temperatures to keep it all around until spring. Snow is beautiful when it's falling and even when it's first on the ground. After a couple days, though, it's nothing but ugly."

I look up from my shoveling to smile at him since I agree with that. Nobody likes seeing those huge mounds of filthy snow with dirt and road salt all mixed in sitting on every damn street corner. They're ugly as fuck, but until warmer weather comes around, that's all anyone sees up here in the Northeast.

That's one thing I didn't miss last year when I got to do a semester abroad in Spain. No piles of ugly snow there for those ten weeks.

"Yeah, I hate that," I say to continue the conversation.

I've never really talked to Jonesy like this, but he's all right. I have to give it to him. This snow may be light, but shoveling it gets tiring after a while. He's kept up with me shovel for shovel this whole time.

When we're nearly finished, I remember we own at least two snowblowers. "Hey, why didn't we just snowblow all of this?"

The groundskeeper stops and jams his shovel into a pile of snow next to him. "I didn't believe the weatherman when he said we could get a storm. They're always saying it's going to be huge, and then you get all ready for it and all you get are a few damn inches, at most. So I gambled that he was wrong, as usual, and didn't gas up either of the snowblowers. Guess I lost that bet."

The way he says that, like it's no big deal and life goes on, makes me laugh. Nothing bothers this guy. I wish I could be like him. Everything fucking bothers me.

"Well, no big deal," I say as I scoop up a shovel full of snow and toss it to my right. "We got this done pretty quickly."

He nods and we get back to work since there's only a few feet left before we reach the door to the kitchen. This hasn't been too bad. I don't think I'd want to do this every day for the rest of my life, but for the past hour, it's been okay.

Even better, it's kept my mind off Ava upstairs in my bedroom.

I glance up at the second-floor windows and focus on mine where she's just a few feet away probably looking at that Playboy magazine. She's not wrong about those women. They don't look real. Not that any man actually cares. Those pictures are just helpful in getting things going.

But even though I buy a new one every month, I barely think about those women when I'm looking through the pages. All I ever think of is the one person I'm not supposed to think about.

Ava Sutton.

When we finish the sidewalk, Jonesy stands his shovel up in a pile of snow and smiles. "Thanks for the help. It was nice to have someone to talk to. Makes the work go by so much faster."

I do the same thing with my shovel and nod, oddly happy about what we did together. "This wasn't bad. Thanks for the stories about all those snowstorms. You know how to make the time pass."

Jonesy slides his hat off his head, revealing a scraggly mess of blond hair. "Thanks. You better go inside. You're not wearing boots, so I bet your feet are pretty damn well frozen by now."

Nodding, I watch him take both shovels as he walks down the path we cleared on his way to the driveway. I should stay out here and help him since I know what's going to happen if I go back upstairs.

I should do anything but go back to where Ava is sitting in that fluffy white robe with nothing on underneath and smelling so good. But I can't stop myself. I've dreamed of being with her for so long, and now to have that fantasy finally close to coming true is too much temptation for me to deny.

AVA IS ASLEEP WHEN I GET BACK TO MY ROOM. Curled up into a comma shape, she looks adorable with her hands tucked under her chin like a little kid napping. My gaze drifts over her body as she lies there so innocently, and then I see her shift position so the robe opens up. There right before my eyes her breasts are on full display, and in seconds, I'm rock hard.

She's not anywhere as huge as those women in the magazines, but she's perfect for her normal body and size. As I watch her knowing I should look away, all I can think of is how I'd never look at another magazine model if I had her for my own.

I shake my head to purge that thought from my brain. No. Of all the females on the planet, she's the only one I can't have.

Turning away, I walk into the bathroom to take a shower. Maybe the hot water will help me get my mind off all the things I want to do with her that I can't.

In truth, it's not an issue of can't. I could be with Ava. Looking down my body as I strip out of my clothes, I see the evidence that I'm physically capable of sleeping with her. My cock is so hard I think it could cut glass right now, so yes, I can fuck her.

I'm just not supposed to.

As the hot water rolls over my head and down my chest, I think back to the first time I knew little Ava Sutton wasn't just the daughter of my father's estate manager. I'd seen her every day for my entire life, but then I looked out the window one night as my brothers and I were fucking around in the game room and there she was wearing that pink satin dress that showed every perfect inch of her body. Some guy I instantly hated picked her up to take her to her junior prom, and her father made them walk up here to meet my father. She looked so perfect and so sweet, and at that moment as she and whatever his name was in his ill-fitting tux that showcased his lack of muscles strolled up the road that beautiful spring evening, I couldn't think of anything else in the world I wanted more than to have Ava as mine.

I never understood why Theo didn't ask her to be his date for the prom. He's been closer to her than anyone for years. When I mentioned it to him, he brushed off the question like it was ridiculous.

"Little Ava? She's not my type."

"Why? You hang out with her all the time. Why isn't she your type?" I asked, even though I had a feeling I knew the answer before he said it.

Screwing his face into a wicked smile, he answered, "Ava Sutton is the type of girl you marry. She's not the type you fuck around with. When it comes time to settle down, I'll look for her. I've told her she's the future Mrs. Theo King, so she knows. Until then, there's a world full of girls to enjoy."

The irony is Theo could have been with her any time he wanted. I never had the choice. Not after that day.

You see, while I was looking out the window at her in that beautiful pink dress that made her look like an angel, someone else was watching me. When I turned around once she and her date drove off, my father was waiting to talk to me.

"I see how you look at her, Matthias. Don't even think about it. Stick with those girls you usually date, but don't touch her."

As usual, what my father said wasn't up for debate.

I didn't know why he'd decided I could never be with Ava while it was perfectly okay for Theo to spend hours with her that any normal person had to believe would eventually develop into something more than friends. All

I knew was he'd decreed that I was never to have Ava, and that was it.

Lost in thought about that day more than two years ago, I don't feel the heat of the water or anything because all I can think of is her. It's been like this since that day. Almost as if telling me I couldn't have her made me want her all the more.

I've obeyed his rule all this time, choosing to be cruel to her when all I wanted to be was the one person who could love her more than anyone else. What else could I do? If I was nice, she'd be her usual sweet self, and I knew how that would turn out.

Exactly as it has today.

The difference now, though, is I'm not going to deny myself the one thing I've wanted for nearly three years. She's here, and there's no Maximilian King or Theo to stand in my way.

Knowing what I want, I turn off the shower and wrap a towel around me to head back out to the bedroom. I silently tell myself if she's still asleep, that's a sign from the Universe that I shouldn't do anything. If she's awake, that's the green light to make a move.

I slowly open the door as anticipation builds inside me. Let her be awake. Please let her be awake.

Stepping into the room, I see her sitting up in my bed staring at me.

Not a red light in sight.

CHAPTER NINE

va

When Matthias walks out of the bathroom wearing only a white towel slung low on his hips, it's like all the oxygen has been sucked out of the room. I can't help but gawk at how incredible he looks standing there still wet from the shower with droplets of water clinging to his muscular chest and abs and that sexy V from his hips angling down toward what hides beneath that towel.

I had no idea the oldest King brother looked like this. I've seen Theo dressed in only a bathing suit during the summer and knew he had a great body, and I've been around the younger King brothers when they're swimming, but somehow I never knew Matthias was so unbelievably built.

My gaze lingers on his gorgeous body for far too long before I look up at his face and see him watching me stare at him. No, not stare. Ogle. I'm ogling him like I've never seen a man's body before.

I'm no better than him with his nudie magazines.

"Hey. I didn't realize you were in the shower," I say, stumbling over my words as the most impure thoughts I've ever had float through my brain.

He nods but doesn't say anything. I want to continue the conversation since it feels awkward just looking at him like he's a piece of desirable meat, but I don't know what to say.

"I must have fallen asleep. Where did you go?"

Matthias silently walks to his dresser and pulls out fresh clothes to wear. "I was outside helping to clear the walkway."

Something about the way he says that so flatly, like there's no emotion in him now, makes me wonder what's changed in him since we talked last. Then he was sweet and kind. Now he sounds like a machine.

"You helped Jonesy shovel the sidewalk?" I ask in surprise since I don't think I've ever seen Matthias help with anything on the estate.

He snaps his head around and glares at me. "Yeah. Why?"

I smile, hoping to diffuse whatever this tension is that's grown between us all of a sudden. "Just wondering. It's just that you don't usually do things like that."

"I do a lot of things you don't know about, little Ava."

And right there when he calls me that nickname, I know something's wrong. "Did I do something? Why are you acting like this again?"

My heart sinks when he turns around to face me and

I see that same cold expression he always wears when I'm around. What did I do to make him change back to this mean person again?

"You should get dressed. The groundskeeper has probably cleared a lot of the road to your house by now, so you can go home."

His words hit me like slaps to the face. He doesn't want me around anymore, even though I don't have a clue as to why. I'm back to being unwanted little Ava who belongs anywhere else other than near him.

"There's no heat at my house, Matthias. That hasn't changed. And my ankle is still hurting," I say, hating how my words sound like I'm pleading to be allowed to stay here even though I'm no longer welcome.

He shrugs in that way that tells me I mean nothing in his world. "Wear a coat. You'll be fine. You should be in your house where you belong."

Those words hit my ears, and it's all I can do to not slap him across the face for being so nasty once again. I jump up out of the bed and hobble across the room toward the door. My emotions are all over the place, so I swear if he says another unkind word, I'm going to lash out and then probably collapse into a teary mess.

God, why does this person have to be so mean to me? And why the hell do I give a damn that he doesn't like me enough to even want to be nice?

Just before I reach the door, I spin around on my good foot and snap, "I hate you, Matthias. You're cruel."

When he doesn't say a single word to me after that, I hobble back through the room to where he stands and push against his bare chest. "I hate you! Are you happy now? Or will you only be happy when you watch me limp through a snowstorm all the way back to my house where someone like me belongs?"

Tears begin to stream down over my cheeks as I wait for him to respond, but he says nothing. It's like I'm not even worth the trouble of answering I'm so low in his mind.

Through my watery eyes, I stare up into his dark eyes and see nothing. No emotion. No kindness. Nothing.

I don't know why, but that makes me feel even worse, and I can't stop myself from exploding. "Say something! Tell me what changed in the time that I was asleep and you were in the shower! Tell me, Matthias!"

Of course, he says nothing. I don't warrant even a murmur. He simply stares at me with a look in his eyes like I'm the one who's being cruel here.

"I bet you're happy to see me cry. I don't understand why, but I bet you are."

For the first time since he walked out of the bathroom, his icy façade cracks ever so slightly and he winces. "No. I'm not happy," he says softly.

I wipe the tears from my cheeks and sniffle as I say, "Well that makes two of us. If that was your goal, congratulations. Good job."

Why this person revels in seeing me miserable, I have no idea, but no matter what he claims, he's enjoying this. What I don't understand and he won't tell me is what I ever did to make him hate me like he does.

I turn to leave once more, crushed at how this has turned out between us yet again. I want to scream or punch something—no, punch him—but it's no use. Some people will never like you no matter how nice you are to them. Matthias King just happens to be one of those people with me.

"Whatever you think I did to you, I'm sorry. I'd fix it if I could, but I officially give up, Matthias. I won't bother you from now on."

As ridiculous as it sounds, I start crying again. I can't understand why my emotions are so all over the place when it comes to him, but this time I don't try to hold back the tears. Maybe it's the pain in my ankle. Or maybe it's the thought of having to walk back home in the blizzard that's still raging outside.

No, it's neither of those things or anything else but the fact that of all the members of the King family, only this one has ever made me feel like I'm not enough. That I'm merely the help he can dismiss whenever he chooses.

I can barely see the door through my tears as I slowly make my way toward it to get the hell out of this horrible person's bedroom. Some part of me keeps thinking he's going to apologize before I leave in a few seconds, but I hear nothing behind me, almost as if he's not even there.

A few years ago, my father warned me to stay away from the oldest King son. I didn't understand why because he knew how close I've always been to Theo, and he never explained what he meant. He just told me whatever I did to not bother being nice to this one.

I thought my father was being overprotective as usual because I was sure even though everyone, including Theo, said Matthias would never be anything but the cold soul he was that if someone showed him true kindness and friendship that he'd reciprocate. But they were all right and I was the one who didn't understand.

Matthias King is simply a mean person who enjoys hurting others. Now I can say I'm one of those he's hurt.

As I reach for the doorknob, I feel something on my shoulder. I look back to see him standing right behind me shaking his head. Did he say something, and I didn't hear him?

"What?"

Typical for him, he doesn't answer me. He stares down at me like he wants to say something, though.

"Do you have something terrible you forgot to say to me? I guess this is your last chance since once I leave this room I never plan to even look at you again, much less speak a word to you ever again in my life. So what is it? Want to tell me I'm ugly or nothing compared to those women in those magazines of yours? Now's your chance because in a second I'm out of here."

"No, I don't think that."

I'm beginning to wonder if he's being charged by the word, but since the Kings have more money than God, I doubt he'd care about paying for every nasty syllable he wants to utter to me. I stand there waiting, but all he does is stare at me with those deep brown eyes that look cruel and sad at the same time.

But I can't let myself get wrapped up in feeling bad for him.

"Fine. Great talk. Thanks for being the person everyone says you are. I'll make a point of telling your brother he was right about you."

For the second time in our current little standoff, something I say makes him wince, and for a split second, I let myself wonder why he looks so unhappy. Then I come to my senses, thankfully. He doesn't deserve to have me care about his happiness. Not after all the terrible things he's said to me today.

"I'm sorry, Ava."

The words come out like someone's pulling them from his throat. Is it really that hard to apologize to me after how rotten he's been today?

"For?"

I don't want to let him off the hook so easily. Normally, all I need to hear are those words and I'm ready to forgive people for virtually anything. Not with Matthias, though. He's hurt my feelings too many times just in the past few hours for me to be my usual kind self.

He hesitates for a moment before answering, "Actually, no, I'm not sorry."

That's it! I've been nice and once again he set me up to knock me down. Now he gets both barrels of my anger.

Spinning around so we're toe to toe, I point my finger up in his face. "You know what, Matthias? Fuck—"

I never get the chance to say the word you before he leans down and presses his lips to mine in a kiss that takes my breath away. In a flash, it's like he surrounds me, and I have nowhere to run.

But I don't want to leave now. I want to feel more of his lips softly touching my lips and his tongue teasing mine.

My head spins as he gently pushes me against the door I couldn't wait to reach just a minute ago. Now I can't think of anything but staying in this room with him.

When he lifts his head and looks down at me, I want to ask what's going on. Or why he's kissing me if he hates me so much that he can't stand to have me around.

Or a million other questions that would help this make sense.

Yet I don't. I simply stare up at him in the hopes that he'll finally say something so I understand him.

Of course, he doesn't. Instead, he reaches his hand out to loosen the belt on my robe, and as I watch, it falls open to reveal my naked body. I don't know why, but I don't move a muscle to cover myself like I would with anyone else in the world. It's like I'm under his spell and I can't do a thing.

His gaze rakes over me from my face to my feet and back up again before he smiles. I'm almost afraid of what he may say he's so unpredictable, so I'm happy when he remains silent as he studies me.

I don't know what to do next, even as thoughts of what I want to happen race through my mind. I'm not a virgin, but I'm definitely not as experienced as he is or, I doubt, as experienced as the other women he's been with.

Finally, I can't stand the silence anymore and throw caution to the wind to risk hearing what he's thinking. "Please say something. I'm standing here naked with you staring at my body. Say something. Anything."

Matthias smiles and looks into my eyes. "You're not naked. You still have a robe on."

The anticipation of not knowing what he'd say makes my emotions unravel inside me, and for a moment, I don't know if I want to laugh or cry. "Really? You have a naked woman standing in front of you, and you want to nitpick?"

"You do have a robe on."

"And if I let it fall to the floor and then I'm buck-naked standing here, will you still have nothing else to say to me?" I ask, silently questioning where that bravery came from.

He shakes his head and leans down to kiss me softly before whispering against my lips, "I won't say anything then either because we'll have better things to do."

His words send chills up and down my spine, and my nipples harden to excited peaks. "Oh. You have something in mind?" I ask, surprised since it seems he's thought this whole thing out between us.

Meanwhile, I'm still trying to figure out what the hell is going on. One minute he's cruel and telling me I don't belong in his house. The next he's being sweet and rescuing me from a snowdrift. And then the next he's back to being cruel and telling me to go away.

Nodding, he doesn't wait for me to drop my robe and slowly pushes it off my body himself. It puddles at my feet, leaving me naked in front of him.

Again, his gaze slides over the entire length of my body, but this time when he reaches my face, he isn't smiling. I instantly brace myself for something hurtful to come out of his mouth, sure I'm dealing with a madman who may have mental problems or at least some kind of split personality issue.

"I shouldn't do this. I'm not supposed to even think about you, Ava." He stops and lets out a heavy sigh before continuing. "The problem is you're all I can think about."

His confession leaves me confused. Relieved he isn't saying anything that will make me cry again, I ask, "Today, you mean?"

Matthias shakes his head. "No. For so long that I

can't remember a time when I didn't want to be right here with you."

His voice falters as he says that, and it's all I can do to not ask any more questions. Those can come later. Right now, we have better things to do.

CHAPTER TEN

va

STILL WEARING THAT TOWEL THAT SEEMS LIKE MORE OF a tease than anything else, he lifts me in his arms and carries me back to his bed, setting me down gently like I'm something important he wants to cherish. I know better than to expect much in the way of talking from him, so I simply watch as he climbs into bed next to me, shoving the Playboy magazine away like it's of no interest to him anymore.

He truly is beautiful lying beside me, his dark gaze fixed on my face like he's searching for the answer to a question he hasn't spoken yet. I move my attention to the towel still wrapped around his hips and smile.

"So one of us is naked, but the other is still wearing clothes. Not fair."

"A towel isn't clothes," he says in a low voice as he traces his fingertip over my shoulder.

"Did you go to school to be a lawyer? You certainly do like to nitpick."

Without answering my question, he leans over and kisses me, and I swear it's unlike anything I've ever experienced in my life. When his lips touch mine, it's as if he's worshipping me, like I'm something he adores. I've never had anyone kiss me like this. As gentle as he was when he was checking my ankle to see if it was broken, he's even more tender now.

I slide my hand around his neck and bury my fingers in his dark hair as I pull his mouth to mine. My tongue playfully dances over his, inching up my desire for him to be rid of that damn towel.

He cradles my face in his hands, sweetly caressing my cheeks. When he lifts his head, I open my eyes and see him looking down at me like he could be happy to just stare into my eyes for the rest of time.

"Why didn't you ever let me know you liked me?" I ask, breaking my own promise I made to myself just a little while ago not to ruin things with questions.

It's just I have to know before we sleep together.

Matthias shakes his head and frowns. "I couldn't."

"Why? If you liked me, why couldn't you let me know?"

When he shrugs, I know I won't get a straight answer about this. Maybe it shouldn't matter. We're snowbound here without another soul around, except for Eleanor and Jonesy. Neither of us have to deal with our families at this moment, so what does it matter what he felt and when?

All that matters is we feel it now.

I slide my hand down over his broad chest and chiseled abs that are hard to the touch until I reach that towel he still hasn't removed. Smiling, I tug at the knot near his hip.

"This may not be clothes, but it's in the way."

He's hard as a rock underneath it, so I can't imagine he wants to keep it on any longer. Does he want me to take it off like he did with my robe?

With a wicked grin, he shifts his body, and it falls away from his hips. Pressing against me, he's long and thick and far more than I expected. Then again, he is nearly a foot taller than me and twice my size. I should have anticipated he'd be hung like a horse.

I can't stop myself from looking down between our bodies, and I feel my eyes grow wide at the sight of him. Oh. My. God. He's even bigger than I thought a second ago.

Biting my lip, I look up at him and know he sees in my expression how much I want him. He smiles so devilishly, sending a jolt of desire through me.

A second later, his mouth is on mine in a kiss that makes me want him more than I thought I could ever want a man. My head swims with how good his kiss makes me feel, and then he gently climbs on top of me. I don't know how he doesn't crush me because he's so much bigger than I am.

I open my eyes when he pulls his mouth from mine, and a second later, one slow thrust of his hips and he fills me so completely I'm practically breathless. He stills inside me as he smooths away the hair away from my face and looks down into my eyes like nothing else in the world matters more than being there with me and making love to me.

Slow and steady, he slides into my body, touching a spot I'd never known existed. Each time he fills me up, it feels like we're made just for each other, pieces fitting together to create a perfect whole.

The sound of his breathing fills my ears, and its warmth heats the skin of my neck as he pumps into me. My fingers tug at his hair, and he makes a guttural noise so utterly sexy I pull harder just to hear him make it again.

I rake my fingernails down his back and sink them into his hips to urge him to go faster. For a moment, he hesitates, but I moan, "Don't stop. God, don't stop."

He doesn't, and with every thrust of his cock into my body, I feel myself inch closer to an orgasm. Wrapping my legs around his waist, I press my heels into his spine and arch my back, desperate to feel every inch of him against me.

"God, I'm so close. Right there…"

He lifts his upper body off me even higher and balances himself on his hands next to my head as he stares down into my face, the intensity in his dark eyes so sexy I can't look away. I don't want to, though. I want to drink in every beautiful expression as he fucks me. For one of the few times with Matthias, I know exactly what he's feeling because of the look in his eyes.

Need. The need to have me completely for himself.

No one has ever looked at me like that. Friends have told me about having their boyfriends look at them like that and how incredible it made them feel, but I've never had it happen to me before.

Like he sees the entire world when he looks at me.

Dipping his head, he kisses me long and deep as his movements became more jagged, fucking me with shallow jabs instead of languorous strokes. I sense he's close like I am and tilt my hips to help us topple over that delicious edge into ecstasy. Just a few more hard thrusts, and that's all it takes for my release to rush through my entire body.

Matthias groans as my body tightens around him and then comes seconds later, his back arching as he fills me one final time. He looks like the very essence of maleness. Strong. Powerful. Imposing.

And in complete possession of me.

We lay in each other's arms not saying a word as a feeling of utter satisfaction takes over me. He holds me to him like I'm the most precious thing in the world.

Like I'm his.

The aftershocks from my release shake my body when he eases out of me and rolls off to the other side of the bed. Flush with pleasure, I close my eyes and let out a deep breath, completely satisfied.

"Ava?" he whispers in a deep voice that hits me exactly on the spot he touched inside me with his cock.

I turn my head toward him and open my eyes. He looks so different now I can barely remember that person who I swore I would hate forever just a few hours ago.

"Uh-huh."

I wish I could say something else, something sexy or romantic, but after what we just did together, I can barely think of any words to say.

Turning to face me, he smiles, and I question how I

could have ever missed how sexy he could be. "Are you okay?"

With a nod, I sigh. "Definitely okay. You okay?"

His smile widens, and he nods in return. "I'm definitely okay too."

He wraps his arm around my body and pulls me close. Resting my head on his chest, I listen to the sound of his heartbeat, loving the way he feels so strong beneath my cheek. He kisses the top of my head, letting his lips linger for a moment before he tightens his hold around me in a way that makes me feel like the entire world can fall away as long as I'm here with him.

Matthias returns to saying nothing, but now, I'm not concerned about his silence. In a strange way, it comforts me and makes this moment mean more than I could have ever imagined possible.

CHAPTER ELEVEN

$\mathcal{M}$atthias

FOR AN HOUR, AVA AND I LIE IN MY BED SAYING little. I suspect she wishes I would talk about something after our time together, but all I can think of is how perfect this feels with her in my arms. I don't want to ruin it by saying the wrong thing.

I turn to look out the window and see the snow still falling. I'd forgotten it was even still a blizzard out there. That's what she does to me. Everything ceases to exist when I'm with her.

Finally, Ava lifts her head up off my chest. A pink blush colors her cheeks, making her even more beautiful than usual. "So, I feel like neither one of us knows what to say now."

"Do we have to say anything?" I ask, sincerely

hoping the answer is no because dissecting what we just did would likely steal all the magic from it.

She thankfully shakes her head and smiles. "No. I just thought someone should break the silence."

I can't help but think she's worried now, but she'd have good reason if she is. My emotions when it comes to her haven't exactly come off as being even-keeled. I know that's my fault. She has no idea how hard I had to fight wanting to be with her before I finally surrendered to the reality that I'm crazy about her.

Then an idea comes to me. Maybe if she knows about something I don't share with most people she'll see she can trust me not to turn into that dick I've been far too often with her.

Reaching around her, I open my nightstand and pull out my sketchbook. Ava looks at it and then at me like she doesn't understand what's going on.

"Planning on writing something? Seems like a strange time to do that," she says with a nervous giggle.

I push myself up as she sits cross-legged next to me. Setting the book on my lap, I open the cover to the first page where there's a sketch of some trees I drew one day five summers ago. She looks down at it and then lifts her head to look at me again.

"You draw? I didn't know you drew. This is really good, Matthias," she says sweetly.

With a nod, I smile, proud of what is actually a pretty basic sketch. "It's not bad. This was the first drawing I made when I got this sketchbook. I have others full of landscapes and objects I've toyed around with."

She shakes her head in amazement. "I had no idea. How long have you been doing this?"

I think about that question for a moment and shrug. "Ten years? Maybe longer. I don't know how I even started, to be honest. One day I just found myself doodling like I always did when I was bored, but the doodle turned out to be an actual picture and not just scribbles like usual. My mother saw me, and like she always did whenever she saw one of us get good at something, she ran out and bought me a sketchbook just like this. From that day on, whenever I can, I work on getting better. These trees aren't very good compared to what I can do now."

"Can I see more?"

Like always, Ava is eager and sweet, and for one of the first times ever, I don't hesitate to show off what I've drawn. Most people have no idea I do this in my spare time. It's not something I want to share with the world.

But I want her to see them, so I begin to flip through the pages, narrating what I was doing and when I drew each image as I get to it. She listens intently, like she's truly interested in everything I have to say, and compliments the ones she likes the most.

It's the first time sharing my sketches with anyone outside of my brothers and my mother. My father doesn't have any interest in this hobby of mine, as he likes to call it. Art isn't going to make me any real money, according to him, so it's not something I should waste my time on.

"I wish I had a talent like this. I bet this is good when you're feeling bad, isn't it?" Ava asks.

With a shrug, I avoid admitting how much it helps having the ability to express myself when I feel like shit and there's nobody to talk to. Instead, I turn the focus to her talents.

"You have soccer. I know you love that, right?" I say as I turn the page to a picture of a bowl of fruit.

Ava sighs. "Yeah, but I haven't had that since I graduated. That's the worst part of taking this year off. No soccer. Nothing to keep me busy or in shape."

I scowl at her mention of not being in shape. "Trust me. You're in great shape."

That makes her blush again, and she tries to smile as she says, "Thank you, but I miss playing all the same. My afternoons and weekends were always either practicing or playing in a match, but now that I'm not on a team since I'm not in school, I don't have anything to keep my mind busy."

I know what she needs to be distracted from. The same thing that made me realize how much I needed art.

"I'm sorry about your mother. I know that must be rough."

She nods, swallowing hard as her eyes fill with tears. "Thanks. I was just thinking the same thing about you. It must have been difficult when your mother passed. I know you two were close."

I force a smile as a sigh escapes my throat. "She was the one person who always told me I had talent. My father sees no use for this whatsoever. It's a waste of time in his mind. My mother, though, always encouraged me. She bought me my first sketchbook, and whenever she saw me drawing, she always made sure to tell me how good it was, even when what I was drawing was shit. I miss that."

As those last words leave my mouth, I realize I've never told a soul that. Not even any of my brothers.

Ava tries to smile bigger now, but she wipes tears

from under her eyes as she says, "I know what you mean. My mother always cheered me on at every match. She was right there in the stands no matter what the weather was like or what else she had to do. I always knew no matter how bad things were going I could look up and see her smiling face as she waved at me. That's one of the reasons why I miss it so much, but when I do get back to it, I don't know how I'm going to handle not having her there for me. I just know I'm going to look up into those stands because that's where she always was for every match, and when I don't see her there, it's going to kill me."

I hate seeing her sad, so I quickly flip through the book to find one of my worst drawings. An apple I tried to capture but ended up making it look like a beach ball.

Pointing at it, I say, "This is an apple. Don't worry if you can't make it out. It sucks."

That makes her giggle. "Oh, well, maybe I could see an apple there."

"You don't have to be nice. It's not good. That's okay, though. Not everything is going to be great all the time. My mother used to say that to encourage me when I felt like everything I was drawing was terrible. She'd say, 'Honey, don't give up. If this doesn't work, try again.' So I'd try again, and she was right. The next thing I tried usually turned out better."

"Do you ever draw people?"

I turn to a drawing of my brothers I was working on earlier today before they left with my father to go to the city. Spinning the book around, I hold it up so she can see. "It's not finished, but those are Marius and Kellen shooting pool, and that's Theo standing with a pool cue.

That outline over there is Ronan. He wasn't doing anything but sitting on the couch texting his girlfriend like he always does, so I figured I could finish him some other time."

Ava studies the image for a long moment before looking at me. "I love how you got their expressions so perfectly! Theo always does that thing with his tongue when he's thinking about something or watching something intently. He sticks it out and focuses really hard. You captured that precisely as he does it!"

I can't help but laugh at her description of exactly what my brother does when he's thinking hard about something. "He's done that all his life. I swear he did it when he was a baby."

"No kidding! I remember him doing it when he was just a little boy and we started playing our hide and seek game. I'd look out from where I was hiding and see him looking for me, his face all serious and that tongue poking out of his mouth. He's too funny when he does that."

"He gets it from my father. He does that tongue thing too when he's really focused on work. I'll walk into his office and see him sitting there reading some specs with his tongue sticking out."

Ava gets quiet for a long while as I continue to show her my drawings until she asks, "Would you draw me?"

Since I don't want to come off as a stalker, I don't tell her I've drawn her before as I sat in the window and watched her goof around with my brother or when she would run up and down the road that surrounds the estate to train for soccer. That would only make her question why I've been so rotten to her for so long, and that's not something I want to talk about.

"Okay. Only if you're sure, though."

Instantly, she tugs the comforter from underneath me and pulls it up to her chin. "I'm sure."

I shake my head. "Nope. Nude or nothing."

She points at the sketchbook and pleads, "But you don't have any other nudes in there."

"This will be my first."

Lowering the covers down to just above her breasts, she tilts her head to the right and smiles. "We aren't in Titanic, Matthias."

"Nude or nothing."

She frowns even as she inches the comforter slightly lower. "I don't know."

"Don't you trust me? We just had sex."

"And right before that, you were acting like you hated me."

I pull on the comforter so it drops down to her waist, exposing her beautiful breasts. "Come on. You can trust me. No one but me will see it. I promise."

"Says the person who has acted like he hated me until two minutes before we had sex," she jokes nervously.

Reaching out, I yank the covers completely away so she's uncovered again. "I never hated you."

She doesn't cover up as she mumbles, "Could have fooled me."

Finally willing to pose naked, she leans back against my legs and smiles up at me. "Do you mind if I lie down? If I'm sitting, there's this roll here around my belly button that I don't think I want anyone drawing."

"We can do it whatever way you want, but choose

now since once I begin, that's where you need to stay, at least until I get the outline of your body done," I say as I reach over into my nightstand to get a pencil.

"Okay. This works," she says as she rests her head on my knee. "By the way, I hope this doesn't sound weird, but you have great legs."

I begin drawing this gorgeous girl lying naked in my bed and resting against me as she compliments what I've always thought was one of my best parts. It seems surreal that it's Ava here as that girl saying those words, and all I can do is smile.

"You probably hear that all the time," she says. "But they're very nice. Long. Toned. Muscular."

Looking up from my sketch, I nod. "Well, you aren't so bad yourself. Legwise, I mean. Well, actually, all of you, but since we're talking about great legs, yours are pretty damn nice. I remember seeing you walking up the road one day in a blue sundress and flip flops that showed off your legs and thinking soccer might not be such a boring sport to watch after all if the players had legs like yours."

Of course, like all people who love soccer, she immediately gives me a look like I've just committed some kind of horrible crime by saying it's boring. I let her go on for a while about how it's the most exciting sport around and don't bother arguing with her since I've had this discussion before with other soccer fans and know how it ends up. They're all goddamned fanatics, but for this one, I don't mind the lecture about the finer points of the sport.

When she finishes, I hurriedly change the subject and

say, "In fact, I've seen you a bunch of times going out and you always looked beautiful."

Ava draws her eyebrows in like my statement makes her unhappy. "Why didn't you ever talk to me like this? You always seemed to hate me."

I don't respond because that explanation would ruin the time we're spending together, and that's the last thing I want to do. When I don't fill in the silence, she continues to talk about one time she saw me when I was wearing a tux.

"You looked great, but you didn't look happy."

While I sketch out the area around her hips and legs, I explain why I was wearing that tux. "I was a groomsman in my cousin's wedding. She left three months after the ceremony. They'd barely gotten back from their honeymoon when she told him she met some other guy twice her age. A real love match they were."

I glance up from my work and see Ava frowning. "Oh. That's terrible for him. Is he okay now?"

Rolling my eyes, I nod. "He's fine. He met some girl online who likes to dress up in anime costumes and they go to cons all the time. I don't even think he knew that shit existed before her, and now he's all in on it. She'll probably leave him for a Pokémon character or something equally as bizarre."

"You sound like you're not a huge fan of love, Matthias."

As I start drawing her breasts, I tilt my head left and right. "I'm not not a fan of it."

That makes her giggle. "Sounds like a ringing endorsement to me."

When I finish the basics of the drawing that I'll add

to later, I turn the sketchbook around so she can see. "It's not done since I have to fill in more, but what do you think?"

She takes the book out of my hand and sits up to look at the sketch of her. For a long moment, Ava doesn't say a word. She doesn't even move a muscle. All she does is stare at that page with my drawing on it.

And when she finally looks up, I know even before she says a single thing that she likes it. "It's incredible, Matthias. I can't believe how wonderful this is."

"It's just how I see you. Nothing big."

"It is big. It's beautiful. Can I have it when it's finished?" she asks so sweetly that I hate having to tell her no.

Shaking my head, I take the sketchbook from her. "No. I want to keep it. You can come visit it anytime you want, though."

Suddenly, she looks shy, and concern fills her eyes. "Please promise me you won't show anyone else."

"I promise. This is our secret."

Still not convinced, she asks, "Doesn't anyone look at your sketches? Don't you show people?"

I set the book on the nightstand, along with my pencil. "No. Nobody cares about this. All anyone cares about when it comes to me is my taking over the family business when my father retires."

Once again, she frowns. Touching my leg, she says, "I'm sorry. They don't know what they're missing with your drawings. Thank you for doing me."

For a second, I don't know what she means, but when her face turns bright red, I figure out she was referring to drawing her, not fucking her. She looks adorable and so embarrassed as she covers her face with her hands, though.

"Oh, my God! I didn't mean it that way. I meant thank you for drawing me."

I pull her to me and kiss the top of her head. "You're welcome. For both things."

That makes her laugh, and when she drops her hands from her face, she's more beautiful than ever.

CHAPTER TWELVE

va

I open my eyes and it takes a second or two to remember I'm not in my own bed. After Matthias and I spent time talking about his drawings and he sketched my picture, I must have fallen asleep.

Looking over toward the window, I see it's still snowing. This really is a blizzard. Thank God I made it up here when I did, or I might be buried alive out there.

I see his sketchbook sitting on his nightstand and look around for any sign of him, but he's not in the room. I could rip out that naked picture of me and take it so I can be sure no one will ever lay eyes on it since I don't know how I'd explain that. As I sit up to reach for the book, though, I decide not to steal it.

He promised me he'd never show a soul, and I believe him. As he said, it will be our secret.

Wide awake now, I search for the white robe and find it carefully folded on the back of the chair at his desk over near the door. He must have done that when I was sleeping. Slipping it on, I tie the belt and walk out into the hallway to find him.

After peeking into every one of the bedrooms and not finding him, I make my way down the hallway to the last room to check on this floor, the game room where the King boys spend nearly all their time when they're home. But he's not there either.

Did he go back outside to help Jonesy? I smile at that and imagine the groundskeeper is going to think he died and went to heaven with all the assistance today since I know all the men who usually work for him are off for the holiday week.

I walk downstairs and hear someone talking, so I follow the sound and end up just outside the living room of the King mansion. An enormous room with more furniture than I think we have in my entire house, the main attraction during this time of year is the fourteen-foot Fraser fir Christmas tree decorated with all white lights and silver decorations standing in front of the bank of floor-to-ceiling windows so anyone driving up to the house can see it. I've never seen that many ornaments anywhere else but the King family tree.

Matthias paces back and forth across the width of the room as he speaks to someone on the phone. Dressed in light gray sweatpants and a black T-shirt, he's as stunning as when I saw him dressed in a tux that time.

I watch as he listens to whomever he's talking to and see his expression grow darker as the minutes pass. Unsure if I should walk in or stay outside in the hallway,

I wait near the doorway until he finishes and tosses his phone on the sofa closest to the fireplace on the far side of the room.

When he sees me, he waves me in, but he still looks unhappy. "That was my father. He and your father and my brothers have to stay in the city because of the storm. I told him about the heat going out in your house, and he said to make sure you're comfortable in one of the guest bedrooms."

Matthias sounds so cold as he tells me all of that. His voice devoid of emotion, he once again reminds me of a machine. I had hoped after we had sex that he wouldn't revert to being that way, and I have a hard time hiding how disappointed I am.

"Oh. That's nice of him," I mumble as I look past him at the tree and its sparkling lights.

He grabs his phone off the sofa and walks toward me as he says, "I'll take you up to your room."

My room? I had hoped I'd stay with him in his room. What's happened to make him change back to this unfeeling creature again? Did I talk in my sleep and insult him in some way?

I want to ask, but he doesn't give me a chance before he breezes out of the living room and begins walking down the hallway. Hobbling to catch up, I reach him at the top of the stairs when he stops at the first bedroom on the second floor.

"Eleanor makes sure her people keep all the rooms clean, so this should be okay," he says flatly, like he's talking to a perfect stranger.

He opens the door and walks in with me following behind him. It's a beautiful room, just like every other part of the King home, but I'm not even paying attention to it. All I can think of is asking Matthias what's changed between us.

Instead, I make a split-second decision, and when he stops just inside the door, I tug on his arm to get his attention. He turns around, and standing on my tiptoes, I kiss him, even as fear fills me that he's going to push me away.

When I step back, he smiles down at me, and he's that same guy who laughed with me in his room earlier. "I'm guessing that's because you like the room?" he jokes.

I shake my head. "No. That's because I like you. I thought you might be angry with me, but I couldn't imagine why. Did I talk in my sleep or kick you and you fell out of bed? I move around a lot when I sleep."

Cradling my face, he kisses me again. "No. I'm sorry if I seemed off downstairs. Talking to my father always puts me in a weird mood. He had me on the phone for twenty minutes explaining things to me like I'm some goddamned simpleton. He made me promise three times to make sure you're okay."

With a smile, I laugh and ask, "Did you tell him you knew I was okay because I was sleeping in your bed?"

A look of utter dread fills his expression. "Jesus, no. I think if I said that he'd have your father drive all of them home right now, blizzard or not."

I open my mouth to say something about us staying together in that room tonight when Eleanor calls out from the stairs, "Ava! I talked to Mr. King, and he told me I'm to make sure you're happy and given whatever you want. Do you need anything? Where are you? I can't find you anywhere!"

All I want is right here.

Matthias grabs my hand and nods toward the door. "Come with me!"

"I can't move quickly. My ankle. Remember?"

He turns around and crouches down in front of me. "Get on my back."

I willingly do as he says, and he hurries out of the room. My arms wrapped tightly around his shoulders as he holds onto my legs, he runs down the hallway toward the back stairs as Eleanor reaches the second floor. My heart races with excitement, and when he turns to look at me, I swear I see happiness like I've never seen in him before.

We duck into a room I've never known about before in all the times I've been in the King house. He shuts the door behind us and flicks on the light switch to reveal a room full of cabinets containing collectible porcelain figurines.

He sets me down gently on my feet, and pressing his fingertip to my lips, he whispers, "Shhhh. Don't make a noise or she'll find us."

Outside in the hallway, I hear her walk past calling my name. I hate the idea of worrying her, but there's nowhere I want to be more at this moment than right here alone with him.

When the coast is clear, he smiles and says, "That was close."

I look around at the hundreds of figurines housed in the wood cabinets that line the walls. "What is this room?"

Matthias takes a deep breath in and lets it out slowly. "This is where my mother kept all her porcelain dolls and collectibles. I don't think anyone but the housekeepers have been in here since she died."

His voice trails off, and I instantly wonder if we should leave this room. It feels wrong thinking about being with him again here.

"They're very nice," I say, not knowing the right words at this moment.

"My father hated every single one of these things. She brought them out one time, and within a few days, they were all back in here. When she got sick, she stopped coming to this room."

"I'm sorry," I whisper against his back as he looks around and sighs.

When he turns back to face me, he kisses me softly and whispers against my lips, "I say we make this a place at least someone enjoys again."

Before I can ask what that means, he lifts me up by my waist and sets me on one of the empty built-in cabinets that runs the length of the one wall. My heart races again, and a second later, he leans in to kiss me once more.

He unties the belt around my robe and opens it, and I tug his shirt up over his head. Lifting my legs to circle his waist, he kisses me long and hard as I nudge his sweatpants down over his ass. His cock springs free, and he tugs me toward him until it presses against my needy pussy.

We fuck fast and hard, both of us desperate for one another. I cling to his neck as I ride him, my body lifting off the cabinet so he has to hold me up by my ass. His fingers squeeze my flesh and move up to my hips where he sinks his fingertips into my skin while he jackhammers into me.

This time there's no softness or words. Just the desire in both of us to feel joined again. Every nerve ending in my body feels like it's alive, and with every low moan in my ear, I inch closer and closer to coming.

His body flexes against my hands, his neck tightened as he pumps into me. I ride him and he fucks me, our mouths devouring one another in a frantic race to that perfect moment when we come.

I reach it first, my body tensing with the first rush of my orgasm pulsing through me. He holds me tightly in his arms, and even as I try to keep quiet, I can't silence the sound of pure ecstasy as I buck against him and revel in every moment of my release.

A minute later, he stills against me, and I feel him come. He sighs heavily near my ear, almost as if he can finally breathe again.

"I never hated you, Ava. Never."

His words make my heart soar. So full of emotion, they're the true version of him I've grown to care for in the hours we've spent together today.

Matthias presses his forehead to mine and whispers, "I'll come to your room later on when Eleanor falls asleep."

A million things run through my mind in response, but I don't say any of them. It's too soon for that. Maybe next time we're together I'll tell him how I feel. For now, I simply nod before he kisses me and sets me on my feet.

I hurry off to my room for the night, eager for when I'll see him in a few hours. I've never felt like this before.

It's as if I'm as light as air and I could fly up the stairs if I wanted to. He makes me smile, drives me crazy, and then makes me happy all over again.

I don't know if this is love, but if it isn't, then I'm content to enjoy whatever this is between us.

By nine o'clock, my mind is filled with nothing but Matthias. When I saw Eleanor at dinner, she mentioned she was feeling tired and would probably turn in early tonight after all the excitement of the day. I was sure he'd come to see me by now since I know she's gone to bed already.

A sinking feeling interrupts my anticipation at seeing him again. Did he regret our time together today so he's not going to come to see me tonight? He's so mercurial that it wouldn't shock me.

Disappoint me, yes. Shock me, no.

Lost in thought about what makes Matthias King like he is, I don't realize there's someone at my bedroom door until I see him enter the room. My heart leaps in my chest at the sight of him smiling as he walks toward where I sit in bed.

"For the record, I knocked," he says before stopping a few feet away from me.

"I thought maybe you forgot, or you didn't want to…"

My sentence trails off as I silently chastise myself for being insecure. He's here now, smiling and happy, so why did I even say that?

Matthias sits down hard next to me on the bed,

making the mattress shift so I fall into him. Wrapping his arms around me, he kisses me long and deep, and it's all I can do to not rip his T-shirt and those gray sweatpants off his body.

He leans back after another mind-blowing kiss and sighs. "Sorry I'm so late. I know you probably thought I was back to being the world's biggest dick, but I swear I wasn't. This snow has me all messed up, and I fell asleep, even though I didn't think I was tired."

Every word makes me happier than I thought possible, and I can't keep the smile off my face. "It's okay. Snow days are like that."

Turning to glance at the TV, he asks, "What are you watching?"

I shrug, unsure what show it is. I just turned it on to keep my mind off him not showing up. "Not sure. I think it's some mystery show."

Matthias looks over at me and nods. "Do you like those kinds of shows?"

"Yeah. They can be interesting. Do you?"

"Sure. I'll watch anything, as long as it isn't some stupid love story."

I sit up and cross my legs on top of the covers. "You don't think much of love, do you? Seems to me if your cousin who lost his wife after three months can believe in love, you certainly could. I doubt you've ever been abandoned like he was."

That makes him chuckle and shake his head. "Don't be so sure. You have no idea what kind of women I've dated."

A jolt of jealousy spikes inside me, so I plaster a smile on my face to hide my feelings. "True, but considering what you look like, I doubt you've ever been in a position like your cousin was."

At that, he smiles, and he's more stunning than usual. "He is sort of an ugly guy. Maybe that's why she bailed on him after ninety days."

"Aww, that sounds worse when you say it that way. I felt bad for him when I was thinking his wife left him after three months, but ninety days is so harsh."

With a shrug, he leans over and kisses me softly on the center of my mouth. "He's okay, so don't worry. He's got the anime girl."

I stare into his deep brown eyes and feel myself getting lost in them, but I want to know why he's so anti-love. "Well, that's good, but you're still very much not a fan of love from what I'm hearing."

Pursing his lips, he nods his agreement. "Maybe I just haven't met the right person."

"Maybe."

Part of me can't help but wonder what he feels for me, but I can't ask anything about that. We're barely twelve hours from him making me think he hated me. With how quickly his moods change, who knows what kind of answer I'd get.

We sit in silence watching whatever show is on the TV until he turns his body to face me. His expression serious, he stares into my eyes but says nothing.

Uncomfortable, I force a smile and say, "Is there something wrong?"

He shakes his head and smiles. "No."

"I just figured since you were looking at me but not saying anything that maybe I had something on my face or hanging out of my nose."

"No."

"Okay. Well, can you tell me why you're staring at me like this? Because I'm feeling more than a little self-conscious right now."

"Just having a hard time believing we're here together."

If any other guy said that to me, I'd immediately think they were lying, but something about the way Matthias looks when those words come out of his mouth makes me think he's honestly in disbelief that we're sitting here like we are at this moment.

Not that I can blame him. If anyone had asked me this morning if I could ever imagine myself spending time with Matthias King, I would have laughed in their face and asked what kind of drugs they were doing. I've believed the oldest King son hated me for years, so imagining us together like we are right now would have been impossible.

Yet here we are. Even more incredible is how we spent the day together.

"Should I pinch you? Would that make it more believable?" I ask, reverting to my usual defense mechanism, humor.

For a few seconds, he looks at me like he can't figure out if I'm sincere or not, but then his smile returns, brightening up his entire face. "I don't think you have to do that. I mean, unless that's your thing. If it is, I don't mind getting a little rough."

Now it's my turn to stare at him in disbelief. "Did you just make a sex joke?"

He shakes his head and chuckles. "No. A sex joke would be something like why does Santa Claus have such a big sack?"

I shake my head as not a single answer comes to mind. "I have no idea."

Grinning, Matthias says, "He only comes once a year."

My mouth drops open in shock as his joke filters through my brain. "Oh my God! You just told a dirty joke about Santa."

He shrugs and says, "I'm a guy. We know a million dirty jokes. Girls have makeup and hair stuff. We have dirty jokes."

"Naked women and dirty jokes. I'm finding out all sorts of things about you today."

"You had to know I probably liked both of those things. I am a guy, you know."

Shaking my head, I say, "To be honest, I don't think I knew anything about you before today, Matthias. Well, other than you never looked happy whenever I was around."

He winces and then gently pushes me back down onto the bed. Easing his body on top of mine, he looks down into my eyes and quietly says, "I was never unhappy when you were around, Ava. No matter what I looked like, I wasn't unhappy."

That's the second time today he's mentioned that how he's always acted around me was just that—all an act. But why?

"Oh. So you were just pretending to hate me more than all the evil in the world?" I ask as he leans down to kiss me.

Matthias nods and whispers against my lips, "Yes."

I press a finger against his mouth to stop him from

kissing me and ask, "So you wanted to be like this the whole time?"

He sucks my finger between his lips and flicks his tongue against it before nodding his answer. My eyes flutter closed at the sensations he's creating inside me as an ache forms between my legs at the thought that he might use that tongue somewhere else on my body.

With a final tug, he sucks hard on my finger and then lets it slide out of his mouth. "No falling asleep on me. We have all night for that."

I look up at him and shake my head. "I wasn't falling asleep. I'm not even tired, to be honest."

"Good. After that nap I took, I'm not either."

"So what are we going to do? I bet we can find a good mystery show on TV," I say with a smile, hoping to God he doesn't answer that he'd love to watch some TV and nothing else.

"I had something else in mind. I think you do too, so no TV for us tonight."

As he finishes speaking, he tilts his hips up and presses his cock between my legs. I like where he's going with this.

CHAPTER THIRTEEN

*M*atthias

SHE'S SO BEAUTIFUL LYING BENEATH ME IN THAT WHITE robe. So beautiful and so sweet. I can't get enough of her. It's like she's a drug, and after only one day, I'm addicted to her.

But that's not the truth. I've been crazy about Ava for years. I just haven't been able to do anything about it.

Until now.

I know if my father finds out, he'll probably exile me to some far corner of the earth. If he doesn't have a branch office of King Industries at the Arctic Circle, he'll order one opened immediately. I don't know why he doesn't want us together, but whatever the reason is, it's serious for him.

Too bad. I don't want to give up feeling this way. Ava makes me happy. She makes me smile. She makes me want to be the kind of person who she'd be with. How could that be something bad?

"Please tell me you aren't having second thoughts because that would be cruel."

Her words tear me out of my thoughts about being shipped off somewhere for being with her, and I shake my head at the very idea that I wouldn't want to be with her right now. "Sorry. Just thinking about Santa's workshop at the North Pole."

Ava draws her eyebrows in, and for a second, she looks like a mixture of confused and angry. "Are you going to tell me another dirty joke that involves the word pole and Santa? Because I don't know if I can take that right now, especially since you're nudging up against me and all I can think of is your pole."

I had no idea she could be this cute. I don't want to laugh and ruin the moment, but I can't help myself. "Did you just call my dick a pole?"

"Yeah."

"That's funny."

She rolls her eyes and shrugs. "That's me. Funny Ava. I guess I've killed the mood, but in my defense, you were the one who was talking about Santa Claus while you're getting me all hot and bothered here."

I push my hips forward and press against her pussy through her robe. "I like that about you. You didn't kill my mood. I'm ready to go."

Sliding her hand between us, she reaches for my cock and wraps her hands around it through my sweatpants. "Good because I am too."

Something in the way she doesn't play any games when it comes to us being together makes me want her even more. So many women try the cat and mouse thing, teasing and toying with a guy, but Ava is straightforward. Mystery's nice on TV, but give me a woman who lets a man know what she wants any day.

"I do love a woman who isn't shy about palming my cock."

For a second, she stares up at me like I've said something odd, but then I realize what's wrong. I said love. It's not that I don't feel that for her or some version of it, but I didn't want her to know that.

Not yet, at least.

But then she smiles and tightens her hold on me as she says, "I like that better than thinking you hate me."

Leaning down to kiss her, I whisper against her lips, "I never hated you, Ava. Never."

"I'm happy about that."

I slide my hand under her robe and open it to reveal her naked body to me. I don't move, my body still as I stare down at her in awe at how beautiful she is. After all those fantasies about what she'd look like if we were ever together, I can't help but think I suffered from a lack of imagination every time.

"Is something wrong?" she asks in a worried voice.

Shaking my head, I lower my mouth to hers and kiss her. "Not a thing."

Her hands cradle my face as she looks up into my eyes with concern. "Oh. I thought maybe something had changed from before since you aren't moving."

I know I deserve that question since I've been nothing but a miserable bastard to her until today, but I hate that she thinks there's something wrong with her because of me. I never meant to cause that to happen.

As much as I wish I could explain myself and why I acted like I did for so long, I can't. I just have to try to make her understand that who I pretended to be isn't the person who's crazy about her and has been for years.

"Don't ever think you're anything less than incredible because of me, Ava. No matter how I act, now you know the truth. I never hated you. I never will, no matter what it seems like."

She stares up at me with a look that tells me she doesn't understand, but I hope she takes my words to heart because I know I'm going to have to pretend to hate her when my father returns. I don't want to be like that with her ever again, but knowing how he feels about us being together, I won't have a choice.

I sense she wants to question me about why I might act differently in the future, but instead, she pulls me to her and kisses me as she tugs my sweatpants down my legs. I get lost in the feel of her lips on mine as my body takes over and I gently push into her. She's like heaven, and I don't want this to ever end.

Even though I know it must.

I GLANCE OVER AT THE CLOCK ON THE NIGHTSTAND and see 12:33. Time flies when I'm with Ava, and more than anything else, I hate that. I want to revel in the moments with her, but they race by so quickly that I'm sure I'm going to forget some detail about our time together when I'll need to find some measure of happiness once I'm consigned to the life I'll be forced into in the coming days.

Ava shifts against my side and turns to look up at me. "You aren't really into this show, are you?"

"Honestly, I haven't been paying much attention. You seem to like it, though."

She sits up and turns her body to face me, crossing her legs under her. "It's okay, but I don't want you to feel like you're stuck watching something you don't like. We can change it. I don't mind."

I shake my head and shrug. "I'd actually like to talk, if you're not going to watch the show."

That seems to excite her, and she nods as her eyes open wide. "Okay! What do you want to talk about?"

"Anything."

In truth, I don't care what topic we choose to talk about. I just like talking to her. It's like I've got a million conversations stored up inside me that I can't speak about to anyone but Ava.

"Okay. What are you going to do for New Year's? Are you going to a big party or keeping things low-key?" she asks in an excited tone that tells me she really wants to know.

The problem is I have no idea. I've never been a huge fan of that holiday, so the idea of spending it with a bunch of strangers getting hammered as we count down the moments to the new year sounds less than appealing.

"I'm not sure. I'm not really a big New Year's Eve person."

She tilts her head left and right, as if she's weighing the truth of that statement before saying, "Me neither. I actually find New Year's kind of sad, but I think that's because my mother got sick in January. Before we knew it, she was gone."

Her sadness sinks into me, but I'm not unhappy about that. Ever since my mother died, it's like I'm drawn to people who feel like I have from the moment she left us.

"I don't blame you. I think I'm sort of like that about springtime. I used to love when winter would finally break, but ever since my mother's death, all I can think about once the snow goes away is the day my father sat us down and told us she was terminal. It's like all the good things I felt about that time of year were pushed aside and replaced by sadness. I hate that too because I used to love that first day when the temperature gets up into the seventies and my brothers and I would go outside and play catch, or my mother would pack us all up and drive us into the city to see my father at his office. Springtime in Central Park was always my favorite thing. I haven't been back there since she died."

Ava frowns as I explain my feelings about spring since my mother passed away, nodding like she understands. I think she does.

"Is that why you didn't want to go with your father and brothers today?"

I shake my head, happy to explain why that trip held no appeal for me today or any other day. "No. I didn't want to go because that's the first step in my father trapping me into being who he wants me to be. I figure the longer I can put off being anywhere near King Industries, the longer I'll be free."

Looking down at her hands resting on her thighs, she softly says, "Maybe he'll decide he doesn't want you to go into the family business."

With a sigh, I tell her what I've told myself every

time I let hope seep into my thoughts. "That's never going to happen. I had the bad luck of being born first, and because of that, I have only one future."

When she lifts her head, I see sadness in her eyes. "I'm sorry, Matthias. I can tell it's not what you want to do."

"I have no choice," I say, hating that truth more than anything else about my future.

"Will you have to move to some other city when you go to work for King Industries?"

"I'm not sure."

Actually, I'm pretty damn sure if my father finds out I was with Ava, he'll send me to an office so far away from here that I'll be lucky if I can even communicate with others without going old school and writing letters.

"Oh."

"Would that bother you if I did move away?" I ask, unable to stop myself from hoping she will miss me if I'm forced to go.

She turns to look at the TV as she answers, "Well, yeah. I mean, I'm just getting to know you, so I wouldn't want you to move away."

Not exactly the heartfelt answer I was wishing to hear.

But then she turns back to face me and says, "That's a lie. It would bother me. I'm not saying I expect anything to be permanent after today because I don't, but I like spending time with you, Matthias. Now that you aren't that guy who's always grimacing whenever I'm around, I was hoping we could hang out again. You know, when it's not snowing a foot an hour and maybe we could go into town or drive into Manhattan for the day."

I reach out to take her hand in mine and bring it to my mouth to kiss it. Her skin is soft like a rose petal against my lips. "Don't you hate having to be so tentative with people when you really want to say you like them? I do. My mother and father used to tell us about how they met, and I don't think they ever felt like they had to make excuses for wanting to be together. I don't know why we do these days."

As I talk, her face lights up from her smile. "I know! My parents used to tell me about when they started dating, and I swear never once did they say anything so wishy-washy. Maybe they edited those things out of their stories, but I don't think so. My father was crazy about my mother, and she was crazy about him, although it took her a little longer than it did for him. But still, there was none of this 'well, if you ever wanted to maybe we could if it isn't too much of a bother' stuff. Why is everyone our age so unwilling to say what they mean?"

"I don't know. Maybe everyone's afraid," I suggest. "They don't want to get hurt, so they figure if they couch everything in maybes that will keep them safe."

"For me, it's that I know you probably have other girlfriends you see, so I don't want to think that one day with me means anything to you."

She stops talking as her face turns bright red. "I mean, girlfriends. Not other. That would mean I think I'm one of your girlfriends, and I don't. I know this is just one day."

I can't let her think she's that unimportant to me, even if I can't tell her how much I've wished for a day like this to happen. Pulling her to me, I take us both down onto the bed and hold her face in my hands.

"There are no other girlfriends. As for what this is, I don't know what we should call it, but I haven't been this happy to be around someone in a long time, Ava."

"Really? Me too."

And just like that, whatever this is between us moves from sex to something more.

CHAPTER FOURTEEN

va

I wake up alone and missing Matthias. Sitting up, I look out the window and see it continued to snow all night and we got at least another foot of snow. At this rate, my father won't be able to drive Mr. King and his sons back for days.

That doesn't make me unhappy, though, because that means I may have another day with Matthias.

I'm nude under the covers, so I look around the room for my robe and see it folded on the chair near the window. He did that, I'm sure, unless I've taken to folding clothes in my sleep.

The last thing I remember is the two of us lying back on the bed after talking. I must have dozed off, and he left after that. I wish he had stayed, but I bet he was worried Eleanor might find us this morning.

I wonder why he's so concerned about anyone knowing we're together. We're both adults. Admittedly, my father has told me more than once to not be around him, but I have no idea why he would say that since now I know Matthias isn't that grumpy guy he always appeared to be. Maybe if my father saw that person instead he'd be happy that we're hanging out together.

I think about my father finding out I slept with Matthias and instantly know he wouldn't be happy about that. But not because of who he is but because I'm his daughter. To my father, I'm still that little girl he thinks he needs to worry about and watch over constantly.

The house is quiet when I walk out into the hallway, and I wonder if anyone's up yet. I didn't see what time it was when I woke up, but it's light out so it has to be at least eight o'clock.

As I walk down the stairs, I smell coffee and know Eleanor is already hard at work in the kitchen. It's warm and welcoming, so I inhale deeply and let the scent fill my nostrils while I head to where she's busy probably making breakfast.

I don't hear any voices, which means Matthias is likely still asleep. A twinge of disappointment nips at me as I walk down the hallway to the kitchen. We can talk later. I'm sure we'll have time today before our fathers and his brothers return from the city.

When I turn the corner into the room, I see Eleanor at the stove cooking pancakes and there at the table is Matthias looking like he's already showered and ready for the day. How is it possible this person always looks good? I instantly worry my hair is a matted mess and wish I had done more than open my eyes before coming down here.

"Ava, good morning!" Eleanor chirps sweetly. "I have pancakes for Matthias, but I can make you anything you'd like. You name it and it's yours. There's coffee too, but I can't remember if you drink coffee or not."

I sit down across from him and pat the sides of my head in case my hair is a disaster. "Thanks, Eleanor. I'll do pancakes too, and I'll get myself a cup of coffee."

"Pancakes it is! And you just sit right there, honey. I'll bring a cup of coffee to you."

Before I can thank her, Matthias quietly asks, "Did you have a nice sleep? Any problems in the guest room?"

Out of the corner of my eye, I see Eleanor curiously watching the two of us interact. We must look unrecognizable compared to yesterday.

"It was okay. Thanks," I say, answering his questions vaguely. Lowering my voice to barely a whisper, I add, "I was disappointed to wake up alone, though."

He smiles broadly and nods as he whispers, "Same here."

Eleanor sets a mug of coffee in front of me and points toward the sugar and cream containers. "Everything you need is right here. I'm happy to see you two have resolved your differences. Like I said to you yesterday, you two have a lot in common."

Matthias and I look up at her smiling at us and then turn to face one another. I can see by his expression he isn't sure if she knows what we've been doing to pass the time on our snow day yesterday. I don't either. Something tells me she suspects we've been doing more than watching TV, though.

When she walks away, I cover my mouth to stop my snickering at his grinning at me. Under the table, he taps my knee with his foot, which makes me want to giggle even more. We're like two kids, and I don't think I've ever felt happier than at this moment.

"Jonesy found some gas in the shed, so he told me he plans on getting the snowblower going this morning. He was waiting until everyone woke up," Eleanor says over near the stove. "I think once I get these pancakes done that I'll let him know he can start anytime now."

Looking across the table at Matthias, I ask, "Are you planning on going out to help him again? I bet blowing snow is easier than shoveling it."

The look in his eyes as they get big at my mention of blowing snow makes me blush. I didn't mean anything sexual by that. It would technically be called blowing snow since it's a snowblower, wouldn't it?

I glance over at Eleanor, who doesn't seem to think anything of how I phrased that, so at least she doesn't think I'm some perv. Matthias, though, can't stop himself from chuckling at my slip up.

"I'm not sure if I'm going to help him. He might only have enough gas for one blower. I think I have other things to do anyway. Not that blowing doesn't sound great."

Now it's my turn for my eyes to get big. I feel them practically bulge out of their sockets at how obvious he's being with Eleanor just feet away. When I look over at her, though, I don't see any reaction. Thank God she's more interested in the breakfast she's making than listening to us.

"Okay, here are some pancakes to warm you up on

this cold December morning," she says as she sets a pile down on my plate and then moves around the table to give the remaining pancakes on the plate to Matthias.

"I'm going to tell Jonesy he can start now. I'll be right back."

I watch as she slips on her coat and walks out the back door before I turn to face Matthias, who is already feasting on his breakfast. I kick his leg under the table to get his attention, and when he looks over at me, he seems genuinely confused.

"What's that for?"

"The blowing talk! What are you thinking? I can't believe she didn't say a thing to that."

He takes a forkful of pancakes into his mouth and chews for a few seconds before washing it all down with coffee. "What is she going to say? 'Gee, Matthias. Are you trying to tell Ava that you'd love to see her down on her knees with your dick in her mouth going to town?' Something tells me Eleanor isn't the type to think that."

My cheeks heat up so they must be bright red at his graphic description of me blowing him. "You are bad, you know that? I'm just going to eat my breakfast and try to act normal over here."

Matthias cuts up another chunk of pancakes and stabs his fork into them. "I can't help that I have an active imagination," he says with a smile that's as guilty as sin.

I imagine this charming thing he has going on has made any number of women do exactly what he wants, including being down on their knees giving him whatever his heart desires. I wish I wasn't jealous, but just thinking about those women makes me wonder.

"Are you angry at me?" he asks after a minute or so of my not saying anything.

Shaking my head, I continue to eat. "No."

"Trust me. She has no idea what I was talking about."

"It's not that," I say as I stand up to take my plate over to the sink.

I really don't want to tell him exactly what it was that made me turn so silent, so I busy myself at the sink for a few seconds. Thankfully, Eleanor returns from her talk with the groundskeeper so I don't have to explain my sudden change in mood.

"All done already? Do you want another helping? I can whip them up in no time," she says sweetly.

As I turn to face her, I see Matthias watching me. I give her a smile and answer, "No, I'm stuffed. I think I'm going to go back up to my room. Any news when everyone is coming back?"

She gently pats me on the shoulder and nods. "Not until tomorrow morning at the earliest. It seems the roads between here and the city are clogged with stranded cars making them impassable. It sounds like a lot of people didn't believe the weatherman when he said this storm was going to be big. You don't have to worry, though. Your father and Mr. King, along with the boys, are all at the Ritz, so they're safe and warm like you two here. I'm thinking of making a ham for dinner tonight. You like ham, don't you Ava?"

I don't have a chance to answer her question before she turns to look over at Matthias still sitting at the table. "I know you like ham. It's been one of your favorites ever since you were a little boy."

"Thanks, Eleanor," I say as I hurry toward the hallway to leave. "Ham sounds great."

"Take your clothes," she says, calling after me. "I left them in the laundry room. They're all clean and ready to wear."

I look back at her, avoiding his intense gaze that's practically burning a hole through me. "Thanks. I appreciate it."

After grabbing my clean clothes, I hurry upstairs to my room to take a shower. I don't know why I got so jealous down there. It's stupid, and I know it. Matthias has been with lots of women. Of course, he has. He's gorgeous, wealthy, and sexy as sin. Why wouldn't he sleep with anyone who wants him?

I'm being silly. I need to stop whatever this jealous thing is right now. We had a good time together yesterday. From the way he was acting at breakfast, he wants it to continue today. So do I.

So I need to forget thinking about all the other people he's been with. Either that or not hang out with him today, which is definitely not what I want. I like him. Actually, I more than like him. I don't know if what I'm feeling is love. It probably isn't. What is that word my mother used to use all the time when I had crushes on boys?

Infatuated. That's it. I'm infatuated with Matthias.

That's okay, though. Nobody said this was going to be anything permanent. We're just two people enjoying spending time together while we're essentially snowbound. It's actually romantic if I think of it that way.

I toss the white robe over the back of the chair and

head for the bathroom. When I open the glass door to the shower, I'm surprised to see shampoo and conditioner I can use, along with a brand-new bar of soap. That Eleanor thinks of everything.

The hot water beating down on my back feels so good that I forget all that silliness I was feeling at breakfast. I have to tell my father we need to get a showerhead like this one. I swear it has ten jets that make a shower feel more like a massage. I'd be the most relaxed person in the world if I got to experience this every morning.

After I wash and condition my hair, I just stand under the water and close my eyes to let myself enjoy the heat against my skin. I definitely need this in my life on a daily basis.

"Are you sleeping standing up? I think that might be dangerous in the shower."

My eyes fly open to see Matthias standing in front of me, naked and smiling. "What are you doing here?"

"Watching you enjoying a shower more than I think any other person in the world ever has. Who knew ecstasy could be found from some water rolling over your head?" he says casually, as if walking into my shower is perfectly normal.

"Do you always barge in on people when they're washing up?"

He grins like he finds my exasperation charming and takes a step toward me. "Actually, this is my first time."

"Why are you here? Don't you have your own shower in your room? I know you do since you took a shower yesterday and walked out wearing only a towel."

None of what I'm saying makes sense, but I'm so

flustered I don't know how to react to him joining me in here. On top of that, he looks incredible. Again. Is there no situation where Matthias King doesn't look entirely perfect?

"You seemed mad downstairs, so I came up to talk to you. Except you weren't in your room, so when I heard the water running in here, I figured I'd come in and talk to you. I hadn't planned on getting into the shower with you, but you looked so good standing here that I couldn't stop myself."

"That sounds like an impulse control problem, if you ask me."

I don't know why I'm so defensive. It isn't as if I haven't seen him nude before this or he hasn't seen me. We've been having sex in the past twenty-four hours. Repeatedly.

"So you were mad. What did I do? Tell me so I can fix it and we can get back to having a good time."

He takes another step toward me and stops, just far enough out of reach that I can't touch him but close enough that water droplets begin to form on his skin, making him look even more incredible. It's like he can't look bad.

Meanwhile, I suspect I look like a drowned rat standing here.

"You didn't do anything. Well, that whole blowing thing in front of Eleanor wasn't great, but she didn't seem to notice, so I guess it's okay."

"Then why are you so cranky with me now?"

"Maybe I don't like people joining me uninvited in my morning shower."

One more step and he's close enough for me to touch. "I don't believe that."

Tilting my head back to look up at him, I ask, "You don't believe I dislike people just joining me in the shower without asking first?"

"Nope."

"Pretty big ego you have there."

Matthias arches a single dark eyebrow. "Is that what girls are calling it now? Ego?"

As much as I don't want to look down, I can't stop myself. I glance toward his cock and see he's rock hard and ready to go. Is this guy ever not turned on?

"See? You like my big ego."

I squint, pretending to be disgusted by him. "Let's call a spade a spade. I don't like your big ego. I like your big cock."

A moan that hits me right between the legs escapes from his throat before he licks his lips and leans in to kiss me. "God, that's sexy. I think you might be the perfect woman, you know that?"

"Really? And what gets me that special designation?"

Matthias tilts his hips so his cock glides over my pussy and clit. It's all I can do to not close my eyes to revel in how good it feels. God, he makes it hard to be upset with him.

I wait for his answer, but instead, he slides his arms around my waist to pull me against his body. Before I can protest, or at least pretend I don't want what's about to happen, he kisses me long and deep, sliding his tongue that tastes like coffee and maple syrup into my mouth and teasing me so all I want is to feel him inside me.

"You aren't going to tell me why I'm the perfect woman?"

He shakes his head and grins like the Cheshire cat. "Later. Right now, we have better things to do than talk."

I want to say something, but my mind is blank, except for the single thought of how much I want him right now. He doesn't make me wait and lifts me up so I'm positioned at the perfect angle for him to slide inside me. It all happens so fast that all I can do is enjoy how incredible it feels when he fills me completely.

As I wrap my legs around his waist and he begins to slowly pump in and out of me, I moan in his ear, "I should be mad at you."

"No, you shouldn't."

"Yes, I should. Oh, God…you didn't even ask if you could join me in here. What if I didn't want you to?"

He stops and leans back to look into my eyes. "You were mad at me downstairs. Tell me why."

Damnit! I should have just kept my mouth shut.

"I wasn't mad at you."

Matthias stares at me intently, and I know he's not going to let this go. "Then tell me what's wrong."

I try rocking my hips to get him to continue, but he pushes me against the tile wall to stop me. "Nice try. Tell me why you were upset."

Looking away to avoid his gaze, I fix my attention on the back of the shower where a towel bar hangs. "Please don't do this. Let's just get back to what we were doing."

"No."

I snap my head back to face him, shocked he just told me no. "Are you saying you don't want this?"

"I'm a red-blooded, heterosexual male with a hard on

that could cut glass. Trust me. I can't think of anything but fucking you right now, except for finding out why you were upset with me at breakfast. So just tell me so we can get back to having a good time."

I want to fight him. I do. Mainly because I don't want to admit what I was feeling before. But he makes it impossible to put him off, and truth be told, I want to get back to us having sex, so I swallow my pride and tell him the truth.

"It wasn't anger or even me being upset before. I was jealous. Okay? Jealous, which is stupid, but there you go. So how about we get back to that good time you were mentioning a few seconds ago and forget everything else?"

Matthias narrows his eyes and shakes his head, clearly not understanding what I mean. "Jealous? Of who? There's only you, me, and Eleanor in this house. Trust me. I don't have a thing for her."

"Now you're just being stupid. Put me down. I'm not in the mood anymore."

So much for having a good time. Now I feel sillier than I did before, and I don't get to come. I should have just lied. At least then I'd get to enjoy myself.

He doesn't fight me and sets me down on my feet. A second later, I hurry out of the shower, leaving him standing in there alone with the water still running. All I want to do is forget I ever said a thing.

But he's not going to let that happen.

He follows me out into the bedroom and catches me just as I'm getting dressed. Grabbing my arm, he spins me around and pulls me to him so I have no choice but to face him.

"Tell me what you were jealous about. I can't figure it out. You were okay with knowing I have Playboy in my bed, but something at breakfast made you jealous? That makes no sense."

I try to push him away, but he refuses to let me go. After a few attempts, I give up, sagging against his hold.

"Exactly. It makes no sense, so let's move on."

That was never going to work, so I'm not surprised when he shakes his head. "No. Tell me. I didn't wait this long to finally be with you to have some jealousy problem ruin everything."

For a second, I try to understand what he means by that, but my brain quickly switches gears and I blurt out, "Fine! I was jealous when I thought about all the women you've been with. Okay? I'm stupid. It's stupid and I'm stupid, so there you go. Can I get dressed now? I feel a little silly standing here with one pant leg on."

But still he won't let me just get dressed and run away from my embarrassment.

Cradling my face, he kisses me softly and whispers against my lips, "You aren't stupid, but don't think about anyone else I've ever been with. They don't matter. All that matters is you."

He doesn't let me think about that or anything else before he pushes me back onto the bed and climbs on top of me. Tugging my jeans down my leg, he tosses them onto the floor and then pulls my panties off, sending them to the same place he sent my jeans.

I don't know if I should want to keep talking and discussing what he said, but all I can think about is how hard he is and how much I want him inside me again. As if he's reading my mind, he doesn't wait before thrusting his hips forward and filling me completely once more.

His mouth covers mine in a kiss that takes my breath away, and I cling to his shoulders as he begins to fuck me. It's frantic and raw, but it feels perfect at this moment.

"It's only you, Ava. Only you," he groans in a husky voice that hits me deep inside.

This time neither of us takes very long, and when my orgasm washes over me, my entire body shudders in ecstasy. He follows me seconds later, thrusting hard one final time before he stills as he comes.

As we lie there, all I can think about is how he said it's only me and he waited so long to be with me. I know he mentioned that he'd never hated me like he pretended to, but those things made it sound like he actually cared about me all that time.

When he lifts his head to look down at me, I consider asking what he meant. I don't, though. Maybe another day after we've spent more time together.

CHAPTER FIFTEEN

va

"So what should we do today?" Matthias asks as I get dressed.

"You mean other than what we just did?" I joke and then my cheeks heat up from a blush.

He shakes his head as he seems to study me for a long moment. "I like the way your face gets all red when you refer to sex sometimes. Not always, which seems odd. Just sometimes."

I press my palms against the sides of my face to make that stupid blush go away and say, "It's nothing. Probably just because I'm so pale during the winter months."

That makes him laugh. "Sure. What I don't understand is why when you were looking at the magazine you didn't get embarrassed but when you're referring to us having sex again you do."

Feeling more than a touch defensive, I walk over to the TV to turn it on so we can stop this discussion. "I don't know. Can you just drop it?"

Matthias winces like what I said hurt him in some way and gets up from the bed to come over to stand behind me. Wrapping his arms around my waist, he rests his chin on my shoulder and plants a tiny kiss on my neck.

"I wasn't making fun of you. I'm just curious."

When he whispers that in my ear and his warm breath dances across my skin, I can't help but close my eyes. Yesterday, I swore I'd hate him forever, but today, I can't imagine ever saying that. This person I could never hate.

I don't say anything, so he quickly adds, "I'm sorry. Do you forgive me?"

Nodding, I smile and answer, "Yes."

"I won't ask about it again. It will just be one of those idiosyncrasies you have."

As I open my eyes, I turn in his hold to face him. Looking up into his eyes, I see he's genuinely sorry for upsetting me. He really can be very sweet.

"So what are we going to do today? And if you say what I think you're going to say, I'm going to go downstairs and tell Eleanor I insist on helping her clean and I won't see you for the rest of the day."

My threat works, and he smiles and says, "Since we're basically trapped here, we could watch movies or TV. Sleep. Or fuck."

"Except for the watching movies and TV part, we sound like people from the nineteenth century."

"We could help Jonesy with the snow blowing. The guy has miles to do before everyone gets back. There's just one problem with that. There are only two snow blowers and three of us."

Before he can continue, I cover his mouth with my hand. "If you start talking about me doing some other kind of blowing, I swear to God, Matthias King, I will walk out of this room and do what I said I'd do with Eleanor."

Beneath my palm, he smiles and then flicks the tip of his tongue against my fingers. "Fine. No blowjob jokes."

"So now that we got that settled, do you have any suggestions on what we can do all day?" I ask as I drop my hand from his mouth.

"Since you've ruled out talking about sex, I guess it's sleeping, actual sex, and watching TV and movies for us."

With a shrug, I turn to leave, but he pulls me back to kiss me. "And if you're good, maybe we can do another drawing."

"If I'm good?"

"Well, you can be bad, if you want, but you're the one who told me no more sex talk. If you've changed your mind, I have this idea of you on your knees in the shower and me—"

I quickly stop him from finishing by covering his mouth again. "You have a one-track mind, you know that? What about a game of pool? Theo always says you're pretty good. Maybe you can teach me."

Again, he smiles beneath my hand before nodding. "I

can do that. If my brother has taught you anything, though, I'm going to have to undo that because he's a terrible pool player."

I turn and begin walking toward the hallway to get my first pool lesson underway. "He hasn't really. I'm a complete billiards newbie."

"Ooooh, a virgin," he jokes behind me.

When I turn around, I see him grinning. "You really do have a one-track mind."

Shrugging, he smiles bigger. "I'm a growing boy. What can I say?"

I roll my eyes at that. "You're twenty-three. That's a man, not a boy."

He opens the bedroom door for me and sneaks a kiss just before I walk out. "Fine, I'm a growing man. In fact, if we keep talking about sex, I'm really going to be growing."

I look back at him and roll my eyes again. "First my pool lesson and then we can see what we can do about your growing, okay?"

Never before, other than with his brother, have I felt this comfortable with any guy. Theo and I never talk about sex, though. For us, it's purely platonic.

As we walk toward the game room, Matthias slides his arm around my waist and pulls me to him. It's a tiny gesture, but considering our past, it feels like something special.

MATTHIAS TEACHES ME THE BASICS ABOUT SHOOTING pool, including how to hold the cue stick, but try as I might, I don't seem to be any good at this game. Every shot he attempts ends up with a striped ball going into the pocket, and every shot I try either ends up with the cue ball sailing off the table or the solid ball I want to get in roaming around the table like some lost tourist in a foreign country.

After my third attempt to get the four ball to go in any pocket, I sigh in defeat. "I'm not very good at this."

He nods as he stands at the other end of the table leaning against his pool stick. "I think I finally understand why you and Theo hang out so much. You're very much alike, especially when it comes to pool. He sucks too."

I pout at hearing that harsh opinion of my pool shooting skills. "I suck?"

Instantly, he knows he's hurt my feelings. Walking around the table, he stops behind me and nuzzles the side of my neck. "Yes, but unlike my brother, I think I can help you to be better."

Turning my head, I look back at him. "Really?"

After kissing me softly on the lips, he nods. "Really. I think the problem starts with how you're holding the cue. I showed you how to position your hand on the table to steady it so when you take a shot the stick doesn't wobble all over the place, but you're just like Theo and insist on holding it the other way. I think you learned that from him, didn't you?"

I nod, forced to admit the truth. "Well, he showed me a little about the game one day. I didn't think I actually learned that much."

Matthias rolls his eyes. "I swear my brother couldn't shoot pool to save his life, so I don't know why he thinks he should be teaching anyone anything. Here, let me show you how to do it."

He leans me over the table, his body pressing against my back and ass, and I have a hard time focusing on what he's trying to teach me. All I can think about is how he's hard behind me. I swear he walks around with a hard on constantly.

I close my eyes and listen to him explain how to hold the cue as his warm breath skitters over my ear and neck. So much for actually learning how to shoot pool.

While I revel in how good he feels against me, Matthias positions my fingers correctly on the green part of the table and slides the cue through my thumb and forefinger. I doubt I'm going to remember any of this when it comes time to actually put it into practice, though. My mind is too focused on his hard cock pressing against the inside of my thigh.

"So that's all you have to do. Think you can try it?" he asks before backing away from me.

Slowly, I stand up to my full height while my body misses the feel of him against me. I watch him walk around to the side of the table, knowing he expects me to take a shot like he just taught me. I try to do exactly what he showed me, but since I wasn't paying much attention, the shot turns out like all my others.

Lousy, with the cue ball barely rolling toward my solid ball.

"I'm sorry. If I'm being honest, I was having a hard time focusing on what you were saying. You were so close, and I couldn't help thinking about something else."

I feel my cheeks heat up from a blush as I admit that, but Matthias simply shakes his head and smiles. Walking around the table, he stops beside me and takes the pool cue out of my hand before setting both his and mine on the table.

He turns me around to face him and smiles down at me. "Tell me what you were so distracted with."

My eyes lower so my gaze drifts south toward his crotch before I look up again at him. "One guess. You know, I'm beginning to wonder if you have some sort of medical condition. You're always hard."

Matthias bites his lip, making him look even sexier than usual, before he dips his head to kiss me. "Not usually, but when I'm near you, yeah."

He slowly pushes his hips forward so his hard cock presses against the front of my pants. Even with the fabric between us, my pussy gets wet.

"What about Eleanor?" I ask, not really caring if anyone sees us together, to be honest.

But he pulls away suddenly and nods. "You're right. No sex in the game room."

I can't help but be disappointed, but a moment later, he takes me by the hand and hurries me out into the hallway. Unsure what he's doing, I ask, "Does this mean the pool lesson is over?"

Turning to look at me, he smiles. "Yeah, but I've got something better in mind. Come with me."

As I hurry to keep up with him, he rushes us back to the guest room where I stayed last night. Closing the door behind us, he pulls me to him and kisses me long and deep.

Against my lips, he whispers, "We're taking a risk since she'll probably be up here soon to clean up your room."

"What are we doing that's so risky?" I ask with a giggle, hoping he might finally explain why he doesn't want anyone to see us together.

With a sinful smile, he answers, "This." A second later, he crouches down in front of me and tugs my pants and underwear down my legs, leaving me naked from the waist down.

Before I can say a word, he presses his mouth to my pussy and slides his tongue up the length of me, making my eyes roll back in my head. Oh. My. God.

I stuff my hand into his hair, loving how silky it feels against my skin. I struggle to get my right foot out of my pants so I can open my legs more and enjoy his mouth completely. While he flicks his tongue against my sensitive skin, he helps me free my leg and then lifts my left foot onto his shoulder, opening me up to him.

Looking up at me, he sweetly asks, "Is your ankle feeling better today?"

"Yeah," I answer, even as I can't concentrate on anything but how much I want his mouth on me.

The few times I've had a guy do this to me I felt self-conscious and awkward, but never before has anyone gone down on me like this. I balance myself on his right shoulder, afraid if I don't that I'll go crashing to the floor when I come.

Matthias leans back away from me, giving me a momentary break from the delight his tongue was performing, and smiles. "Don't worry. I've got you."

He slides his right hand behind me and cups my ass before tilting forward again to return to the incredible attention he's paying to my pussy. With every delicious swipe of his tongue over my clit, I feel like I'm going to explode. God, I love it!

I don't know how long we go like this, but when he gently sucks my clit between his lips, that's all it takes. The top of my head feels like it blows off, and every inch of my body comes alive as I come hard against his mouth. Matthias rides my orgasm as if he's a master at this, his tongue never relenting until I finally sag against him, exhausted and utterly satisfied.

A heavy sigh escapes from me, and he looks up with a smile that says he enjoyed himself too. "I've been dying to taste you like that since breakfast."

My right leg shakes like it's about to give out, so he lowers my other leg to the floor before standing up to kiss me. I taste myself on his lips, something so utterly sensual that I've never experienced before with any other guy.

"Thank you."

Matthias raises his eyebrows in surprise and leans down to kiss me. "No need to thank me. I enjoyed it as much as you did."

Suddenly feeling shy, I lean down to pull my clothes up. "Well, I've never had anyone do that like you did."

When I finish getting dressed, he cradles my face in his hands and kisses me softly. "Really? No one?"

I shake my head as my inexperience makes me wince. "Nope. No one."

With a smile, he takes my hand to lead me toward the bed. "Good. I like that I was the first one to make you feel that way."

I don't say anything, but that's not the only time he's

been the first one to make me feel something. This may not be love. In fact, it very well might be merely infatuation, but I've never felt this way about anyone before in my life.

And I don't want it to end once the snow clears and everything returns to normal again.

SOMEONE KNOCKING ON MY DOOR WAKES ME OUT OF A sound sleep, and I sit up to get my head straight before jumping out of bed to answer whoever is there. When I open the door, I see not Matthias but Eleanor.

"What time is it?" I ask, still groggy from sleep.

She smiles and says, "It's eight o'clock. I know you probably like to sleep later in the morning, but I made breakfast. I hope you don't mind, but I came up here early this morning and got your clothes. They're all fresh and cleaned and ready to wear."

When she hands them to me, I shake my head in disbelief. It can't be morning already. Why didn't he come see me again last night?

"It's eight in the morning? How is that possible? I must have slept through all night."

With a chuckle, she says, "You must have been tired. Now come down to the kitchen and get some food in you. Jonesy has the entire driveway and road cleared, so when Mr. King and your father get here, they'll call the repairman so you can go home. Staying somewhere new is nice, but I know I always love to go back to my own cozy bed. Now come on. Get dressed. Breakfast will be cold if you don't hurry."

She rushes away toward the stairs as I close the door behind me. Why didn't he stay all night?

I do as Eleanor said and hurry up to get dressed. I want to go to his room to see if everything's okay. Halfway down the hallway, though, I hear Mr. King and all of the King boys come into the house, so I turn around and run downstairs before anyone can see where I was.

"Ava! I heard about the heat in your house," Mr. King says as he hands his coat to Eleanor. "Your father is down there right now, and if he can't get it fixed, then you're just going to have to stay here for another night. How does that sound?"

He gives me a big smile and a wink, and for a moment, I can't help but wonder if he knows what his son and I have been up to. I nod like I know I have to, but then he points at Theo as he walks into the room.

"I'm sure Theo will be the perfect host if you have to stay over again, right Theo?"

My closest friend in the world gives me a big smile. "Of course. Ava, I have to tell you about this guy I met in the city. He's a racecar driver, and he's going to get me set up to start racing. Pretty great, right?"

"Yeah, pretty great," I say as I search around me for any sign of Matthias.

Where is he?

As Theo and Marius begin to tell me about this racecar guy and we make our way to the kitchen for breakfast, my father walks in looking downright unhappy. The electricity must still be off. God, I hope the pipes didn't freeze.

Mr. King walks into the room and asks him, "Were

you able to get the heat back on?"

When my father nods, I'm stunned. Wasn't it out because of the electricity being off? I want to ask, but he looks so displeased at this moment that I don't dare and risk him reprimanding me in front of the entire King family.

"Time to go, Ava."

I get up from the table without saying a word. My father makes some small talk with Mr. King, and then we leave without me being able to see the only person I want to speak to this morning. Where could he be?

Neither of us says a word as he drives back to our little house, but once he closes the front door behind us, he gives me a stern look I don't understand. "Did you lie about the heat being off so you could go up to the main house and not be alone?"

I'm stunned at his accusation. My father knows I wouldn't lie to him. Not about that or anything else.

Well, that's not true. I plan to lie to him about Matthias, but that's different. That's my own business. Mine and his.

"Dad, I swear I didn't. Why would you say that?"

"Because when I came home all I had to do was turn the heat up and it kicked on with no problem. What did you do while you were up at the house?"

I shake my head, surprised he's so angry about something Mr. King constantly says I can do anytime I want. "Nothing, Dad. I hung out with Eleanor. She made me hot chocolate like she used to when I was a little girl. I watched TV. I promise I didn't do anything that would make Mr. King unhappy. I wouldn't do that. You know that, don't you?"

"What about Matthias? I know he stayed home yesterday. Did you two spend any time together?"

His angry gaze fixes on my face, and I don't think I can lie like I know I need to. So I fudge the truth a little.

"I saw him. Yes. We hung out for a little while. It's okay, Dad. He was very sweet. We had a nice time."

As I say those words, his expression grows darker and darker. When I finish, he grimaces and shakes his head. "You're going to go stay with your aunt in New Hampshire for a while. She's been asking to see you since your mother died, and I think now's a good time for a visit. Go pack your things."

I can barely hold back the tears at hearing I'm being banished to New Hampshire with my Aunt Jessie. Not that I don't love her, but she lives in the middle of nowhere. I don't even think she has internet there, and half the time when I'm at her house, I can't even get my phone to work.

"Why? I didn't do anything wrong, Dad. I swear the heat was out. What does it matter if I went up to the main house because I didn't want to be alone anyway? Mr. King thinks the world of me. He's always saying I should come up and hang out with Theo and his brothers."

"Theo isn't Matthias. Go get packed. I'm driving you up there today," my father says before storming away.

I know there's no point in arguing with him. My aunt lives alone and probably misses my mother even more than we do since they talked nearly every day and the two of them were closer than any two sisters I've ever heard of. Still, I don't want to be the good daughter who does as she's told this time.

After rushing to get packed, I hurry up to the King house to see if I can talk to Matthias before I go. Like earlier, he's nowhere to be found, but I see Theo still in the kitchen sitting alone on his phone.

I sit down next to him and can barely hold back the tears at my news. "My father is taking me to my aunt's in New Hampshire. I don't know how long I'll be gone."

He makes a face like he just bit into a lemon. "That sucks. Thank God for computers and phones, though."

"That's the problem. I don't think she even has internet, and my phone doesn't always work there. It's like I'm going to be transported back in time."

"Jesus, Ava. That sucks even worse. When are you coming back?"

I shake my head as I struggle to hold back the tears. "I don't know. I need you to do me a favor, though. Would you?"

Theo gives me a big smile that lights up his face. "Anything for my little Ava."

"Would you tell Matthias where I went and that I didn't have a choice? That I had to leave."

My friend gives me a strange look. "Why does he need to know?"

"We hung out yesterday, and for the first time, it seemed like he didn't hate me. I don't want him to think I didn't even have the manners to say goodbye. I wanted to this morning, but he's nowhere to be found, it seems. Did you see him?"

"He's probably out. You know how he is. I wouldn't be surprised if he snuck one of his girls into the house under Eleanor's nose last night. Did you hear anything strange while you were in the guest room?"

I shake my head while all I can think of is I was the girl he snuck around with last night. "No. I have to go, Theo. Will you do that for me? Just tell him I had to go because my father made me. If I can get my phone to work up there, I'll call you, so you better answer because I'm going to be stuck out in the hinterlands."

That makes him laugh. "Got it. Tell big brother you were exiled to the hinterlands with no phone or internet, and you're living like you're Amish now."

Rolling my eyes, I throw my arms around him to give him a hug goodbye. "Promise me you'll answer your phone if I can actually call. I won't forgive you if you don't, Theo King."

He wraps his arms around me and holds me tightly to him as he says in my ear, "Of course, I will. You're my Ava. I always answer when you call. Always have and always will."

Tears well in my eyes as the thought of having to leave both my best friend and the person I'm crazy about becomes a reality. I hurry out of the King house back down the road, and twenty minutes later, my father and I pile into his car with my three suitcases full of clothes and essentials.

As he drives me off the estate, I look up toward the windows in Matthias's bedroom and can barely stop myself from crying. For the first time in my life, I feel like I'm in love and now I have to leave him and everything I care about behind for God only knows how long.

Maybe it won't be for more than a couple weeks. Then I can come back, and Matthias and I can pick up where we left off last night.

CHAPTER SIXTEEN

*M*atthias

MY EYES ARE BARELY OPEN WHEN I REALIZE I FUCKED up. I don't know why, but I fell asleep as I was filling in Ava's picture. Throwing off the covers, I jump out of bed as my sketchbook sails through the air and lands on the floor. I don't have the time to pick it up, though. My father and everyone else will be back this morning, and I want to see her before they all storm in and I can't talk to her at all.

I run down the hall to the guest room and fling open the door, but there's no one in the bed. It looks like Eleanor has already been here to fix the room.

Christ! Ava is going to think I went back to being a dick to her. I have to find her and explain.

I hear my father and brothers making their usual

noise, and my heart sinks. I'm too late. Even if I do find her, we won't be able to talk with all of them around.

Hurrying to the kitchen, I find Eleanor cleaning up after breakfast. When she sees me, she immediately launches into what I can choose to have to eat, but I wave off her suggestions. I don't give a damn about eating right now. All I care about is finding out where Ava went to this morning.

"Eleanor, I'm fine. I'm not really hungry. Where's Ava?"

She dries her hands on the dishcloth near the sink and smiles. "She woke up and left as soon as your father and your brothers came home. I think Theo saw her, though, because she came back up to talk to him. That was about a half hour ago."

I need to go to her house to talk to her and explain I didn't mean to fall asleep and forget about her. Grabbing my coat from near the front door, I start to get ready to head down to the carriage house when I hear Theo behind me.

"Where the hell are you going to?" he asks with a chuckle.

"Out. I need to take care of something."

He walks up to me as I open the front door and asks, "In the snow? Everything's shut down. It was a blizzard out there. Did you sleep through the entire thing? I don't think anything's open for fifty miles."

I turn to look at him, wondering why he's telling me about the goddamned snow. "It couldn't have been too bad. You guys made it back."

Rolling his eyes, he says, "That was Mr. Sutton. I swear he's a maniac. We could have stayed in the city all day today, but once he heard Ava was up here because the heat was out in their house, he swore up and down to Dad that he could get us back safe and sound. I have to give it to him, though. He did just that. You should have seen all the cars stranded on the side of the road the whole way back here. It was a fucking mess, but he kept on driving like he was a man on a mission."

None of this matters to me. All I care about is finding Ava.

"Good for him. Maybe Dad should give him a raise. Speaking of the Suttons, did you see Ava this morning? Eleanor said you and she were talking in the kitchen."

My brother nods and gives me a shrug. "Yeah. She came up to tell me she's leaving to go to her aunt's in New Hampshire. No, maybe it was Vermont. I don't know. I just know she said it's out in the boonies and she didn't think she'd have internet there. Sounds pretty fucking lame to me, to be honest."

Leaving? What's he talking about? Ava isn't going anywhere. She lives here on the estate. Why the hell would she go to stay with some aunt who doesn't even sound like she lives in civilization? She didn't mention anything about that, and we talked about everything under the sun in the time we spent together.

I need to act casual, though, or Theo will know something's up.

"Yeah, that sounds like it's going to suck for her. When's she leaving?" I ask, struggling to control my emotions as I attempt to look as calm as possible.

Turning on his heel, he starts walking toward the stairs. "She left already. Packed up her things and drove off with her father a little while ago."

I want to ask if she gave him a message for me or maybe asked for my number when she came up to see him, but I can't without making him wonder why I'd give a damn. I've pretended to dislike Ava Sutton for years, so suddenly being upset about her leaving would throw up red flags all over the place.

As I take off my coat and hang it back up, I pretend like it's no big deal that the only person I wanted to see today has left and I have no idea when I'll see her again. "I just remembered. I have something to do before I go out," I mumble as I pass him on my way back to my room.

"You're acting weird, dude. Did something happen here while we were gone?"

I look back at him and shrug as my foot hits the first stair. "Not that I know of. What could have happened? All it did was fucking snow like a foot or two."

"Well, you're acting strange."

There's no way I can tell him or anyone else in this house what happened between Ava and me, so I simply wave off his mention of my acting strange and dismiss it without saying another word. By the time I get back to my room, I can't shake the feeling that she left without even saying goodbye. She didn't even leave a note or anything.

Maybe she won't be gone for long. I mean, how many days can you stay at your aunt's out in the middle of nowhere?

Two weeks have gone by, and she's never called or texted or even told Theo to give me a message. Nothing. I thought we had something special. It sounds stupid even thinking that since I've been with dozens of women I couldn't give a damn if they ever contacted me after I slept with them, but Ava's different.

Or at least I thought she was.

I can't get my mind off her. For the first time in my life, it wasn't just about sex with a girl. I thought we had a good time together. Yeah, things started off a little rocky because I felt like I had to keep up the lie that I hated her, but we got past that.

Didn't we?

For two weeks, I've waited for some word from her. I've checked all her social media, and it's clear she does have some way of getting online at least every so often. She's posted a few times about having to be at her aunt's house in the middle of the woods or something. She can do that, but she can't call the house here to talk to me?

I open my sketchbook for what feels like the hundredth time and look at her picture. She seemed like she was having a good time. We talked about losing our mothers and how much we miss them. I never talk about that with anyone.

Not until her.

With every passing day, I feel more like shit. Forgotten shit. Easily dismissed shit. I keep waiting for Eleanor to say the phone's for me or get some message online from Ava, but nothing ever happens.

A knock on my bedroom door tears me out of my misery, and I yell for whoever the hell it is to come in as I stuff my sketchbook under the covers. Theo strolls through the doorway like he doesn't have a care in the world. Typical Theo. He always looks like he's got the world by the tail and he's enjoying every minute of it.

"Hey, big brother. What's up? You've been holed up in this room for weeks since the blizzard. You sick or something?" he asks as he sits down in the chair near the window.

"No. Just avoiding Dad," I say, only half lying about that.

The last thing I want to do is have to face the fact that my freedom is about to come to an end. My father has let me slide for months since I graduated from college last May, but that day of the blizzard when he mentioned learning about the business was the signal that he's not going to let me just hang out around this house for much longer. He's going to expect me to take what he calls my rightful place at King Industries so I can one day be the head of it when he decides it's time to retire.

"I can understand that, I guess," Theo says nonchalantly. "As the oldest, he's going to want you to join the family business. I'm actually surprised he's let you avoid that for this long."

He's not wrong. I thought my father would have demanded I join him at the company months ago. Whatever's keeping him preoccupied is bound to end sooner than later, though, and that's the day I lose all of my freedom.

"What are you doing here?" I ask, remembering it's almost mid-January. "Shouldn't you be back at school already?"

Theo shakes his head and smiles. "School doesn't

start until later this month. Unlike you at your nice Ivy League school, those of us at state schools get a break. I'm not even sure I want to go back. I'm never going to use that degree. I'm getting into racing, so what the hell will a degree in business do for me with that?"

I can't help but envy him. He's got a world full of options he can choose from. He wants to race cars? Everyone will think it's great. Best idea ever. He'll be fantastic at it. Go Theo! He wants to climb Everest and write a travel book on the expedition? My father would probably buy a publishing company to ensure his work got published.

The world is Theo's oyster. The same for Marius, Kellen, and Ronan. Whatever they want to do with their lives is fine with my father.

Me? I get no choice. I'm the firstborn son of Maximilian King. I get to take over the family business. It's that and nothing else.

That's why being with Ava was so wonderful. She loved the fact that I had my art. She didn't care about me taking over King Industries. In fact, I think she would have been happy to see me spend the rest of my life drawing and doing what I love.

And then she left like none of it meant a goddamned thing.

I can't stop myself from asking Theo about her, even though I know I shouldn't. My father gets one whiff of the possibility that she and I were together and he'll make sure I'm sent to some office for the company at the ends of the earth so I never see her again. Still, I have to ask if he's heard from her at all in the past two weeks.

"Have you heard from your little friend?" I ask with a shrug, trying so hard not to look like I care.

"Who's that?" he asks.

I point toward the window and the carriage house where she used to live. "You know. Your little friend who's stuck out in the wilderness with no internet."

He laughs at my description of her and nods his head. "Oh, yeah. She might not have much in the way of communications up there in New Hampshire at her aunt's, but she can't go a day without calling me."

"Oh yeah?" I say, even as my heart sinks.

So she can speak to people. Just not me.

"Sure. Ava's good like that. If she's thinking about someone, she makes sure they know about it. That's how you can tell if she cares. She's all about the calling and texting. I hear from her all the time."

That's it then. She cares enough about Theo to call and text him, but I get nothing because she doesn't give a damn about me.

I swing my legs off the bed and stand up to leave. My brother watches me like he doesn't understand what's going on.

"Was it something I said? Where the hell are you going in such a hurry?" he asks as I march toward the door.

"I have to talk to Dad about something."

Behind me, he says, "I thought you said you were avoiding Dad like usual."

"Change of plans."

I storm down the hallway to the stairs, taking them by two on my way to my father's office. He's been working from home for the past few weeks, so I know he's around.

With a quick knock on his office door, I throw it open and walk in. He looks up from his desk, shocked to see me since I usually avoid this room like the plague.

No more, though. Ava can call and text Theo, but she can't be bothered to even try to contact me? Fine. Fuck her then. It's time I accept my fate. I thought for a few precious moments when she was around that I could be happy, but that obviously wasn't the case.

I can't stay here forever thinking of what could have been with her. If I'm going to be trapped in a life I hate, at least I can do it on my time and no one else's.

"Matthias? What's going on? Why are you here?" my father asks with pure confusion in his voice.

Stopping in front of his desk, I take a deep breath and say, "You told me once that if I wanted it, I could have a position with the company in London. Is that still an option?"

My father's expression is the definition of shock. For a few moments, he doesn't seem to know how to answer me. He merely stares up at me like I've just told him I plan to go to Mars.

Finally, he smiles and nods his head slowly, like he wants to savor this moment when his firstborn son capitulates and gives up his life. "It is."

"Good. Sign me up."

"That's great! I actually plan to be in London starting next week and lasting until late spring. I can make sure you get settled and trained for the job of leading that office. What changed to make you want to go to London?"

I shake my head knowing he can't know the real reason I want to get the hell away from this place and the memory of Ava. "Just time to get started on what I'm going to have to do eventually anyway. When do we leave?"

He begins to explain how excited he is to have me join the company and how much I'm going to love the people in the London office, but I'm not listening. I don't care about King Industries or the employees in any of the dozens of offices he has around the world.

I don't care about anything anymore.

All I want to do is forget her. If that means going to London, then so be it. I'll go anywhere just to stop feeling like I have for the past two weeks.

For a short time, I was truly happy. I finally got to be with the one person I'd wanted for so long. But it wasn't meant to be, and now all I want is to be as far away from anything that reminds me of Ava Sutton.

CHAPTER SEVENTEEN

va

FIVE YEARS LATER

The front door closes, alerting me that someone's arrived. The King house feels alive again after so long, and even though everyone is returning for a terrible reason, I'm happy they're coming back. I've missed all the King boys, but especially Matthias. Five years have gone by, and I can't deny I'm nervous about seeing him again.

Mr. King stirs in his sleep, a common occurrence in the past few weeks. He's seemed downright restless since Thursday when they gave him the news that he didn't have long to live. I have a feeling he's eager to see his sons again and maybe feeling a little regretful for how he's lived his life. Not that he's been a bad man, but there's a reason it's been years since any of his sons returned to their childhood home.

The nurse gives me a smile as I gently smooth the covers over his chest, careful not to wake him. I mouth that I'm going to walk downstairs to see who just arrived and she nods, whispering, "He'll be asleep for a while. I gave him a shot, so take your time."

I smile back at her and quietly walk out of the room, careful to close the door softly. My spirits soar at the sound of a familiar voice, so I hurry down the stairs and see Theo standing in the foyer. Dressed in jeans and a light blue T-shirt, he looks the same as the last time I saw him that day when my father hurriedly whisked me off to my aunt's house in New Hampshire over five years ago.

His face lights up when he sees me as I hit the last step, and he opens his arms wide. "Little Ava Sutton! My God, you're a sight for sore eyes. Come here and give me a hug."

I run into his arms and wrap mine around his muscular body, noticing how much bigger he is now than he used to be. "I missed you, Theo."

"Me too, Ava. Knowing you were back here taking care of Dad, I made sure to get the earliest flight possible. I landed at JFK and raced up here without even stopping in at my place in the city."

He lets me go, and I step back to look at him. No taller than the last time I saw him, he looks like a man has replaced the boy he used to be. Still as handsome as ever with those gorgeous brown eyes and chiseled features every one of the King brothers has, Theo has turned into the person I always knew he would.

"You look incredible," he says before I can

compliment him. "I'm sorry I didn't keep in touch this past year or so. Sometimes it feels like I'm never in the same place for more than a couple days. I guess I got too caught up in my life and forgot about you and this place. I'm sorry, Ava."

I hold my hand up to stop him from looking so sad as he says that. "It's okay. You're allowed to live your life. It hasn't been all bad for us back here. Until your father got sick, I was going to school and loving it. I only have one semester left before I graduate with a bachelor's in nursing."

His eyes open wide before he takes me into his arms for another hug. "That's great! You should tell them this counts toward your credits."

I take a deep breath, inhaling the scent of his skin and the cologne he's wearing into my nostrils. Leaning back, I look up into his face and smile. "You smell great. When did you start wearing cologne, Theo King?"

Throwing his head back in laughter, he pulls me into him for yet another hug. "I love how you don't hold anything back. I've missed that about you, Ava."

With a roll of my eyes, I turn out of his hold and shake my head. "Please. I bet the cologne is for your current girlfriend. What's her name? Mattie? Mari? Your father told me she could be the one."

Theo's smile fades, and he shakes his head. "Not the one. Not even close. I think my father just has this wish that he'd see me happy before he dies. I'm sorry to tell him that's not going to happen, although I can say I'm honestly happier right now than I've been in a long time. That's all thanks to you, little Ava."

I stand up as tall as I can, making sure I'm not

slouching at all as I say, "I think we can stop with that little Ava business. I'm not tall, but I'm definitely not a little girl anymore."

He nods, and I watch his gaze slide down my body. I wish I had worn nicer clothes. The jeans and tank top look I've been going with since it's getting warmer out now isn't great, even if it is comfortable when I'm taking care of his father.

"You are definitely not a little girl anymore, Ava. Definitely not."

Pushing my fingertips into his bicep, I nudge him before turning to walk toward the kitchen. "You must be hungry. Let's get something to eat. I think I saw Eleanor mixing up a batch of muffins before."

He walks beside me down the hall as he asks, "She's still here? I thought she might be gone by now."

I turn to look at him in horror. "Are you wishing poor Eleanor dead? She's not that old, Theo!" I whisper, hoping she can't hear us.

That makes him laugh, and he slips his arm around my shoulders. "No. I'd never do that. I guess I just figured when all of us moved away that she would retire or something. What exactly does she do now?"

"The same thing she always has. Just for fewer people. Now be nice. I don't want her to think you're wishing for her untimely demise."

As we step into the kitchen, Eleanor turns around from lifting a batch of blueberry muffins out of the oven and practically drops them on the floor in her surprise. "Theo! Oh, look at you. You aren't that boy who left here to go be the world's most famous racecar driver."

He smiles, and I can't deny he's just gorgeous now. Not that he wasn't handsome before, but five years away has done wonders for him.

"Hi, Eleanor. I don't know about world famous, but I do okay."

She catches herself and stops smiling a moment later. "I'm so sorry about your father, honey. If it's any consolation, Ava here has been taking great care of him. She and the nurse they sent out make sure he's never in pain and always has company, no matter what time it is, day or night."

Theo turns to look at me and pulls me tightly next to him. "That's my Ava. Always caring."

"Would you like a muffin? They're blueberry, and they're right out of the oven," she asks as she begins to lift them out of the tin.

"They smell too good to say no." Pulling out a chair, he sits down before Eleanor sets a fresh muffin on a plate in front of him and places the butter dish down nearby.

"How about a drink?" she asks, happier than I've seen her in ages. "There's soda, milk, water, juice. You name it, we have it. I'm not sure why we have this much to drink, but I must have thought since all you boys would be coming back that I should stock up when I went to the store yesterday. So what will it be?"

He takes a bite of the steaming muffin, and his eyes roll back in his head. "Oh my God. I'd forgotten how good your food is, Eleanor. Milk would be great with this. Are these fresh blueberries?"

I watch her beam happiness at his mention of how great her cooking is. "Yes. I got a few quarts of them because Ava and the nurse told me your father needed more fruit. I guess I went a bit overboard, though, so I figured I'd make some muffins with the berries. I'm so happy you like them."

A charmer, just as he's always been, Theo smiles and takes a drink of milk from the glass she places next to his plate. "Like? No. This is love right here. I knew I missed something about this place. It's you, Eleanor."

His compliment makes her blush, and she waves it off before turning back to the oven. When he looks over at me, he quickly says, "Not that I didn't miss you too, Ava. You knew that, though, right?"

"I'm sure," I say with a chuckle.

From the foyer, the sound of the front door closing makes my heart skip a beat. Maybe it's Matthias. Theo looks at me, and I swear we hold our breath as we wait to hear who it is. A few seconds later, a voice calls out, "Where is everybody?"

"We're in the kitchen!" Theo yells before turning to look at me. "The last time I saw Marius, we were both in France. I was racing, and he was taking pictures of something or another. Wait until you see him."

I look over toward the doorway as I watch for the middle King son to appear. When he does, it's like I'm taken back in time to those days when the three of us would play on the estate's grounds from early morning to late at night every summer.

Unlike his brother, Marius doesn't look like he's changed much at all since I saw him last. Still lean, he may have filled out a little in the past five years, but as always with him, there's a hint of something dark in his expression, even as it brightens when he sees me.

"Ava Sutton, you're a sight for sore eyes after a flight from hell and that drive from JFK," he says as he opens his arms to hug me.

"When did you fly in? If I knew you were taking a flight close to mine, I would have waited and we could have driven up together," Theo says.

I step back from Marius and smile as he sits down next to his brother and immediately begins picking at his muffin. "That's what you get for not keeping in touch, you know."

The two of them laugh, and then a second later, they begin pushing one another to get to the muffin. Eleanor shakes her head before setting a fresh blueberry muffin in front of Marius.

"No need to fight. I made two dozen."

"They're as good as you remember," Theo says as he breaks off a piece of his brother's. "Now we're even."

I can't help but chuckle at how much has changed yet these two are still the same as they've always been. As Eleanor sets a glass of milk down in front of Marius, Theo begins to talk about how good it is to be back, even though it's for a bad reason.

One by one, the King boys return to their childhood home. Kellen and Ronan arrive together a few minutes after Marius, and with each time someone walks into the kitchen, it's like we're all transported back in time to when we were kids. We laugh as each one brings up a story they remember, the past flowing into the present with ease for all of us.

All except Matthias.

I wait as the minutes tick by and he doesn't show up.

Finally, after we've all talked for over an hour, I begin to wonder if he's ever coming.

Leaning in, I quietly say to Theo, "Where is Matthias?"

He shrugs and looks down the table at the rest of his brothers. "We're missing one. Anyone know where Matthias is? I figured he'd be back by now."

They all shake their heads, and it's like the mention of his name brings an end to all the laughter. I hate that for him. Yes, he could be miserable, but I've seen his happy side. His brothers have too. I know they have.

Yet even one of them saying his name changes the mood of the group.

"He is coming. Isn't he?" I ask as my hopes begin to fade I'll get to see him and have a reunion like I've had with his four siblings.

None of them have the answer. Each one in turn says that he hasn't talked to Matthias for over a year, and all I can think of is how sad it must be for him to never speak to his brothers for all that time.

We start to talk about happier times, and once more, everyone is laughing and reliving the old days. Eleanor busies herself with making more muffins, and for a time, I forget how much I wanted to see the one King brother I've missed more than any other.

In the middle of Theo telling all of us about his last race where he crashed and miraculously walked away without a scratch, the oldest King brother appears in the doorway to the kitchen. He doesn't say a word, but the very presence of him chills the mood for everyone, and they fall silent.

"About time," Theo says as he stuffs more muffin into

his mouth. "We thought you might have bailed and left this whole thing to the four of us."

I watch Matthias stand as still as a statue, not even cracking a smile at his brother's poor attempt at a joke. No one else speaks, and while I wait for him to say something to any of us, I can't help but notice how angry he looks.

But he's as stunning as he was the last day I saw him right here in this house. His hair is a little longer, but it's still nearly black. His beard looks about a couple days old, and as he scans the room, I see not a hint of happiness in his dark brown eyes.

It's as if being back with his family makes him feel nothing.

Even more, it's as if seeing me makes him feel nothing.

And then he opens his mouth, and it's like I'm back in that room upstairs on that snowy day and he's telling me I'm not welcome in this house.

"What is she doing here?" he says, each word dripping with nothing but pure hate.

His anger stuns me. After the time we spent together, I thought he'd be kind to me like he was that last day I saw him.

Theo immediately comes to my defense, thankfully. "She's been taking care of Dad. You know this, Matthias. Sit down, take a load off, and eat some fucking muffins to get that frown off your face."

No one says as word as Matthias narrows his eyes to angry slits and shakes his head. "I'm not interested in muffins."

I stand up and smile, hoping he'll lighten up, but he

simply stares down at me with a look of pure disgust in his eyes. "I need to speak to you," I sweetly say as I start moving toward the hallway so we can have some privacy for our conversation.

But he shuts me down. "No, you don't. Get out."

"Matthias, what the hell is wrong with you?" Marius asks, clearly disapproving of his brother's behavior. "Ava has been taking care of Dad, so telling her to leave is shitty, to say the least. On top of it, she's like one of the family after living here for years. Lighten up, dude."

In a flash, Matthias whips his head in his brother's direction and snaps, "No, she's not. Dad has a nurse. Whatever she's been doing isn't necessary, so she can go. Now."

Lowering my head, I stand there embarrassed for a long moment as time seems to stop. Theo once again tries to defend me, but I stop him. There's no point. Whatever I've done for their father and whatever the rest of his brothers feel about me, it's clear the oldest King doesn't want me around.

"I have to go. It was nice seeing you all again."

All four brothers try to stop me, but I hurry out, humiliated by how awful Matthias treated me. I should go back upstairs to check on Mr. King, but instead I run out of the house down to the carriage house where my father is, desperate to see a friendly face.

As soon as I open the front door to our house, my father looks up from his desk and smiles. "Hey, I didn't expect you back this early."

When I don't answer because I'm on the verge of tears, he stands up and hurries over to me. "Ava, what happened? Is it Max?"

I shake my head, sorry for alarming him. "No, Dad. He's still with us. I just had to get out of that house."

"Why? Is he having a bad day?" my father asks as he gently guides me into the living room to sit down.

"No. Mr. King is having the same kind of day he's had since they gave him the news. I had to leave because when Matthias arrived after all his brothers, he ordered me out of the house. I don't understand, Dad. Forget about the fact that I've been with his father taking care of him for months since he first got sick. Why does Matthias King hate me so much? After we spent that time together during that snowstorm, I thought things had changed. I guess I was wrong."

I close my eyes and will the tears to go away. I don't want to cry today. It's just that I was so excited about seeing him again after all this time. I know he's married and there can't be anything between us now, but I thought he'd at least be nice to me.

My father wraps his arm around me and gives me a squeeze that means the world at this moment. "Honey, take it easy on Matthias. He's had a lot to deal with in his life."

Turning to look at him, I roll my eyes. "Oh, I'm sure. He has more money than I or anyone I know will ever see, he's gotten to live the high life in Europe, and he's about to inherit more when a man he doesn't even care about leaves him a ton. Poor Matthias. Boo-hoo."

To my surprise, my father shakes his head. "He's had to live with expectations that would have crushed other men. He was forced into his marriage, and from what I hear, it isn't a happy one. Even worse, Matthias never wanted to work at King Industries. He didn't have the temperament for it. He's got an artist's heart, and that doesn't mix with a business mind."

I look at my father, stunned. "I didn't know you knew about his art."

With a smile, he nods his head. "I know a lot of things you don't know about. When his mother was alive, she encouraged him to follow his passion and kept his father from pushing him into the business. When she died, that protection ended. I knew it wouldn't be long before Max decided he had to follow in his footsteps. Matthias not only lost his mother. He lost the person who championed his talent. Without her, it was only a matter of time before he would be forced to work at King Industries."

My heart hurts for Matthias, even as I hate him for treating me so cruelly earlier. I can't imagine being stuck in a life I never wanted.

"You sound like you admire him. Why did you always tell me to stay away from him then?"

My father pats my knee and sighs. "You two come from very different worlds. You don't belong together."

"But Mr. King always liked me. He treated me like I was good enough. All those gifts he gave me."

"He adores you. Always has. You're the daughter he never had. He would have loved you to be with Matthias. He's told me many times that he and his wife thought the world of you and hoped you two would get together. But I didn't want you saddled with all the anger and resentment he has over not being allowed to live the life he wanted. Any woman he ends up with will get nothing but misery. I didn't want that for you."

"I've seen him happy, Dad. He's not always miserable."

Shaking his head, my father frowns. "He never had a chance to find happiness. His father had his entire life planned out before he was even a year old. Matthias had the misfortune of being born first, so while his brothers get to do whatever they want, he always had to be exactly what Max expected. He had to attend the same university his father did. He had to major in business, even though he never had any interest in that. The pressure on him to be the next head of King Industries would have broken others, so in some ways I admire Matthias. I also feel sorry for him. I even tried to talk to Max about it, but once Elizabeth died, there was no chance Matthias would ever have a life he wanted. So I made sure Max knew you and his oldest son could never be."

I tell him I understand, but the truth is I don't. I don't know why Matthias had to follow in his father's footsteps instead of doing what made him happy.

"Why couldn't Mr. King just have Kellen take over King Industries? He's always wanted to be in the business. He's about to graduate with an MBA, for God's sake. Wouldn't he be a better person to head the company than Matthias?"

With a smile, my father sighs. "That makes sense to us, but not to Max. He wanted his firstborn son to take over the family business. Kellen isn't that, so it fell on Matthias."

"Well, even if he is unhappy about his life, he didn't have to take it out on me," I say, sulking.

"Just remember, Ava. All that money the Kings have

doesn't buy happiness. It just buys stuff, but that's not going to make anyone happy."

Standing, I give him a kiss. "I'm going to go outside and get some sun for a little while. I can't remember the last time I spent any time outdoors recently."

"That'll be good for you. Try not to be too hurt by what he did. Some people just can't be happy."

I walk outside to clear my head, but I can't stop thinking about how angry Matthias was. As I walk along the road, I wonder if we'll ever get back to the way we were that day.

"Ava! Wait up!" Theo calls from behind me, and I turn around to see him jogging to catch up.

"Hey, did you see your father?"

He shakes his head. "No. He was sleeping, so I figured I'd take a walk around the estate. Turns out I miss a lot of things about this place. I don't think I ever realized how beautiful it is in springtime, you know that?"

I look around at all the trees with their green leaves and all the flowers the groundskeeper planted and have to agree. "It is. I think I never saw how incredible this place was until last spring. Something about the flowers and how they seem to go on forever. It's just beautiful."

As we walk, he quietly says, "I'm sorry about before with my brother. I don't know what his problem is."

"His problem seems to be me."

When I look up at Theo, he's smiling and shaking his head. "Well, then Matthias is dumber than I thought. And blind."

I think for a moment that I should explain that his brother and I spent those days together and I don't understand how he could be so horrible to me after that, but I don't. Pressing my lips together, I keep the words in.

There's no point in dredging up a past only I remember and care about.

CHAPTER EIGHTEEN

*M*atthias

I SLAM THE DOOR AND STEP A FEW FEET INTO MY bedroom before memories of my time with Ava wash over me. Fuck, I don't want to think of that. Not now. Not ever. Just the sight of her sitting there with Theo like they're two happy peas in a fucking pod made me want to kill someone.

Looking around at the room I spent so many years in, I have to laugh. I hated this space for no good reason. I understand that now that I'm back here again. This house always felt like a prison.

How foolish I was back then. I had no idea of what a prison really felt like.

I walk over to the bed and sit down, exhausted from the trip back here. Well, that's only part of it. All those hours spent getting here were made worse by all my thinking about the past.

About Ava.

Christ, it was a mistake coming back here. My father doesn't need to see me before he moves on to the next life. We haven't spoken in ages, unless I can count King Industries memos and the company Christmas card everyone receives around the holidays.

Closing my eyes, I don't stop my mind from drifting back to that one Christmastime I can't seem to forget. Twenty-two of them came before it, but I can barely remember a single thing from any of them. Five of them have come after that day, and not one of them made me as happy as that time I spent with her.

I've tried to forget. God knows I have. I knew it wasn't fair to marry Jillian when I was still in love with Ava. I thought I could be the husband I needed to be to make it work, but she's not stupid. She knew. Jillian didn't know who always made me keep her at arm's length or how much I couldn't stop myself from thinking about the time I spent with Ava those two snowy December days, but she sensed I wasn't hers, even though I asked her to marry me.

Not that it was ever my idea. Our marriage, like everything else in my life once I joined King Industries, happened because it was good for business. My father and her father decided merging our two families would benefit their bottom lines. So we got married two years ago, even though I still loved someone else.

I look up at the ceiling and try to remember a time when I wasn't so unhappy. All that comes to me is that time with Ava. How is it possible that a few hours could mean so much to me? I've had thousands of hours since then. Why couldn't a single one of them bring a smile to my face like those I spent with her?

Fuck! It's like she haunts me, and I don't know how to get rid of her. My life would be so much better if I never had those days with little Ava Sutton.

Lying back on the bed, I take a deep breath in as the truth echoes through my brain. No, my life wouldn't be better. It would merely be empty, and I'd have no reason to ever want to come back to this place.

When I found out from my father's estate manager that his illness had reached a point that there was no hope, all I could think of was seeing Ava again. Even after all the hurt, I only thought of her. I can't help my father. His cancer is going to end his life, and that's the simple fact.

I considered not even returning here. What's the point? I did everything my father asked, and in return, he thought he gave me the world. Should I now tell him in his final days that all he did was ensure I'm the most miserable person anyone could ever meet because I did as he demanded?

He got what he wanted, and in return, I'll be the head of King Industries at the ripe old age of twenty-eight. I'm sure it seemed like a fair deal in his mind. It's not like I ever had a chance to do anything else. He wanted me to go to college for business, so that's what I did. And when he wanted me to join the family company, that's what I did. So now when he dies at barely sixty years old, never having the chance to retire and enjoy life outside the walls of King Industries headquarters, I'll again do as I must and take his place.

Every time I think of that eventuality, I feel like someone's placed a thousand-pound weight on my chest and I can't push it off. It threatens to smother the life out of me, but how different will my existence be once I step into his shoes and take over as head of King Industries? I have little else in my life other than work. My wife and I barely talk to one another anymore. We have no children, thank God. I can't imagine bringing a child into the sham we call a marriage. I have no real friends. They've all fallen away in the past few years.

So not much will change once my father dies. I'll get his office. That will be different, but it's meaningless. Much like everything else in my life.

My mind drifts back to those days Ava and I spent in this room talking and laughing. And sleeping together. After all those months of wishing I didn't have to obey my father's rule of staying away from her, I finally threw caution to the wind and took a chance she could forgive me for being rotten to her for so long.

She should have told me to go fuck myself and kicked me in the face when I was crouched down in front of her taking off her wet shoes. I deserved at least that much nastiness from her.

But that's not who she is. She forgave me without making me grovel or humiliate myself like other women would have. Her gentle nature left her no choice.

And for that, I repaid her sweetness with what I did today. I should have forgiven her by now for leaving me. I know in my heart she never meant to hurt me, but seeing her again brought all those emotions to the surface, and as I always do, I lashed out.

At the only person in the world I love.

The memories of that time do their slow march through my mind. Her face down in that snowbank. Me carrying her up to this room as she fought me the entire way. The way she smelled so perfect and innocent because of her perfume that reminded me of flowers. Her being her sweet self and me trying to push her away.

Me finally giving in to what I'd wanted for so long and never believed I could have.

Then the memory of her letting me draw her pops into my head, so I reach over to open the top drawer of my nightstand. I know Eleanor has the housekeeper clean all the rooms every week, not that they need it since none of us live here anymore. I wonder if my old sketchbook is still here.

I feel around and it's right there on top where I left it. Lifting it out, I hold it in front of me, running my fingers across the front cover. Nothing made me happier than when I could draw back then. How long has it been since I sketched anything? Not since I moved to London. My wife doesn't even know it's one of my favorite things to do.

When I open the sketchbook, I see the picture of those trees I drew when I knew nothing about shadow or depth. I was just drawing because it made me happy. With each page I flip to, I see myself growing in my ability to capture what I saw. I can't help but be proud. My mother was right. She always said if I kept at it, I'd get better and better.

Twelve years she's been gone, and still the thought of her smiling at me and handing me that first sketchbook makes my breath catch in my chest. She had no idea what that gift gave me. I always knew my destiny as the firstborn son of Maximilian King. It was set in stone the day I was born.

But art gave me a reprieve from my sentence.

I continue to flip through the book, knowing what sketch is last. I haven't drawn a single thing since that time. Consumed by unhappiness at my fate and losing her, I never bothered again.

When I reach that page, I want to keep moving, to ignore her like I've forced myself to for all this time. I can't, though. She's as beautiful in my sketch as she was that day. As she is today. I don't know how I possibly captured her gentleness and that hint of shyness she showed me as I drew her that snowy afternoon, but there it is on full display in every stroke I made.

I swear if I close my eyes right now, I can smell her flowery perfume still hanging in the air.

Why didn't she say goodbye? What made her leave without a word to me after what we shared together? Was it because I fell asleep and didn't get to go to her that morning? Why didn't she try to get in touch with me like she did with Theo?

I've asked myself these same questions hundreds, if not thousands, of times since that day I woke up and never saw her again. Until today. Sometimes I think I know the answers, and other times I'm utterly clueless as to what happened.

All I know is every time I ask myself them, I feel the same way. I hate her. Then I love her. Then I hate her again for infecting me like some virus I can't shake even years later.

What is it about little Ava Sutton? She's not the most beautiful woman in the world. I've met better. I've had hotter. But her looks were never all she was. Even now, I have to admit that.

To this day, I don't know what it is about her that I can't forget. It's everything about her, not just what she looks like.

I can't keep chasing ghosts like I have. Being back here at this house makes me hate myself more than I usually do. All I want is to be free of the memory of her.

But that's a lie I tell myself when the loneliness gets too much. I don't want to be free of Ava. Ever. And that's the problem.

Frustrated, I throw the sketchbook across the room. It slams off the wall next to the bathroom door and hits the floor with a thud.

Closing my eyes again, I try to think of anything but her. Why does she torment me like this?

My phone vibrates against my ribs, so I fish it out of my suit jacket and hold it up in front of my eyes. Jillian. Jesus, I can't take another fight with her right now.

But maybe it won't be like that this time, so I answer it. "Hey, I got here. When are you coming? The airport was a goddamned nightmare, so whenever your flight is, get there like three hours early."

The phone is silent for so long that I wonder if it dropped the call, but finally, Jillian quietly says, "I'm not coming."

"Oh. Okay."

What the hell else can I say?

"In fact, I won't be at the house when you come back, Matthias. I've packed my things and I'm leaving."

"Oh."

Again, I have nothing.

"I know you're not going to be bothered by this. We haven't been happy, so it's not like this should come as a surprise. We got married for our fathers, not because we loved each other. Now that your father is going to be gone, there's nothing keeping us together."

In her quaint British accent, her news sounds strangely charming. It's certainly not a surprise. Nothing she's saying is untrue. Her timing isn't great, but then again, it's not like I'm close to my father.

"Good luck, Matthias."

"Yeah, you too."

And with that, the call ends along with my marriage. It's been a hell of a day, and it's not even three o'clock in the afternoon.

I toss the phone onto the bed and return to staring up at the ceiling. I don't know why. It's not like any of the answers I need are up there.

So my marriage is over. Not exactly a shocker. I should feel something about that, but that would have required me to care about Jillian in the first place. It's not good when you go into a relationship still hung up on someone else.

My wife's been cheating on me for the past six months, so she'll be fine. She has a warm place to land. If I'd been smart, I would have done the same thing, but I had no interest in finding another woman. I never wanted the one I married because she wasn't the woman I'm still in love with, so why would I bother with finding something on the side?

I roll over and stare out the window at the grounds on the estate I'm about to inherit. Neither Jillian nor I are going to want the house in London, so that's going to have to be sold. I can run King Industries from here, if I want to. My father has for years. Maybe it's time I came home for good. I'd be lying if I said there was nothing here for me.

For a few minutes, I let myself daydream about Ava and me together here. Could that still happen? After my behavior this morning, I'll have to work overtime to get her back.

In the distance, I see her and Theo standing on the grass laughing. Instantly, every good thought I let myself have about her evaporates, replaced by the reality of what she did five years ago.

The reality I've lived with every day since then.

Balling my hands into tight fists, I watch the two of them having a good time together as rage builds inside me. "Don't bother, Theo. She'll just disappear on you."

CHAPTER NINETEEN

va

COOLIGAN'S LOOKS THE SAME AS IT HAS SINCE I WAS A little girl and my parents would bring my brother and me for dinner here on special occasions. I always liked the crisp white tablecloths, which looked so clean and fresh. My mother used to say with Andrew and me, she didn't dare to put a white tablecloth on the dining room table since it would be dirty before the first meal was served.

I look around at the dark walls with the large metallic gold squares and beautiful wall sconces in the middle of each one as Theo and I are shown to our table in the corner of the restaurant. It's been a few years since I came here, and I'm looking forward to enjoying one of their delicious steaks I remember being the best I've ever had.

We sit down across from one another on the black leather tufted chairs I've only ever seen at Cooligan's, and I open my napkin to set it across my lap. A waiter dressed in a black and white uniform quickly joins us to fill our water glasses while all I can think about is what happened between Matthias and me this morning.

"There's a restaurant in the south of France that always reminds me of this place," Theo says with a smile as he unfurls his napkin and sets it on his lap. "Every time I go there, I think of Cooligan's."

"Is it because of the gold squares on the black wall?"

He nods as he chuckles. "It is! How did you know?"

I shrug and answer, "It's the part of this restaurant that always stands out to me. Anytime anyone describes this place, it's always by the dark walls and the thin gold square lines."

Theo leans toward me and whispers, "No offense to anyone here, but that place in France makes this beef dish that's better than sex."

My cheeks instantly heat up at his mention of sex. I sensed he was flirting with me earlier today when we were walking around the estate, and now this and the way he seems to have a twinkle in his eye tells me he may be doing it again.

As close as he and I have been for nearly all our lives, I don't know how I feel about Theo being anyone but my best friend. He always teased that I was the future Mrs. Theo King, but I never took that seriously, and I doubt he did either. That was simply a joke a boy made to a girl he cared for like a sister.

Or at least that's all I ever considered it to be. If I had

thought we were ever more than just friends, I would have never been with his brother.

Not that Matthias and I had anything close to a relationship. It was only a couple days, but I can't lie. That time still means more to me than I can explain, although by his actions today I think I can safely say it didn't mean anything to him at all.

Theo taps the top of my hand as it rests on the table, bringing me out of my thoughts. "Hey. Where did you go there for a minute?"

I shake my head and force a smile as the last tendril of memory from those snowy days recedes into the back of my mind. "Sorry. I was thinking about another time here with my parents," I lie.

He nods solemnly like he always has when any mention of my mother comes up. The two of us have both lost our mothers, so we have that in common on top of everything else we share.

"For a second there, I thought it was because I said something about sex."

Again, my cheeks heat up with a blush I'm sure is making him think I'm embarrassed. I'm not, so I don't understand why this keeps happening. This is Theo King, the person I've been friends with for so long I can't remember a time when he wasn't in my life. Even gone for the past five years traveling around the world racing cars, he and I have kept in touch through texts and calls, so it's not like he's never said anything about sex before. I mean, he's told me about many of the women he's dated all the way back to when we were teenagers.

I wave away his concern and take a drink of water.

Maybe that will stop my face from getting red over and over again during this meal.

"We've known each other forever, Theo. You can say anything you want to me. It's all fair game between us, right? We've never held anything back when it comes to anything."

He nods and a slow smile lights up his face. "Good. That's the way I was hoping things would continue to be. I mean, I know we've only texted for the most part, except for a few calls here and there in the past few years, but you're still my Ava and I'm still the same Theo for you, right?"

"Always."

I can't help but notice that when he smiles he reminds me so much of how his brother looked those days we spent together. I liked seeing Matthias that happy. He's never been as carefree as Theo, but seeing him truly enjoy himself made me realize how beautiful he was.

A waiter stops at the table and hands us the menu in enormous black leather books. When he walks away, I stand mine up in front of me and peer over the top at Theo.

"I've always thought it's strange that the print is so little in these menus since they're pretty much made for giants," I say, giggling.

He stands his up in front of him and smiles over the top of it. "I know. God help anyone who doesn't have perfect vision. Between the dim lights and the tiny print in the menu, you'd think you're ordering a steak and you'd get clams in red sauce instead."

I cringe at the thought of that mistake. "That would definitely ruin my meal."

The two of us fall into silence as the room fills up around us with other diners and we look over the menu. I know I want to get the filet since it's been my favorite since I was fifteen. Something about the way they season it makes it the best steak I've ever tasted.

Since I don't have to decide on what I plan to order, my mind drifts back to the house. It's like old times with everyone back at home, and I guess that the way Matthias acted toward me is also just like it used to be. I need to stop thinking he changed for a long time and the way he behaved today was some aberration.

The truth is those two sweet days that December were the aberration. Not even an entire week. Just a few hours, if I'm being honest.

Once the waiter takes our order, Theo and I talk about how we and Marius used to play every day, rain or shine, snow or searing heat, and before long the two of us are laughing about old times. I can always rely on Theo to make me laugh. No matter how bad my day ever was, all it took was a few minutes with him to make me happy.

"Tell me about racing," I say as the waiter brings me my glass of red wine and him his glass of scotch neat. "I want to hear all about it."

He sighs and shakes his head. "I don't want to think about that now. Tonight, I'm with my favorite person in the entire world back home where nothing else matters."

I study his expression for a moment and find something dimmed in him. Could it be he's not happy racing cars all around the world? He always sounds like he's having the time of his life whenever he texts me to say hi and ask how things are back here. I thought he'd love telling me all about his exciting times.

"Okay."

Once more, we settle into silence, but this time there are no menus to hide my discomfort. The elephant in the room is we wouldn't be even on the same continent if it wasn't for his father dying. I've spent the last few months taking care of him, so I'm happy to tell Theo anything he wants to know, but all day he hasn't asked a single question about it.

Finally, I say, "I'm sorry about your father, Theo. I want you to know I've been doing all I can to make his final days as comfortable as possible. I'm not a full-fledged nurse yet, but I've done what I could, even if it was just sitting with him and listening to stories he's told me."

Theo nods, but I see no real sadness or remorse in his face. "Thank you. I'm glad he's had someone so kind with him these past months. I'm sure I speak for all my brothers when I say it's greatly appreciated."

I shrug as I say, "I'm just happy I could be there for him. He's always been very kind to me and my family."

"He always did think the world of you. He considers you the daughter he never had."

"That's what my father always says. Your father has always been so thoughtful too. The diamond tennis bracelet he gave me when I graduated is something I'll cherish forever, and every year for my birthday and Christmas, he always makes sure to give me something wonderful. That's why when he got sick, I figured it was the least I could do after all the things he's done to show me how much he thinks of me."

Theo sighs again and leans back against the leather chair. "You had two great father figures then. That's pretty good. I can tell you your father has done an incredible job running the estate. The place would have fallen apart if it wasn't for him."

As much as I'm sure my father has been helpful, I know Theo is being too kind now. "That's sweet of you to say, but I'm sure your father managed most things. He was always a very hands-on kind of businessman."

"He was, but not always," he says before taking a drink of his scotch. "When my mother died, things got bad. I never told you about it, but if you'd been inside our house, you would have seen a very different situation than when she was alive."

I shake my head, stunned by his comment. "I had no idea. Why didn't you tell me things were bad then?"

Theo forces himself to smile, but it's obvious the memory of that time is painful still to this day. "They weren't that bad. I was still living in a mansion most people would give anything to call home. My father just didn't care for a while after she died. I think he was so devastated to lose her that he couldn't find it in him to handle a lot of stuff that had to do with all of us. He was left with five sons who needed to be taken care of, but he was too consumed with grief to do it. So that job fell to other people for that first year after she passed away, like your father and Eleanor."

My memory of that time period is hazy, but I vaguely remember not going up to the King house for a long time. Theo would come out, joined by a few of his brothers, and we'd still run around the estate, but unlike before his mother died, he didn't ask me to come up to the house for months.

"I had no idea. I'm sorry. I wish I knew."

"It's okay. Your father was a godsend, though. He handled a lot of things my father simply didn't want to deal with. I remember one time the principal at school gave Matthias a letter to bring home. He and I, since we were the two oldest, walked into my father's study where he spent nearly every day and night for months after my mother died, and gave it to him. He didn't even open it. He just threw it onto the table and told us to leave. It was a letter about our tuition and how it needed to be paid for all of us. Your father was there that day and picked it up. It was him who took care of the problem. I know that because we never got another letter about our tuition again."

I smile at the idea that my father was able to take care of the King boys when Mr. King couldn't because he was so torn up about losing their mother. "I'm happy he could help. He's always cared about your family more than just as an employee."

"When my father finally came out of it, he knew who watched over things while he couldn't. If it wasn't for Eleanor handling the day-to-day stuff with us and your father making sure we didn't get thrown out of school and dozens of other things I'm sure I don't even know about, we five kids would have been a mess. That's why I know he's going to leave your family and Eleanor money in his will. He knows he has a big debt to pay back."

I take a drink of my wine at Theo's mention of my family getting anything in the will after his father dies.

"He's going to need it if your brother fires him and throws him out of his house."

As much as I don't want to sound alarmed, I'm afraid of what Matthias will do once he has control of the estate. After today's little performance, I'd say it's a sure thing he's going to make things as hard as possible.

Strangely enough, though, Theo shakes his head like he doesn't agree. "My brother can be heartless, but he's not that bad. He knows how dedicated your father has been to our family all these years as the estate manager. He saw what he did to make sure we didn't have to worry about our tuition that time."

I wish I could be as confident as Theo that Matthias isn't going to be the world's worst ogre when the time comes. "I wouldn't be so sure of that. I thought he and I were friends, and you saw how he was with me today. The first time seeing each other in five years, and he acted like I was his mortal enemy."

"I know. I couldn't believe he said those things to you. What was that all about?"

Shrugging, I pretend not to know the reason, but I think I do know why Matthias seems to hate me again. "He's going to be the executor of your father's will, though, and I worry that means my father will be out on his ear as soon as Matthias can send him packing. He's lived there all my life, Theo. I don't know where he'll go."

"Or you. Don't forget that's your home too. I can't believe my brother would be such a dick. Do you want me to see what I can do? He might listen to me. If it looks like he's going to make things hard for you guys,

I'll talk to him and remind him of all your father's done for our family."

"Thank you. I'd appreciate that."

Theo's smile returns, that big grin that never fails to brighten my mood. "Then it's settled. For now, no more talk about Mr. Miserable, who never fails to bring down the vibe. Let's enjoy tonight and have great meal."

I agree, happy to know my father and I have someone in our corner with Theo.

CHAPTER TWENTY

atthias

ALONE IN THE ROOM WE CALLED THE GAME ROOM when we all lived here, I sit in the dark watching some show on TV. I didn't bother to change whatever it is when I turned it on, but I'm not really paying attention to what's happening in the show. It's more background noise for me as I try to process this day.

I still haven't gone to my father's room to see him. I've been here for nearly twelve hours, but I can't bring myself to do it yet.

He's got my brothers Ronan and Kellen there with him, so it's not like he's all alone. One King son is as good as another.

Whatever this is on the TV shows me a couple in love strolling through some park on a beautiful sunny day, and all I can think of is rolling my eyes. What nonsense.

Love is a joke. "Don't do it, man. Stay free," I say to the guy on the screen, but it's no use. He's already lost.

Another single man bites the dust.

I can't watch any more of this, so I grab the remote and say, "Violence."

The TV instantly switches to something I'm guessing is about the mafia if all the guys dressed in black suits hanging around a bar is any indication. It doesn't matter what it's about. I just don't want to see people smiling and kissing like it's the happiest day of their fucking lives.

"Take that shit somewhere else, Romeo and Juliet," I mumble as I toss the remote onto the sofa nearby.

I've spent the last hour or so thinking about my marriage ending, and fuck if I can't find it in myself to be sad. I feel nothing about it. Jillian's been sleeping with that guy for a while, so I guess I should be happy? Or maybe angry since she was stepping out on me.

I feel neither emotion. I don't know if she suspected I knew about whoever the guy is, but the truth is I just didn't care enough to do anything about it.

Why should I? It wasn't like we were ever in love. Our marriage was a business arrangement set up by our fathers, and as she said, now that one of them is about to leave this earth, what's the point of staying together? We barely slept together the entire time we were married. In truth, we were more roommates than husband and wife, so it's like when my college roommate moved out to live with his girlfriend.

My mind switches to him and the news I heard a year or so ago that she left him for some yoga instructor. He should have cut and run when he had the chance and she told him she was moving to fucking Decatur for a job after college. That was his out, but instead, he moved there to be with her, and they got married. Less than five years later, she's fucking Mr. Bendy Legs behind his back and my former roommate is drinking every night and wondering where it all went wrong for him.

"You believed in love, you sucker. Don't make that mistake again," I say into the darkness.

My brother interrupts my misery when he strolls in, turns the lights on, and sits down in the chair next to me. His usual happy-go-lucky self, Theo flashes me a grin and puts his feet up on the table in front of us.

"What's with sitting in the dark alone?" he asks with a chuckle.

As if anything in this house at this moment is fucking funny. Read the room, Theo. Someone's dying on the other side of the building, for Christ's sake.

Then I smell a familiar scent on him. I'd know that perfume anywhere. He's been with Ava tonight. How fucking nice for him.

"Did you come in here to annoy me?" I ask. "Because that's what you're doing."

Again, he smiles, irritating me more. "No. I came in here to see what you're up to. Why were you sitting in the dark?"

"I'm practicing my mourning. You might try it."

My brother looks at me oddly and nods his head. "Okay."

Thankfully, he doesn't continue trying to talk to me since I'm not in the mood for idle chit-chat. After realizing he's been with Ava tonight, I'm not only miserable but angry as all fucking hell.

The silence only lasts for a few minutes before he insists on talking again. "So what's going to happen with the estate once Dad is gone?" he asks, immediately raising my suspicions.

I lean forward in my chair and look over at him. "What the hell do you care? You'll get all Dad promised you."

"I'm not worried about me," he says with a chuckle.

Christ, he's grating on my nerves right now. That way he has of making even the most serious things sound like they're all fun and games bothers me. He's always been the good time guy who never worries about everything. Maybe if he had to live up to our father's standards about anything and had to marry someone he didn't fucking love to please him, he wouldn't be so goddamned happy all the time.

"Why are you asking if you're not worried about you?"

He shrugs off my question and gets up to grab the remote off the sofa. As he's surfing through the channels, he casually answers, "Just curious. There are a lot of people who will be affected when Dad dies. That's all."

What is his angle tonight? Who is he talking about in this lot of people who are going to be affected when our father leaves this earth?

Then I catch another whiff of that flowery scent on him and know what he's doing. I stand up and walk in front of him, stopping so he can't see the TV and has to face me.

"This has to do with our father's estate manager, doesn't it?"

Theo tilts his head up to look at me. "His name is Joe

Sutton, as you well know, and he's known Dad our entire lives. Mom adored him, if you remember. Stop acting like he's some unnamed servant nobody gives a fuck about."

Jealousy surges inside me as all I can smell right now is that fucking perfume of Ava's clinging to every inch of Theo. "Well, I don't give a fuck about him."

"What the fuck is your problem? You seem to be hell bent on being a dick to anyone with the last name Sutton. Let me remind you how much our dying father adores him and Ava."

I turn to walk away as I say, "Dad has always cared too much for the help."

Before I can take two steps, Theo's on me, spinning me around to face him. "Stop acting like such an asshole. They're like family, Matthias."

We stand toe to toe in each other's faces like at any moment we're going to start fighting. I'm pretty much in the mood to rip someone's head off, so if my brother makes the mistake of pissing me off any more, he's going to get a fist in his mouth.

"If she's family, maybe you shouldn't act like a horny schoolboy whenever she's around."

Theo shakes his head and takes a step back. "What is your problem with Ava? I swear you act like she killed your best friend."

I ignore his comment and walk out into the hallway before I let him get under my skin anymore. He doesn't need to know what my problem is with Ava Sutton. That's between me and her, and sometime soon, she's going to understand what she did.

Ronan and Kellen meet me in the hallway, and all I

see is sadness in their faces. Grabbing my arm as I pass them, my youngest brother quietly says, "Dad was asking about you. Are you going to go see him now? He's awake and pretty coherent."

With a shrug, I nod and start on my way down the hallway again. "I guess."

WHEN I OPEN MY FATHER'S BEDROOM DOOR, I SEE HIM sitting up in bed and looking pretty good for someone who's supposed to be close to death. His pale color looks about the same as I remember from the last time I was around him, and he waves me in when he sees me in the doorway.

It's when I hear his voice that I know he's not well. Weak and trembling, his words seem to have to fight their way out of his mouth.

"Matthias, I'm glad to see you."

I walk in and sit down in the chair near the window as far away from him as possible. I've avoided this all day, and now I know why. Seeing my father like this unnerves me in a way I'm not prepared for.

We sit in silence, neither one of us uttering a word until he finally speaks again. "I hear you're giving Ava a hard time. Why? She's taken care of so much for me, and I thought you two were close."

"We're not anything," I say, barely able to contain my rage as I speak that little nugget of truth.

My father seems confused by my anger. "Really? I thought you, Theo, and Ava were as thick as thieves."

His inability to correctly remember the past when it comes to Ava Sutton only further pisses me off, so I remind him of that conversation all those years ago when he told me I wasn't to even think about her. "You were the one who told me not to even look at her. Remember that? So what makes you think we're close?"

He frowns and turns to look out the window, and for the first time, I notice how old he looks. He's barely in his sixtieth year, but right now, he seems decades older.

"That's not what I wanted, Matthias. I remember how your mother used to talk about how wonderful it would be if Ava and you ended up together."

I stare at him wondering if he's delirious. "Then why did you forbid me from even thinking about her?"

Not that his warning ever stopped me. If anything, it only made me think about her more.

"That wasn't my decision."

"Whose was it then?" I ask, needing to know who kept me from the only woman I've ever truly cared about in this world.

He doesn't answer at first, but then he turns his head to face me. "Don't blame him. I put so much pressure on you that he was worried anyone you ended up with would be miserable. I'm happy you and Jillian turned out so well, though."

For a moment, I consider whether I should tell my father what happened between us. On one hand, he doesn't need to be thinking about how my life is falling apart as his is ending. On the other hand, though, maybe he should know that the person he forced me to marry didn't turn out to be the wife he thought she would.

"Jillian called. She's not coming, but she's divorcing me. Not that it matters. You liked her more than I ever did."

I watch as my father's expression darkens. So much for a happily ever after for his firstborn.

"I'm sorry, Matthias. For so much. Once your mother passed, I did so many things wrong. I hope you can find someone and be happy now."

Standing, I begin walking toward the door, needing to get out of this room right now. Under my breath, I say, "I found someone, and she left too. I should have listened to you when it came to Ava Sutton. I wish I never laid eyes on her."

CHAPTER TWENTY-ONE

va

My phone chimes to let me know my brother's calling, so I answer it, excited to hear when he's arriving. I know he was scheduled to fly out early this morning.

"Hey, Ava. Is Dad around? I tried his phone, but it went to voicemail," Drew says.

"He's up at the house with Mr. King. He asked for him today. I think he's getting close."

I can't bring myself to say he's close to dying. I'm too emotional lately, and simply saying those words will make me cry.

"Oh. Well, I wanted to let him know my flight was cancelled. We've got a hurricane coming, so I don't know when I'll be able to get up there."

"This early in the season?" I ask, disappointed to hear my brother might not arrive before Mr. King passes. My father's going to need all of us around him when it happens.

"The days when hurricane season was only June through November are long gone, Ava," my brother says, correcting me. "If you lived down here, you'd know that."

"Oh. Do you think you guys are going to be okay, or will you have to evacuate?" I ask, suddenly worried about my brother, his wife Mika, and my two nieces.

In a somber voice, he answers, "I'm not sure. We don't usually get a direct hit, but each storm is different. So how is everything up there? Did all the King kids get there yet?"

"Yeah. All five showed up yesterday. It was like the old days with all of them back. The only one missing here is you."

"How are they handling things?"

I think about how each of the King sons seems upset. Well, all but Matthias, who only seems to be angry, as usual. I debate whether to mention to my brother how he acted toward me, but there's no reason to put any more on his plate. He already has enough to worry about with the storm, keeping his family down there safe, and maybe getting a flight out at some point.

"Tell them I'm sorry. I'll keep trying to call Dad, but can you tell him what's going on, Ava? If I can get there sometime soon, I will. I'm sorry you're having to deal with all of this on your own. If it wasn't for this hurricane, I'd be there with you."

"It's okay, Drew. Tell Mika I said hello, and tell Tara and Tasha that their Aunt Ava loves them and I'll see them soon."

"I will. Talk to you soon, okay?"

"Yeah. Stay safe."

I end the call and sit back on the couch, closing my eyes. My father is going to be disappointed Drew isn't able to get here. It's been nearly a year since he saw them, and having his son around at this time would have helped him deal with the loss of Mr. King, who's not only my father's employer but also his friend.

My father walks into the house fifteen minutes later, and I can tell by the deep frown etched into his face that things aren't good. I don't want to heap more bad news on top of everything else, so I don't mention my brother not being able to get out of Florida because of the hurricane.

He sits down next to me and sighs before saying, "Mr. King is asking for you, honey."

"Did something happen? Rachel's still there with him, isn't she? She's the official nurse. If he needs something, she should handle it."

Patting my knee, my father shakes his head. "No, she's still there, but he's not asking for you for anything medical. He wants to talk to you. I don't think it'll be long now, to be honest."

Confused, I look at him, hoping he'll explain why his boss wants to speak to me. I'm not family. In his final hours, I can't imagine why he'd look for me.

"Why does he want to talk to me?"

"I don't know, but he was adamant about it. He wants to speak to you."

For some reason, I think my father is holding back from telling me the truth. I think he knows why Mr.

King is asking for me but doesn't want to tell me. Why makes no sense, though.

"Dad, when I was at the house yesterday, Matthias pretty much chased me out. I'm not sure I can handle being treated like that again."

"You have to, Ava. It's Max's dying wish."

Rarely has my father referred to Mr. King by his first name with me. That tells me this must be serious.

I hang my head, unsure how I'm going to handle dealing with Matthias if he's around but not wanting to deny Mr. King one of his last requests of me. "Okay. I'll go now."

With each step I take up the road to the main house, a feeling of dread fills me. I'd known for weeks that this time would come sooner than later, especially after the doctors told Mr. King there was nothing else they could do. I've tried to be there for him, even if it meant simply sitting by his bedside as he slept so he never had to wake up alone when Rachel had to step out of the room.

But none of that compares to his actual family members being there for him.

When I get to the house, I look around but see no one. Thankfully, Matthias appears to be out. I walk up the stairs and follow the sound of muffled voices at the end of the hall in Mr. King's room.

I softly knock, hoping not to interrupt him with his sons on what may be one of his last days, and wait for someone to answer. When no one does, I slowly open the door and poke my head in to see him sitting up in bed and looking better than I've seen him look in days.

Did my father make a mistake?

"Mr. King, my father told me you wanted to see me?" I tentatively say as I step into the room.

From behind the door, Matthias appears, and the look on his face is pure disgust. Before I or his father can say another word, he snaps, "Get out! You don't belong here."

He sounds even angrier than yesterday. I shrink back away from him, turning to leave, when his father speaks up and says, "I asked for her."

His voice barely reaches a whisper, and its softness makes him sound so frail. The man I've always thought of as so powerful now seems so small and weak.

Matthias shakes his head as he glares at me with pure hatred in his dark eyes. "You shouldn't use your time left speaking to her."

God, every word out of his mouth hurts more than the last one. I don't even get a name. I'm just her, and the way he says that word makes it sound like a curse.

But Mr. King still possesses some strength and says, "I'm fine. I want to speak to Ava in private, if you don't mind."

Matthias turns to face his father and then me, and if looks could kill, I'd be dead right here in Mr. King's bedroom. His rage unnerves me, and it takes every ounce of confidence I have in my body not to run out of the room.

Furious, he storms out, slamming the door so hard it shakes the pictures on the wall. I stand there embarrassed at how much he loathes me, even as I honestly can't be sure what I did to deserve this much anger.

Mr. King gives me a feeble smile and lifts his hand to

wave me over to the chair beside his bed. "Come here, Ava. I want to talk to you."

I do as he asks, still ashamed by how his son made me feel. Even more, I feel sad for Mr. King. A dying man shouldn't have to deal with that much rage in his final hours.

"I'm sorry for that. My son's behavior stems from the stress of what's about to happen, I'm sure," he says, but I don't think either one of us believes that excuse.

"I'm sure he's under a lot of pressure as the eldest son. I just don't know why he hates me so much."

Mr. King gives me a tiny smile and reaches for my hand. "I do, but that's for another time. Just know Matthias has had to sacrifice more than anyone knows."

Although I don't say it, I'm not sure he's seeing things clearly when it comes to that son. Matthias has lived a charmed life, wanting for nothing. If he had to sacrifice at all, I'm sure he was compensated more than enough with even better things.

"Now I don't have much time left, so let me explain why I asked you to come see me."

CHAPTER TWENTY-TWO

$\mathcal{M}$atthias

I WAIT FOR AVA TO COME OUT OF MY FATHER'S ROOM for nearly thirty minutes, my anger inching higher and higher until I swear I want to put my fist through a wall. What the hell could he want to say to her? She's only the daughter of his estate manager, a man who's going to be out of a job and a home the second I'm the one in charge of this estate.

Little Ava Sutton definitely has a way of weaseling herself into this family. My brother can't make a move without her since he's gotten back, and now my father is using some of the precious final moments of his life to talk to her.

Well, whatever she thinks she's doing, I'm going to put a stop to it.

I march down the hallway to his room, but right

when I'm about to throw the door open and put an end to whatever the hell she's up to, she walks out and nearly runs straight into me. For a second, I look down into her brown eyes and see the sweetness I saw that time we spent together five years ago.

But it doesn't take long for me to remember that sweetness isn't who she really is. "What were you two talking about?" I ask, wanting an answer before I go back in to speak to my father.

She doesn't respond and instead tries to push past me. No way. She's not getting out of this house until I get some answers.

I grab her by the arm and force her down the hall and into my room. Slamming the door behind us, I block it so she can't leave. I will know what that little conversation was all about, and I'll know right now.

Ava stands in front of me, a tiny thing I could break in half if I chose to, but in her expression I see defiance. So much for the sweet little Ava act she puts on for the rest of my family.

"I asked you a question. What were talking about with my father?"

"He asked for me, so I went up to see him. That's it."

She tries to step around me to open the door, but I push her back by her shoulders. "No, that's not it. What did he say to you?"

Tilting her chin up, she stares up at me, and I swear I see a hint of a smile as she answers, "That's something you'll have to ask him. I don't think it's right to share what he told me in confidence."

I feel my blood pressure rise like the top of my head is about to blow off. "In confidence? What the hell could he have to say to you that I can't hear? You're not family. Hell, you aren't even one of his goddamned employees. You're the child of one of the help, even though no one else in this fucking house can seem to remember that fact. So I'll ask you again. What did you and my father talk about?"

She opens her mouth to answer me but then closes her lips like she decides against it. I loom over her like a beast since I'm twice her size, but she never looks away or backs down.

"Why do you treat me like you hate me?"

"Because I do. Now answer my question."

"Why do you hate me? I thought after the time we spent together during the blizzard—"

I interrupt her. "You thought wrong."

Expecting her to ask me something else about those days or probably break down and cry, I wait as she stares up into my eyes. She doesn't speak for so long that I wonder if I'm just wasting my time standing here talking to her when I could just ask my father what he said to her.

Finally, she steps toward me so our bodies are practically touching and says in a soft voice that hits me square in the chest, "You're lying. I don't know why you're acting like this, but you're lying. You don't hate me."

I lower my head so I'm at her eye level and stare into those brown eyes so full of confidence right now. "You don't know me. You have no idea what I'm feeling. You're just some stupid girl who can't seem to remember her place."

Tears fill her eyes, and a twinge of guilt stabs at me

for being so cruel to her. I push that down to that place inside me where all my memories of that time we spent together exist, refusing to let myself feel anything for her even now.

Wiping the tears as they roll down her cheeks, she pushes past me as she sobs, "I hate you, Matthias King."

The sound of her trembling voice makes me wince even more than the words she says. I deserve for her to hate me for all I've said to her. I accept that. What's harder to take is how hurt she sounds right now.

I won't feel bad for that, though. I can stack up the hours and days and months I spent questioning why she never even tried to contact me after our time together against her hurt feelings over my unkind words, and I'd win hands down.

Stepping out into the hallway, I watch her run away toward the stairs. Good. Run from me, little Ava. That's what you do. You're actually pretty good at it.

But then she stops and glances back at me, and the look in her eyes makes my heart skip a beat. All that hurt in them, and it's all because of me. I shouldn't fucking care. I'm not the one who left and never even bothered to text or anything. That was her.

Still, I can't seem to stop myself from feeling bad about how I've treated her.

"I hate you. Why do you have to be like this?" she softly asks before turning around and hurrying downstairs.

I don't have an answer for her.

Walking back into my room, I slam the door shut. She might hate me, but I hate how she somehow has this power to make me forget all those nights I stared up at the ceiling wondering why she never even tried to get in touch with me. I know she's kept talking to Theo all these years, and not once could she tell him to give me a message. Yes, I know we were supposed to be keeping things secret, but a fucking message to say hi was too much?

Almost like I'm on autopilot, I sit down on the edge of my bed and open the top drawer of my nightstand to get my sketchbook. I know exactly what page her picture is on—the last one I ever drew.

I stare at it almost as if looking at her this way will make things better between us. I don't want to be so cruel to her, but every time I see Ava, all I can think of is that moment when Theo told me she was always in touch with him after she left.

Ava's good like that. If she's thinking about someone, she makes sure they know about it. That's how you can tell if she cares. She's all about the calling and texting.

And then all the moments after where she entered my mind even though I didn't want her to, crowding out every chance I could ever feel anything for another woman.

Somehow, in this sketch, she's not that person who walked away and never looked back. She's just Ava, the only person who ever made my heart soar. I get lost in her picture, loving the intimacy she offered simply by letting me draw her. I don't know how I captured that along with the hesitation I knew she felt the whole time, but it's there as clear as day in her expression and in those beautiful dark eyes of hers.

My mind drifts back to those moments that changed my life as all the hate and anger subside. It's like someone finally lifts the thousand-pound weight off my chest, and I can breathe again.

Ava smiles up at me as I flip through my sketchbook to find the drawing of that huge pine tree we've always called the Christmas tree. It seems like the right time of year for it.

When I stop on the page, I turn the book around and say, "Any guess what this is?"

She studies it for a long moment and then looks at me, her eyes wide with excitement. "I'd know that anywhere! That's the Christmas tree! You captured it perfectly, even the one part on the right side up near the top where that odd section is. Is that another tree growing out of it or something else?"

I shake my head, unsure what's happening with that part of the Christmas tree on the back part of the estate. "I don't know. It's odd. I sat there for hours staring at that tree before I began drawing it, and I never figured out what that is."

Sitting up, her knees brush against mine and for the first time I notice how smooth her legs are. She really does have beautiful legs.

Without a word, I run my palm up her shin and stop at her knee, amazed at how soft her skin is. She giggles, and I look up from where my hand is to see her smiling.

"Someone's ticklish."

Ava covers my hand with hers to stop it, weaving her fingers through mine and setting our hands on her thigh. "I am, so stop it. Now tell me about what you do when you want to sketch something. Do you stare at it for a while like you did with the Christmas tree, or does something come to you like a bolt of lightning and you start drawing?"

I think about her question for a few moments before answering, "It depends. I studied the Christmas tree all that time because I felt like I needed to. Other times, I just pick up my pencil and draw. That mostly happens with the sketches I do when my brothers and I are all hanging out."

"That's probably because you've been looking at them your entire life, right?"

Nodding, I think about how I've drawn her like that many times. Then again, I've been looking at Ava for what seems like my entire life too.

She stretches her legs out in front of her so they overlap mine right below my knees. She's as light as air on top of me, but the feel of her skin on mine excites me. I've dreamed of being with her for so long, never believing it could ever happen, and to have her sitting with me in my bed like this feels like one of those dreams.

If it is, I pray to God nobody wakes me up.

"You got quiet there," she says as she taps her finger against my forearm.

I shake my head to push the thoughts out of my mind and smile. "Just didn't have anything to say for a few seconds."

What I'd love to say to her I can't. Not yet, at least. Maybe someday, though.

My life is going to change soon when my father finally decides my months of avoiding joining King Industries are over. I'll be in the city every day, forced to join the ranks of the working businessmen of the world. Ava's life is going to change too in the coming months. She'll probably start college soon, and that means playing soccer again, I'm sure.

But I hope with all that happening for both of us that we'll be able to find time to spend at least a few hours a week together. I'm already dreading my life as part of the family business being trained to take over the company when my father retires, so having the ability to be the person I am with her right now for a few precious hours sounds perfect.

I wish I could talk to her about this, but for her, this thing *between us is brand new. She has no idea I've fantasized about her as more than just my brother's best friend and the girl who lives in the carriage house. Telling her any of this likely would make her run away in complete terror since she'd think I was some stalker or something.*

So for now, all of my plans and hopes for what's going to happen come the new year will stay with me. Maybe by spring I'll be able to share them with her.

My chest aches like someone's carving into it as I think back to how happy I was that day with her. All my dreams had finally come true, and I thought we had a future together.

And then she left, and all those hopes were dashed. Now five years later, I'm back here to deal with my father's imminent passing, but I feel like part of me is dying every time I see her. I want to grab her by the shoulders and make her stand in front of me as I shout, "Why did you leave me?"

But like with nearly every other part of my life, I can't do that. So I sit here in my anger and hatred wishing I felt neither because all I want to do is have her back with me so I can feel the way I felt on those snowy December days again.

CHAPTER TWENTY-THREE

va

As I storm out of the King house, I slam the front door and instantly regret it since it probably disturbed Mr. King. Fucking Matthias! I hate him. Yes, actual hate. Not the kind of thing people say when they're angry and then take back later.

Oh, no. This is full on, one hundred percent, makes me want to punch something hate for him.

Tears roll down my cheeks as all of today finally becomes too much for me. It's likely the last day Mr. King will be alive, and his terrible oldest son chooses today to berate me for talking to his father.

What a bastard!

Marching across the grass toward the road, I swear I could push a car out of my way I'm so furious. Of course, I always cry when I get truly angry. That asshole

Matthias probably thinks I had tears in my eyes because he hurt my feelings.

Well, fuck him. He can believe what he wants. He's going to anyway. It's not like he bothers to consider that other people have feelings. No. He just acts whatever way he wants, and the rest of the world be damned.

I mumble to myself how much I hate Matthias King, finding some relief from my misery in my cursing him out. Next time he does something like that—and there will be a next time because he seems hell bent on making my life as awful as possible—next time I'm going to give him both barrels. I don't know how I'm going to control this silly crying thing that happens every time I get mad, but I'll find a way. And when I do, I'm going to tell him exactly what kind of awful son of a bitch he is. I might even include how I hope he ends up alone and miserable in his big house full of all the money in the world around him.

"Ava! Wait up!" Theo calls out behind me.

I turn to look at him for a brief moment but don't stop. I'm too damn angry right now, so I need to keep moving.

He catches up to me a few seconds later, full of happiness and giving me one of his typical Theo smiles. How on earth he and that shithead of an older brother can be related is beyond me. It's a mystery of modern-day science how an entire family full of good people can have one utterly rotten one too.

"Hey, what's going on? You look like you could punch a bear right now."

I turn to look at him and can't help but laugh. "Punch a bear? Have I ever punched any animal, much less a bear? I don't even think I could punch a person, although your damn brother might have a good chance at that happening. I swear to God, Theo, one of these days I'm going to tell him exactly what I think of him, and then he'll be left standing there with tears in his eyes."

My friend jumps in front of me and stops me, holding me by the shoulders. Staring down at my face, he frowns. "Did he make you cry? What did he say?"

Hanging my head, I sigh since crying and feeling bad is a constant in the history of Matthias and me. "Your father called me up to talk to him. Your brother was furious about it, and when I left your father's room, he grabbed me and demanded to know what we talked about. Since your father told me it was something he wants me to keep to myself, at least for a little while, I refused to tell him."

I stop as tears well up in my eyes again. "He said I'm just some stupid girl who doesn't know her place."

When I lift my head to look at Theo, he's still frowning. I hate that I'm the one making him look like that. He's always so happy and fun, and he's barely home two days before he's looking as unhappy as that asshole brother of his.

Theo gently sweeps the pads of his thumbs across the tops of my cheekbones to dry my tears. "Don't listen to him, Ava. He's the most miserable fuck around. I don't know what his problem is with you specifically, but who cares? I'll make sure if he decides to do something to your father or you that he won't get away with it."

I take a deep breath in and hold it in my lungs for a long moment before I let it out slowly, willing the negativity dealing with his brother forces on me to leave my body. "Thanks. I'm not super worried about it now, but thank you."

He cradles my face in his hands and smiles. "Now let me see you give me a smile, or I'll think I failed completely at this attempt to cheer you up."

My smile pushes my cheeks up against his palms, and the warmth of his skin makes me feel new again, like I can forget all that terrible business with his brother and focus on being happy that I can do what Mr. King asked me to. I can't tell Theo or anyone because he said to keep it quiet for now, but when it comes time, I'll be able to fulfill his last wish from me.

"I'm okay. Thanks for listening to me bitch."

He waves that away, rolling his eyes. "That's bitching? I'm sorry to tell you, Ava, but that's minor league bitching right there. You're going to have to step it up a bit if you want to be thought of as a real bitch."

I'm not sure I want that. Well, it might serve me well for when I have to deal with his brother, which unfortunately after what I learned today is going to be far more than I would like.

"Maybe I can take bitch classes. Do any of the local colleges offer that?" I ask with a chuckle.

Letting his hands slide off my cheeks, he laughs, and I'm so thrilled to see him happy again. "I think Bitchery 101 is generally taught in high school, to be honest. I'm thinking you might be too old to learn. I guess we're all stuck with sweet little Ava Sutton."

Instantly, my mood darkens. Poking my finger into his chest, I say, "Don't call me that ever again. That's your brother's nickname for me, and as of today, it's officially off-limits."

Theo lifts his hands in front of him like he's surrendering. "Got it. Not more little Ava. You're not really little, so it doesn't fit anymore anyway. Matthias is going to need to work on some new material to keep up with the times."

I look back at the house, glancing up at his bedroom windows and scowling in case he's looking out. "Matthias can go fuck himself and the horse he rode in on."

When I start walking away toward my house, Theo laughs and joins me. "Damn. You really are angry at him. I don't think I've ever heard you say someone can go fuck himself. And you even ventured into bestiality too."

Turning my head, I give him a look of complete disgust. "Gross."

"I wasn't the one who said he should go fuck a horse, which by the way I think is correctly termed the Catherine the Great treatment."

Leave it to Theo to say that.

"Really? I swear you must have gotten some education in the world in the past five years."

That makes him throw his head back in peals of laughter. "Just the usual stuff. To be honest, I've known that about Catherine the Great having sex with a horse since I was a teenager. Fifteen-year-old boys love that story."

"I think I hate all men. You know that?" I say as I imagine a bunch of his friends and him sitting around getting excited by the idea of a woman having sex with a horse.

"Even me?" he asks in a hurt voice as he stops walking.

I turn around to look at him and shake my head. "All except you. And not your father, my father, my brother, Marius, Kellen, or Ronan either. Or the groundskeeper."

That brings a smile back to his face, and he takes a few giant steps to reach me. "So basically the only man you hate is Matthias."

"Yeah. Let's not talk about him anymore, though, because if I see a bear, I'm going to punch it straight in the nose, and then you and I will have to run away fast because he's going to be pissed."

Theo nudges his elbow into my arm, pushing me a little off to the side as we head toward my house. "I think we need to give you a lesson in what bears are actually like."

"Don't ruin this for me. I'm enjoying the idea of being brave enough to punch a bear. I'd just pretend it has your brother's face."

Right before we reach my house, Theo stops me. "Hey, I was wondering if you'd like to go out again tonight. The Spring Festival wraps up today. I thought we could go check it out and see if anything's changed from the last time we went together."

With all the events happening on the estate lately, I'd forgotten about the Spring Festival. I've never missed going even a single year, but this year has been so busy, it completely slipped my mind.

"I'd love that. Do you think we should be away from the house, though? The doctors don't think your father has long, Theo."

He nods, and a somber look comes over him. "We've

said our goodbyes. There's not much more to do. It's not like my father and I were ever that close. He seems far more interested in having Ronan and Kellen there with him, to be honest. Even Marius mentioned it to me. I think he has a lot more regrets when it comes to them because they were so much younger when our mother died."

"I'm sorry. I'm sure he loves you."

"Oh, yeah. I know. Marius knows too. But that's why the idea of sitting around waiting for someone to die sounds pretty damn awful. We won't be gone long. Just a couple hours. What do you say?"

I can't deny some time away would feel nice. I said my own goodbye to Mr. King when I met with him, and I guess it would be all right for a couple hours to attend the festival.

"Okay."

THE SPRING FESTIVAL WITH ALL ITS COLORED LIGHTS and great food and games lightens my mood after all I had to deal with today. Theo's jokes about my threat to bears make me laugh, and as we walk down the pathway along the river they've lit up with tiny flower lights on the ground, I feel so much better than I did a few hours ago.

This feels like the old days when he and I spent every waking hour together. I listen to him talk about things like where he wants to travel to next and what people are like around the world, and all I can think about is how nice it is to spend time with someone who's so fun to be with.

"You're particularly quiet tonight, Ava," he says as he gently pushes his arm into my arm. "Something wrong?"

With a smile, I shake my head. "No. Just listening to you. Your stories are very interesting."

He disagrees with that, waving away my compliment. "Not really, but that's very kind of you to say. I swear there's not another girl in the world like you, you know that?"

I look up at his gorgeous face that's only gotten more beautiful in the years he's been gone and wonder why some beautiful French woman hasn't gotten Theo to settle down with her. He's successful, comes from money, and stunning. In addition, he's sweet but just enough not to make him seem like a pushover.

"So tell me, why aren't you with some movie star or supermodel? I thought I heard something about you and a woman named Celeste a while back."

"You were always too fond of me, Ava. I don't think movie stars and supermodels even notice me, not that I spend a lot of time around those two groups of people."

He intentionally avoids telling me anything about that woman I know he was dating.

"You're a world-famous racecar driver. I thought that was the best occupation to meet famous people," I say as he slips his arm around my waist to keep me from stepping in a hole on the pathway.

I lean against his side as he laughs at my assumption. "Not exactly. The only people I usually meet are racing fanatics, who tend to be men, and mechanics, who also tend to be men."

We walk a little further before I broach the subject of

the girlfriend again. "So about this Celeste woman. Any truth to the rumor?"

He shakes his head and grins, which tells me there is some truth to it. "You act like I'm the lead story on TMZ every day. Trust me. If you heard rumors about me, they probably aren't true, but I can't imagine who would be telling you that."

Unable to remember where I heard he was serious about some Celeste woman, I say, "It doesn't matter where I heard it. Maybe your father told me. It could have been Eleanor. She's very in tune with all the racing info and rumors, believe it or not."

Theo stops walking and stares down at me. "I don't believe that. Fine, since you want to know, I'll tell you. Yes, I was dating a woman named Celeste. She wasn't a supermodel or movie star. She was a racer like me, actually. It didn't work out, though, and that's pretty much the end of the story."

I search his expression for any sense he still cares for this ex-girlfriend of his, but I find nothing to say he's upset they aren't together anymore. "Oh. Well, should I say I'm sorry you two broke up?"

"I'm not, so you shouldn't think you should be. It was just something that happened for a while, and now it's over."

The way he can be so casual about things has always impressed me. I wish I could be like him and treat endings so calmly. For me, when something doesn't go the way I wanted it to, I fixate on it, always wondering what went wrong.

Then again, maybe he didn't want it to turn out as his happily ever after with this Celeste. That's a possibility.

We walk along in silence as the crowds around us thin out to just a few people ahead of where we are. It's a beautiful spring night with just a hint of chill in the air that still comes with evenings in this part of the country. I shiver a little when a tiny breeze through the trees makes me wish I had brought a sweater with me.

"You'd think I'd spent my entire life down where my brother lives and I didn't know it would get down into the fifties here at night in early May," I say as I wrap my arms around my body.

"Do you want to go back?" Theo asks, his voice full of concern.

Shaking my head, I keep walking. "No. I'm fine. I just wish I brought a sweater."

He slides his arm from around my waist up around my shoulders and pulls me to him. "I'll keep you warm."

It's a sweet gesture so typical of the person he's always been with me. I can always count on Theo to take care of me, no matter what I need.

"You're so nice, Theo. Thank you."

I feel him press a kiss to the top of my head. He really is the best person in the world. That Celeste woman doesn't know what she lost.

"You don't have to thank me, Ava."

A man and a woman approach us, and I instantly recognize them as Carrie Mondale and Jake Roberts, two of the most popular people from high school. The memory of her never really talking to me flashes through my mind, so I'm surprised when they smile and stop to chat with us.

"Theo King!" Jake says as he sticks out his hand to shake his. "How the hell have you been?"

"Great! Just living the dream," Theo says with a chuckle. "How about you?"

"Same. You remember Carrie, right?"

Before Theo can say a word, she flashes him a huge, toothy grin and says, "I knew you two would end up together. You guys were always joined at the hip. How have you been, Ava?"

Since she never cared enough for me to be interested in my well-being before, I assume she's simply being polite and answer, "I'm good. Thanks."

Then I realize what she meant and look at Theo, expecting him to correct her about us being together. But he doesn't. Instead, he pulls me close to him like we're actually a couple.

"Some things are just meant to be. What about you guys?" he asks them.

Carrie holds up her left hand to show off her engagement ring. "Getting married in two months. I can't believe it!"

I notice Jake doesn't look as enthusiastic as she does about their impending marriage, but he was always more low-key about everything. They're complete opposites, but maybe that's why they fell in love.

"Congratulations! Good luck to both of you."

Jake nods like he's used to hearing those words, and Carrie squeezes his arm before giving him a kiss on the cheek. "Thanks! Same to you guys. It was great seeing you!"

They walk away, leaving Theo and me alone again. He turns to look at me and smiles. "Did you get the feeling he's not as happy about getting married as she is? I thought he was going to crawl out of his skin when she flashed that engagement ring of hers. Maybe he's uncomfortable because it's so tiny."

I jab his side with my elbow and shake my head in fake disapproval. "You're so bad."

"Just call them like I see them. He comes from nearly as much money as my family. I think he could have sprung for a decent sized rock."

Looking back at them as they walk away, I see they aren't holding hands anymore. "They seem happy enough."

"Jesus, that's an indictment of a relationship if I've ever heard one."

I turn back to face him and shrug. "Just calling it like I see it."

"At least she wasn't a bitch to you like she used to be."

We start walking again as I laugh at his comment. "Well, I guess that's nice. That was high school, though. People change. I can respect that."

He shakes his head and smiles at me. "You don't."

I have no idea if that's a good thing. He seems to think it is, but I'm not sure.

In a woodsy part of the path, he stops and gently moves me in front of him. For a moment, I wonder if he's okay, but then I realize what he's doing.

All the time we've spent together in our lives, Theo and I have never been anything but friends. Best friends who watched out for one another and took care of each other, but nothing more.

When I look up into his dark eyes, I see something in them that says that's about to change. After all the sadness with his father's illness and all the cruelty from

Matthias, I can't help but welcome this sweet change from Theo.

He doesn't say a word before dipping his head to kiss me softly on the lips. I don't think twice before kissing him back, even though I have to admit I've never even thought about what it would be like to feel his lips on mine. He was always just Theo, my best friend.

After a few seconds, he lifts his head and smiles. "That was nice."

"Just nice?" I tease him, loving how I can be playful right now instead of feeling awkward.

"More than nice," he says, grinning. "I think we should do it again just to make sure."

I watch as his face dips and his lips press against mine in a kiss that's unbelievably sweet. It's almost as if he doesn't want to scare me off, but he doesn't have to worry. I've cared about Theo for so long, I can't remember a time when he wasn't one of the most important people in my life.

Slipping my tongue past his lips, I tease him for a few seconds before pulling back to look into his eyes. For the first time, I know he's seeing me not as little Ava Sutton, that girl he's been best friends with since we were small, but as a woman.

He doesn't say a word but slides his hand around my head and pulls me to him in a kiss that's nothing as sweet as the last two. This one is full of passion and the promise of so much more than friendship.

And I'm so ready for that.

CHAPTER TWENTY-FOUR

M atthias

TWO DAYS AFTER MY FATHER CALLED AVA UP TO HIS room for their little secret meeting, he fell asleep at six that night and it was over. Ronan sat in the corner where the nurse had been watching over my father, and when the doctor pronounced him dead, I heard my youngest brother begin to cry.

I can understand why he felt sad. He had the least amount of time with both our parents, even if he was the favorite. Never pressured to be anything but who he is by his nature, Ronan looked at our father in a way I never got to experience. So naturally, his death hit my brother hard.

It seemed to hit all of them hard but Theo. While Ronan cried and Kellen and Marius fell silent, Theo wasn't even in the room when it happened. I don't even know if he was in the house. When he finally showed up in the kitchen downstairs and I told him, he merely nodded but said nothing.

Not that he and my father were terribly close, but I guess I expected something more from him than a nod and silence. Perhaps he didn't know how to act since his usual happy-go-lucky style didn't seem appropriate for the moment.

Whatever he felt, he didn't tell me, and a few minutes later, he left the kitchen, and I haven't seen much of him since that day nearly a week ago. He was at the funeral with his best friend right by his side, of course, sobbing like it was her father who died. I'll see Theo and everyone else today since it's the reading of my father's will. I expect my father's office to be full to the brim with people to hear what his attorney has to say about who gets what.

It's not really a secret. My father always told us we'd be taken care of, and as the eldest son, I'll be expected to act as the executor of his will. He as much said that the last time I spoke to him the day he died. He was in and out of it that day, sometimes making no sense like when he made me promise I'd remember to be kind when dealing with carrying out his final wishes.

I didn't understand what he meant, but I suspect he simply wanted reassurance the money he planned to bequeath to his favorite charities would, in fact, find its way to them. He didn't need to worry. I can be a son of a bitch in business and even to some people in my life, but I'm not heartless.

As I walk toward my father's office on the first floor, I see all my brothers, along with all the people who work here at the house, including Ava's father. Of course, she's tagged along too, probably hoping to get something for her time playing nursemaid to my father for the past few months.

We all jam into the room that always seemed so big until nearly fifteen people needed to be here. I position myself near the window right next to my father's desk where his attorney Lucas Manion sits unloading his briefcase of all the papers involved in the end of my father's life. A heavy man with gray hair for as long as I've known him, I don't think he's more than a few years old than my father. He used to remind me of Santa Claus when I was a little boy and he'd stop over at the house.

I give him a little smile when he looks over at me with nothing less than dread in his eyes. I can understand that. He's known my father and our family for decades. I imagine even though this is his job that it's hard to deal with the death of someone who wasn't only a client for all those years but a friend too.

"If I can have your attention," he says to begin, his normal booming voice sounding a little softer today. "There aren't a lot of surprises in Max's final will, but I want to make sure we do exactly as he wanted. It's the last thing I get to carry out for my friend, so this is important."

As I suspected, Lucas is struggling to deal with the loss of my father just like the rest of us. I look around the office and wonder what surprises my father has in store. He always did like to keep people on their toes.

"Okay, first I think we should start off with how Max wanted everything handled. I will continue as his attorney in this matter, and I'll be assisting the executors to carry out his final wishes."

His words hit my ears wrong, and I stare at him waiting for a correction. Executors? Why did he say that like there would be more than one, which is me?

I open my mouth to ask that very question when Lucas turns his head to look at me. "Your father established that you and Miss Sutton would be the executors, Matthias."

Every word comes out shaky, like Lucas fully expects some pushback on this ridiculous idea. Me and Miss Sutton? Why the hell would my father do that? I'm his eldest son. Why would he invite some person who isn't even family into handling his affairs?

I'm speechless, even as that old familiar rage I feel for her surges inside me so my head feels like it's going to explode. From the back of the room, I hear someone mumble, "Did he just say Matthias and Ava are the executors?"

"This has to be a joke. Why the hell would my father make her an executor of his will? I won't allow it," I say to Lucas, who looks like being here is the last place in the world he wants to be at this moment.

"I'm sorry, Matthias, but this is what your father wanted."

Furious, I march over to my father's desk to glare down at his lawyer. "Then I'll challenge it. He probably changed his will to include this ridiculous thing in the past few months, didn't he?"

"Actually, he included Miss Sutton as co-executor five years ago right before you moved to London. Perhaps he was concerned you wouldn't be able to fulfill your obligation and he wanted someone who lived here to assist you."

Five years ago? What the fuck?

I spin around to face her and see she knew this before even walking into this room today. It's written all over her face.

"Five years ago, Miss Sutton wasn't even living here. She had run off to wherever her aunt lives somewhere in New Hampshire, so why the hell would my father put her as an executor of his will?" I ask no one in particular.

Lucas quietly answers, "I don't know, Matthias. I don't think he intended on causing you any stress by doing this, though."

I glare at her like I've never done before in my life and bark, "This is why he called you up here the other day. You knew."

She doesn't look away, defiantly staring me down as I seethe with rage. I should have expected my father to do something like this. His final attempt to make me the most miserable fucking person on the planet.

Thanks, Dad.

I don't need to hear any more of this bullshit since I'm going to be in charge of carrying out his final wishes —or half in charge since I have to do this with her— so I storm out of the room and head down to the living room to pour myself a drink. After the day I've had, I deserve it.

Two bourbons later, I'm at least calmer than I was, even though I hate what my father did. Marius finds me out on the patio off the living room enjoying my drink and trying to forget that I have to work with her on doling out all my father's bequests.

My brother sits down next to me and lights up a cigar. Blowing a huge puff of smoke into the air above him, he smiles and then turns to look at me.

"Exciting time, huh? Leave it to Dad to make one more thing difficult for you."

At least this brother understands. Our father always seemed to give the two of us challenges he never forced the other three of us to deal with.

"I swear to God he's looking down and smirking, the son of a bitch," I say before talking a gulp of bourbon.

"Any idea why he thought you'd need the help of little Ava to handle his will?" Marius asks, shaking his head.

And just like that, my mellow mood disappears.

"I have no fucking idea, but if anyone thinks I'm going to be conferring with her on anything, they're crazy. She isn't family, so the old man must have been out of his mind when he decided to include her. She doesn't know a damn thing about his charitable efforts and who gets what."

Marius doesn't say anything for a long while, choosing to thankfully sit there quietly and puff on his cigar. When he does speak again, he sounds as confused as I am about the timing of our father's decision to include Ava.

"Yeah, but if he was crazy, that was five years ago, according to Lucas. What the hell was going on five years ago that made him want to include Ava in his final affairs?"

I've thought about that very question ever since the words came out of his attorney's mouth that this wasn't a decision my father made while he was sick but something he chose to do all that time ago right after I decided to accept my fate and go work for King Industries in London. Why would he think including Ava as executor then was something he needed to do?

"I have no idea."

"Are you curious about who got what? You left before any of the good stuff happened."

Whatever good stuff Marius is referring to I don't give a damn about, so I ignore him and keep drinking. Maybe if I get drunk enough, this day will just become a blurry memory I can try to forget.

"Well, we all got what Dad said we would. I got the house in Spain. Theo got the one in France since that was always his favorite. Kellen got the penthouse in London, and Ronan got the place in Rome. That leaves you with this house, the place in Florida, the other house in Italy, and Grandma's house."

Great. Maybe I'll move into the place in Italy. It sounds a hell of a lot better than staying here.

"I was a little surprised to find out he left Eleanor so much, but she's been good to him and to us for so long she deserved it."

I know he's holding off telling me about what Ava and her father got like it's some kind of suspenseful game we're playing, but I truly don't care. As long as I have enough to live on, who cares what everyone else was left?

Finally, he blows a big ring of smoke into the air and turns to face me. "Mr. Sutton, Ava, and Andrew were left enough money to set them up for the rest of their lives. Dad also made sure they never have to move from that house, as long as they want to live there."

Fucking fabulous.

"Good for them," I say, using every ounce of strength I possess to sound like I don't care.

"Yeah. Mr. Sutton's been Dad's estate manager and friend for as long as we've been alive. That was nice of him."

How kind of my father to be nice to everyone. Everyone but me, that is.

"I'm going to be staying for a while, Matthias. I've got a shoot lined up in Fiji in a few months, but until then, I think I want to stick around. I think Ronan and Kellen plan to go tomorrow, though."

I nod, envious my other brothers have lives they like enough to want to return so quickly to them. Not that I could fly back to London even if I had a loving wife waiting for me. Handling my father's estate means I'll be staying here for a few weeks, at least, too.

"I'm not sure about Theo, though. I get the feeling he's in no hurry to get back to racing."

My brother looks for me to comment on that, but I have nothing to say. I have a suspicion I know why Theo wants to stay here on the estate. He and Ava have been spending every waking minute together, and I heard Eleanor mention to him this morning that she would have his picnic lunch ready for him after today's meeting with the lawyer.

I should warn him about her. Let him get away before he falls in love so he doesn't go through what I did.

CHAPTER TWENTY-FIVE

heo

FOR TWO WEEKS, I'VE WAITED FOR THIS NIGHT WITH Ava. Now that everything has been settled with my father's passing, I can finally be with her like I've wanted to since I returned home.

I always said she was the future Mrs. Theo King, and while she seemed to think I was joking, I was dead serious. I knew I loved her years ago when I was far too young to do anything.

Now everything is different. I'm successful and have more than enough money to give her everything she deserves. Not that she can't afford whatever she wants on her own. My father took care of her and her family in his will, which I have to say was a nice ending for a man I never figured was the thoughtful, caring type.

I'm glad he did that, though. She deserves it, along

with her father, and now money doesn't have to be an issue between us. Not that it ever was. I've never once thought of her as less than us because she didn't have King money. Unlike Matthias, who seems to delight in referring to her as "the help" like she's a lowly fucking servant and he's an actual king, I've always seen Ava as just Ava. Her social status didn't mean a damn to me. She was my best friend who lived close by so I never had to worry about not being able to see her.

It must be eating him up inside to know she's wealthy now and he can't talk down to her anymore. I honestly don't understand where the hell he got that elitist bullshit from. Neither of our parents ever treated anyone as beneath them based on how much money they had. It was probably those assholes he hung out with in school. Montclair Prep had its fair share of snobs who looked down on anyone who didn't live in some huge mansion or drive the right kind of car.

Thinking about high school makes me cringe when I remember how many times I had to push around some guy for treating Ava and her brother like they didn't belong. God forbid anyone try to get an education without having to put up with that superior crap so many of those kids had going on. She didn't deserve that kind of nonsense.

As the sun dips below the horizon and dusk begins to come around, I see her walk out of her house and head down to meet her. I'd hoped we could have gotten together before this, but with my father's passing and then everything else culminating in the funeral, it's been days since I kissed her at the Spring Festival.

She waves at me, so I start to jog toward her, dying to

get our date started. When I reach her, I lean in to give her a kiss. I want her to know that night wasn't a one-off.

"Why didn't you just wait for me to come up to the house like we planned?" she asks in a suspicious voice.

I shrug, not having any real reason why. "I don't know. I didn't feel like staying inside to wait for you, so I figured I'd sit by our tree and wait until you walked out of your house."

Ava turns to look over at the enormous maple tree a few hundred yards from my house and smiles. "I haven't called it that in a long time. I think since you've been gone."

Sliding my arm around her waist, I pull her to me. "Well, I'm back and I missed it, so I spent some time over there telling it all I've been up to in my travels. It's all caught up on my news now."

With her usual sweetness in her eyes, she gazes up at me and giggles. "Oh yeah? Did it just listen, or did it have anything to say?"

"It just listened. Trees aren't notoriously big talkers."

I watch as her expression turns slightly darker and she asks, "So the tree gets to hear all about your life away from here, but I don't? That doesn't seem fair. Why does the tree rank and I don't?"

She's being sort of playful, but I can tell the fact that I haven't told her much about my life away from here bothers her. Ava doesn't need to hear what I've been up to. Far too much of it involves women who only cared to be around me because they thought I had some kind of fame. They weren't supermodels by any means. Just racing groupies I had a good time with but never wanted anything permanent from.

Those women were good for one thing. They weren't like Ava. Some women you sleep with. Some you care about but can't imagine spending the rest of your life with.

And then others are the whole package. Like Ava.

"Men don't worry about boring trees senseless. I'm trying hard to make a good impression here," I say, half-joking.

She narrows her eyes and looks at me funny before saying, "You don't have to impress me, Theo. You're my best friend. I've thought the world of you since I was a little girl."

Jesus, I need to get this date back on track or we're going to get stuck talking about how we're friends. That is definitely not where I plan to have this night end up.

"Let's go up to the house. I've got a surprise for you," I say as I begin to guide her up the road.

I can't pinpoint exactly why, but she seems hesitant about walking up to the house. That seems strange. We've hung out there too many times to count over the years.

Then it dawns on me. This doesn't have to do with the house or either of us.

Stepping in front of her, I walk backwards and ask, "Hey, is something wrong? You don't seem to want to go up to the house tonight."

Her expression gives me my answer before she does, and it's far more truthful than her words. "No. Why would I have a problem with going to the house? I've been to your house a million times, right?"

All the while she says that worry is etched into her face around her mouth and on her forehead. I hate that she feels like she's not welcome in a place that's been like her second home for her entire life.

Fucking Matthias!

"You don't have to be concerned he'll be there. Eleanor told me he's gone for a few days. Probably having to tie up loose ends with that soon-to-be ex-wife of his."

Ava stops walking and stares at me like I just told her the worst thing in the world. "What do you mean ex? I thought his wife just didn't come for the funeral."

"No, she left him the day he got here. I guess she gave him the news they were over when she called to tell him she couldn't be bothered to come. Pretty cold, huh?"

She frowns and shakes her head. "Wow. That is cold."

I shrug, already tired of talking about my miserable brother. "If you ask me, he had it coming. If he acted like he does whenever he's around us, no wonder she walked out on him. I think her timing was shitty, but if they've been unhappy for a while, no time is going to be a good time to say it's over."

Taking her hands in mine, I pull her forward so we can start walking toward the house again. She doesn't fight me, but now she looks sad. I don't know why. Matthias has been nothing but a complete ass to her from the moment he fucking walked into the house that first day. He doesn't deserve her sympathy.

"Cheer up. He'll land on his feet. He's now the head of a multinational corporation worth billions. I don't think he'll be alone for long. Worst comes to worst, he can pay women to sleep with him. He's got more than enough money to afford hookers."

I don't say that I think they're the only ones who will tolerate his moods since that might seem like piling on. That Ava cares at all that he got dumped over the phone on the day he arrived to prepare for our father's death tells me she's as sweet and kind as I always believed she was.

Scowling at my mention of him paying women to fuck him, she gives me that look of disapproval she's had since she was just a little girl. It never fails to stop me dead in my tracks.

"Please smile, Ava. You can't be mad about my little joke about him. He has it coming to him, don't you think?"

She forces the corners of her mouth to rise, but her smile doesn't reach her eyes. "I just don't like kicking people when they're down. You should know better than anyone else how it feels to lose a parent."

I nod, agreeing with most of that. "Yes, but I also know when you're a bastard to everyone you come in contact with that it's going to come back around on you sometime. If he's unhappy, he's merely getting a nice dose of karma. Maybe if he hadn't been so shitty to you, his wife wouldn't have told him she wants a divorce over the phone later that day. Just saying."

"You're right. I know. I just don't like reveling in his misfortune. Isn't that going to go bad with our karma?"

Christ, I swear my brother is going to somehow ruin this goddamned evening for me, even though he's miles away.

"Well, I don't know about my karma, but you're the nicest person I've ever met, Ava. Your karma is stellar.

So I'm not worried about us. Now let's get up to the house so I can show you my surprise."

That convinces her neither one of us is about to have a run of bad luck or have a terrible accident that will maim or disfigure us. With a smile that's genuine because this one reaches her eyes, she picks up her pace and hurries toward my house.

"You know, I'm not Mother Teresa or some kind of saint. I have done some things in my life that might give me some iffy karma."

I look over at her, intrigued that my perfect Ava might have a little tarnish on her halo. "Do tell."

"No. I don't think I should. You look like you're about to enjoy it too much."

"I just like the idea that perfect little Ava Sutton has a dark secret she won't share. That's all."

Drawing her eyebrows in toward her nose, she grimaces, and I remember I said I wouldn't use my brother's nickname for her anymore. "Sorry. Perfect Ava Sutton has a dark secret she won't share with me. I still love it."

"It's not a big deal. It's not like I killed someone, Theo."

I spin around and take her hand, walking up the driveway toward the kitchen door. "I think you should tell me. I didn't realize we had secrets between us."

When I look back, her eyes are as big as saucers. "Hello, pot. This is kettle. You're black."

"What's that mean?"

Ava levels her gaze on my face. "It means you haven't told me a single thing about your life in the past five years, but you're bothered that I won't tell you this one secret I have. Seems pretty hypocritical, if you ask me."

Since I don't want to fill her head with thoughts of me with other women on the very night I want us to sleep together for the first time, I quickly change the conversation. "So any idea what my surprise is?"

For a long moment, she stares at me like she's angry I won't give in and tell her about the past five years of my life, but then she smiles, and I know we're back on the right track. "Is it animal, vegetable, or mineral?"

That makes me stop to think of which a surprise candlelight dinner would be considered. "Vegetable, I guess?"

For that, I get a look of confusion. "Oh. I'm not sure what I thought you'd say, but for some reason, I wasn't expecting that. So my surprise is a vegetable?"

"Not exactly. Maybe we should just wait since you'll see it in a few minutes."

When we walk into the kitchen, Eleanor's got the table set just for us. I made sure to tell Marius to stay away tonight, and since Matthias is gone for a few days, there's no chance of him busting in and ruining things.

"Hello, you two!" Eleanor chirps in her usual happy tone. "Everything's all ready for you. All I need to do is set the bread out, which will happen in a second or two when the timer goes off."

As if on cue, a beep sounds, and she hurries over to the oven to take out a beautiful loaf of French bread I bought specifically to complement tonight's meal. It became my favorite after I got to enjoy it a few months back when I spent that few days in a cute little seaside hotel with the most incredible café. I couldn't believe it when I found a bakery a few towns away from the house here that specialized in French bread and knew it would be perfect for tonight.

I look over at Ava and see her eyes wide as she scans the table. "Wow! What is all of this?"

As I escort her to her chair, I explain, "I got to enjoy this when I was staying at this cute inn on the south coast of France." I point at the salmon right in front of her and continue. "We'll start with salmon tartare. Have you ever had it?"

She smiles, but I see something strange in her eyes. "Tartare? Doesn't that mean uncooked?"

I nod but quickly add, "Yes, but this is just smoked salmon. Don't worry. It's good."

Relief washes over her, and she leans forward to look at the dish. "It looks great."

Turning to look at the other end of the table, I point at the salad bowl with a variety of greens and say, "There's also a salad. The French don't do a huge thing with salads if they aren't the meal, so it's just some mixed greens with an incredible vinaigrette."

That makes Ava's smile return. "Oh, good! I always love a good salad."

"Of course, there has to be wine. I had this merlot and loved it. I know you like red wine, so you're going to love this!"

I pour her a glass and then one for myself before lifting mine in the air to make a toast. "To an incredible meal with my favorite person in the world."

A blush makes Ava's cheeks turn a soft pink. "To Theo and his wonderful meal!"

I sit down and take some of the salad before handing

her the bowl. "Wait until you see the main course. Rougail Saucisse. You're going to love it!"

Ava nods and in a low voice repeats the name of the dish. "Rougail Saucisse. I had two years of French in high school, but I don't know what that is."

Before I can tell her, Eleanor excitedly answers her question. "It's the most delicious sausage and rice dish I've ever seen! I may not have cooked it, but it's been filling this kitchen with the most delightful smell since Theo brought it into the house this afternoon."

With a smile, Ava nods as she takes a bit of her salad. "That sounds great!"

Eleanor quickly says, "I'm sorry, Theo. I didn't mean to butt in like that."

I wave off her worry and chuckle. "No apologies needed. The Rougail Saucisse does smell fantastic."

If I was being polite, I'd ask her if she wanted to join us, but my plans tonight don't include hanging out with anyone but Ava. Eleanor senses the bread being finished is her cue to leave, and hurriedly excuses herself, thankfully.

Ava and I eat our salads, but I notice she's not interested in the salmon. Maybe if she had some bread to go with it.

I grab the loaf off the island and set it down in the basket at the center of the table. "Try this bread. It's incredible!"

She looks around the table for a long moment before turning her head to look at me. "There's no knife to cut with and where's the butter?"

Leaning over, I lift the loaf up and tear off a piece. "No need for a knife. Just rip off as much as you want.

As for butter, the French don't use it like we do for bread."

Ava sighs but gives me a smile before she breaks off a chunk of the loaf. "Oh. Okay. Well, great bread doesn't really need butter anyway."

I sense she's disappointed, so I quickly stand up. "I'll get it. We don't have to act like this is an actual meal in France."

"No, that's not necessary, Theo. I'm good. Really," Ava protests, so I stop halfway to the refrigerator and sit back down across from her at the table.

"Good, because there's nothing as bad as cold butter ripping through a piece of bread. I've never understood why we keep it in the refrigerator here. Everywhere else I've gone it's left out so it doesn't shred whatever you put it on."

We eat in silence for a few minutes before it's time for the main dish. It was fully cooked by a French restaurant next to the bakery I found, so all Eleanor had to do was keep it warm for the past few hours.

"Ready for the entrée?" I ask Ava as I walk over to the oven. "You're going to love this! I know it."

"You went to so much trouble for this, Theo. It's so nice. Thank you."

Looking back at her at the table, I shake my head. "No trouble. I just wanted you to experience what I got to enjoy at that inn. You should have seen it, Ava. The water was so blue, and you could see it from the balcony of the room we were in."

As soon as I finish speaking, I realize I said the room *we* were in. Not exactly great since I'm trying to use this meal to seduce Ava.

She doesn't say a word, but I know she heard it, so after I take the dish out of the oven and bring it to the table, I quietly say, "I think you're really going to love this."

With a smile, she looks up at me. "You don't have to worry, Theo. I don't think for a second you were alone for the past five years. It's okay that you got to have all of this with someone else."

"I just didn't want you to think…"

Jesus, I'm fucking this up royally. She hates the salmon, and now I've mentioned enjoying this same exact meal with another woman at a cute little French inn. Smooth Theo. Real smooth.

She reaches across the table and gently squeezes my hand. "It's okay, Theo. You're allowed to have a past. I have one. Everyone does."

I smile, thankful she's so sweet, but she has no idea about my past or how many women I've been with in my life. That's all over now, though. I've done enough playing around with other women. I want to settle down with the only one who's ever meant a thing to me.

Eager to change the subject, I point at the bowl of Rougail Saucisse. "I can't wait for you to taste this. It's a little spicy because it's more creole than traditional French food, but it's so tasty."

After scooping out hers and mine, I wait to see what she thinks. I watch as she takes a forkful into her mouth.

"Oh, that's delicious!"

"Not too spicy?"

Ava shakes her head and takes another bite. "No. I can taste the garlic and onions, but there are a lot of spices too that I can't place just yet. It's so good, Theo. Thank you for this."

I take a bite of my meal and revel in the taste as the flavors hit my tongue. "I was a little worried because sometimes they put a lot of cayenne pepper in this dish, but that restaurant seems to have gone easy on it. I'm so glad you like this."

She nods and takes another bite. "I love the rice too. Mmmm…so good."

For the next hour, we enjoy this incredible meal and our wine, and I'm sure everything is back on track. Tonight's going to be the night Ava and I finally sleep together. After all my playing the field around the world, I've come home to the person I've loved for years.

And then as if fate has something against me, Ava breaks into hives. I see them appear before she notices anything, and my heart sinks. Is she allergic to something in the Rougail Saucisse?

"It feels really hot in here tonight, don't you think?" she asks before fanning her face.

"It's okay. We can go for a walk, if you like. It's a beautiful night out."

If I can just get her outside, maybe she'll feel better and we can spend the rest of the night together like I planned. A little fresh air will do us good.

But when Ava stands to leave, I know it's not going to happen. "Just let me freshen up a little. Then we can go."

A few seconds later, I hear her scream when she sees her face and neck covered in hives. I rush into the powder room in the hallway to find her staring in horror at reflection in the mirror.

"Oh my God! Have I looked like this all night?" she asks with tears in her eyes.

I shake my head and lie, hoping I can salvage my plans. "No, not all night. Maybe you're having a reaction to one of the spices in the dish. I'm sure you'll be okay."

She splashes cold water everywhere the hives are, but that does nothing. I watch as she gets discouraged at how she looks, but she doesn't need to worry. I don't care about that.

"I need to go home. I'm sorry, Theo. You aren't mad at me, are you? I feel terrible that you went to all that trouble with our dinner, and I have to leave early."

When she turns to face me, I take her face in my hands and kiss her softly. "It's okay. I'll see you tomorrow. Feel better."

She hurries out of the bathroom, and a few seconds later, I hear the kitchen door close. As disappointed as I am, I can't be upset with her. She's my Ava. So tonight won't be the big night. It'll happen and soon.

I know it.

CHAPTER TWENTY-SIX

va

Lucas and I wait in the office for Matthias, who is now twenty minutes late for our first official meeting as the executors of Mr. King's estate. I knew he'd pull something like this. First, he delayed us even having this meeting for two weeks by suddenly needing to be away for some reason neither the attorney nor I know about, and now he's kept us waiting like idiots sitting here staring at each other for almost a half hour.

"Maybe we should give him a little longer," Lucas says in his professional way.

I look away toward the window and roll my eyes. All I want to give Matthias King is a piece of my mind. He deserves nothing else.

In the short time that I've been with Theo, I've come to finally understand that whatever I thought I had with his brother was nothing compared to the years of friendship that have grown into a romance I thought might only exist in movies. I never have to wonder if I've done something to upset Theo. He's only interested in having fun, which is so much better than being a moody, broody bastard who snaps at people for no reason, never taking into consideration that maybe they have feelings too.

It's been eye-opening, to say the least.

When it reaches thirty minutes past the time we were supposed to meet here with Lucas, I stand up, tired of giving the oldest King brother any more chances. "I'm going to find out where he is and remind him that we had a meeting."

The attorney smiles and nods but says nothing. He probably doesn't feel it would be professional to tell me he's sick and tired of waiting, but I wouldn't think he was wrong for not appreciating sitting here for nothing. He's a busy man, and I'm sure he has dozens of clients he could be working for instead of waiting for Matthias.

I march upstairs to his room and knock on the door, expecting him to fling it open and bark at me, like usual. I swear the man has one emotion. Rage. At least when it comes to me.

When he doesn't answer after about half a minute, I knock harder a second time and loudly say, "Matthias, I know you're in there. We had a meeting with Lucas at nine o'clock. It's very rude to simply decide to stay in bed when people are waiting for you."

But he says nothing. All I get is silence. So I slowly turn the doorknob and open the door before I step into his room. For a second, everything about those snowy days comes flooding back into my mind, but I push it out, refusing to think about that time or him in any way other than regret now.

"Matthias, I know you're going to say I shouldn't be in here, but you should be downstairs in the office for our meeting with the attorney."

I take another step and then another until I can see his bed, but he's not there. Where the hell is he then?

By the time I get down to the kitchen, I'm so angry about having to play hide and seek with a grown man to get him to accept his responsibilities that I nearly snap at Eleanor when she offers to give me a cup of coffee. God, this person has the worst effect on me.

"Thanks, but I'm good. I'm looking for Matthias. He and I had a meeting scheduled with Lucas Manion at nine this morning. He never showed."

Eleanor looks up at the clock on the wall and then at me. "That was nearly a half hour ago. Did you check his room?"

Great minds think alike, obviously. I nod and say, "He's not there either. Did you happen to hear him say he was leaving and when he might come back?"

She walks over to the kitchen door and looks out before turning to wave me over. "He's still here. Or at least his car is. See?"

I join her at the window and see his silver Maserati sitting there. "Okay. So he's somewhere here in the house?"

"Or on the grounds," she suggests. "I can look in here if you want to go take a walk around to see if you can find him."

"Thanks, Eleanor. I swear to God this man is the biggest hassle."

I walk out through the kitchen door grumbling about how much I can't stand Matthias King and how my world would be better if his father had never forced this executor job on me. I still have no idea why he would have thought I'd be the perfect person to help his son with anything, never mind the distribution of his money and carrying out his final wishes. And why would he have decided I was the right one for this job when I wasn't even living here that winter when he made the change to his will?

Resigned to the fact that I'll probably never know, I trudge across the lawn looking left and right to see if he's anywhere nearby. It's a beautiful, sunny day, thankfully, so at least I don't have to search for him as rain drenches me to the bone.

Mick the new groundskeeper looks up from a flower bed he's planting with beautiful white and pink flowers, the same ones the Kings always have every year because they were Mrs. King's favorites. "Hi, Ava. Out for a walk on this gorgeous spring day?"

A man in his late forties, I'm guessing, Mick never fails to talk about the weather whenever he sees me. I figure it's an occupational hazard since so much of his job depends on what it's doing outside on any particular day. He's a pleasant soul, so I always make sure to say hi to him whenever we run into one another.

"Hi, Mick! I'm supposed to be in a meeting, but the third member of our trio is AWOL."

The groundskeeper gives me a blank stare, clearly not understanding what I'm talking about, so I quickly add, "You haven't seen Matthias this morning, have you?"

That makes his smile return, and he turns to point toward the back of the house. "I saw him walk back there about an hour ago."

Thank God someone noticed where he went since he didn't bother to tell a damn soul his plans. "You're a lifesaver, Mick. Have a good one!"

I trot off toward where he pointed, and as I turn the corner of the house, I see Matthias sitting under a tree in the distance. How nice for him that he's decided to lounge around enjoying nature while Lucas and I get to sit waiting for him inside on this gorgeous day.

As I get closer, I see he's not simply sitting under the tree but has his sketchbook with him. He appears engrossed in whatever he's drawing, and as much as I wish I didn't have to interrupt him since I know he loves doing this, I can't forget that the attorney and I have been left to do the job Matthias is supposed to do with us.

"Did you forget our meeting?" I ask as I stop a few feet away from him.

He sits in a pair of black shorts and dark red Cornell T-shirt, and I'm surprised to see he doesn't have shoes on. Matthias isn't a barefoot kind of guy. He's never been that.

Did he just roll out of bed and walk out here to sketch some trees?

"Matthias, did you hear me?"

He ignores me for the second time, not even looking up when I ask that question or the previous one. Has he had some kind of psychotic break? He looks like he belongs back on his old college campus and he's not even taking the opportunity to be mean to me.

Something is definitely wrong with him.

I watch him continue to draw something in the landscape around us for a few moments before I again attempt to get his attention. "Matthias, can you hear me? We're waiting for you to have our meeting. You know, the meeting we need to have in order to start handling your father's affairs the way he wanted?"

Still nothing.

Checking to make sure he doesn't have earbuds in and actually can't hear me, I see nothing to indicate why he's acting utterly oblivious to my standing right in front of him. "Why are you acting like this?"

He doesn't answer immediately, instead closing his sketchbook and then standing to finally face me. Like always, he looks down at me with such hatred in his eyes that I feel like I want to turn away.

"What do you need me for? You and the lawyer can handle everything. That's how it was supposed to be, except I was supposed to be the one dealing with what my father wanted."

Looking up into those dark eyes so full of loathing for me, I try not to let myself feel bad for what he's going through. "I didn't ask for this job. I hate it almost as much as you seem to hate me."

He looks around like he's searching for something and then returns his attention to me, glaring like always. "Where is your new boyfriend? He always seems to be nearby, so I'm surprised he isn't trailing right behind you like a puppy."

"Why would you say something like that about

Theo? You two have always been close. Do you hate him now too?"

He doesn't bother to answer, walking away like I don't even deserve another word. I follow him, running to catch up to him as he marches away with long strides toward the house.

"So you don't hate him? Just me? Why? I thought after—"

He cuts me off, spinning around and stepping so close to me that his lips are practically kissing mine when he leans down to get into my face. Oddly enough, his dark eyes don't look utterly full of hate for once.

"After what, Ava? After we spent a couple days fucking? Why would that mean anything to me?"

His words are cruel, but his voice hitches when he says the word anything. Why does he seem so emotional about this if it meant nothing to him?

I have to wonder if the person he was back then even exists now. I stare up into his eyes wishing I'd see some hint of that Matthias, and for a moment as we look at each other, I think I see something in them that says he's in there.

As much as I want to snap at him for how cruel he's been to me since he returned here, I say, "The more you work with the lawyer and me, the sooner you get to leave and never see me again. I'd think that would be motivation enough for you."

He winces when I mention him leaving but doesn't say another word before simply walking away. I follow him, unsure where he plans to go, and I'm surprised when I realize he's actually going to where the attorney is waiting for the two of us.

Lucas stands from his chair and turns to look at me in amazement, probably at how Matthias is dressed like some frat boy. I begin to apologize for our late start, even though it wasn't my fault, but I'm interrupted before I get more than a few words out.

"What do I have to do to get this over with?" Matthias snaps at him.

Stunned at how nasty he's being, Lucas answers, "Just follow through on your father's final wishes. He made them very clear, so if there's no one contesting the will, it shouldn't be too much work."

"Why the fuck should anyone contest the will? My father, in his misguided generosity, seems to have left something to every goddamned person who's ever stepped foot on this estate."

Lucas and I give one another the side eye but say nothing to Matthias's outburst. I know that was a dig at my family and me since we're merely the help and the kids of the help.

And just in case I wasn't sure that's what he meant, he throws me a dirty look before turning on his heel and storming out of the office. "I'll be back. Get things started because I don't want this to take all day. I have better things to do with my time."

CHAPTER TWENTY-SEVEN

va

THREE HOURS LATER, MATTHIAS WALKS OUT OF OUR meeting after announcing he's finished with this nonsense, leaving Lucas and me sitting there at the table in the office staring at one another in shock. I shouldn't be surprised. After all, this seems to be all he does whenever I'm around. If he's not barking at me, he's storming out in disgust.

"I guess we're done?" I ask, unsure if we can even continue our work without him around.

Lucas slowly nods, and I get the sense that he feels bad for me. "Let's set a meeting for early next week. I'll email you and Matthias, and hopefully, he'll be able to make it."

"Okay. Thanks. Sorry we didn't get a lot done here

today, but I think Matthias is still dealing with a lot of stuff."

Why I bother to make excuses for his bad behavior, I don't know. Maybe it's because it might be true. In all that's gone on in the past couple weeks, I think Matthias might be having a hard time dealing with some of it, especially considering that he found out his marriage ended right before his father died. I don't know the particulars of his relationship with his wife, but those two events one on top of another surely must be causing him grief.

Or maybe he's just a terrible person who likes to make everyone around him miserable. I'm not sure which of these is true, but because I choose to be a good person, I'm willing to entertain the possibility that some of his behavior might be because of all that's gone on recently.

Probably the part involving Lucas. Everything Matthias does involving me is driven by pure hate. Unfortunately for the attorney, he's caught in the middle.

I walk out of the office and exhale a sigh of relief. Yes, we only got a few things done, but my time with him is over, thankfully. Now I can be with the King who doesn't hate me.

As this thought runs through my head, Theo comes up behind me and wraps his arms around my waist, pulling me back against him. Already hard, he plants kisses up and down my neck as he asks me how my day is going.

"Trust me, you don't want to know. It's much better now, though," I answer, turning my head just in time to get one of his kisses on my lips.

"I was thinking about you and hoping that even if you were only on a little break that we could sneak off together. How long do you have before you must go back and deal with all that executor stuff?" he asks as he nuzzles my neck just below my ear.

Spinning around to face him, I say, "As long as you want me for. Your brother stood up and left after telling us he'd had enough of this nonsense today, so my executor duties are done for the day."

Theo smiles and slides his tongue across his lower lip, leaving it wet and making him look so sexy. "Well, thank you big brother. I guess he's not a complete son of a bitch. But enough about him. Let's go up to my room and spend the day together."

He punctuates his suggestion by tilting his hips so his hard cock presses against my body. He's always such a good time. I love that about him. Everything about Theo is fun.

The way he cheers me up. The way he shows me he cares. The way he can't wait to be with me. All fun and exactly what I need after a morning full of Matthias.

"Okay!"

Taking my hand in his, he runs down the hallway to the staircase leading to the second floor. We sound like two wild kids stomping through the house laughing and having a good time, but I don't care.

By the time we reach the top of the stairs, I'm nearly out of breath he's made me run so fast. Looking back at me, he says, "No giving up yet. We're just a few feet away."

I push myself to keep up with him, wanting nothing more than what he's got planned for us when we reach his room. A few seconds later, he flings his bedroom door open and pulls me into the room, slamming the door behind us.

"Do you know how many times I fantasized about doing that?" he asks as he takes my face in his hands, cradling my face and looking down into my eyes.

"Today or since you got back?" I ask, not sure what he means.

Theo shakes his head and kisses me softly. My heart practically skips at beat he's so sexy, and then he answers me and my heart soars.

"No. I mean for years. I've wanted to do this since we were teenagers."

There's no time to ask him if he means it because he's already busy undressing me. His fingers quickly unbutton my blouse before he slides it off my body, letting it fall to the floor as he kisses me. I fumble around with his T-shirt, trying to get it off him but having no luck since his arms are busy at the moment.

"I guess I'm going to have to let you undress me and then I'll undress you since trying it at the same time isn't working."

He smiles and practically rips his shirt off his body, yanking it up over his head before tossing it across the room. "There. Now you can concentrate on the jeans. I'll handle your shorts after that."

For a long moment, I don't move a muscle as I stare at his body. Toned and muscular, Theo's chest, shoulders, and arms look like an athlete's. I guess I shouldn't be surprised. He is a race car driver. That's a sport, right?

My gaze slides down his torso, and all I want to do is explore the peaks and valleys of his washboard abs.

Somewhere in the back of my mind I try to remember if he's always looked like this. I don't remember feeling like every part of me got weak whenever I saw him shirtless when we were younger.

I run my fingertips across his stomach from hipbone to hipbone, loving how he trembles as I graze across his silky soft skin. He stares down at me with pure need in his eyes, as if he can't figure out why I haven't ripped his jeans off him yet.

"Everything okay down there?" he asks with a chuckle.

Nodding, I glance down at the spot just below his belly button and sigh. "Everything's great. Just admiring the view."

"Cool, but we haven't even gotten to the good stuff yet."

So typical Theo. Even our first time having sex won't be serious. It's not his style. He loves to keep everything lighthearted. I like that, though. No pressure. Just having a good time.

I roll my eyes at his attempt at humor. "You're too funny. You know that? The good stuff is what's in your pants, I'm assuming?"

Clearly wanting to move things along, he smiles as he unbuttons his jeans and slides the zipper down. "That's what I've been told. You'll have to give me your opinion after."

He tilts his hips forward, pressing his hard cock against my belly as thoughts of what's about to happen next run through my mind. I've loved Theo all my life. He's been my best friend, my confidant, my soul mate forever. We're made for each other.

For a split second, I wonder if I should have told him about Matthias and me, but I push that out of my head immediately. There's nothing to tell. What happened between us is ancient history. Two incredible days in a lifetime that meant something to me but obviously meant nothing to him. Telling Theo would serve no purpose since it's nothing that has to do with us or how we feel about one another.

"Ava?"

His voice tears me out of my thoughts, and I look up at him to see concern in his eyes. "Sorry. I got lost for a moment there. You shouldn't tease me with the good stuff."

Theo dips his head to kiss me long and deep, pushing my shorts and underwear down my legs at the same time. I'm left in my bra, which suddenly makes me feel very self-conscious. I don't have much time to think about that, though, because a second later, he eases me back onto his bed. I stare up at him as he makes quick work of his clothes and climbs on top of me.

Cradling my face, he kisses me and whispers against my lips, "I love you, Ava. I always have. You've always been my Ava."

"I love you too, Theo."

The moment makes my heart fill with happiness. Theo and I have always been meant for each other. I've always known this.

He pushes into me as he kisses me again, and it's perfect. Just like him.

I wrap my arms around his shoulders and pull him to me, wanting to feel all of him against my body. His muscles tense under my touch as he pumps into my body, and it doesn't take long before we find our rhythm. Our lovemaking is fast and hard, but it's also sweet. In my ear, he moans about how perfect I am and how he's dreamed of this for so long. I know it's just sex talk and not true because I'm definitely not anything close to perfect and I doubt he's thought of this for that long since he's been with other women, but I love that he says those words anyway.

When he gets close, he lifts himself off me and pumps faster into me. Every time his cock slides into my body, it's like a jolt of lightning hits me. I feel myself getting near to my release, so I wrap my legs around his waist to keep him right where he is.

Just a few more thrusts and I'll be there.

I stare up at him in awe at how beautiful he is. My Theo. I've thought of him like that for years, but never before was he actually mine. This incredible, sexy, gorgeous man loves me, and I love him.

It's perfect. We're perfect together.

Just as it was always meant to be.

He closes his eyes when he comes and sags against my body, breathing heavily in my ear. I can feel my orgasm right on the edge. I only need him to keep pumping into me for a few more times.

But he doesn't. He falls still, and no matter how much I move my hips to give him the hint, he doesn't move.

When he finally lifts his head, he smiles down at me and kisses my lips. "That was incredible. Just as I imagined it would be."

I nod, unsure if I should tell him I didn't come. I don't want to ruin our first time. It was incredible, exactly as he said. So incredible that I want to tell him how much. It's just that it ended about three thrusts too soon for me.

"You didn't come?" he asks, and I can tell he's disappointed.

With a quick shake of my head, I say, "It's okay."

"No way. Sex without coming is like an ice cream sundae without hot chocolate."

Before I can say anything to that, he slides down my body and pushes open my legs. Positioning himself between them, he looks up at me and gives me a sinful grin.

"Time to give you that hot chocolate."

I watch as he buries his face between my legs, and a second later, I feel his tongue slide up my pussy. My eyes roll back in my head at how good this feels, and when he flicks the tip of his tongue over my clit, it's like colors explode behind my eyelids.

And then he slides his finger inside me and it's like I'm in heaven. Now this is the good stuff.

Theo brings me to the very edge of ecstasy and then lifts his head. Grinning like some Cheshire Cat, he licks his lips and says, "I thought I'd take a break."

"A break? I was so close, though," I say, practically pleading for him to get back to business.

"Oh. Then I guess I better continue."

God, he can be so cute. And so frustrating at the same time.

He returns his mouth to my pussy, and less than a minute later, I feel my release begin deep inside me. A few seconds later, I arch my back as the most incredible orgasm races through me. I grab hold of his head to keep him right there, just in case he has any ideas about taking another break.

When the final aftershocks subside, he lifts his head and kisses the inside of my thigh. "Feel better?"

"Yes, but I think I want an ice cream sundae."

Sitting back on his heels, he throws his head back in laughter. "That's too funny. I was just thinking the same thing. What do you say to getting dressed and going down to that ice cream place in town?"

"Scoops?"

"Yeah. I've never had a better sundae anywhere than that place."

I sit up and kiss him, tasting myself on his lips. "Remember when you and I went there that summer day during the heat wave like ten years ago and you ate your ice cream so fast you had an ice cream headache for nearly fifteen minutes?"

Theo cringes. "I can still feel that pain."

"Promise me you won't gulp your sundae down like a puppy, and I'll go."

He nods and kisses me. "I promise."

We hurry up and get back into our clothes, laughing about another time he reminds me of when his mother took all five of the boys and me for ice cream when we were all under the age of ten. She must have had a will of steel to handle all of us, but I remember Marius making a mess with his ice cream and wearing more of it than he ate.

"I haven't thought about that in years. Those were good times," Theo says as we hurry out into the hallway.

And just then, almost as if the universe decided we'd had enough fun for one afternoon, Matthias walks out of his room and sneers at the two of us. He practically seethes his hatred for not only me but his brother.

"Hey!" Theo says to him as we walk by. "Cheer up. We're leaving."

Matthias says nothing, but when I look back just before we walk down the stairs, I see him staring at us with so much loathing I shudder. Now he doesn't just hate me. He hates the one person in his family he's been closest to all his life.

I think about saying something to Theo about it, but I don't want to ruin our time together. Matthias is who he is. There's nothing either one of us can do to change that.

CHAPTER TWENTY-EIGHT

M atthias

WEEKS OF HAVING TO WORK SIDE-BY-SIDE WITH AVA on this damn estate bullshit while she and my brother are together every waking moment makes me want to kill someone. Obviously, Theo has decided it's time to settle down since he always said Ava wasn't the type of girl you mess around with but definitely the kind of girl you marry.

I've never been jealous of that brother. He was my best friend growing up. Out of all of my brothers, I'm closest to him.

Or at least I was.

Now I can barely look at him without being filled with envy. I should want him to be happy. I love him. Yet I can't bring myself to feel that way.

We're drifting apart further and further every day,

and there's nothing I can do about it because it's all my fault. I'm consumed with jealousy over him being with Ava. I can't tell anyone about it because the only two people I would tell are involved.

It's tearing me up to have to be around her and not be able to have any chance to ever be with her again. I moved thousands of miles away to try to forget her, but it didn't work. From the moment I saw her that first day back, all I wanted to do was tell Ava how much I missed her.

But then the memory of how I felt that day after Theo told me she left comes rushing back into my mind, and I'm blinded by hate. That's all she ever sees, but hidden away deep inside is what I've always felt for her.

Love.

I had hoped with a little time I'd be able to push aside my emotions and be around her without wanting to lash out. If I could do that, then maybe she'd see the person I was with her back then still exists.

All that became impossible once she and Theo got together.

Now it takes every ounce of strength I possess to even come out of my room because I know at some point I'm going to see the two of them kissing or being playful somewhere in the house. I walked into the kitchen yesterday and she was practically sitting on his lap as they ate lunch. All I could do was turn around and walk out in disgust.

But it's never disgust I feel.

The jealousy eats at me twenty-four hours a day. It makes sleeping next to impossible, so I spend night after night staring up at the ceiling trying to convince myself I truly hate Ava Sutton with all of my being.

That's not even the tiniest bit true.

I don't hate her. I've never hated her. Even after she left without even saying goodbye and even when I knew she was keeping in contact with Theo but didn't bother to talk to me, I didn't hate her. I wanted to. I tried to. God knows I tried to change my love to hate, but it never worked.

Every time I say something cruel to her, I have to stop myself from saying I'm sorry. It takes everything I have inside me to pretend to loathe her. It's exhausting. If I wasn't so consumed by jealousy that she's with my brother, I'd sleep like a fucking baby I'm so tired.

Living so close to her is pure agony. I'd give anything for the pain to stop. I have more money than I know what to do with now, but no amount can make my life better because I don't have her.

I cautiously walk to the kitchen, looking around the corner to see if the lovebirds are here before I get excited about grabbing something to eat. Eleanor stands at the island chopping up something that looks like a salad. Probably for Ava since Theo and Marius wouldn't touch a salad if their lives depended on it, and I can't remember the last time I had any green leafy vegetables.

"Matthias, there's chicken salad for lunch. Would you like me to make you a sandwich?" she asks when I sit down at the table on the other side of the room.

Nodding at the thought of one of Eleanor's famous chicken salad sandwiches, I walk over to the refrigerator to get a drink of iced tea. "Yeah, that would be good. Thanks."

No sooner do I pour myself a glass and sit back down, I hear footsteps coming toward us. Dread fills me, followed immediately by anger. Can't I even have a fucking sandwich for lunch without being subjected to those two?

I hold my breath as I wait to see who it is, and when Marius rounds the corner, I nearly jump up and hug him I'm so relieved to see his face. "Hey, what's up?"

My brother looks at me oddly, not surprising since I sounded downright gleeful to see him. "Hey, what the hell are you so happy about? I thought your thing was being the most miserable person in the world."

"I'm not happy," I say, lying as I silently thank God for the reprieve from Theo and Ava and their romance show. "Well, maybe a little to see you, but we're brothers and I don't hate you, so it's only natural."

He sits down at the table across from me and studies my face for a few seconds. "Everything okay with you, Matthias? You're acting weird."

"So much for brotherly love," I say with a chuckle before taking a sip of iced tea.

"Marius, I'm making your brother a chicken salad sandwich. Do you want one too?" Eleanor asks.

My brother's eyes light up. "With dried apricots and scallions? Chicken salad à la Eleanor?" he asks with a big smile.

She beams her pride in her take on a pretty common recipe and nods. "That's the one."

"Any chance we have wheat bread? It tastes best on that wheat bread Mom used to love."

Eleanor points at the bread container and walks over to it to grab the loaf of bread. "I've got it. The usual way you like it? I know you're more particular than Matthias there, who doesn't care what kind of bread I use."

Marius cranes his neck to see what she was chopping over on the island. "Any chance you have some arugula over there? I think that would go great with it."

"Who are you and what have you done with Marius King?" I joke.

He turns to look at me like I'm some barbarian who doesn't know good food. "What?"

"Arugula? Seriously?"

"Just because my palate has grown from macaroni and cheese or peanut butter and jelly sandwiches when I was six doesn't mean there's anything different about me. I'm sure you found some foods over in the UK you liked that I'd find strange."

I shake my head. "Not a one."

He laughs as I grimace at the thought of English food. "You look like you're going to be sick. You okay?"

"Just bad memories. So now you're an arugula guy. It's like I don't even know my own family anymore."

"Theo seems the same. Everything's a good time, and he's stuck to his best friend like they're joined at the hip. Sounds like every day of his life growing up, don't you think?"

His mention of those two makes my mood sour, and I hurriedly stand up to leave, sending my chair sailing across the floor behind me. "I changed my mind about the chicken salad sandwich, Eleanor. Maybe later."

She and Marius look at me like I'm out of my mind, but I don't care. I don't have an appetite anymore.

By the time I get outside, that old familiar rage I've felt every day I've been here is back, tearing me up

281

inside. Christ, I don't know how I'm going to handle this for much longer.

Not that I imagine I'll have to. Once we're done with the executor bullshit, I'm sure Theo will be taking Ava with him. He told me he's got a race two months from now, so he's going to have to get back to his life soon.

A life that now includes her.

I stop walking and realize I'm halfway out to my favorite spot on the entire estate. Looking up, I see the sky is perfectly blue with only a few wispy white clouds. I can't think of a better day to sit under that tree and sketch. Fuck work and everything to do with King Industries for the rest of today. Same with anything having to do with that executor job and anything else here that's driving me insane.

Ten minutes later, I'm right where I want to be for the first time in a few days and happier than I thought I could be nowadays. Two birds chirp above my head having their own private bird conversation, but other than that, it's quiet. Nobody's telling me they need me to do this or expect me to do that. It's simply perfect and all I want at this moment.

I left my cell inside, so no one can contact me. For the first time since I returned to this place, I'm free to do what I want, and the only thing I have any desire to do is sketch.

Pushing every other thought out of my mind, I focus on a rabbit sitting perfectly still under a hedge nearby. For a few moments, I wonder if it's one of those garden statues the new groundskeeper seems to love. He's placed them around the estate, often in some of the oddest places like that duck he's set out on grass near the back of the property. There's not a drop of water anywhere near him. He looks lost, like the rest of the ducks in his life all left and he's not sure where to go.

I see the rabbit's ears twitch ever so slightly, and I know he's not one of the groundskeeper's new toys. The creature doesn't move any more, almost as if he knows I want to draw him and he's happy to pose for his portrait.

Sure I don't have long before he hops away, I quickly begin sketching his head and body, resigned to probably having to fill in the rest later because he'll be long gone by the time I can sketch his fur. That's okay, though. I understand the urge to get away from others.

Ten minutes later, he's disappeared to another part of the estate, but I'm happily drawing his little face and enormous ears. I haven't seen a lot of rabbits, but as I begin to complete his features, I have to admit he's a beautiful animal.

I work to capture the softness of his brown fur and the innocence in his dark eyes, wanting to do him justice since he so kindly sat for so long while I drew. Focused on that, I don't hear someone interrupt my peace and quiet until they step on a branch resting on the ground nearby.

Instantly irritated, I lift my head and see Ava standing a few yards away. Dressed in a pink sundress with little white polka dots and wearing black flip flops, she looks like she belongs at the beach. She's got her long brown hair up in a ponytail and looks sweet as she stares at me.

Everything about her looks innocent. It's all a lie, though. Nobody knows that more than me.

"I'm sorry. I didn't mean to bother you."

As usual, every ugly thing I can possibly think of to say to her fills my head, but this time I don't utter even a single one. I simply remain silent as I look at her, trying to convince myself she was never anything to me.

Now we're both full of lies.

"I'm happy to see you're drawing. I know that makes you happy."

She stops after her second mention of happiness. That word shouldn't be a part of any of our conversations. When it comes to Ava Sutton, I've felt exactly the opposite of happy more often than not.

Taking a few steps toward me, she stops and looks down at the grass before lifting her head and smiling. "Can I see what you're drawing?"

"No."

The answer comes out of my mouth before I can stop myself, and instantly, I regret it. I was doing so well until she asked that.

Disappointment shows on her face, filling me with more self-loathing. I try to think of something to say to take away the sting of my rejection, but my head is filled with cruelty, like always.

"Oh. Okay. I'll leave so you can get back to your sketching."

Every word sounds sad. I did that. I should be happy. I've wanted to make her feel like I do this whole time, and now that I have over and over, I've triumphed.

But I'm not happy seeing her like this. I'm never fucking happy when I hurt her.

She turns to walk away, so I jump up and follow her, leaving my sketchpad and pencil behind under the tree. When I catch up to her, I touch her shoulder, and it's like lightning races through my fingers all the way up my arm.

Ava stops and turns around to face me. Christ, she's small. Tilting her head back, she looks up into my eyes, and a flash of memory from those December days races through my mind.

"I'm sorry. I'll show you my drawing if you still want to see it."

A huge smile lights up her entire face, making her the most beautiful thing I've ever seen. "I would. You know I would. I love your drawings, Matthias."

"Hang on."

I hurry over to where my sketchbook sits and grab it before hurrying back over to her. "It's not done yet. I had to rush to get as much of him done before he hopped away. Probably had a rabbit meeting or something to go to."

She giggles, and I swear it feels like my heart is about to explode out of my chest when she reaches for the book and says, "Here, let me see it. Is he wearing a suit for this rabbit meeting? I wonder if they discuss carrots and lettuce at their meetings?"

I let her take the sketchbook out of my hand and watch as she looks at my rough drawing of that rabbit. Looking up at me, she says, "It's very good, but all your drawings are so good, Matthias. I bet you have some great ones from your time in London."

Shaking my head, I take the book from her hold. "No, not a one."

"Really? I would have bet you drew a lot there. I mean, there's so much to see that would be perfect for you to do."

"No. I never sketched the whole time I was there."

My admission brings our pleasant conversation to a screeching halt. Fuck. I never do things right when it comes to her.

We stand there in awkward silence until she says, "I'm sorry about your marriage."

Not a single hint of cruelty or gloating can be found in her words or her tone, but still her feeling sympathy for the breakup of my sham marriage annoys me. She must have heard about that from Theo, and they probably had a good laugh between them about my wife divorcing me.

"No need to be sorry. Neither one of us wanted it to continue. We weren't happy like others I know."

My poorly veiled reference to her and my brother is too obvious for her to miss, and she forces a tiny smile in her discomfort that I've brought him up. Why, though? She should be happy to hear any mention of their bliss.

"I'm sorry anyway."

God, I hate her feeling pity for me. I have everything a man could want in this world. Power, money, position. How dare little Ava Sutton feel bad for me?

"Speaking of sketches, how do you think your boyfriend would feel knowing I still have that nude drawing of you?" I ask as my rage and jealousy mix into a potent poison filling me until it practically oozes out of every one of my pores.

"You still have that?" she asks, but I get no sense she's truly surprised.

Why should she be? I told her I wanted to keep it.

"Yes," I say with a smile that takes every ounce of my

energy to force. "I wonder if he'd be happy that I have something like that with his girlfriend."

Calling Theo her boyfriend was hard, but calling her his girlfriend makes my mouth taste like I've been eating ashes. The two of them make me sick with their happy romance constantly on display no matter where I go in this house.

My fucking house.

Ava's expression turns dark, and she looks away as she answers, "Your brother isn't like you. I doubt he'd care."

"No, he's not. I'd more than care if another man had a picture of the woman I'm crazy about. Theo, though, is all about being a good time, isn't he? He couldn't be bothered to be unhappy, even if he saw that sketch. That's the difference between us."

When she turns back to face me, I see hurt in her eyes, just like I always find whenever I speak to her. "There's nothing wrong with being happy and fun like Theo is. You might want to try it sometime. You might be surprised at how good it feels."

Nothing wrong with being happy and fun like my brother. She has no idea how many times throughout my life I've wished I could be like Theo. He's never had anyone breathing down his back, watching to make sure he did exactly as they expected and eager to let him know when he failed. He's been allowed to be whatever he wanted to be for every day of his life.

"I'm sure. Tell me, Ava. Does he know we were together before you two started dating?"

I watch as the hurt in her eyes morphs into utter

terror, even as she shrugs off my question and casually answers, "That's ancient history. It means nothing to us."

Us? Which us? Ava and me? Or Theo and her? Because it fucking damn well means something to me.

Before she can say another word, I pull her to me and kiss her hard. Fully expecting her to pull away, I move quickly, sliding my tongue inside her mouth as years of missing her threaten to consume me.

But she never pulls away. She kisses me back, her tongue sliding over mine and making me want her more than I thought possible after all this time I've spent trying to hate her. Her hands don't push against me to make me leave her alone. No, she's as willing as I am as we stand here kissing in broad daylight.

I step back and grin. "Yeah. Ancient history. Keep lying to yourself, Ava."

Flustered, she shakes her head, but her denial is half-hearted, at best. Pure happiness fills every inch of me as I realize she still cares about me after all this time apart and after all I've done to make her never want to speak to me again.

I watch her scurry away, looking back right before she reaches the house. I never let myself believe Ava cared at all, and once I began being so cruel to her, I was sure I'd chased her away for good.

Now I know I was wrong.

Pressing my lips together, I revel in the memory of her kissing me. For the first time since I came back to this place, I know what I want to do.

Win Ava back.

CHAPTER TWENTY-NINE

heo

FOR WEEKS, I'VE WATCHED AS AVA BECOMES MORE and more upset about having to deal with my older brother. I can't fathom what his problem is, although to be honest, I don't care. So what if he doesn't get to be the sole executor of our father's estate? Who fucking gives a damn about that kind of thing? Doesn't Matthias have more important things to do with his time? He's the CEO of King Industries now. You'd think he'd have his hands full dealing with that and would appreciate not having to handle all the details of my father's will all on his own.

Yesterday, when she came back from running down to her house in the afternoon, she looked like she wanted to cry. She refused to say it was because of him, but who else on this entire estate makes her feel that way?

I've had enough of my brother's being an asshole. When I see him today, I intend on making it clear to him that whatever his problem with Ava is, he needs to get the fuck over it and immediately. I won't let this vendetta against her go on any longer.

Until then, I plan to enjoy my day.

Marius stands at the end of the pool table surveying the balls still left on the table after his break. "Not bad. I'm a little out of practice, but it's all starting to come back to me."

A little out of practice for my younger brother means he isn't running the table for every game. He still beats everyone he goes up against. When we were younger, I was sure he must be cheating to constantly win no matter who he was playing against. Kellen and I even spent hours one afternoon checking out every inch of the table because we suspected he had something rigged.

We found nothing. We had to accept Marius is just a damn good pool player. Not that he ever keeps that a secret. My brother is nothing if not proud of his abilities, as proven by how he likes to gloat after winning every time.

"You've beaten me like twenty times in the past week. Not bad?" I ask as I chalk up my pool cue.

He looks over at me and smirks. "Theo, no offense, but you suck at this. You always have. You and Kellen are two of the worst pool players I've ever met. Ronan isn't very good either, but he doesn't have as much practice as you two, so he has an excuse. The only worthy opponent in this house is Matthias, who I bet is still able to give me a run for my money even though he doesn't play much anymore."

I roll my eyes at his insult on my playing and then his mention of Matthias. Marius, who seems to have chosen to ignore virtually everything that's going on in this house lately, shakes his head like he doesn't understand my disgusted expression.

"Tell me I'm lying. You may be a great driver, but sorry, man. You suck at pool."

"Just take a shot, okay? I didn't agree to play with you just to hear how bad I am at this for the hundredth time."

He leans over the table to line up his shot of the six ball in the far right corner pocket and mumbles, "Touchy. You'd think getting laid all the time from that pretty girlfriend of yours would put you in a better mood."

Two seconds later, the six ball drops into the pocket, and Marius stands up straight like some goddamned conquering hero. "That's how it's done."

"Whatever." I walk around the table as I try to figure out what my shot will be. He's left me nothing to work with, as usual. "And getting laid isn't the reason I'm in a bad mood."

My brother throws his head back and laughs. "I wouldn't think it would be."

I take my shot, and the fifteen ball bounces off the side before rolling aimlessly into the center of the table. Jesus, I really do suck at this. Frustrated, I stand back and prepare for Marius to sink every ball now and end the game.

"It's Matthias who's making me upset. I swear to God he's hell-bent on making Ava's life as miserable as he is."

"What's his problem with her again?" Marius asks

before taking his shot and sending the four ball into the left side pocket.

As he moves around the table to size up his next shot, I say, "Fuck if I know. He's always had a problem with her. Asshole refers to her as the fucking help, or at least he used to. Where the hell did he get that shit from? Mom and Dad never looked down on anyone who had less money than them. None of us do it, but he acts like he's some royal asshole and she's some servant girl and it's the goddamned fourteenth fucking century."

My anger makes my brother laugh right before he bends down to send two fucking balls into the same pocket. Fucker is going to run this damn table like always.

"Not that I'm defending him, but cut Matthias some slack. He's dealing with the breakup of his marriage, for Christ's sake. That can't be easy."

"I'd leave that bastard too if he was as miserable as he is all the time. Anyway, I never got the feeling it was a love match between him and Jillian. The one time I saw them when I stopped over in London on my way to Amsterdam I had dinner with them, and I swear to God, Marius, it was like hanging out with Mr. and Mrs. Snowman. I don't think either one of them cracked a smile the entire time we sat there together, and I was telling her some funny shit from when we were all small. Even Dad looked uncomfortable that night."

Marius shrugs and aims at the white cue ball in front of him. "It still has to hurt to have your marriage end by long distance. Eight ball in the side pocket to set me up for the win."

I watch as his prediction comes true a second later

when he sinks the eight ball to end the game. Good to know some things never change.

Tossing my pool stick on the table, I sit down hard in the chair nearby. "Yeah, I guess it might suck, but he probably brought it on himself. Have you seen how nasty he is to everyone since he got back?"

Marius gloats over his win before crouching down to collect the balls. As he racks them, he says, "He was nice with Eleanor the other day when she was making us her famous chicken salad sandwiches."

"That's because she's the help, as he calls them, and she was doing exactly what she's supposed to do, according to him. I swear, Marius, he's turned into some elitist asshole."

Standing, he points at the triangle of balls and silently asks if I want to break. I nod and walk around to where he's standing, nudging him out of the way. Pulling my cue back, I push it forward, but the break is weak and only a couple balls roll away from the pack.

He pushes me out of the way, laughing. "Okay, new house rule. No more breaking for you. As for Matthias, why don't you say something to him? Sounds like he needs to have someone set him straight about Ava."

A minute later as I'm proceeding to lose my second straight game to Marius, the oldest King walks in and sits down to watch. "Kicking his ass like always? Theo, I don't know why you keep playing this game. You can't win, especially against someone who's so good at it like Marius."

I glance over at him and frown. "I'm a glutton for punishment."

Marius laughs and takes another successful shot

before Matthias says, "That's a wonderful description of you, Theo. I couldn't have put it better myself."

Something snaps inside me, and I throw my pool stick down on the table, ruining the game for Marius. Normally, he'd bitch up a storm about it, but this time, he merely steps back out of the way.

"What is your fucking problem, Matthias? You've been acting like an asshole for weeks. What the hell is wrong with you?" I ask, ready for this fight.

He doesn't bother standing up. Instead, he sits back in his chair and looks up at me with a smug expression I swear makes me want to push my fist into his face.

"I don't have a problem. You seem to though, Theo. What could it be? Trouble in paradise?"

My anger practically propels me across the room, and I take two giant steps to where he sits. "What the hell does that mean? Forget it. I don't care. All I want to know is why you insist on being such a dick to Ava."

Matthias doesn't answer for a long moment, and when he does, I swear I want to pound the fuck out of him. "Is Ava so fragile that she needs her boyfriend to stand up for her? Maybe she should bow out of being the executor of Dad's estate if she's so delicate."

I glare down at him, shaking my head. "Stop busting her balls, Matthias. This is your only warning."

He grins in that arrogant way that has never failed to get under my skin. "I didn't realize Ava had balls. How does that work out when the two of you are getting busy? Who's the guy in your couple?"

"What is your problem with her? She's never done anything bad to you, so why are you like this?"

"I don't have a problem with her."

There's a lie if I've ever heard one. I don't care if he's smiling or not. He's got some issue with her, and I want to know just what the fuck it is.

"Then you've just decided to be a dick to her for no reason?"

He shrugs, and finally that insufferable smile fades from his face. "I have my reasons."

Jesus, it's like talking to a wall. I want to fucking smack the hell out of him right now.

"Is this about Dad making you two co-executors of his estate? She never asked for that, you know. You being a shit to her isn't necessary and doesn't make things any easier."

"So now you decide what's necessary for little Ava? Did she give you that job, or did you take it upon yourself to proclaim yourself her guardian and protector?"

I swear every word out of his mouth is him practically begging for me to fuck him up. "What does it matter to you if I want to defend her? Someone has to. Everyone's noticed how ugly you are to her, Matthias."

He stands up so we're toe to toe with one another and then looks over at Marius standing across the room. "Is that true? Have you noticed that, Marius?"

Turning to look at my other brother still standing there with his pool cue, I see him shake his head and take a step back. "I'm not getting involved in this. You two need to settle your differences when it comes to Ava Sutton. Leave me out of it."

Behind me, Matthias laughs. "I don't have any differences with little Ava Sutton. Trust me on that."

I spin around to look at him and get into his face.

"Then why the fuck do you act like you fucking hate her?"

We stand there silently glaring at one another, and I swear I see something like hurt in my brother's eyes. What the hell does he have to be hurt about? I'm just trying to get him to stop being a shit to the woman I love.

Finally, Matthias steps around me and smiles. "Well, I guess there's no doubt about it then. I hate little Ava Sutton."

He walks out, leaving Marius and me standing there staring at him as he heads down the hallway. Looking over at my brother, I hope he has something to say that makes sense of what just happened.

When he doesn't say a word, I shake my head. "See? What the hell is wrong with him?"

"I have no idea. He acts like she killed Dad or something. What does she say about why she thinks he's acting like this?"

With a sigh, I answer, "Nothing. She has no idea either. It's like he's decided for no reason that she's the person he's going to make his mortal enemy."

Matthias can feel whatever damn way he wants, but the days of him mistreating Ava are over. The next time he says even a single unkind word to her, I'm going to do what I should have done weeks ago.

Let's see how cocky he is with a mouth full of blood and a broken nose.

CHAPTER THIRTY

va

TWO MONTHS OF BEING WITH THEO HAS MADE ME happier than I ever thought possible. He hasn't said much about when he plans to get back to his life, but I'm hopeful he'll ask me to join him when he leaves. I think we have something great, and I'd hate to see it end.

I see Mick tending to the flowers along the sidewalk on this beautiful day and wave to him as I walk up to the main house. "Looking good!"

"Me or the flowers?" he jokes, laughing.

"Both. I love those pink flowers especially. Have a good one!"

"You too, Ava!"

I remember Eleanor telling me she was planning on cleaning the kitchen floor today, so instead of going in the back door, I walk around to the front door of the

King house. The sound of two voices yelling hits my ear the second I get inside, and it doesn't take me long to realize who's making all the noise. I'd hoped it would never come to this, but obviously, Theo had a different idea if he and Matthias are fighting.

Racing up the stairs, I find them in the hallway taking swings at one another. One of Theo's hits Matthias in the jaw, and a second later, Matthias slams his fist into Theo's cheek, sending him reeling backwards into the wall.

"What are you doing?" I scream, but it's like neither of them even hear me.

Theo lunges at Matthias, and the two of them tumble to the ground with a loud crash. I watch in horror as they slug it out, both of them getting shots in and blood coming from God only knows which one.

"Stop! Someone's going to get hurt!" I yell, again to no avail since they aren't listening.

I grab Theo's shoulder and try to pull him off his brother, but as I work to separate them, Theo lurches back and I'm sent flying backwards. I land hard on the floor, hurting my tailbone.

"Are you all right?" he asks as he pushes Matthias away and stands up to help me.

Theo offers me his hand, and I take it, thankful for the assistance. "I'm okay. I just hurt my butt."

When I get back up on my feet, I see Matthias glaring at me. There's such venom in his eyes that I have to look away. I've never seen him so full of hate for me.

"Why were you fighting?" I ask Theo, praying it had nothing to do with me but knowing better.

This has been coming for weeks. I've dreaded the

very idea of it, but I knew it would happen sooner or later if Matthias kept acting the way he's been toward me.

He answers instead of Theo. "My brother seems to think he needs to defend your honor. Is that true, Ava?"

Every word out of his mouth seems filled with more viciousness than usual, especially when he says the word honor. I shake my head at his question, unsure what he means.

Theo wraps his arm around me. "Don't bother talking to him. It's a waste of time. The only thing he understands is a fist to his fucking face, which will happen again if you say another goddamned word to her."

For some strange reason, that makes Matthias smile. Turning his attention from me to Theo, he says, "Fine. I'll talk to you then. Did your girlfriend ever tell you about the time we spent together? We had a good time. Didn't we, Ava?"

Instantly, the hallway seems like it's shrinking, and the walls are closing in on me. I swallow hard, feeling like I'm going to be sick.

Horrified, I shake my head. "P—p—please, Matthias. Don't."

Theo stares at me with the purest look of hurt I've ever seen in my life. It's like his gaze is cutting into my chest and I can't turn away because I don't want him to feel any more pain.

He lets go of my hand, and when I search for it, he won't let me hold it again. I see in his eyes that he isn't sure what to think, so there's a chance this will be okay.

"Oh, yeah. Right down the hallway in my bedroom.

Snowbound together with nothing else to do but stay in bed all day. We barely came up for air, so we didn't really care about the weather, though."

With every word he says, my heart sinks. I should have said something to Theo when I had the chance all those weeks ago. He asked me what I thought his brother's problem was with me, and all I had to do was tell the truth. It was two days, for God's sake. He would have understood. I could have made it seem like it was a mistake, and he would have been able to accept it. Maybe we could have had a laugh about it and then moved on.

But none of that happened because I couldn't find a way to say the words without being obvious about how much I care about Matthias. God help me, I hate that I do, but I knew I wouldn't have been able to hide it.

So I said nothing, and our fate was set in motion, finally coming to fruition today in this horrible moment with the man I care so much about looking at me and waiting to hear me say it's all a lie.

"She didn't tell you?" Matthias asks, his cruelty making each word so painful before he mocks me. "Ava's been a naughty girlfriend it seems."

"Tell me he's lying. Just say it and I'll believe you over him."

Tears fill my eyes, making Theo get all blurry. All I can do is shake my head. This is what I've feared for weeks, and it's so much worse than I ever imagined.

"Little Ava isn't a very good liar. I don't know how she kept the secret for this long. The truth is written all over her face. Jesus, Theo. She's been lying to you the whole time."

Theo spins around and snaps, "Fuck you!"

There's so much hurt in his voice that my heart breaks. I try to get him to listen to me, but he won't even look at me.

"Please, Theo. I can explain. It had nothing to do with us. It was five years ago. It's nothing compared to all the time we've spent together."

Matthias sneers at my attempt to make Theo see he shouldn't care about this. "Yeah, a whole couple months. Not exactly a lifetime of dating bliss."

I keep reaching for Theo's hand, but he won't let me touch him. All he does is sadly shake his head.

"Please, don't let him ruin what we have," I plead.

Finally, he says in a voice full of hurt and betrayal, "What do we have, Ava? You've been lying to me this whole time. What else haven't you told me? How can I believe anything from you now?"

"Don't say that! Please, Theo," I beg, still reaching out for him, but he won't even let me get close now. "We can figure this out. It's not important. Not like everything we are together."

He steps back from me, taking all my hope he'll forgive me with him. "I feel like I don't even know you right now."

I can't hold back the tears at hearing that, and as they stream down my cheeks, he turns to leave. "Don't follow me. I don't want to talk to you right now."

Devastated, I watch him walk away and then turn to face Matthias. "Why would you do that? What do you get from hurting him?"

Full of anger, he snaps, "I did him a favor. He'll thank me someday."

"Why do you hate us?"

"I don't hate Theo. I hate you," he answers with venom dripping off each word.

Wiping my tears, I ask the question I've wondered about since he returned to this house. "Why? What did I ever do to you to make you hate me?"

Matthias doesn't answer immediately. I watch as he walks toward me and fear what may happen next. When he stops in front of me and stares down into my eyes, I'm not sure he won't hit me like he just did with Theo.

Then I see hurt in his eyes. Why is that there? How could he be hurt after what he just did?

"The first chance you got, you left without even saying goodbye. I shared parts of myself with you that I've never shared with another living soul. That time we spent together was some of the happiest of my life. But it obviously meant nothing to you since you ran away the first chance you got."

I'm stunned by what he's saying. "I didn't run away. I had to leave. My father sent me to my aunt's house. I didn't want to leave, Matthias. I didn't have a choice."

"So why didn't you even try to call or email or anything? Nothing in five years, Ava. Not a single fucking word."

I step back, confused. "That's not true. I told Theo to let you know I had to leave because my father was making me. Doesn't that count for something?"

In a low voice, he answers, "He never told me you said a word."

That can't be right. Theo promised me he'd give Matthias my message. Why wouldn't he?

All the years apart from Matthias come rushing back

to me. I thought about him so many times, but he's right. I never really tried to contact him.

He takes a step closer to me and says, "I thought about you every day you were gone. I wrote you letter after letter with not a single response. I tried to run away myself, willing to take the job my father had for me in London, but it didn't matter. You followed me there too."

What does he mean he wrote me? I never received a single letter.

"I'm sorry. I didn't mean to hurt you. I swear I didn't."

"You didn't hurt me. You cut my heart out, and then you haunted me. I can't tell you how many times my wife asked if there was someone else. She was sure I was in love with another woman. We were doomed from the start because of you. Then when she told me she was leaving, all I could think of was now we could have another chance."

He abruptly stops talking and looks away. I don't know what to say to all of this. Never in my wildest dreams did I think I mattered this much to him.

"I didn't know, Matthias."

He snaps his head around to face me, and all I see in him is anger again. "Well, now you do, and now you're as miserable as I've been for every moment you've been with my brother."

With another glare, he turns on his heel and storms away, leaving me alone in the misery we now share. I don't know if I can ever make up for what I've done with him, but I know I have to try with Theo. He didn't deserve to go through this. I have to make him see we can still be happy.

His door is closed, so I knock softly and say, "Theo, please open up. Talk to me. Please, Theo. I can explain. Just give me a chance."

A second later, he throws open the door and stands there staring at me like I'm some stranger and not the woman he said he loved. "I don't want to hear anything you have to say right now, Ava. Just leave me alone."

"I can explain. Please, Theo."

His dark eyes stare at me like he's seeing into my soul. "I gave you every chance. I asked you so many times why he was acting like he was, and every time you said you didn't know. But you did."

Before I can say another word, he slams the door in my face. My tears roll down over my cheeks as my heart breaks in two.

My best friend, the one person I've cared about my entire life, won't even talk to me. I doubt he'll ever forgive me, and I have no one to blame but myself. For as awful as Matthias was in telling Theo what happened between us, I'm the one who could have made sure none of this ever happened and he never got hurt like he just did.

Crushed, I walk back downstairs and leave the King house. For the first time since that snowy December day, I don't feel like I'm welcome here.

CHAPTER THIRTY-ONE

$\mathcal{M}$atthias

As I try to take my mind off all that's happened today by watching some TV, Marius walks into the game room and stands in front of me so I can't see a damn thing. Does no one in this house have any respect for anyone else?

Pushing him aside, I grumble, "What the fuck? Can't you see I'm doing something here?"

He glares down at me like I've done something to offend him, but I have no idea what his problem could be. "I'm trying to figure out what you're doing, Matthias, because I don't get it. Why did you do that to Theo and Ava?"

I look up at him for a moment before turning my focus back to the TV. "Mind your own business."

"You know what I think? I think you care about her."

I'm clearly not going to get to watch this show, so I turn to look at him, hoping this conversation can be over soon. One look at his face tells me he's serious.

"You don't know what you're talking about."

"Don't I? You're in love with her."

That gets him a well-deserved eye roll. "That's insane. I hate her."

"No, you don't. It was killing you that Theo was with her because you're crazy about her. From what I heard, you've loved her for years."

I say nothing to that. I'm tired of denying how I feel. I've pretended to hate her for far too long. I can't do it anymore. Whatever people want to think, let them.

Yes, I love Ava Sutton. I have for so long I can't remember not being in love with her. And yes, I'm a son of a bitch because I pretend to hate her.

When I don't respond, Marius says, "You know, you don't have to do things like that. You don't have to push people away all the time."

Great. Now this brother has decided to get on my last fucking nerve. I swear to God this is why I've sometimes wondered what it would have been like if my parents stopped at me and made me an only child.

"Nice of you to try your hand at counseling, Marius. Stick to photography."

But still he continues.

"I wonder if you even know you're doing it, to be honest. Ever since Mom died, you've been a miserable fuck. I get it. I miss her too. But you don't have to work so hard to be unhappy, Matthias."

I don't want to listen to any more of this, so I stand up and walk out. Everyone in this damn house thinks they know what's right and it pisses me off.

Since I can't seem to escape my family today, I figure I'll have to hole up in my room. All the better. It will mean I have less grief, at least for one day.

On my way there, Theo walks out of his bedroom. He's holding his suitcase, which means he's going.

When he sees me, he thrusts an envelope into my hand and without looking me in the eye, says, "Give this to her. I'm leaving."

"She says you were supposed to give me the message that she had to leave that day after the blizzard. Why didn't you?"

He shakes his head as he glares at me. "Because I knew that meant she fucking cared about you. She was mine, Matthias. Mine! You knew that."

"Yours? And that's the reason you left her here while you went off to live your life?"

My brother doesn't answer my question before he walks away. He's right. He always said he'd marry her when he was ready to settle down.

I want to do something to stop him, but after all I've done today, that's unlikely. I watch my brother—the person I've always been closest to in the world all my life—and I can't think of the words to say even if I could undo the damage I've caused.

Theo stops right before he gets to the stairs but doesn't turn around. His head hung and his voice tinged with more pain than I've ever heard in him, he says, "You should have told me you were in love with her when she and I got together. I'm your brother, Matthias.

You didn't have to do it like you did. I wouldn't have done that to you."

An ache like I've only felt once before when I found out Ava left five years ago fills my chest until it hurts to take a breath. How could I have done this to him? Are my feelings for her any more real or important than his are? In truth, he deserves her more than I do. He's been her best friend since they were children. What have I been to her that could compare to that?

I've been nothing but terrible to both of them, never once thinking about their happiness, and now he can't even look at me when he says he would have done something I never could.

I've been cruel for no reason other than I was jealous. I have no other excuse than that. And now that jealousy that's been eating me up inside for months has hurt Theo.

CHAPTER THIRTY-TWO

va

FOR A WEEK, I'VE HIDDEN AWAY UNDER THE COVERS and cried more than I thought possible for a human being. Just when I think I'm coming to grips with all that happened, a memory of my time with Theo washes over me and the tears come once more.

I had hoped to hit the anger stage by now, but that doesn't seem to be anywhere on the horizon. I don't know if I should be angry at Theo, though. All I felt when I watched his car drive away from the house was emptiness.

Like the most important thing in my life had just disappeared from it, leaving a hole inside me I can't imagine ever being filled again. He was my best friend since we were young enough to not know anything but how much we made each other smile. We spent hours every day together playing, and as the years passed, he never threw me aside for new friends or because he chose a girlfriend over me.

I loved him before I even knew what love was. Theo was the cornerstone of my life here on the King estate. When he had to go away on vacations, he would text or call me every day to tell me what he was doing and how much he wished I was wherever he was to share in his fun.

Even as an adult, he and I kept in touch. Maybe during the past five years the texts and phone calls hadn't been as frequent, but he was always in my heart and on my mind.

Yet now, he won't answer a single text I've sent in the past week. Day after day has passed with dozens of texts telling him how sorry I am, how I love him, and how I'm begging for forgiveness, but he hasn't responded to even one. I've tried to find the words to make him see I never meant to hurt him. All I want to know is he's still my Theo, still the person who's cared about me for all my life. If he doesn't love me because of what I've done, I'll understand even though I'll be crushed, but if he can't even talk to me because he can't stand what he now knows about me, I don't think I'll be able to go on.

I type out a text and send it, my hopes still soaring with each time I wait for his response. A few minutes go by, and I make the same excuses I have for the past seven days. He's busy. He didn't get the message yet. He'll text back as soon as he gets it. Theo always does. No matter what, he answers.

But then a half hour has passed, and he still hasn't said a word. I question whether he received it, so I check my phone to see if it was actually sent. It was. Then I check to see if he got it. He did, a few seconds after I clicked SEND.

Staring at my phone, I silently will him to respond. Answer me. Please. Just give me a single word to let me know you're thinking of me like I'm thinking of you. Say something so I know you don't hate me.

He will. I know he will this time. My Theo, my best friend, always responds.

When I check the time and see an hour has gone by, I know the truth. Just like with every text over the last week, he received it. Maybe he read it. Maybe he immediately deleted it, unable or unwilling to see what I have to say.

He can't forgive me.

My heart sinks as I admit that to myself. Will he ever be able to forgive me? He has to. He's my Theo. Every other time we've had a fight, he always forgave me, and I always forgave him. That's what friends do.

But that's the problem. He's not forgiving me for something I did as his friend. This is different. I need him to forgive me for something I did as his girlfriend.

What if he can't?

I feel so empty, like I've lost the most important part of me, and I may never get it back. What will I do if Theo can't forgive me? How will I live knowing he's in the world somewhere and refuses to talk to me or see me ever again?

My phone finally vibrates against the pillow, and I pick it up as my hopes soar. No matter how angry Theo is, he sent me a text back. He's not ignoring me anymore.

But the message isn't from him. It's from Lucas, the

lawyer. I've neglected my duties as an executor all week. I've begged off, claiming I'm sick. He's understanding, as always, and when I text back that I'm still under the weather, he immediately responds with a message telling me he hopes I feel better.

I'm not sure I'll ever feel better if Theo never answers me.

My thoughts drift back to that moment as I watched him drive away. He never said goodbye or anything. He just packed his things and left. My heart sank at the thought that he couldn't even tell me he was going.

The irony that Matthias likely felt something similar the day I left without even a word to him isn't lost on me. If he felt anything like I do, I deserved all of his hate. But I did tell Theo to let him know I had to go to my aunt's. Why didn't he relay that message?

If only he had, maybe what happened could have been avoided.

Taking a deep breath in, I lay my head back down on the pillow as the truth fills my brain. No, even though Theo never gave his brother my message, it isn't his fault that everything happened as it did. That's my fault. Even Matthias isn't totally to blame. I hurt him, and since that day, he's held a grudge that made him lash out every time he was around me. All I had to do was tell Theo the truth. If I had only been honest with him and told him Matthias and I were together five years ago, all of this misery could have been avoided.

This is my fault, and I'm the one who has to make things right. I don't have control over that, though. Only Theo does, and if he never answers my texts and calls, then his silence will be my punishment.

I call him for the third time today, and when I hear his voice in my ear saying, "You know what to do," I wish I did know how to fix this. I hate the thought of him sad because of me.

At the beep, I wait for a moment and then say the same words I've said every time I've called. "Theo, I don't know if you're getting this message, but I hope you are. I'm sorry. Please forgive me. I never meant to hurt you. If you could just call me or answer any of my texts so I can know that you don't hate me, I'd be the happiest person in the world. I'm so sorry, Theo."

I end the call and set my phone on the pillow next to me as I turn onto my side and watch for any text or call. He has to answer me sometime. I know he's hurt, but he'll call or text. I know he will.

Another hour goes by, and my phone doesn't make a sound. I know exactly how Matthias felt that day I left.

Unloved. Unwanted. Unimportant.

I don't know what to think about him. I should be furious and hate him for ruining things between Theo and me. Every time I say that, though, the truth comes rushing to the front of my mind. Matthias didn't lie in a single word he said about our time together. I may not like that he told Theo about us, but if he did that because of jealousy, how am I to blame him?

The truth is I haven't only been crying about what happened with Theo. I'm sad about Matthias too. I never wanted to hurt him either. That time we spent together meant something important to me. I didn't mean to break his heart by leaving.

A soft knock on my bedroom door tears me out of my sad thoughts. It's my father, just like it's been him a few times every day since everything happened and I came home and crawled into bed.

Every time, I've told him I don't want to talk and to please leave me alone. And every time, he's quietly walked away to leave me with my misery.

I know he wants to talk and try to make me smile. He wants to tell me things look bad but they're going to get better. He told me that every day after my mother passed away, even as he was struggling to not hide under the covers and let grief consume him over losing her. I needed those words then, but now I'm not sure they're true.

Things may never get better. If Theo won't talk to me, I'll have lost my best friend in the world. How can things be better if that happens?

"Ava, honey? Are you awake?" he says against my bedroom door.

"Yes, Dad. Come in."

The door opens slowly, and when he steps into the room, he looks almost afraid, like he doesn't know what to expect. He's surely heard me crying day after day, so he probably isn't sure what kind of condition I'll be in when he sees me for the first time in a week.

"Honey, are you okay?" my father asks with a gentle smile meant to cheer me up.

That question makes tears well in my eyes again because I'm not okay. I'm not sure I'm ever going to be okay again.

"What's up, Dad?" I ask, hoping to change the conversation so I don't start bawling again.

Tilting his head toward the door, he says, "Matthias is downstairs. He wants to see you."

Surprised, I sit up in bed at that news. I hadn't expected that to come out of my father's mouth.

"Do I have to?" I ask, afraid if I don't see him that he'll do something terrible to my father.

My question gets me a look of confusion. "Why would you have to talk to him?"

"Because I don't want this to cause a problem for you."

I don't explain what I mean because I don't want to scare him. He shouldn't have to worry that at any moment Matthias will swoop in and try to take the house from him. Mr. King made sure that we can stay here as long as we want, but I've worried about upsetting Matthias and him retaliating. Even worse is the fear that he'll fire my father. Mr. King left us money, but my father's job means the world to him.

My father walks over to the side of my bed and sits down next to me. "Max took care of me and you and your brother, honey. This house is ours for as long as we want it, and we have enough money to tell anyone we want we don't want to speak to them. That includes Matthias King."

I breathe a sigh of relief at that news. Mr. King has made us safe from everything, and for that, I can't thank him enough.

"But I will say this. He doesn't look like himself."

My father has a tendency to be far too kind, even to people who don't deserve it. His claim Matthias doesn't look like he usually does makes me wonder if he's been suffering for the past week because of what he did.

"What do you mean?"

"I'm not sure. He just seems different today."

I think about that for a few seconds before saying, "Fine. Let him up. A different version of him might be better."

My father stands up but hesitates before leaving. "Do you want me to hold off sending him up for a few minutes?"

Confused, I shake my head, but then I catch a glimpse of myself in the mirror above my dresser and understand what he means. Ordinarily, I'd be bothered by looking like something the cat drug in, but today's not a normal day. I don't care if this isn't my best look.

"No. He deserves to see the consequences of his actions. Let him up whenever you feel like it, Dad."

As I wait for Matthias to come upstairs, I look down at the clothes I've worn for seven days straight. My pale green T-shirt with the little turtle on the breast pocket and jean shorts probably smell to high heaven.

Oh well. If he doesn't like the view, he doesn't have to look.

A minute later, I hear a knock on my bedroom door. "Come in."

When he opens the door and walks in, I immediately see what my father meant. He does look different than usual. Something about him looks almost lost as he stands in front of my bed.

"What do you want, Matthias?" I ask, not even trying to be pleasant.

He sets a white envelope down on the comforter and looks over at me. "Theo asked me to give you this. I was going to give it to you when you came to the meeting with Lucas, but you never showed up, so I figured I'd come down here today."

I glance down at the envelope as fear races through me. All this time I've wanted to talk to Theo to explain how sorry I am, but now that I have the chance to see how he truly felt that day, I'm not sure I can read it.

Then he turns to leave, and I ask, "Is that it?"

Matthias doesn't look back at me as he remains silent for a long moment before finally answering, "I'm sorry."

He leaves without another word, and for a few minutes, I stare at that envelope next to my leg. Tears fill my eyes as I think about what Theo could have said.

When I can't hold off reading his note anymore, I slip it out of the envelope and instantly I'm sadder than I thought I ever could be.

AVA,

The time we spent together was some of the happiest in a long time for me. I wish I was the one for you, but that didn't turn out to be.

Goodbye.

Love,

Theo

I SOB INTO MY PILLOW, CLUTCHING HIS NOTE WHILE regret fills me. This can't be goodbye. Theo and I can at least be friends again, can't we? We've been through so much together all these years. I was there when his mother died, and he sobbed like a baby in my arms. He held me when my mother died and all I could do was cry. With every good day and bad, Theo and I had each other.

This can't be the end.

Grabbing my phone, I try to type out a text to him, but my tears make seeing my screen nearly impossible. I dry my eyes and try again, this time trying to find a way to make him see how terrible I feel about hurting him.

I'm sorry for what happened. I never wanted to hurt you. I loved the time we spent together, Theo. I hope someday you can forgive me.

Love,
Ava

I stare at my phone waiting for him to respond. He never does. After a while, I set my phone on my nightstand for the first time in a week and close my eyes.

Theo can't forgive me.

CHAPTER THIRTY-THREE

*M*atthias

A NOISE DISTRACTS ME FROM MY PHONE CALL, AND I look up from my laptop to see Ava standing in the doorway to my office. It's been a week since I walked down to her house to give her Theo's letter. A quick glance tells me she's doing better than she was that day, thankfully.

"I'm sorry. I didn't mean to interrupt. I'll come back later," she says quietly.

Shaking my head, I hold my hand up to stop her. "I'll be done in a minute. Please stay."

Confusion fills her expression, along with what I think may be suspicion at my attempt to be nice, but she stays all the same. She has no idea how happy I am to see her up and out of bed now.

I listen as the head of the petroleum division of King

Industries continues to talk about some issue she's been asking to meet with me about for three weeks. Distracted by Ava as she sits on the couch on the other side of my office, I nod and hum every few seconds to make it seem like I'm listening.

I'm not. All I can think about is how beautiful Ava looks today. Something about her seems different somehow, as if she's changed since I saw her last.

If only I could tell her that. I've never been that way, though. Theo has always been the one King who could flatter and charm better than the rest of us. It's why everyone loves him from the second he walks into their lives.

No wonder she fell in love with him.

Jennifer Sayton finishes telling me what she thinks I need to know, so I say, "Okay, get your section heads together and we'll have a meeting on Monday at eleven a.m. I'll read the reports you've sent and be up to speed by then."

Happy to be finished with my call, I hang up and walk over to the couch to sit down on the opposite end from Ava. She looks even more suspicious now. I can understand why she wouldn't trust me to be nice or kind today or any other day.

Except for those days we spent together, I've never been anything close to either of those things. I've made her pay over and over for leaving, but that's over. I don't want to hurt Ava anymore.

"I'm guessing you're here for the work we need to do with Lucas regarding the estate."

Ava nods and then hangs her head. "I'm sorry I

haven't been living up to my part. I just needed some time."

"Well, no worries. I made sure to take care of everything. I told Lucas you were sick and wanted us to keep going. He was fine with it. I didn't want anyone my father left things to in his will to have to wait. The charities especially need that money, so we went ahead and expedited everything."

For a moment, I don't think she understands what I mean. Then she shakes her head and says, "So all the money will be distributed, and we're done?"

I force a smile even as I have to say something that's tearing me up inside. "All done. You can leave and go wherever you need to."

Where she plans to go isn't a mystery. She'll be going with Theo now. As much as I want to stop her, I have no right. She loves him, and he loves her. They should be together. It's as if that's what was always meant to be. Her days with me were just a moment in time compared to the years they've cared for one another. It would be wrong to try to get in the way. I see that now.

My heart sinks when she stands up to leave. Some tiny part of me had hoped maybe she'd stay here with me, but after how I've acted toward her, that was a foolish thought.

"Thank you. I appreciate this, Matthias."

Pretending I'm fine, I shrug like none of this matters to me. Not her. Not seeing her leave. It's all fine.

"You're welcome, but it was no problem."

She walks out of my office, taking my last possible chance that she and I can ever be together with her.

Likely she'll leave to go be with Theo today. I can't think of that anymore. I've known this would happen once I gave her that letter. He probably told her he just needed a little time, like he always does when he gets angry. But now that he's had time to think about things, he'd be crazy if he hasn't called Ava begging her to come be with him.

All I can do is try to forget her and everything I feel. We were never meant to be. I see that so clearly now.

But I'll never be able to forget Ava or that time we spent together. It's just that now she and my emotions will stay in a place deep inside me so I can't hurt her or my brother ever again.

THE ATTEMPT TO SIMPLY ACCEPT THAT AVA IS NOW with Theo turns out to be harder than I thought it would be, and by nine that night, I'm standing outside his apartment staring up at what I'm pretty sure is his front window. I don't see any lights, which probably means they're together up there.

I don't know why I need to torture myself like this. How will knowing she's with him now make the sadness I feel go away? I'm happy for him, even if it's killing me inside. Isn't it enough to know they were able to overcome all that happened?

Fishing out a key he gave me a few years ago from my pants pocket, I head up to his apartment, knowing this is a mistake. I just need to see that they're together and then maybe I can go on with my life. At least that's what I keep telling myself as I ride up in the elevator to the eighth floor.

With each step I take down the hallway toward

apartment 813, my stomach clenches tighter and tighter. I shouldn't do this. Ruining their first night back together will only make things worse.

But I keep walking anyway and stop when I reach his apartment. I put my ear to the door to see if I can hear them, but there's nothing but silence. I slide the key into the doorknob and turn it to open the door, and when I step inside, it's all dark. I listen once more for any sign they're here, but his apartment is empty.

I ride down in the elevator as my mind fills with thoughts of Ava getting to travel the world with Theo as he races. She deserves that. Life on the estate was never enough for someone like her. She dreamed of excitement and fun, exactly what my brother offers.

This is how it should be. Ava and Theo living the life two people in love are supposed to have. She'll get to experience all sorts of wonderful things with him. He's got money, success, and now he has the one person who makes his life complete.

On my way out of his building, I see the doorman. I don't know why I need to ask him if he's seen them. It's just another way of torturing myself, but maybe I deserve all the pain I can feel for all I've done.

"Excuse me, do you know Theo King? He lives in apartment 813," I ask the man as he holds the door open for another tenant.

He smiles, just like everyone does when they hear my brother's name. "Oh, Mr. King! I absolutely know him."

"I'm his brother, Matthias King. I was upstairs looking for him, but he doesn't seem to be home. Did he and a woman leave recently?"

With a shake of his head, the man says, "Oh, Mr.

King, your brother left yesterday. He told me he was looking forward to a race in France somewhere this weekend. He had no lady with him when he left, though. He was all alone. I wished him luck, and then I got him into a cab to take him to the airport. I'm guessing he's already in France by now."

I smile halfheartedly and shake the man's hand. "Thank you for all your help. I appreciate it. Good evening."

As I walk down the street, I take one last look up at Theo's apartment as sadness fills me. He didn't wait for her. Why didn't he wait? He must know she's devastated at losing him. Didn't he tell her he just needed time in his letter?

I stop at the corner and take my phone out of my pocket to send him a text.

YOUR DOORMAN TOLD ME YOU'RE RACING THIS weekend. Good luck.

THERE'S SO MUCH MORE I WANT TO SAY BUT SENDING it in a message doesn't seem right. He never replies to my text, and I don't try a second time.

After what I did, I deserve it if my brother never speaks to me again.

CHAPTER THIRTY-FOUR

va

MY FATHER AND I SIT AT OUR MODEST KITCHEN TABLE we've had since I was only a little girl. It routinely feels like it's going to collapse, and the chairs creak whenever anyone sits down on them. Still, I think it reminds my father of a time when my mother was still here and all four of us happily lived in this house.

"So? Any plans for what you want to do now?" he asks in a chipper voice.

I shake my head and force a smile. "I'm not sure. I guess I could do anything, right?"

"Pretty much. Max always cared for you like one of his own children, so now you get to have all the advantages they have. I thought maybe you'd fly to Europe like you used to talk about."

The mere mention of Europe makes me want to cry.

That's where Theo is. I know he's racing this weekend in France. I could fly there and try to see him, but I won't. His letter told me it's over, and I don't have a choice but to accept that.

Another shake of my head is followed by another forced smile. "Not now. Maybe another time."

Sadness fills my father's eyes, and he frowns. "Oh. I just thought that since…"

He doesn't finish his sentence, thankfully. I don't think I can hear Theo's name out loud right now. It's still too soon and my emotions are too raw.

"You could travel somewhere else. How about Italy? You always said you'd love to visit Rome and Pompeii. Now that you have money, you can go in style. First class all the way for you, Ava."

I chuckle at how he says that. "Yeah, I guess. I hear first class flights include some nice perks. Drew told me he got upgraded one time and there were free drinks, extra snacks, and even warm towels to clean his hands."

My father's eyes get big. "I had no idea. I think the next time I fly down to see him, I'm going to fly first class then. Extra snacks are always a good thing to me."

Taking his hand in mine, I give it a squeeze for how cute he can be sometimes. "You're definitely first class to me, Dad. You deserve to have only the best after all these years working for Mr. King."

He gives mine a tiny squeeze and says, "It wasn't bad, though. Max was great to work for. He never treated me like an inferior. I was his friend and someone he could rely on. That's why he took care of us in his will. I think he hoped you'd finish school so you can be a nurse. It meant a lot to him that you took time away from your education to take care of him."

"I didn't do much. Rachel did all the real nursing work with him. Most of the time I just sat with Mr. King so he wouldn't be alone."

"Well, it meant the world to him. So will you go back to school? You don't have long to go before you graduate."

My father sounds so hopeful that I don't want to disappoint him by saying I don't think I'm ready for school yet. I need to be able to focus, and just like right after my mother died and I had to take time off, I feel the same way now.

I've come to realize I feel sad not only because of losing Theo but also because of Mr. King's death and all that's happened with Matthias. It's been a hard few months, and until I'm able to put at least some of it in the past, I can't even consider the idea of returning to school.

"Someday, Dad. I promise I'll get my degree. Just not right now. I'm still pretty down about everything, so I'd be no good at school. But I'll get back."

He smiles and pats my hand. "I know you will. That's how you are, Ava. You feel things so strongly, so when it gets too much, you need a break. It's smart, actually. I think more people would be in better shape if they did like you do. But I also know you're focused, and you'll get back to your studies and graduate just like Max hoped."

Eager to change the subject, I take a deep breath and ask, "So what do you plan to do with all your money he left you? Are you planning on traveling down to see Drew and the family soon?"

A guilty grin tells me he's been hiding things from me. "I'll definitely go down there, but I have news I wanted to share with you first. I've made a decision."

I love when he teases me like this. His decisions always turn out to be something small, like he's going to paint the living room a different shade of blue. He can be so playful at times.

"Oh yeah? Let me guess? You're going to get a new range and refrigerator? Not to pry, but I saw you left some pictures of appliances on the table in the living room."

"I was looking at new refrigerators, but not for here, honey. I've decided it's time for me to leave this house. I stayed here long after your mother and I planned. We wanted to travel when I retired, but then she died, and all those plans went up in smoke. Now that Max is gone and I don't have to work anymore, I'm going to buy a cabin on a lake somewhere and live out my days fishing and relaxing. He made me swear to him I wouldn't work until my final days like he did, and I plan to live up to that promise."

My father's announcement hits me like a truck. Leaving here? I never imagined my father would live anywhere else but in this house. He loves it here. This is where he and my mother lived the entire time they were married. How can he leave?

"Are you sure, Dad? I mean, you've always loved living here."

Nodding, he smiles. "I loved it here because I was working for Max. I'm not working as the estate manager anymore. I don't even think Matthias is going to have one. It's time for me to move on, and a cabin on a lake where I can fish and you kids and my grandkids can come visit sounds like the perfect retirement to me."

I love that for him. After all these years doing for everyone else, my father is finally going to live for himself. He deserves that.

"That's great, Dad. I guess I'm the last Sutton to leave."

Even as I say that, I feel sad. This has been my home my entire life. It seems like a lot of things I've relied on since I was a child are leaving me.

"You'll go when it feels right. I know you will."

"Have you found a place yet? I'd love to hear about it."

He pulls out his phone and says, "As a matter of fact, I have. A nice place on a lake in North Carolina. I'll be halfway between Drew and you, assuming you choose to stay here in New York. It's got a dock and three bedrooms I hope will be in use more often than not."

As he swipes through the pictures of this lake house he's found, I want to be happy for him, but all I feel is sadness. Everything's changing so quickly. I'm not sure I'm ready to lose another person in my life so soon after Theo and Mr. King.

Even more, when I leave, my connection to this estate will be broken forever. I'll have no reason to return if my father isn't here. That means I'll never see Matthias again.

I don't understand after all that's happened why that makes me sad. I should hate him for what he's done. I just can't. Too much of what happened is my fault.

When I finish looking at the pictures and hand my

father his phone, I ask, "Have you told Matthias you're going to be leaving?"

He nods and quietly answers, "I told him today. He seemed to take it almost somberly, to be honest. For the first time, he reminded me of his father when I gave him the news."

"Oh. That's good. I didn't know if he'd give you a hard time or anything."

My father stands up from the table. "I think after what happened, he's changed, Ava."

I say nothing to that. Maybe he has. I don't know.

"Well, I'm off to bed. I need to get to sleep early tonight. Your brother and the girls are going to FaceTime me in the morning, and I swear those two require me to have at least two cups of coffee beforehand to understand them."

He's so cute when he talks about his granddaughters. They are like two tiny sacks of dynamite. "Okay, Dad. I'm going to stay up for a while. I feel like I spent a month in bed, so going to sleep early is the last thing on my mind these days."

Leaning over, he kisses the top of my head. "You're young, Ava. You shouldn't even be thinking of sleeping at all at this age. Go out and have some fun, honey."

I nod, knowing he's right. The problem is I don't know if I can have fun anymore. Even more, I don't know if I deserve to have any fun after what I did.

Maybe if I took a walk I'd feel better.

Before he goes upstairs, I ask, "Dad, when I was away at Aunt Jessie's, did I get any letters?"

He nods and grimaces. "I don't know if what I did

was right, but I wanted to save you from heartache. I hope you'll understand."

So Matthias did write to me.

"How many letters did he send, Dad?"

My father shakes his head. "I lost count, honey. I'm sorry."

"Were there a lot?"

Looking down at the floor, he quietly answers, "Yeah."

I don't know what to say. I can't be angry with my father, even though I hate that he worked so hard to make sure Matthias and I were never together. If only I knew how he felt all that time.

It feels like so much of my life recently has been if onlys.

"I wish you hadn't done that, Dad. Those were my letters. I deserved to know about them."

My father nods, and I see sadness in his face when he looks at me. "I'm sorry, Ava. I thought I was doing the right thing. I see now I was wrong."

He walks up the stairs as I try to find something good that's come from all that's happened. But I can't. Worst of all, the one person I'd talk to about everything isn't there anymore.

After slipping on my flip flops, I head outside into the warm June night. The smell of honeysuckle in the air fills my nose, bringing back a million memories from all the times I spent playing on the estate. I try not to think of my longtime playmate because that just hurts too much. He's off living his life, and I have to live mine.

Even if I don't know how to move on.

I find myself up at the main house and notice the office light is still on. I walk in through the kitchen door and see that Eleanor has quit working for the day. I'm actually surprised Matthias has kept her on since it's just him and Marius now, and his brother will probably be leaving soon.

Everyone has a life to get back to, it seems. Everyone but Matthias and me.

When I reach his office, he's sitting behind the desk still dressed in his dark suit after a long day at work. I see he's got a glass of whiskey in front of him, but he doesn't seem to be doing much in the way of drinking it.

My father was right when he said Matthias had to give up more than any of his brothers. They get to come and go as they please, choosing what to do with their lives based entirely on what makes them happy.

But not him. He's here running King Industries, even though I know he'd rather be doing something else. Like his art.

"Ava, is something wrong? Would you like to come in?" he asks, pulling me out of my thoughts.

I walk into his office and sit down on the black leather couch. I feel like I'm intruding. "My father told me he's leaving to go enjoy retirement in a cabin by a lake in North Carolina. Do you have plans to move a new estate manager into the house any time soon?"

His father explicitly stated in his will that the house was to be ours for as long as we wanted to live there, but if Matthias intends on hiring a new estate manager to replace my father, then they'll have to stay somewhere. I wouldn't blame him if he said he needed me to find someplace else to live.

Matthias smiles and shakes his head. "No. I don't

intend on having an estate manager since all my brothers will be living elsewhere."

"Would you be okay if I stayed then? It's really the only home I've ever had, and I'd like to keep living there." I stop and then add, "At least for a little while."

For some reason, he looks surprised when I say that. "I thought you'd be in a hurry to leave once you got your inheritance."

I shrug, knowing that's probably what my father thought too. "I'm not sure what I want to do, to be honest. So I thought I'd stick around for a little while until I figure it out."

Lifting his glass of whiskey to his lips, he takes a drink and swallows it so his Adam's apple bobs up and down before he says, "Feel free to stay as long as you like, Ava."

No meanness or cruel words. Just normal conversation.

"Thank you."

He smiles and returns to his work as I watch and realize my father was right. There is something changed about Matthias.

CHAPTER THIRTY-FIVE

va

PEOPLE STREAM BY AS EDEN AND I SIT OUTSIDE HER favorite restaurant and I try not to let myself get down again about everything. She called me so many times in the past few weeks, and every time I said I couldn't meet her.

Until today.

This morning when she called, I finally felt like maybe I could venture off the estate and act like a normal woman in her mid-twenties and not the pathetic mess I've been since Theo left. It actually felt good to say yes to Eden's invitation to get together, and although she has no idea how worried I was I would regret it, I'm enjoying myself for the first time in far too long.

"Are you going to eat more of your sandwich, or

should I assume you're on some hunger strike or something?"

I give her an eye roll she deserves and take a bite of my turkey club. Setting the quarter of the sandwich back down on the plate, I shake my head. After swallowing it, I frown at her.

"Better?"

"I guess. I mean, almost half a club sandwich eaten is better than nothing. So do you want to talk about things yet, or are we going to pretend you're fine?"

Leave it to Eden to cut to the chase not halfway through lunch.

"What do you want to talk about?" I ask, knowing full-well she, like my father, thinks that if I talk out my feelings that I'll feel better.

Maybe I will. I'm just afraid if I start talking about Theo now, I'll start crying right here on this busy street surrounded by all these people.

She leans in toward me and whispers in front of my face, "Well, the options are my work, which may be the most boring thing on the planet, or how you're doing. Your choice."

I focus on her stunning green eyes and know she's not going to give up. Maybe it's time to talk about everything.

"For the record, I think your work is interesting. You're the assistant to the president of one of the largest banks in the country. Stop acting like you're boring. But since you're going to keep pushing because that's who you are, fine, let's talk about how I'm doing."

Stopping to take a sip of my water, I watch her level her gaze on me as she waits not-so-patiently for me to continue. After a few seconds of silence, her eyes open wide as any hint of patience disappears.

"Is this my cue to start asking questions? Because I have a ton, and I'm happy to start peppering you with them like I'm some idiot reporter on the red carpet and you're some star who just hit it big."

I shrug. "Feel free."

"First and foremost, why did you and Theo break up? You two have been best friends forever, so I just figured when you told me you guys had gotten together that it would be the world's greatest love match. I mean, everyone says relationships are so much better when you're best friends with the guy you love. So what happened?"

With a heavy sigh, I answer her question. "He found out something terrible about me and couldn't forgive me."

Eden's mouth drops open, and for a few seconds, she just stares at me like some fish gasping for air before she shakes her head in total disbelief. "That is bullshit. You tell me right now what he couldn't forgive. Theo King couldn't forgive you, Ava Sutton? I refuse to believe that."

"Well, it's true."

After all that's happened, I should just tell her. I'm not embarrassed of what I did with Matthias. Yes, I should have told Theo. It was a mistake not to. But what his brother and I did those two snowy December days wasn't, and I won't say it was.

Eden tilts her head to the right and screws her face into a grimace. "Do I have to ask politely what you did that Theo can't seem to forgive? Just tell me already. I'm dying here!"

I take a deep breath and let it out slowly through my nose as my heart begins to beat wildly. Why am I nervous about admitting the truth? It's not like I killed someone or anything. I had sex. A lot of sex. With a certain person. So what? People have sex all the time.

Finally, I have no more air in my lungs to expel and say, "I slept with his brother."

My friend looks like someone's hit her with a stun gun. She shakes oddly for a few moments like she's twitching from a jolt of electricity, and then she sits back in her chair and opens her mouth to speak, but nothing comes out.

When she seems to recover, she utters only a single word. "What?"

"You heard me. I slept with his brother."

A woman passing by our table looks down at me as I say that and gives me a smile. Nice to know I can amuse perfect strangers with my messed-up life.

Eden leans in toward me, still unsure about what I said. "You slept with his brother?"

The shock in her voice is unmistakable. I guess I'm not the type of person anyone expects to hear those words from.

I nod, sighing again. "Yeah. I slept with his brother."

Now that she's heard me say that a few times, she seems able to string together some thoughts and says, "When? Where? Never mind. Forget those minor details. Who? Which King brother did you sleep with?"

As soon as the question leaves her mouth, she reaches

over and shoves my arm. "Oh, my God! You slept with Marius King!"

I shake my head almost violently as memories of her wanting to do exactly that march through my mind. "No! I did not sleep with Marius."

"Kellen? I mean, I could see it since he's got those King looks, but he's always seemed so much younger than us. I know it can't be Ronan. He's way too young compared to you, isn't he?"

Now that she's listed every King brother but the one I actually slept with, I wait for her to finally figure it out. She doesn't, though. She simply keeps talking about how the youngest two King brothers are the last people she would have ever thought about in a sexual way.

Frustrated, I swat at her as she moves to shove my arm again and snap, "No, I didn't sleep with Kellen or Ronan! It was Matthias. How could you not figure that out?"

My outburst surprises her and leaves her speechless once more. Odd that she never even considered the oldest King brother.

After nearly a minute, she says, "Matthias King? I didn't realize you two even hung out."

"We didn't. Not until one snowy day between Christmas and New Year's that last time you were at your grandmother's."

Once again, Eden's face twists into a confused grimace. "My grandmother died almost five years ago, Ava."

Nodding, I shrug. "I know."

"And this is what got Theo's shorts in a tangle? You slept with his brother once five years ago? I know you haven't continued to sleep with him since he moved away, didn't he? He went to London or somewhere else in Europe, right?"

"Yes."

"I don't understand, Ava. You and his brother slept together five years ago, and Theo can't forgive that? He was a manwhore all through high school, and something tells me he hasn't stopped being that, especially since he became a world-famous race car driver. Were you supposed to sit at home doing your nun routine while he slept with anyone who smiled at him?"

Anger begins to seep into Eden's voice now, which I expected once I told her the truth. It's not that she never liked Theo, but every time I've ever joked around with her that he always said I was the future Mrs. Theo King, she never failed to point out that my friend who was planning for us to be married one day was busy fucking anything with legs and a nice rack.

"I don't know. All I know is he found out, and he won't talk to me now. He left the estate right after he found out, and ever since then, he won't answer my texts or calls."

Tears begin to fill my eyes, but I turn my head to stare off at two men arguing in front of a building nearby so I can force my sadness away. I promised myself I wouldn't cry over Theo anymore. He's made his choice. I can't change that.

"What a dick Theo King is! I know you think he's the next best thing to sliced white bread, honey, but this is pure dick behavior right here. Five years pass after you sleep with his brother for one night and he can't forgive you? He can go fuck himself is what I say."

Desperately needing to lighten the conversation so I don't burst into tears, I turn back to look at her and sigh. "It wasn't just once, if I'm being honest."

Yet again, Eden stares at me in shock. "You didn't just sleep with Matthias once? What the hell, Ava? I thought we were best friends. I've never kept a secret from you, and now I find out you've kept this torrid love affair hidden for five years. Forget Theo and his fragile male ego. I want to know every dirty detail about you and his brother."

"I might need a drink," I say with a giggle.

"And now you're saying you need alcohol to tell me? Get the hell out of here! Spill the tea now, girl. You start talking while I get the waiter. I want to hear every detail."

I'm thankful Eden is the way she is and our conversation has veered off into gossiping because if she had been serious about what happened with Theo, Matthias, and me, I don't think I could have taken it. She waves over our server and orders us two white wines before setting her elbows on the table and leaning toward me with nothing but curiosity in her expression.

"It was that day you called me from your grandmother's house. The electricity went out in my house because of the blizzard—well, actually, it turns out it didn't, but I'm not sure what happened there."

Her green eyes get as big as saucers. "Enough with the minutiae! Get to the good stuff. Where did it happen? Was he good? Oh, my God! I remember Maia talking about Marius. Is Matthias big too?"

My cheeks heat up from a blush as I think back to our time together. "Yes, he's good. And yes, he's big. I went up to the main house because I didn't have any electricity, and he was there. All his brothers had come into the city with my father and Mr. King, so it was just us and Eleanor. Jonesy was there too. He was the gardener."

"Unless you're about to tell me he joined in, I don't give a damn about the gardener. So you and Matthias just hooked up? I can't believe it! What's he like? He was so far ahead of us in school I don't think I know a thing about him. Well, other than he's hot and a billionaire. Oh, and he's hung like a horse, assuming what you said means the same as what Maia used to say about Marius."

I think for a moment about how I want to describe Matthias, and after the waiter drops off our glasses of wine, I say, "He's intense. Yeah, that's the best way to describe him. I don't think I've ever met anyone who feels things like he does. He's also an artist. I had no idea until that day, but he showed me some of his drawings. They're really good. He drew me."

For a second, I stop and then add, "Nude."

Eden nearly spits out her mouthful of wine at that little piece of information. "He drew you nude? Oh, my God! Maybe Theo has a good reason for breaking up with you. I mean, his brother must have been pretty incredible to get you to pose nude for him."

"Theo doesn't know that. He just knows we were together," I say quietly.

"Who told him?"

"Matthias."

A smile lifts the corners of Eden's perfect mouth. "So he sees you with his brother for the past few months and then tells him about your little tryst five years ago? Sounds like Matthias wants things to start up again between you two."

Shaking my head, I think about the few times he and I have spoken since that fateful day. "I don't think so. I live right there on the estate, and he barely speaks to me when he sees me. If he's interested in me, he has a funny way of showing it."

As I say that, I think about all that time he spent acting like he hated me when he actually wanted to be with me. Is it possible Matthias does want us to start over?

"I bet he does, but since you're moping around like some sad sack over his brother, that's not exactly giving him the green light."

"I think he feels guilty that he broke Theo and me up and chased his brother away."

God, this conversation might require more than a single glass of wine.

"You want to know what I think?" Eden says with a big smile. "I think Theo is an ass, and I say you go back to your house, get dressed up in something gorgeous, and march up to that main house and show Matthias what he's missing."

She says that with such strength, but I don't have much of that lately. I don't even know if Matthias and I would work together, and if we made a mess of things this time, I might end up homeless.

I shake my head at her suggestion. "No. Things are just as they're supposed to be. He and I are acquaintances, just like we always should have been. I

343

just hope he and Theo can make amends someday. Then maybe we can all be friends."

Eden tilts her glass back to swallow the last bit of her wine. "Fine, but something tells me things aren't over with you and Matthias King, no matter what you think."

CHAPTER THIRTY-SIX

M atthias

EVERY DAY, I SEE HER OUT MY OFFICE WINDOW, AND each time she takes my breath away with how beautiful she is. It's been a month since she asked me if I would mind if she stayed in the carriage house when her father moved away. It took everything in my power not to tell her how it's going to break my heart when she finally goes. She's the only thing that makes living in this house bearable, even though I rarely talk to her anymore and only get to see her from a distance.

This is my punishment for what I've done. She's so close, but I never let myself speak to her. I don't deserve it anyway, and there's a very good chance if we did speak again, she'd tell me to go fuck myself after all the heartache I caused her.

I have that and so much more coming that I'm surprised she hasn't said anything to me yet. Whatever she does isn't half of what she ought to do to me. Ava's too kind to exact the kind of revenge I deserve.

So I do it to myself by letting myself see her but nothing else.

This morning, instead of dealing with whatever problems cropped up overnight for King Industries, I watch out the window as she talks to that groundskeeper. Dressed in white shorts and a red T-shirt, she looks like she's gotten some sun recently. Her legs are tan, and as I let my gaze drift down to her ankles, I can't help but remember the two of us complimenting one another on having nice legs.

She seems to get more beautiful with every passing day. I can't imagine what's going through my brother's head to leave her for all this time. If I knew she loved me, there wouldn't be a creature or machine powerful enough to keep me away from her. Theo's being stupid, but he refuses to respond to my calls and texts, so I can't tell him what he's missing. He should know. That he doesn't makes me wonder about him.

Is his pride worth so much more to him than her love? If so, then he's beyond help.

As I stare out the window at her laughing with the groundskeeper, I wonder what they're talking about. He looks genuinely happy to be with her, but that's not surprising. Ava has a way of making even the most mundane things seem special when she's a part of them.

"I'm guessing this is the hardly working part of that saying?"

I slowly turn around in my chair to see Marius smiling at me. "What are you talking about?"

He points toward the window. "You know. Working hard or hardly working? I'm thinking you're a fine example of hardly working. What's so interesting out there anyway?"

Shaking my head, I pretend it's nothing. "Just looking at the grass. I guess I'm easily distracted today."

Marius doesn't believe that for a second, as he shouldn't. I've never been a fan of anything concerning the lawn. Walking toward my desk, he leans over to the right and sees what I've been watching for the past fifteen minutes.

"Ah, that explains it. You know, if you're that crazy about her, why don't you actually make some effort to be with her instead of doing your stalker routine in here?"

I don't answer his question. Anything I say would sound stupid anyway to Marius. A lot like Theo, if he cared for Ava, he'd just walk out there and talk to her. Then again, he wouldn't have been the meanest fucker in the world to her either.

My brother sits down in the chair in front of my desk and folds his arms across his chest. "So you're actually happy just watching her from afar? Is this some kind of self-imposed penance you've got going on?"

Since it's clear I'm not going to be able to escape this conversation, I might as well be honest. "Yes. I'm sure you find that ridiculous, but you're you and I'm me."

He arches a single eyebrow and hums. "Hmmm… sounds pretty fucked up to me."

As I shuffle papers around in front of me to look like

I'm busy and he's now interrupting me, I ask, "Did you come in here for some specific reason, Marius?"

"Just to say hi. We do live in the same house for the time being, Matthias."

I stop pretending to appear like I'm busy and look over my desk at him. "Hi. Anything else?"

For some reason, that makes him laugh. "No, but I'm starting to feel like I'm talking to a robot right now. I just thought you might like to hang out for a little while."

"I can't. I've got a ton of work I need to do," I say, returning to my paper shuffling.

"So I saw when I walked in. Tell me, Matthias. Don't you think you've paid enough for who you are?"

That makes me stop what I'm doing and stare at him in confusion. "What does that mean?"

Marius looks over the things on my desk and shakes his head. "You never wanted to be this. You were forced to be what Dad wanted. If Mom hadn't died, you may have escaped this life, but once she was gone, it was like Dad saw nothing but remaking you in his image. The four of us watched it and were sure you would rebel because we knew you hated the very idea of working for the family business. You never did, though."

Listening to my brother narrate the past five years of my life makes me feel like someone's put that familiar weight on my chest that threatens to suffocate me if I don't do something to remove it. No, I never wanted this. That didn't matter. As the oldest son, I had no say. This was my fate.

I don't look at him when I say, "I didn't have a choice."

"That's what I'm talking about. Once Mom wasn't around to keep Dad from forcing this on you, your choices were gone. Don't you think that's enough punishment for you? You care about Ava. Let her know that."

He has no idea what he's talking about. Things are always so easy for him. He doesn't make mistakes that hurt everyone around him.

"Not after all I've done to her. She may have been able to forgive me for all the cruel things I said, but now that she's lost Theo, I can barely even face her. I don't know what the hell is wrong with him. He should have come back here already and taken her away."

When Marius doesn't say anything, I look over and see him wearing a strange expression. "What? Do you think I'm wrong?"

"Theo can't forgive her, Matthias. He can't forgive you either, but I think you know that. But he's not coming back for her," my brother quietly says.

"You've spoken to him? What did he say?"

Marius blows the air out of his lungs and shrugs, but I can tell what he has to say bothers him. "Just that he can't forgive her. You know Theo. Everything is absolutes with him. He loved her since they were kids, and I don't think he ever thought she grew up. To him, Ava was that girl who adored him. When he found out she wasn't that person he'd created in his head but a real person who does things he doesn't agree with, I don't think he could handle it."

I toss a pen across my desk as I listen to his explanation, shaking my head. "Then he's a goddamned fool. She and I had a couple days. That was it. Theo and Ava have a lifetime together. Anyway, it isn't like she cheated on him or anything. Fuck, he went through girlfriends like they were water even before he became the famous driver he is now. All the while she was here adoring him, just like you said. This is what you get when you think someone is going to wait until you're ready. He should have seen what she was to him instead of saying over and over that Ava was the type of girl you marry, not the type you mess around with."

"See, that's the problem. He put her up on a pedestal and then expected her to act like that perfect girl. The reality that she would have been with you isn't something he can accept because he still thinks she should behave like he thought she should."

Disgusted, I sit back in my chair and stare up at the ceiling. Theo needs to stop thinking Ava's imperfect because she didn't live up to his idiotic standards.

"You need to tell him he's fucking up. Tell him to forgive her and take her away from here. She'll go."

"And you won't do a thing to stop her? Don't you think what you feel for her is important enough to even try?"

Leveling my gaze on him, I answer him truthfully. "No. She loves him. I have to accept that."

"You know, I think you're wrong. She has all the money she could possibly want now after Dad left her and her family enough to live very comfortably. She can afford to go anywhere, including where Theo is. She hasn't gone anywhere, though. Why? I don't think they have the love match you think they do if neither one of them is willing to go after the other."

My brother has no idea what he's talking about. "She's giving him space after what happened. What he should be doing is putting his fucking pride aside and forget everything I said. I can't believe he's not coming back for her."

"I don't think he ever loved her, to be honest. He loved this fantasy girl he built up in his mind, and when it became clear she had feet of clay, he bailed. That's not love, Matthias."

Standing from my desk, I look down at Marius as I walk out, tired of talking about this subject. "Then he's a bigger fucking fool than I ever thought possible."

Behind me, he says, "From where I'm sitting, both of you are being foolish when it comes to her."

I need to get away from him and that office to clear my head. Heading outside to the beautiful August afternoon, I make my way around the back of the house as the heat of the day surrounds me. After only a few minutes, my black suit becomes stifling, so I take my jacket off and find the nearest tree for some shade.

Closing my eyes, I try to push what Marius told me out of my mind, but I can't. Theo isn't coming back for her. Every damn day I've waited to see him drive up the road, knowing the only reason he'd return to this house was to get her. I've emotionally prepared myself by repeating those terrible words I said, a constant reminder of what I did.

He can't make this mistake. It will haunt him for the rest of his life.

I take my phone out of my jacket and call him for what feels like the fiftieth time since he left that day. He never answers my calls, but maybe if I leave him a message, he'll finally realize he's losing the best thing in his life.

When he actually answers, I'm stunned into silence for a second. "I would have thought you'd have something to say after calling me for weeks on end, Matthias," Theo snaps.

"Why haven't you come back here for her?" I blurt out, unable to pretend with mindless talk of the weather or polite questions about what he's been doing since he left.

"I'm not interested in talking about this. If that's all you called about, I'm going now."

God, he sounds so closed off. I've never heard him like this. He seems like a stranger to me.

"Don't do this, Theo. Don't let your pride get in the way of being with Ava. She's here. All you have to do is come get her. She'll go with you."

"You sound like her. I swear to God she's texted or called me at least ten times a day for weeks."

The way he talks about her trying to reach him is so cold. What's wrong with him? Why doesn't he see the mistake he's making?

"Then why haven't you talked to her? Jesus, Theo. She loves you. Don't let a couple days out of a lifetime make you do something stupid."

"Says the person who made sure I knew about those couple days."

I'm not getting through to him. I have to, though. It's the least I can do for both of them.

"I'm sorry. I've told you that in messages and voicemails until I'm blue in the face, and I accept that you don't want to hear it. Fine. But you're fucking this up, and you're never going to forgive yourself if you don't come back for her, Theo."

He falls silent, and I hope he's thinking about what I'm saying. All he has to do is call her, and I know she'd forget his silence for the past weeks. I know she would.

"If it was anyone but you..." he says, his voice dropping to barely a whisper.

"Why does that matter? So she's not a vestal virgin. You couldn't have thought she was waiting for you all these years."

Theo doesn't say anything, and after a few seconds, I wonder if he's still there. Then in a quiet voice, he says, "Marius I could have handled. Not you."

"Why? What does it matter?" I ask, unsure what he means.

A heavy sigh fills my ears. "I knew that morning we came back from the city after the blizzard. She was way too upset about having to go up to her aunt's, and when she told me to let you know she had to go, I knew. Something had happened during the storm. Anyone else in the world and I wouldn't have cared."

"Why does it matter? It was two days, Theo. You and she have a lifetime together. She and I had two days."

My brother doesn't respond, and I feel my chance to convince him of the colossal mistake he's making begin to slip away. I don't know what to say to make him see what he's losing by not coming for her. I don't understand him at all.

Finally, he says, "I'll tell you what, Matthias. You have her. She would have told me about what happened between you two if she didn't care about you. You remember that I know her better than anyone else, right?

That's how I know those couple of days meant something to her. There's nothing in your way now. She's right there and all yours. I wish you two good luck. Have a nice life."

The call ends, leaving me sick to my stomach that I utterly failed to make him see he's making the biggest mistake of his life. I could try again, but by the sound of his voice, I know he's made up his mind.

I sit there for hours trying to accept what my brother said. He made it sound so easy. She's all yours. As if Ava doesn't remember all the terrible things I said and did. Damnit, he doesn't seem to know her at all.

Then after a while, a tiny flicker of hope ignites inside me. Maybe he and Marius are right. Maybe she could at some point forgive me. I'd have to show her I deserve it and I deserve her. But that's assuming she wants me like I want her.

"I guess I'll never know if I don't try," I mumble to myself before standing up from under the tree.

As if my feet have a mind of their own, I find myself walking down toward the carriage house a few minutes later. I'm not sure what I plan on saying to her. I have no plan at all, in fact.

When I see her sitting on the porch reading a book, I almost talk myself out of this. No. I have to at least try.

I stop at the end of the sidewalk that leads up to her house and take a deep breath in, letting it out in an excited rush before I say, "Ava, would you like to come up to the house for dinner tonight?"

She lifts her head and stares out at me oddly for a long moment before saying, "Tonight? Okay. Is it some special occasion? You've never asked me to eat dinner with you up there before is why I ask."

"Just thought you might like it. That's all."

Ava thinks about the offer for a moment or two and nods. "Okay. What time?"

My heart skips a beat when she agrees to come to dinner with me tonight. "Seven."

"Okay. I'll be there. Thanks!"

I hurry away back up to the house and make a beeline to the kitchen. Eleanor is busy peeling carrots for what looks to be a stew she's cooking, but she'll need to stop that because I have no intention of giving Ava stew for our dinner together.

"Ava is joining me for dinner at seven. I want you to make all her favorite foods, Eleanor."

The older woman nods before a smile lights up her face. "Okay. What about you? Do you have anything you want me to make that you like?"

"No. Just concentrate on all of her favorites. I'm sure I'll be fine with whatever you make. As long as she likes it is all that matters."

"All of her favorites at seven it is. I'll make sure to bring up a bottle of wine from the cellar that will complement the meal since she drinks wine."

I nod, thankful Eleanor remembers things like that. I don't drink wine, so I would have never even thought of what would go with the meal.

"Thank you."

"You're welcome, Matthias."

Something in the way she's smiling at me makes me think I'm not the only happy person in this house today.

I don't know how I'm going to focus on work for the rest of the day, but I don't care.

Ava and I are having dinner together. I think this can be technically considered a date.

Now to see if she can forgive me for all I've done.

CHAPTER THIRTY-SEVEN

va

I watch him practically run back to the main house and wonder what's going on. Yes, he's been nicer since Theo left, but he's never invited me to dinner. Maybe he's just trying to be neighborly. We do live on the same estate.

That's probably it, though there seemed to be something different in the way he looked at me when he asked if I wanted to come up to the house for dinner. Wait…is this a date? Is that why he looked like that?

Since Theo left, I haven't even considered going out with anyone. Not that I have that many opportunities when I don't leave this estate very often. My friends call and want me to come out with them to clubs, but it's felt like it's too soon. My lunch with Eden yesterday was the first time I left the estate since everything happened.

If I'm being honest, at least for the first few times my friends invited me to go out, I was still hoping Theo would come back. I've given up on that. He's not coming back for me. He's never responded to my texts or voicemails. Not a single one. Nothing I've said has worked.

He can't forgive me.

Like always lately, I tear up at the thought of Theo. I can't believe I'm never going to see him again. That doesn't seem possible.

Maybe when enough time has passed he'll surprise me one day by calling me or dropping in to see me. I can't help but smile as I think about him just showing up after months and in his typical Theo fashion acting like nothing was ever wrong. He'll probably say something like, "Hey, Ava! Where have you been hiding yourself?"

That's so him. I bet he will someday. Then we can get back to being friends, even if we can't be anything more.

In the meantime, I have a dinner to attend tonight.

RIGHT BEFORE SEVEN, I WALK UP TO THE KITCHEN door at the main house and see Eleanor busy cooking. She smiles when she sees me, pointing at my dress as if she's impressed.

"You look beautiful, Ava! I love you in blue. Matthias is somewhere in the house. I haven't seen him since he gave me the menu for dinner. I think you're going to like it."

"Oh, yeah? Anything I might like?"

She wipes her hands on her apron and nods.

"Everything you like. I made sure to pick your absolute favorites for tonight. His instructions."

"Should I be worried he's planning on poisoning me or something? This dinner invitation seems like it came out of the blue. I don't want to be suspicious, but you know him. His moods change like lightning. One minute he's inviting someone to eat a meal with him, and the next he's making them wish they never said yes."

Some of that is joking, but I can't stop myself from being apprehensive around Matthias. We haven't spoken much since all that happened with Theo. I don't know what to expect tonight.

Eleanor shakes her head at my sad attempt at being funny. "Oh, I don't think so. I think he's very much looking forward to this dinner tonight."

"Well, whatever this is about, I'm just glad to not have to make a meal. Since you're the one making the dinner, I know it'll be great. Definitely better than my usual macaroni and cheese and cereal."

A look of horror settles into her face. "That's what you eat for dinner?"

I shrug, trying not to feel like too much of a failure as an adult. "Well, it's only me down there now, so cooking feels like a waste of time."

"Well, I think from now on, you should come up here to eat dinner every night. And I mean whether you're eating with Matthias or not. I'm always happy to have the company, and you know I make a full meal every night. Not that he or Marius eats it. I swear they pick like birds. I don't know how either one of them isn't as thin as a reed."

Laughing as I think about the size of both the King brothers living here, I ask, "Is Marius joining us too?"

She shakes her head and smiles. "No. I saw him drive out a couple hours ago. I'm thinking this is just you and Matthias. He had me set the table in the formal dining room for only two places."

The formal dining room?

I glance down my body and wonder if I'm underdressed for this dinner. My blue sundress with the tiny white flowers isn't exactly formal wear.

"Well, I guess it's almost time. Wish me luck," I say as I walk out into the hall and head for the dining room.

The table is set just as Eleanor said, although she didn't mention she used the fine china that was the pride of Mrs. King. White with gold around the edge, it's usually only brought out for holidays and special occasions like Mr. King's parties.

My mind drifts back to those days long ago when all the King boys lived here and my parents would bring Drew and me up for holiday get-togethers. After dinner, we'd all go play upstairs or outside. Well, almost all of us. Matthias rarely bothered with his brothers when I was around, it seemed.

I smile at those old days, even as tears fill my eyes at the memories. Those were good times. If only we had all been able to stay kids.

Matthias walks into the room and clears his throat to let me know he's there. When I turn toward him, I see he's wearing a suit. God, I really am underdressed for this tonight.

Then again, he wears a suit to work here at the house every day, so maybe he just left the office.

"Did you just finish work?" I ask. "We can start dinner a little late if you want to change."

He smiles and comes around the table to pull out my chair. As I sit down, he says, "That seems redundant since I just changed into these clothes."

I watch him as he walks a little farther down the table to sit at the end. He just got dressed for our dinner? I've never seen him in that dark green dress shirt before. Is it new? Did he buy a new shirt for tonight?

"You look beautiful, Ava."

"Thank you. I didn't realize we were dressing for dinner tonight. I would have worn something a bit more formal."

He shakes his head with conviction, like he's never heard anything he's ever disagreed with more. "You're perfect."

The way he says that leaves me speechless, but thankfully, Eleanor walks in at that very moment with a charcuterie board. I stare at her in surprise since I hadn't seen that when I breezed through the kitchen a few minutes ago.

My eyes widen at the variety of meats and cheeses alongside a piece of golden honeycomb. "I haven't had this in ages. This is great!"

Eleanor looks over at Matthias and smiles. "It was his idea. Enjoy!"

I turn to look at Matthias and see him nodding. "She's exaggerating, to be honest. I told her I wanted her to make all your favorite foods. She should get the credit."

"So you don't like anything on this charcuterie board?"

He cranes his neck to look at it and smiles. "I'm sure I can find something I like. I'm just happy you like it."

I set about to try every piece of meat, cheese, and dip Eleanor included on the board, in addition to the honey, but Matthias doesn't seem very interested in the appetizer. In fact, all he seems interested in is me, which makes enjoying it awkward.

A short while later, Eleanor shows up with baked ham, baby red potatoes with rosemary, and orange-glazed carrots with dill, all my favorites. Setting each dish full of food down on the table in front of us, she gives me a little wink before she quietly says, "Eat up, but save room for apple pie. I have vanilla ice cream if you want it à la mode."

All my favorite dinner foods and apple pie?

I turn to look over at Matthias smiling. He looks truly happy, something I've witnessed so rarely with him.

"Well, I hope you at least like some of this," I say as I start to fill my plate.

"I'm sure I will. I'm just glad you seem to be happy with the foods Eleanor chose."

"You should give her a raise for picking these out," I joke, but then feel awkward about saying that. "I just mean if you left this up to her and really wanted me to like the dinner, she did a good job."

"Good. Then maybe I will give her a raise. Now dig in and enjoy."

We have an incredible meal, but every time I try to start a conversation with him, he simply smiles and nods. When Eleanor brings out the apple pie and tops it with a big scoop of vanilla ice cream, I'm sure I've never had such a wonderful dinner.

If only the company seemed as happy to be here, but Matthias remains content to sit quietly and watch me eat.

Finally, I ask, "Is anything wrong?"

"No," he answers with a smile.

"You aren't saying much."

His expression grows dark for a moment before his smile returns, but I can tell it's forced. "I'm sorry. I've never been as great a conversationalist as the rest of my family."

As much as I like that nothing's wrong, I'm bothered by his apology because I know he's comparing himself to Theo. He doesn't have to be like anyone else. I care about him because he's the person he is.

"You're fine as you are, Matthias."

That gets me a smile that looks genuine, but he still remains silent. I finish my dessert, commenting on how Eleanor's pies are always the best I've ever tasted, and he nods in agreement but says nothing else.

Finally, he asks, "Would you like to go for a walk? It's a beautiful night out."

I stand up, excited about the possibility that he'll talk more while we walk around the estate. "That sounds great! Let's go!"

Any hope I had for him to talk more is dashed as we begin strolling across the lawn and he doesn't say a word. The warm summer night feels like the perfect time to clear the air between us, but his silence makes me unsure what to say.

So I fill the empty space with chatter about nothing —the weather, the flowers the groundskeeper chose for this season, what my father told me about his new cabin. Matthias seems to know where he wants us to go, though, so I let him lead the way until we reach the tree where I saw him drawing that day.

Right near where he kissed me the last time.

When we reach that spot, he takes my hand in his and looks down into my eyes. In the moonlight, he looks beautiful, just like he did that snowy December day when we first kissed all those years ago.

"I'm sorry."

Confused what he's apologizing for, I say, "For what? Dinner was lovely. You don't tend to say much usually, so if you're sorry about that, it's okay. I talk enough for both of us."

He hangs his head and doesn't speak for a long moment before he finally says, "For what I did that chased Theo away. I'm sorry, Ava."

I know he's trying to make amends, so I reach for his other hand and smile up at him when he looks down at me. "Theo was always going to go. It was just a matter of when."

I've never said that out loud, but in my heart, I've always known it was true. Maybe he would have asked me to come with him, but I'm not sure of that. All I know is Theo was never going to stay here for me.

I expect Matthias to say something else or maybe apologize again, but instead, he dips his head until it's level with mine and presses a soft kiss onto my lips. It's so gentle and sweet, and something ignites inside me. I kiss him back, thinking something more might happen, but he merely takes my hand and begins walking toward my house.

He says nothing more, and although I want to fill the silence because that's how I am, I force myself to remain quiet too. I don't know what's going on, but he just kissed me for the first time in what feels like forever.

When we reach my house, he stops at the end of the sidewalk like he did earlier when he came down to ask me to dinner. I'm not sure what to do, so I ask him, "Would you like to come to dinner tomorrow? Say about the same time as tonight?"

"I'd like that. Seven it is."

I expect him to kiss me again, at least a little peck to say goodnight, but he leaves without doing anything. I watch him slowly walk back up the road to his house, unsure what just happened.

And not being able to think of anything else but kissing him again.

CHAPTER THIRTY-EIGHT

$\mathcal{M}$atthias

FOR THE PAST HOUR, I'VE SILENTLY BEATEN UP ON myself wishing I was the kind of man who has the charm my brothers have. Other than telling Ava her pasta primavera is delicious, I haven't said much more. She doesn't seem to mind, but I do. I want to dazzle her with great conversation so she remembers this night as great from start to finish.

I'm failing miserably at that, though.

"My father loves his new place. He wants me to come visit this winter. I told him I'd love to, but I have to admit I'm not looking forward to the drive," Ava says as she begins to clear the table.

"You can use the King Industries company jet. Just tell me when you're planning on going, and I'll make sure it's ready to go."

She stops on the other side of the table and looks at me strangely for a long moment. "I didn't know you had a company plane. Did your father always have it too?"

Nodding, I smile. "As long as I remember."

Confused, she shakes her head. "Then why did your parents always drive everywhere when you all went on vacation?"

"Because my mother hated flying. I thought everyone knew that."

"I had no idea." She hesitates as she moves to walk toward the kitchen and says, "Oh, now I remember. I did know that. Theo complained about it when you all drove to Florida that one year."

Her mention of his name makes the conversation come to a screeching halt, and she quickly hurries out of the dining room toward the kitchen. I'd hoped we could start over without talking about him, but I know now that's not possible.

I follow her into the kitchen and find her loading the dishwasher. I don't know how to start this conversation because it's the last thing I want to discuss tonight or any time, for that matter. It has to happen, though.

Ava doesn't turn around to face me but says in a low voice, "I didn't mean to make things uncomfortable by mentioning his name."

"I think we need to talk about it."

Shaking her head, she sighs. "I don't want to talk about it."

My heart sinks at how sad she sounds. She still loves him. I've just been fooling myself by believing I could ever be something to her.

"You should have gone to him," I say, hating every

word as it leaves my mouth. But I can't stop now. I have to say what I've been afraid of this whole time. "I'm sure if one of you gave in, you could be happy."

She spins around, and I see hurt written all over her face. "Why are you saying this now? I thought we had a nice dinner. Last night was great too. So what's all this about?"

"I can tell you still love him," I answer, every word tasting like ash in my mouth.

Slowly, she closes the dishwasher door and sighs again. "I'll always love Theo. He was my best friend for my entire life."

I swallow hard as my chest feels like someone's got it in a vise. "Then go to him and never look back."

Tears fill her eyes as she stares across the room at me. "Why are you saying this, Matthias? Is it that you've changed your mind about me? I thought last night meant you wanted to see if we could be together. If you don't want that, then just say it."

I shake my head, hating the very thought of her gone from my life but knowing I can't stop her if she wants to go. I made that mistake because I was jealous the last time. I won't do that again.

"Just say it!" she screams as tears stream down her cheeks.

"I can't because it's not true, but if you want to go, then I won't stop you."

She wipes under her eyes and sniffles. "Why do you think I want to go? Don't you think I could have gone at any time before now?"

I shrug, hating how I've ruined this night for us. Fuck! She deserves better than me. She deserves him.

"Say what's on your mind, Matthias. If you can't be with me for whatever reason, just say it."

When I don't answer, she screams, "Fine! I'll say it! You don't want me because I was with your brother. Well, I'm sorry, but I can't change that. Maybe if he had given you my message that day after the blizzard. Maybe if my father had told me about your letters. Maybe, maybe, maybe. I can't change any of that. I wish I could."

My emotions go wild inside me as I try to find a way to explain I don't blame her for anything but can't find the right words. Finally, I snap, "I'm not asking you to change it! All I'm saying is if you want to be with him, I won't stand in your way. I tried that already and made a goddamned mess of everything, so this time, whatever happens, I deserve it, good or bad."

Christ, I hate this. All I want to do is tell her how much I love being around her, but as usual, I'm fucking it up.

Ava walks over to me and stops before bowing her head. "Is this always going to be between us?"

"I'm sorry."

Ava looks up at me and sighs. "I know, but you don't have to keep apologizing."

"I feel like I do. Like if I say those words enough, that will change what I did. But if that does happen, then I'll have to accept you'll be gone from here with him," I admit, unsure what to do about that difficult reality.

She turns away, avoiding my gaze as she says, "That isn't going to happen, Matthias. He can't forgive me. I've accepted that."

I gently take her chin between my fingers and turn

her head so she has to face me. "Then he's a damn fool. It must run in the King family because I've been one for far too long too."

"Theo's who he's always been. He was never going to stay here for me, and I'm not sure he was ever going to want me to go with him. As for you, I don't know, but I can tell you this. I forgive you for what you did, so you don't ever have to apologize again, okay?"

When she smiles, it's like the world's been lifted off my shoulders. Maybe we can be what I've hoped for.

The words I love you sit on the tip of my tongue, but I don't say them. Not yet. Instead, I kiss her and hope she senses what I feel when my lips touch hers.

"I'm sorry. I know you said I don't have to apologize again, but this one is for something else."

She draws her eyebrows in and shakes her head in confusion. "I don't understand."

Hanging my head, I explain, "I was in a dark place for a long time and took it out on you. I've been cruel to you when I shouldn't have been. It's not your fault my life has turned out like it did. It's just that I was so unhappy, and every time I thought about that time we spent together, I couldn't think of anything but you left me. What I didn't see was your feelings for me weren't where mine were for you. I'm sorry for that."

Ava cradles my face in her soft hands and gently tilts my head back so I'm looking at her. Smiling, she kisses me and says, "You don't have to apologize for that anymore either, Matthias. I understand now why you were so hurt. I don't know why Theo didn't give you my message or my father hid the fact that you sent me all those letters. I just know we have to forgive them too."

After all that's happened, she's right. I just want to forgive and forget, and maybe if she and I can do that, we can be happy together.

"I made something great for dessert. It's a surprise, so go out there and wait, okay?" she says as she slides her hands away from my face, and I instantly miss her touch.

With a smile, I do as she wants. A minute later, she appears in the dining room carrying two bowls. I don't have to wait long to see what's in them, and when I do, my mouth begins to water.

As she sets mine in front of me, she says, "I remember when you were a little boy and your mother would take all of us kids out for a treat. You always wanted peach pie, and I remember how disappointed you were when you couldn't get it. So I made peach crumble for dessert tonight."

"I never did understand why I couldn't get peach pie any time other than a few weeks in the summer," I say as I inhale the sweet scent of the dessert she made just for me.

"Well, dig in. I hope you enjoy it."

With the first spoonful of peach crumble, I savor all the flavors in the dessert. The peach and cinnamon in the filling and the brown sugar and butter for the topping taste like perfection. I devour it, loving it and the person who made it for me.

I push the bowl away and smile at Ava. "That was incredible. Thank you."

She still has half the dessert in her bowl and smiles back at me. "I'm so glad you liked it, Matthias. You looked utterly happy eating it."

I want to tell her I'm happy because I'm with her, but I don't say those words. Not yet.

Ava stands from the table. "I'll be right back. If you want more peach cobbler, feel free."

Something's wrong, but I don't know what. I thought things had gotten better once we sat down to enjoy her delicious dessert she made especially for me.

When she doesn't return after a few minutes, I make my way upstairs to find her staring out her bedroom window at the lawn that connects this carriage house to the main house. My heart sinks as I watch her and know she's thinking about Theo.

"Thank you for dinner, but I think I need to go now," I say as casually as possible, hoping to hide the disappointment filling me.

She turns around and shakes her head. "Why?"

One of us has to admit the truth, and I guess it's going to have to be me. So be it.

"Tell me you aren't thinking about the two of you all those times you played out on that lawn growing up. I know you're always going to love Theo, but it's more than that, and I don't think we can get past what happened."

Shaking her head again, she walks over to stand in front of me. "No, you're wrong, Matthias. I wasn't remembering Theo and me. I was actually thinking about the first time I thought you weren't just the oldest King brother who never really spoke to me. You and Theo were out there with Ronan teaching him to play baseball. He must have been about nine or ten, which would have made you about sixteen. You were pitching to him while Theo caught, and you were so patient with him, even though he missed every ball you threw to him. You just kept telling him to keep his eye on the ball. I watched for fifteen minutes, and never once did you get frustrated. Theo started teasing him, but you stayed calm the whole time."

I can't help but smile at the memory of that spring day. Ronan had asked our father to teach him how to play baseball every day for over a month, but he had no time because my mother was sick. We didn't want to listen to the youngest King whine about not knowing how to play, so Theo and I decided to help him since both of us had played ball in grade school.

"The three of us spent all afternoon out there until Ronan finally got good enough to hit a decently thrown pitch," I say with a smile. "From that day on, he had a glove in his hand whenever the weather was nice out. I like to think we gave him his start."

"And he's been at it ever since. He played right through college, didn't he?"

"He did," I answer with a nod. "I think my mother would have been proud to know he turned out to be a hell of a ball player."

Ava and I fall silent until I ask, "Why were you thinking about that?"

With a shrug, she says, "I don't know. I came up here to go to the bathroom, and when I was passing my room, the memory popped into my head."

"We've been in each other's lives for a long time."

"All my life."

I know what she's saying. She's still mourning the loss of her friendship with my brother. Maybe sometime in the future we can try to be together again, but now it's too soon.

"I'm going to go now. Thank you for dinner, Ava. Maybe we can do it another time."

As I turn to leave, she grabs my hand. "No, please don't go. I know tonight hasn't been great, but it doesn't have to end."

"I just don't think it's the right time."

She frowns and lets go of my hand. I walk away, but before I reach her bedroom door, she asks, "Why didn't you kiss me last night when we stopped in front of the house here?"

Looking back at her, I answer, "I thought we should take things slowly this time."

"Well, maybe I don't want to take things slowly. Maybe I liked the speed we took things last time."

When she finishes speaking, a sexy smile makes her brown eyes dance with mischief. She has no idea how breathtaking she can be.

"I'm worried you aren't over Theo yet."

I wish I didn't have to say that since she's being so sexy at this moment, but it's the truth I can't get past. As much as I want to be with her, I don't want to be her rebound guy. I'm too crazy about her to be that.

Ava sets her hands on her hips and takes a deep breath before letting it out in a rush. "Well, then, I guess it's about time to put that idea to rest. Yes, I will always love Theo just as I've loved him all my life. That won't change. But we weren't right together. I knew that, even though I didn't want to admit it. I know now all this time I was wanting him to forgive me it wasn't because I had been with you. It was because he felt something I didn't, and I should have never let things go on as long as they did."

"You looked pretty happy together. I'm having a hard time believing you weren't having fun."

"I was. I was spending time with my best friend. It felt so good to have him back in my life like he was when we were kids. Then when you were so mean to me, it felt nice to have Theo there to care about me and make me feel better. But I wasn't feeling what he was feeling."

Hearing she turned to him because I was so cruel once again makes my heart ache. If only I hadn't been so quick to want to hurt her.

"I'm sorry I screwed everything up. You would have never turned to him if I hadn't been such an asshole."

With a big smile, she nods and says, "Exactly. So how about you not screwing this up now?"

"Okay. What do you suggest?"

Ava looks around the room we're in and levels her gaze on my face. "We're in a bedroom. I suggest we use it the way it was meant to be used."

"Go to sleep?" I tease, loving this assertive and confident version of her.

Taking a step closer to me, she gives me a look and then says something that makes me instantly hard. "After. First, though, I say we remind each other why we couldn't forget those two days we spent together five years ago."

I slip my arm around her waist and pull her roughly to me. Looking down into her beautiful brown eyes, I smile at how incredible she feels against my body.

"I'm going to remind you all night long."

She stands on her tiptoes and kisses me long and deep before grinning at me. "Promise?"

A tiny hint of fear that she still cares about Theo as more than a friend sits in the back of my mind, but I can't let that stop me from being with the woman I'm madly in love with anymore. I want her so much it hurts not to be close to her. She's all I think about, distracting me from nearly everything else in my life.

I want to make her mine tonight and forever.

Ava quickly unbuttons my shirt before slipping it off and tossing it over onto a chair in the corner of her room. "I figured it was my turn to undress you first," she says with a giggle before moving to my pants.

We only had two days together five years ago, but that brief history blots out all the bad that's happened between us. I smile at her mention of that snowy day and how beautiful she looked wearing only that white robe, furious at me while I surrendered to a fantasy I'd had for so long about her.

When she unzips my pants, I push her sundress down her body. My breath catches in my chest at how stunning she is as she stands in only her panties in front of me. Already hard as a rock, I can't hold back anymore and spin her around toward the bed.

I tug her underwear down her legs and toss them toward where my shirt landed on the chair. Naked for me, she turns her head and gives me a sexy smile, biting her lower lip in that way that makes me want her so fucking badly.

"Are you planning to remain clothed for this?"

"My shirt is off."

"Are we going to do this again?" she asks, and I shake my head.

"Not exactly. Up on the bed on your hands and knees," I say, nuzzling her neck as she moans at my command.

She's open and ready for me, so I set my hands on her hips and pull her back toward me, sliding my cock through her soaking wet pussy and grazing her clit. That makes her even more excited, and she wiggles her ass against me, making the thought of taking things slow an impossibility.

With one smooth thrust, my cock is buried inside her, and I'm in heaven. My fingertips sink into the flesh on her hips as I begin fucking her, my need to mark her as mine more powerful than I ever thought. She's always been my Ava in my heart, and now I'm going to do whatever it takes to make her mine in every way.

I hear tiny whimpers come from her and I continue to plunge into her wet and willing body. She grips the bedspread tightly in her hands and lowers her head to the bed, changing the angle of our lovemaking to something even more incredible.

For so long, I've wished to be with her again and didn't think it would ever happen, so now I can't make this happen fast enough. Sliding my hand up her back, I tighten my hand in her hair, pulling it hard enough so she has to arch her back.

"Oh, God…right there…don't stop…"

When I move my hand around to the front of her neck and begin fucking her even faster, Ava lowers her head and sucks my thumb into her mouth. Something about her tongue and lips against my skin sends me over the edge, and a second later, I flood her with everything inside me.

Her cunt contracts around my cock as I come, and it doesn't take her long to orgasm hard, her body milking me until we're both exhausted and collapse onto the bed. Utterly satisfied, I look at her face down on the bed as she breathes heavily beside me.

"Ava?"

She takes a few moments to react, but when she turns her head to face me and pushes her hair back off her face, I see she's feeling the same thing I am.

"Yes?"

"That was incredible."

Smiling, she says, "I'm going to be walking funny, I think."

"What?"

Ava shakes her head and leans over to kiss me. "Nothing. That was incredible. I don't think I've ever come like that."

I can't help grinning at hearing that. It's petty and immature, and I don't care. I love hearing that being with me isn't like being with anyone else. I can't be her first in most things, but I can't be her last and her best, and that's even better.

Before I can say another word, she rolls me onto my back and tugs my clothes down my legs. With a sexy smile, she climbs on top of me and kisses me long and deep.

"Ready to go again?"

God, I love this woman.

CHAPTER THIRTY-NINE

va

W HEN I OPEN MY EYES, I SEE HIM IN THE BED NEXT TO me smiling. At me. Sure I look like something the cat dragged in, I smooth my hair down and feel myself blush.

"I tend to move a lot when I sleep, which makes my hair look like someone took a hand mixer to it. I didn't kick you or anything, did I?"

Before I start rambling, I stop myself, pressing my lips together. God, why am I so flustered first thing in the morning?

I know the answer even before I ask myself the question. Matthias and I slept together. It was incredible and mind-blowing, but even more, it was something I wanted. I thought I'd never forgive him for what he did to me with Theo. I must have been ignoring my feelings, and when he kissed me the other night, everything came back to me like a dam breaking.

"Are you okay? You seem upset," he says with a hint of concern in his voice.

He seems perfectly fine to be lying naked here in my bed. In fact, I don't think I've ever seen Matthias look so happy.

I look away toward my mirror and see my hair is as bad as I feared. Pressing it down against my head, I say, "I'm fine. Well, other than my hair, which is really bad. You look great, though. Must be nice."

"You look beautiful," he says, wrapping his arm around my waist to pull me back against his naked body. "Come here and stop worrying about your hair. It's gorgeous, just like the rest of you."

As much as I'd love to believe him, I know he's lying. The mirror doesn't tell fibs, though, and what I saw makes me wish I had pulled my hair back in a ponytail before we fell asleep.

After we had wild, fantastic sex.

I turn in his hold and look at him as he lies back so confidently. "We slept together."

He stares down at me like I've just said I've met aliens and then smiles. "I was there. It was great. Just as incredible as I remembered."

Then he stops and his expression darkens before he frowns. "Are you unhappy we slept together?"

Quickly, I answer, "No! Not at all. I was just saying we slept together." Avoiding his intense gaze, I focus on the pillow and add, "I know I didn't have to state the obvious. I guess I'm just uncomfortable because you wake up looking stunning and I wake up like a troll."

His chest expands when he laughs at that. "You don't look like a troll, Ava. You're beautiful. You're the most beautiful woman I've ever seen in my life. Trust me. Your hair isn't bad, and even if it is, I don't care."

"Well, I do. Why doesn't hair ever look like it does when people sleep together in the movies?"

That makes him laugh again, and it's such a wonderful sound that I don't mind that he's probably laughing at me. "Because they didn't really sleep together. They just pretended. We did a whole lot more than pretend."

Oh, God. He's so comfortable talking about this, and I don't know why, but I'm not. Burying my head in his chest, I mumble, "I know. I was there."

"Is there something you want to talk about? You seem to be struggling with this."

Damnit! I know he thinks I'm acting like this because he's not Theo. I need to make sure he understands that's not it at all. I don't know what my problem is, but it's not that.

I lift my head and see worry in his eyes. My ridiculous and very unsexy morning behavior put that there. I need to say the right things to make sure to banish that look forever.

Sitting up, I take a deep breath and say what I have to, no matter how stupid it sounds. "Matthias, I'm not struggling. I promise. Not with a single thing. I loved that we slept together last night."

Before I can continue, he playfully says, "And early this morning. Twice."

"You're not helping."

"Okay. Continue."

"I'm not struggling. Honest. I don't know what's wrong with me. Suddenly, I feel very self-conscious around you. I don't even think I acted like this when we were first together five years ago."

Matthias takes my hand and brings it to his mouth to kiss my knuckles. "Ava, it's okay. I've earned all of this because of the way I've been to you. Deep down, you're probably afraid my mood is going to change, and I'll say something mean. I get it. But I don't want you to worry. I'm not that person anymore."

What he says rings true, but now doesn't seem to be the right moment to say that, so I lean over and kiss him softly on the lips. "I'm glad you aren't because I like this version of you."

When I move to pull away, he stops me. Pressing his forehead to mine, he says, "I love you, Ava."

I stare into his eyes and see so much emotion in them. He lets me go, and I sit up, stunned at what he just said. "You love me?"

With a smile, he answers, "I've loved you since before we were together that first time. I wasn't supposed to even think about you, so I had to find a way to stuff my feelings down so no one would know. But I always knew I loved you. I understand if you can't say it back to me. I've done nowhere near enough to prove to you I'm not that person who was so hurtful to you all those times. It doesn't change the fact that I love you more than I can say."

I kiss him to stop him from saying anymore. He doesn't have to convince me he's a better man now. I already know that.

And I know something else too.

"Matthias, I love you too."

A smile lifts the corners of his mouth and lights up his dark eyes. "You love me?"

Nodding, I wipe under my eyes as tears begin to roll down my cheeks. "I do."

He cradles my face in his hands, and against my lips, he whispers, "You love me."

And just like that, all my worries about my messy hair and how I look in the morning disappear.

FOR THE PAST MONTH, MATTHIAS AND I HAVE SPENT nearly every night together, and I think he'd spend every day with me too if it wasn't for his responsibilities with King Industries. Sometimes we have dinner and then go for a walk like we did that first night. He tells me about his day and then asks me about mine. Other times we go out for dinner at a restaurant and then come back to the estate to stay in his house or mine.

I don't know what made him change, but gone is the man who never had a kind word to say to me. He's a different person now, someone who worries about how I'm feeling and wants to make sure I'm happy.

This morning when we left his bed, he asked me to make reservations at Cooligan's, and for a fleeting moment, I considered asking him if we could go somewhere else. I stopped myself, though. I can't live fearing the past will somehow make me uneasy when I'm with him. Theo and I were together. Nothing can change that. I don't regret a single moment I spent with him, but those days are over. He walked away from me, and while

I accept that I was partly to blame for our breakup, I know we were never meant to be.

He never responded to any of my texts or voicemails. I had to come to terms with that, and I have. Theo has his life, and I have mine, and now I have Matthias. I hope someday we'll all be able to be friends again. Nothing would make me happier than to see the two brothers close like they used to be, and I'd love to have my best friend back in my life.

Only time will tell, but I'm hopeful.

I see Matthias through the window in his office and wave to him like I always do now. He smiles and crooks his finger to beckon me inside. Something in his expression tells me he's feeling playful today.

He's out from behind his desk by the time I walk into his office, and the wickedly sinful look in his eyes stops me dead just inside the doorway. Playful isn't exactly his mood, I see.

"Close the door and come here."

I do as he commands and stop in front of him over near the bar area in the corner of his office. "It's a little early for a drink, isn't it? Or are we celebrating something?" I ask with a giggle, sure he isn't interested in toasting anything this early in the day.

Matthias pulls me to him and kisses me long and deep. Every cell in my body comes alive at his touch, like always.

When he breaks our kiss, I see pure need in his eyes. "So no drink?"

He shakes his head and grins. "Later. For now, I have something else in mind."

"But what if someone sees us?"

Arching one eyebrow, he smirks. "I own this house. I can do whatever I want here," he says as he leans in to kiss me again.

Even as my stomach does flips, I ask, "You don't have to be at work now?"

That gets me a bigger smile. "I own the company. What are they going to do? Fire me?"

"So basically you own everything, and you can do what you want when you want."

Matthias runs his tongue along his lower lip and shrugs. "Pretty much. It's one of the perks of ownership."

I don't say it, but he owns me just as much as this house and King Industries. My heart, at least.

He kisses me to stop my questions, sliding his hand around my neck to hold my mouth to his. He's needy and possessive, and I love it.

I love him.

Sliding his mouth over to my ear, he whispers in a deep voice, "This dress is beautiful. The only way it could be better is if it was off your body."

Before I can say a word to that, he slides his hands over my shoulders, taking my pink sundress with them. A second later, my dress puddles at my feet, leaving me only in my bra and panties I suspect will end up on the floor in a few seconds.

I can't help but worry Eleanor or Mick might walk into his office at any moment, but the need to feel him inside me pushes away those concerns. He moves quickly to strip the rest of my clothing from me until I'm nude in front of him.

"What about you?"

Matthias simply shakes his head and turns me

around so my back is facing him. Nuzzling my neck, he murmurs, "I like having you naked for me like this while I'm still dressed."

I move to turn back so I can undress him, but he holds me in place so I can't, sliding his hand between my legs and up my body to cup my breast. I'm soaking wet and ready for him to fill me with his hard cock pressing against my ass.

As he gently pinches my excited nipple, he moans in my ear, "God, I need you, Ava."

The sound of his zipper opening is followed by the feel of his hand stroking his cock against my ass. I close my eyes and imagine the sensual scene and how beautiful he must look at this moment.

I nudge against his body to let him know I don't want to wait any longer, and a second later, he sets his hands on my hips and squeezes tightly before sliding into my body, filling me so completely the feeling takes my breath away. All I can do is hold on to the edge of the bar as he begins to slowly pump into me.

His right hand releases my hip and slides up my spine until he buries it in my hair, tugging hard as he increases the pace of our fucking. I wish I could see his face and touch his body because the look in his eyes when we're together never fails to send me over the edge. The man I thought was always so angry and hateful is filled with a passion I've never seen in anyone else, and when we make love, it's on display for me to adore.

"You feel so fucking good," he groans behind me before tightening his hold on my hair again.

I arch my back, and the small change in position lets him plunge even deeper inside me. Matthias sinks his teeth into my earlobe and says, "Fuck, you keep moving like that and I'm not going to last much longer."

"You didn't give me much choice," I say as I stare at the half-filled whiskey decanter at the front of the bar. "When you pulled my hair like that, I had to do something, or my neck was going to snap."

"Mmmm…I'm sorry," he moans as he continues fucking me but releases his hold on my hair.

I instantly miss that touch of possession and search for his hand. I bring it around to the front of my neck and place it against my throat.

Without a word, he senses what I want and tightens his grip just below my jaw, sending a rush of need coursing through me. I love that streak of possessiveness in him and how it makes me feel, especially at moments like this.

His body presses against mine, and he begins to fuck me with shallow jabs instead of the long, slow strokes from a few minutes ago. He wasn't lying when he said he wouldn't last long. That's okay. We'll have time together after dinner tonight.

The softness of his silk tie sliding against my back suddenly becomes my focus as he releases his hold on my left hip and slides his hand up to my shoulder. He moves his mouth from near my ear, and a moment later, I feel his teeth sink into the tender skin near my collarbone. It doesn't hurt but instead only increases my desire, and I moan softly to let him know I love it.

"Oh, fuck…" he groans, and I know it's only a matter of seconds before he comes.

I arch my back once more, and he fills me with everything he has until it runs down the inside of my thighs. Matthias slowly pumps into me a few more times before I come, my hands tightly gripping the edge of the bar counter so I don't fall.

He wouldn't let me, though. I know that. I'm safe with this man.

Kissing me softly just below my ear, he whispers, "I love you, and that's got to be the best midday break I've ever had."

I turn my head to see him grinning and smile back at him. "Happy to be of assistance. Let's schedule another session like this for later after dinner tonight."

He presses a kiss to my lips and sighs. "It's a deal."

When he slides out of me, I instantly miss him. I slowly spin around as he finishes zipping up his pants and then crouches down to pick up my clothes. It reminds me of that snowy December day when he took such care with removing my snow-drenched shoes as I sat on his bed wondering what was happening since until that moment he'd been nothing short of my mortal enemy.

I get my clothes back on as he silently watches me with that same expression of fascination in his eyes he always seems to have when he looks at me. Ready to head back outside, I stand on my tiptoes to kiss him softly on the lips.

"Have a good day at work. See you later?" I ask, already sure of the answer.

"Absolutely."

When I move to leave so he can return to work, he stops me by holding me there with him. Unsure why, I shake my head and stare up at him in confusion.

"Is something wrong?"

With a smile that makes him even more gorgeous than usual, he answers, "Not a thing. I love you."

"I love you too, Matthias."

He sighs heavily. "Time for me to get back to work. I miss you already."

"I'll just be outside," I say with a smile before kissing him again. "Feel free to join me. I'm going to see what Mick is planting today."

As I turn to leave once again, he doesn't stop me, but I hear him mumble as he walks back to his desk, "You have no idea how much I wish I could."

I glance back at him as he positions himself at his desk to get back to work and can't help but think he doesn't belong there. He should be outside drawing and enjoying his art.

Maybe I'll be able to convince him to join me later.

CHAPTER FORTY

va

THE GROUNDSKEEPER'S WRIST-DEEP IN TOPSOIL AS HE transplants a rose bush from out near the edge of the property to a few yards away from the back patio off the living room. I asked him to plant some roses there, never thinking he'd actually move an entire bush from another part of the estate to that spot, and I feel like I should offer to help him since he's gone to so much trouble.

"Would you like an assistant? I'm pretty good with dirt, or so my father used to tell me since I never failed to come home filthy as a little girl."

Mick lifts his head and gives me a big smile. "I think I have this covered, but I'd love some company. I sent the rest of the crew out to clean up that strip of land right near the property line today. I don't know how long it's been since anyone paid attention to that part of the estate, but it's a bit shabby back there."

I sit down on the grass near him and watch as he carefully works to make sure the rose bush is transplanted safely. "I don't know. I can't remember the last time I was out there. When we were all kids, neither my parents nor Mr. and Mrs. King liked us to be that far out. I'd bet it's been at least a decade since I saw what that part of the property looked like."

"You and the Kings have been close all your lives? That's nice."

Nodding, I smile as I think about how true that statement is. There isn't a year I can remember when the King boys weren't the biggest part of my life.

"It is. I love them like they're my own brothers."

As soon as the words leave my mouth, I cringe and quickly add, "Well, not brothers. At least not all of them. That came out weird. God, that really sounded terrible, didn't it?"

Mick turns his head to look at me and laughs. "I knew what you meant. They've been like your family all your life. That's still nice."

"Yes, exactly. Like family," I say, happy to agree with the way he phrases it since my way sounded oddly incestual.

Eager to change the subject, I lean over and watch him pat the soil around the newly relocated rose bush. "Do you think it's going to do well here? I'd hate to see it die. I love yellow roses, and there aren't any other yellow rose bushes near the house."

"Oh, it'll be fine. I just have to make sure I give it

extra tender loving care. I'll watch over it for a few weeks to make sure it's taking to its new home, but I think it will be okay."

He stands up and wipes his hands on the front of his pants, covering them in dirt. "But for now, I need to go check on the order of mums for next month. Mr. King explicitly told me that he wants as many as possible, but there must be some shortage because I've had to search high and low to find a nursery that has enough for what he expects."

"Okay. I'm going to hang out here for a bit. Maybe I'll talk to the rose bush. You know, give it a pep talk and tell it how much it's going to love its new home."

Mick nods like what I just said isn't completely silly. "They say plants do better when we talk to them, and a rose bush is just a bigger plant, so why not?"

"Yeah, why not? The way you say it doesn't sound so ridiculous, so maybe I will. Thanks!"

As the groundskeeper walks away with his shovel and tools, he calls back, "Anytime!"

I give the rose bush a big smile and whisper, "I don't know if this is going to work, but I think you'll love it here. I know I do. I promise to come out and see you every day, and I promise to show off your beautiful flowers inside because yellow roses are my favorite."

A few minutes later, Matthias rounds the corner of the house and stops dead when he sees me sitting on the ground having a chat with the newest rose bush on the block. He looks upset, so I quickly jump to my feet to explain.

"This may look weird, but this is a rose bush Mick

brought from out near the property line. I was just giving it some tender loving care since yellow roses are my favorite. I swear I'm not crazy. You can ask him. He agreed with me since talking to plants is so beneficial and a rose bush is technically just a big plant."

Matthias tries to smile as I tell him what I was doing, but it's like he can't make himself. So instead, I stand on my tiptoes and kiss him sweetly, just in case he's having a bad day at work and needs some cheering up.

"By the way, I made reservations at Cooligan's for eight. They didn't have anything for seven, so I figured eight would be okay. Are you upset about something? Are you dealing with problems at work today?"

I stare up at his expression. He looks like he's about to lash out at me. What's happened to make him turn back into that person again?

"What's wrong?"

He shakes his head and grabs hold of my hand. "I just got a call. Something's happened."

Instantly, I squeeze his hand tightly, afraid of what he's about to say. "What? What's happened?"

A million terrible thoughts run through my head. Is it my father? I knew living alone in that cabin on that lake was a bad idea. I should have made him change his mind.

Or is it Drew? Or the girls or his wife? They made it through that hurricane unscathed a while back, but he's always telling me about alligators on their news down there. God, I wish he didn't love that place so much because a state full of alligators is simply terrifying.

"Matthias, what is it? Tell me!"

Now I see nothing but utter sadness in his eyes as I wait for him to tell me what's happened. Finally, in a voice barely above a whisper, he chokes out, "There's been an accident. Theo."

I step back from him in horror, shaking my head. "No. I don't believe you. You're just saying this because you had some kind of problem at work. No."

He takes my hands and holds them tightly in his as he follows me across the grass. "I'm sorry. It's not anything like that, Ava."

"No! Don't tell me he's gone, Matthias. I won't believe you."

His eyes fill with tears as he says, "It was an accident in a race. He hit a wall. His manager called me a little while ago."

I yank my hands from his hold and pound my fists against his chest as I scream, "No! Not Theo. No! He isn't dead. I don't believe you! I don't believe you!"

My brain fills with a single horrible thought I can't believe is true. Theo's dead. No. That's not possible. It can't be.

Matthias tries to wrap his arms around me, but I keep punching him, needing something to take out my pain on. "He can't be gone! No! I never got the chance to talk to him. He can't be dead. Please tell me it's not true. Tell me, and I'll forgive you for being cruel. I promise I will, Matthias. Just tell me he's okay."

He says nothing when I tilt my head back to look up at him. All he does is shake his head no. Please let this be a nightmare and I can wake up so it's not real. Please don't let Theo be gone. Not my Theo.

I let my hands fall to my sides as every ounce of strength drains from my body. Matthias holds me tightly while I sob uncontrollably against his chest, crushed by the news. Theo is gone. No, please God, no. I had so much more I wanted to say to him. How could he be gone? The world will never be the same without him in it.

"Why? Why did it have to Theo? We never got to talk to him again, Matthias. How can I go on without telling him I'm sorry just one more time so he can hear how much I never wanted to hurt him? I can't handle this. Please tell me it's not true. Please."

Matthias presses a kiss to the top of my head and quietly says, "I'm so sorry, Ava."

The tears continue to come as if I can't stop crying. He guides me into the house, but being inside makes it all too real that Theo's gone, and he'll never come back now. I'll never have a chance to see his smile when I say something funny. I'll never get to wrap my arms around him again.

Worst of all, the last time we ever spoke to one another was horrible.

I collapse to the floor, shaking my head as utter sadness fills every inch of me. I never got to show him how much I loved him and how much I miss him, and now that chance is gone forever.

As Matthias carries me upstairs, I sob into his shoulder, desperate to wake up from what has to be a nightmare. Theo can't be gone. I never got to say goodbye or make him understand how sorry I was.

"Rest a while in here," Matthias says before gently setting me down on his bed. "I have to handle things for now, but I'll be back, okay?"

I don't answer him, unable to do anything but cry. My best friend is gone.

Matthias kisses me on the cheek and whispers, "I love you. We'll get through this."

No words come out of my mouth before he walks away and closes the door behind him. I don't know how long I lie there sobbing until my throat is raw and my entire body aches, but at some point I realize this isn't where I should be.

Guided entirely by emotion, I walk down the hall and open Theo's bedroom door. The room smells like his cologne, that woodsy stuff I bought him. He wore it from that day on, claiming it was the only scent he ever liked.

Looking around at the walls covered in pictures, I see one of the two of us from that night at the Spring Festival this year hung over his desk. It was a selfie I had no idea he printed out later. He never mentioned it.

I reach out and touch his smiling face, remembering how he turned to kiss me right after he took this picture. My Theo.

How am I going to live without you?

The image becomes blurry through my tears, so I pull it down off the wall to press it to my heart before lying down on his bed. He can't be gone. Please, God. Don't let him be gone. Bring him back to me so he can know how much I miss him.

I stare up at the cloud that looks like a whale and wonder if things are always going to be like this. "You see the whale?" I ask Theo.

He doesn't answer for a few seconds, and when I turn to look at him, he's squinting his eyes. "I don't see a whale. That looks like a car to me."

Nudging his arm, I laugh. "It's a whale. You're crazy."

"Just because I don't see what you see? You're pretty bossy today, Ava."

I glance over and see him smiling. Theo and I have only had one fight in the entire time we've known each other, and that only lasted a week. It was when he was twelve and I was ten. Since then, we've been thick as thieves again, like my mother says.

"We aren't going to have another fight, are we? Because that's a whale," I say with a chuckle.

Theo rolls over and shakes his head as he looks at me. "We're never fighting again. I told you that. You and I are going to live here forever."

"Best friends forever," I say, happy at the sound of that.

He props his head up on his hand and looks down at me. "We should do something today. I'm tired of staring up at the clouds."

"Aren't you going out with Marley to the carnival later?"

Rolling his eyes, he blows the air out of his mouth like the thought of going out with his newest girlfriend bothers him. "Maybe. I don't know."

"Why not?"

"She's a lot. Not like you, Ava. Every time I go somewhere with her, she wants to do too much. I just want to hang out, and she's got a million things planned. I doubt I'll even get to go on a single ride if I go."

He'll go. He always does. Then he finds me and tells me how much he wishes he didn't go or how he should have just gone with me.

"I think you're going to marry her, Theo. Marley King. It sounds right to me," I tease him.

A look of utter disgust covers his face. "No way. You're the future Mrs. Theo King. She's just someone to hang with sometimes."

In the distance, one of his brothers yells his name, and I

know our time alone has ended. We'll get together tomorrow, though. We always do.

I clutch the picture of Theo and me to my chest as my sobs become uncontrollable again. There's no more tomorrow for us. He's gone, and I don't know what I'm going to do.

CHAPTER FORTY-ONE

$\mathcal{M}$atthias

THE SUN SHINING FEELS WRONG TODAY. I STAND WITH Marius, Kellen, and Ronan on my left as we watch the casket slowly descend into the hole in the earth. I made it through the wake and the funeral, but I don't think I can do this.

Except I don't have a choice. It fell to me to arrange everything since I'm the oldest, and I tried my best to make it all what Theo would want. For days, I've listened to men and women tell me how much they're going to miss him or recount a good time they had with him, and all I could think about was our last conversation. The person I was closest to all my life talked to me like I was a stranger.

Or worse, like someone he hated.

I turn my head and look down the line of my brothers

to see Ronan's head hung. Barely in his twenties and he's lost half his family already. Kellen fights back tears, while Marius is his usual somber self. Whatever he feels, he keeps inside like always.

And me? I can't bear to look in that hole and know Theo is there in that casket soon to be buried.

Unlike Ava, I can accept he's gone. What I can't accept is I never found a way to make him see how sorry I was.

The graveside service ends, and I do my job as the oldest member of the family thanking people for attending and letting them know we'll be having a get-together an hour from now. I can't let on that's the last fucking thing I want to do today. Never much for entertaining, I certainly don't feel like being the host with the most today.

But I don't have a choice.

When the crowd thins, I turn back to look at my brothers. They stand together silently staring off in the distance like they aren't sure what to do now. I know exactly how they feel.

Lost. Like they don't know how to keep living.

I tap Marius on the shoulder. "Time to go."

He nods and nudges Kellen who then does the same to Ronan. Four grown men who have no idea how to do what's expected of them.

When we lost our mother, our father was there. Even consumed with grief, he helped by at least being someone who could handle all the people who came to express their condolences. Then when we lost our father, we could take comfort in the fact that we each still had four brothers to rely on.

The loss of Theo has made us all realize how fragile that bond could be.

PEOPLE MINGLE THROUGHOUT THE HOUSE AT THE GET-together I know I must have after the funeral, even though the last thing I want to do is talk to anyone. Marius, Kellen, and Ronan chat with people, occasionally smiling as they thank them for coming to show their sympathy for our loss. A few people approach me, mainly my father's friends and associates who were here at the house for his funeral not six months ago.

The grief at Theo's death is so much more intense for me than it was for my father's passing. He wasn't old, but he'd lived a full life and accomplished what most people couldn't even dream of in a lifetime.

Theo was young. He had his whole life ahead of him. He had plans he was looking forward to. The worst part of him being taken so soon was I never got the chance to tell him just one more time how sorry I was for what I did. After our last conversation, I meant to call him again. I wanted to make sure he knew how torn up I was that I had hurt him. But I never got around to it.

And now that chance is gone. He left this world thinking I was that heartless fuck I had been that last time I saw him.

For hours, I hold it together, pretending to be the somber oldest brother who has control of his emotions for our guests. I don't. It's just a good act I put on, like always. I've got three younger brothers who are struggling with the loss of their brother and Ava upstairs in Theo's room every day, unable to do much of anything but lie in his bed and cry.

As people gather around telling stories about Theo, I see Ava's father walking across the room toward me. He looks confused as he glances around, no doubt looking for his daughter.

"Matthias, where's Ava? I didn't see her at the funeral, and I can't find her here."

I force myself to smile and shake his hand. "She's upstairs. She wasn't up to attending the funeral."

His sad expression morphs into one of concern. "I'd like to see her."

"Of course. She's..." I hesitate to admit where she is, but I don't have a choice. "She's up in Theo's room."

He nods like he understands and pats me on the shoulder as he turns to leave. "I'm sorry about everything, Matthias. Losing your father and your brother in such a short time must be hard."

I give him another forced smile but say nothing else. It's not only my father and Theo I've lost. Every day Ava stays in that room sobbing, I feel like I'm losing her too.

Before he walks away, he says, "I was wrong about you, and I'm sorry. I see that now."

I don't know what to say to that. I should hate him. He's the person who kept Ava from me. He's the reason I had to live without her for five long years.

Except I can't hate him. He's her father, and I just don't want to be angry anymore. So I nod and try to smile to let him know I forgive him.

By the time the last mourner leaves, I'm exhausted. It's been nearly a week since I got that terrible phone call from Theo's manager, and every minute after has been a struggle to keep it together for all the people who are relying on me.

I walk upstairs and see my brothers sitting in the game room like the five of us did on so many days in this house. There's no laughing or joking around today, though, as the three of them sit silently.

When I join them, they turn to look at me, almost as if I have something to say that will take all the pain away. We've lost our mother, our father, and now one of us. Each time, I was expected to keep myself from falling apart while handling everything for them.

I don't know if I can do it this time.

"Where is Ava? She wasn't at the funeral, and I didn't see her here. I can't imagine she wouldn't come for Theo," Ronan asks.

Letting out a heavy sigh, I say, "She's sleeping. The doctor has her on some heavy medication so she can rest."

The detail I don't include is where she is. Where she's been for the past week. Theo's room. At first, I wanted to bring her back to my room so I could keep an eye on her, but she wouldn't leave his room. When I talked to the doctor about it, he suggested the more important issue was to keep her calm and let her sleep as much as possible after crying nearly nonstop for days.

"Jesus, she must be devastated," Marius says in a sad voice. "She never got to talk to him again, did she?"

I shake my head and add myself to that. If only I had one more chance to talk to him.

"I can't believe we have to go through another will reading not six months after Dad's death," my brother

Kellen says sadly. "I don't give a fuck about that, to be honest. Who cares about money now?"

We all nod, and I wish more than anything else in this world that I knew what to say to make them feel better. Theo would know if he was in my place. He'd tell some story that would make everyone smile and maybe even laugh. I don't know how to do that without falling apart.

The four of us sit in silence until it's too much for me to bear and I walk down to Theo's room to check on Ava. Opening the door only a little, I poke my head in and see her curled up on his bed clutching that picture of them like she has for almost seven days now.

Even though the doctor told me to let her rest, I walk in and sit down next to her on the bed. She doesn't move, which he warned me would likely happen since he basically has her doped up so all she can do is sleep, but I softly touch her shoulder, missing her more than I thought possible.

For five years, I felt like a part of me was lost when she was gone from my life, but now I feel even worse because she's right here with me, yet I can't reach her through all her grief. On top of her grief is mine, along with all the guilt from never being able to make things right with my brother before he died. Some days, it's like I'm being crushed under the weight of all our sadness.

"Ava, I'm here. If you need anything, just let me know," I whisper against her cheek and then press a tiny kiss to her skin.

She doesn't respond, so I ask, "How was your visit with your father?"

I wait for her to say something, but she doesn't move, so I stand up to leave. "I love you."

Silence is all I hear in return.

Maybe tomorrow will be better. I hope it is.

FOURTEEN TOMORROWS GO BY BEFORE SHE COMES OUT of his bedroom to eat dinner with me one night. I'm surprised when she walks into the kitchen and sits down on the other side of the table. Over near the stove, Eleanor lets out an audible gasp.

"Ava, honey, what can I get you to eat?" she asks in a gentle voice.

Turning to look at her, Ava lets out a sigh. "Maybe a piece of bread?"

She looks down at the table and quietly says, "I thought I should get up. I might take a shower."

"That's good. Are you feeling any better?" I ask, letting my hand holding my fork hover over the plate, almost as if I'm afraid to move in fear it might upset her.

When she lifts her head to look at me, I get my answer even before she says a word. No, she's the same as she's been for three weeks since that terrible day we got the news.

"Not really. I don't know. Being hungry might be a good sign, right?" she asks, and all I can think is she's broken.

Not just sad. Broken.

"Mick has a lot of the fall flowers out. Have you seen any?" I ask as I resume eating.

Eleanor brings over a plate with bread and butter

and sets it in front of Ava. "There you go, honey. I'm so happy to see you up and around again."

Ava doesn't answer her but takes a bite of bread without putting any butter on it. After she finishes it, she looks across the table at me. "I haven't seen them, but thank you for having him cut the yellow roses for me and putting them next to the bed, Matthias."

I force a smile even as I know those roses I place in Theo's room every morning aren't from the rose bush the groundskeeper transplanted next to the house a few weeks ago but from the florist in town. Since that day, it's struggled to do anything, and he told me yesterday he's worried it's not going to make it.

Another death. I don't think I can deal with any more. I know Ava can't.

"They're your favorite, so I make sure you see them every day."

She picks at her piece of bread, eating tiny bites before finally setting the crust of that first piece down on the plate a few minutes later. I want her to stay up today. It would be a huge step toward her getting back to normal, but when she stands up to leave a few seconds later, it's all I can do to pretend I'm fine with her going back to his room.

"I think I'm getting tired again," she mumbles as she walks out of the kitchen.

Disappointed, I return to my roast beef dinner and hope maybe tomorrow will be the day she feels well enough to stay out of bed. Eleanor walks over to the table to take Ava's half-eaten plate of bread and gives me a smile.

"That was improvement, right?"

She sounds so hopeful. I wish I felt the same.

With a shrug, I sigh. "Yeah, I guess."

Eleanor pats me on the shoulder. "Maybe if you sat with her since she's up. I think it could do her a world of good."

"It couldn't hurt."

Even as I say that, I don't know if that's the case. The doctor says Ava is suffering from depression on top of grieving. He claims she's gone through the other steps, but he's worried because she appears to be stuck in this one. Every single thing he's said I should do has failed miserably, so I doubt simply sitting with her is going to do much.

By the time I finish my dinner, I'm convinced sitting with Ava won't help, but I'm going to try something new tonight. I walk up to my room and look through the shelf in my closet for my old sketchbooks. The one I want is from when I was only fourteen or fifteen. I find it on the bottom of the pile and take it down to look at. As I flip through the pages, I cringe at a few of my drawings from back then, but it isn't pictures of trees I want to show Ava.

Hopeful for the first time in weeks, I walk down the hall to my brother's room and softly knock on the door before pushing it open. Ava sits cross-legged on the bed and turns to look at me with an expression that says she's surprised to see me.

"I thought maybe you'd like some company?" I say as I close the door behind me.

Her gaze moves to the book under my arm. Pointing at it, she says, "You aren't thinking of drawing me, are you?"

With a smile, I shake my head as I sit down next to her. "No. I just wanted to show you a drawing of mine from a long time ago. I'm thinking I was fifteen, maybe, so keep that in mind."

For the first time in weeks, she gives me a tiny smile when she says, "You're always so humble about your sketches, Matthias. They're good. You should think that way about them too."

I turn the pages until I get to the one I drew of Theo in the pool one hot July day when he was thirteen or fourteen. I don't remember anything about that day, but the picture shows him smiling and laughing while he was playing with a huge beach ball with Marius.

Without a word, I set the sketchbook down in her lap and point at Theo. "I always had a hard time getting his smile just right. He was joking around with Marius and Kellen, and right before I started drawing, he bounced the beach ball off the top of Kellen's head. He got angry and jumped out of the pool, but Marius stayed in with Theo and the two of them were tossing the ball back and forth while I was sketching this."

Ava touches the paper before running her fingertips over my brother's smile. "He was always so happy. It didn't matter how bad a day you were having. If Theo was around, it got better."

"That was Theo."

She exhales a heavy sigh before handing me back my sketchbook. "Thank you for showing me this."

When she lets her hand linger on my leg, I cover it with my hand and give her finger a tiny squeeze. "I just wanted to see if I could make you smile again."

Ava turns her head to look at me and sighs. "You did. Thank you."

I stand to leave, and she says, "I like that you're growing a beard."

When I look back at her, I shrug. "I haven't felt like shaving these past few days."

"It makes you look older, more distinguished. I like it."

She lies back on the bed and closes her eyes, so I return to my room, happy I could at least do something to bring a smile back to her face. It's not huge progress, but it's something.

And I can hope it's the first step.

A WEEK LATER, AVA JOINS ME FOR DINNER FOR A second time. I'm surprised to see her showered and dressed in different clothes from the sweatpants and T-shirt she's been wearing for weeks.

"What is that you're eating?" she asks as she sits down at the table across from me.

"Ham. I was going to bring you some in a little while since I know it's your favorite. Would you like me to get you a plate?"

She nods and gives me a tiny smile. "Yes, thank you. I'm feeling particularly hungry today, and I thought I smelled ham this afternoon. My mouth has been watering ever since."

Out of the corner of my eye, I see Eleanor hurry around the other side of the kitchen preparing a plate for Ava. A minute later, she sets it down in front of her and says, "Ham with boiled baby red potatoes and butter and garlic green beans. Two of them are your favorites, so eat up, okay?"

Ava looks up at her and nods. "I will. And the garlic green beans are one of Matthias's favorites."

"That's right. If I knew you were coming down to dinner, I would have made carrots too, though."

Shaking her head, Ava looks over at me. "It's okay. I like garlic green beans too."

I watch her eat more than she has in weeks, nearly finishing all the food Eleanor put on her plate. Two slices of ham and almost all the potatoes and beans later, Ava nudges the plate away from her and stands up to leave.

"Thank you, Eleanor. That tasted great."

Before she leaves, I scramble to say something that will keep her down here, even for a few minutes more. "There's pie too. Apple pie. Your favorite."

She looks over at Eleanor and smiles. "I'm not hungry anymore, but maybe tomorrow if there's any left I'll have some. I think I'm tired now, so I'm going to go upstairs."

With each time she walks away to go to Theo's room, I feel like I'm losing more of her. More of us. She's trapped in that depression stage, and I don't know what to do to get her out of it.

I OPEN THE DOOR TO THEO'S BEDROOM AND SEE AVA in his bed, like always. My heart clenches in my chest as I stand there watching her and waiting for her to look at me.

She never does.

I feel like an intruder in this room. I don't belong here. I'm not the King brother she wants to see.

When I walk around the bed, I see her clutching that picture of the two of them to her as she sleeps. It's as if inch by inch, she's slipping away from me in front of my eyes.

Every fear of loss and abandonment I've struggled to overcome since my mother's death threatens to overwhelm me. I desperately want Ava to open her eyes and tell me she's still here. She's still mine.

But she remains silent, and my fears begin their vicious dance inside me.

I kneel next to the bed as I try to convince myself this isn't like my mother or my father or even Theo. Ava is still alive. She's right here with me. I haven't lost her completely yet.

Leaning close to her, I gently press my forehead to hers, needing to feel her against me. It's been so long since she's been in my arms. I miss her almost more than I can handle, and I don't know what to do about that because the doctor keeps talking about her depression and how it's important I don't make it worse by forcing her to move on.

I wait for her to open her eyes, but she doesn't, so I remain there in front of her, my forehead pressed to hers as I whisper the truth I live with every hour of the day. "Don't leave me to live this life alone. Please. I can't handle losing you both. Not you and Theo. Stay with me, Ava. I'll do whatever I need to if you'll stay with me."

All I get in response is silence.

I wait for what seems like hours for her to open her eyes and tell me she hasn't left me. She never does. I walk back to my room and prepare to be up all night like I am every night. I sleep in brief spurts that punctuate the hours I spend sketching because it's the only thing that brings me even the tiniest reprieve from my mourning and her sadness.

As I settle in with my sketchbook in my lap, I admit the terrible truth I can't deny. I've begun to lose hope that Ava and I will ever be happy together again.

CHAPTER FORTY-TWO

va

I LISTEN AS THE RAIN BEGINS TO TAPER OFF, THE midday storm finally ending after nearly an hour. The air smells fresh and clean like it always does after a rainstorm. I take a deep breath in and hold it in my lungs before letting it out slowly. When Theo and I were kids, he loved a good, drenching rain. He used to say everything seemed new after a storm.

For a few seconds, tears well in my eyes, but then I look out the window and see Matthias walking the grounds. He's alone, as always, and I can't help but notice his shoulders are hunched a little today. Maybe he's remembering how much his brother loved the rain today too.

I shake my head, still not able to believe we'll never see Theo again. Never hear him joke about something.

Never see him smile that crooked smile that reminded me of a pirate.

My emotions well up inside me as I think of another never we have to live with now. We'll never be able to make him understand how sorry we were for all that happened. I know it haunts Matthias that he and Theo never reconciled. I still can't accept that my best friend won't someday show up at my door wearing a big smile and ask me one more time to play our game.

No, it's too much to bear. I know it's true, but I can't handle that right now.

With one last look at Matthias, I watch him walk out of view before I lie down again. Maybe if I sleep a little I'll feel better.

I OPEN MY EYES AFTER A SHORT NAP AND SEE THE SUN shining in through the window. It's a beautiful early autumn day. Is it really that late in the year?

Two months.

That's how long it's been since that horrible moment when Matthias told me Theo was gone. Two months of crying and regrets, of feeling like I might never be happy again because my best friend was taken from me.

It hasn't been all terrible, though. The time Matthias and I sat looking at that drawing of Theo in the pool made me happy. And getting to eat dinner with him lately has been nice.

Tonight, I'm going to try to not hide away from the world in this room. I'm still mourning Theo, but for the first time today, I don't feel like my grief is smothering me.

I felt this way a few days ago, but then I talked myself out of trying to live like a normal person again because it seemed too soon. I loved Theo for all my life, so two months didn't seem like enough time to say goodbye.

But then I saw Matthias walking across the grass when I looked out the window this afternoon after that rainstorm came through, and as I lay there thinking about never seeing Theo again, it dawned on me that Matthias has had no one to help him mourn the loss of his brother in all this time. Suddenly, I felt like I could breathe again and knew I needed to try to be there for him.

So I showered and put makeup on so I could feel like a person again for the first time in months. Dressed in my navy-blue tank dress, I look in the mirror over Theo's dresser and can't believe how thin I look. That comes from not eating right for eight weeks. What I look like doesn't matter.

All that matters is I don't feel like dying today.

With one last glance around his room, I silently say my final farewell to my best friend I loved all my life. Tears fill my eyes, but tonight, I will them away. I've mourned for Theo, but now it's time to return to living.

After I set the picture of the two of us down on his bed, I turn off the light and in the darkness, I whisper, "Goodbye, Theo."

I pad down the hallway in my bare feet to Matthias's room and knock on his door. As I wait, I think that maybe he won't want to have me back with him. I've spent two months hidden away in his brother's room. It never occurred to me how much that must have hurt Matthias until this moment.

His door opens, and he looks at me with such happiness in his eyes that I know he'll take me back. He says nothing. He simply opens his arms to hug me. When I step into his embrace, it's like I can finally exhale as he wraps his arms around me and holds me tight.

"I'm sorry, Matthias. I'm sorry I wasn't there when you needed me. Can you forgive me?" I whisper against his T-shirt that smells like the lemon-scented detergent Eleanor uses for the wash.

He doesn't say a word, but when I look up at him, he smiles. "There's nothing to forgive."

Taking me by the hand, he leads me over to his bed. His sketchbook is open, and as I sit down, he turns to a new page and begins drawing me.

"Thank you for opening the door when I knocked."

He looks over at me and nods. "Always."

We sit in silence for a few minutes as he continues to sketch me sitting next to him before I say, "You've been here for me this entire time. I'm sorry I wasn't able to be there for you. He was your brother, the one you were closest to all your life."

Matthias holds up his sketch book to show me pictures he's drawn, and as he turns each page, I see they're all of Theo. Some are of him laughing and joking around like he loved to do, while some are serious. Some show him shooting pool and watching TV in the game room as he did so often when he was a kid, and others are of him driving his race car. Each one is a testament to how much Matthias loved him.

With tears in my eyes, I touch his arm. "They're beautiful. I love every single one of them."

He sets the book aside and sighs. "Everyone mourns in their own way. This is my way of saying goodbye to him."

When he returns to the sketch he began when I sat down here tonight, I don't understand. Is he saying goodbye to me?

"Why are you drawing me? I'm not going anywhere."

Matthias lifts his head and smiles. "Because you're my favorite person to draw. It combines two of my loves."

Touched by how sweet he is when I need it most, I lean over and kiss him softly on the cheek. "I love you. Thank you for waiting for me."

"Always."

"I'm so sorry I got lost, Matthias. I couldn't find my way out of my sadness." I stop and shake my head. "No, that's not exactly true. I didn't want to for a long time. I felt like it would be wrong for me to."

He lifts his head and looks at me, and in his eyes I see he's worried tonight is only temporary. "Why?"

"Because I loved Theo for all my life. He was my best friend, and the thought of never being able to make it up to him for what I did made it feel wrong to not be so sad."

Matthias nods and then lets out a heavy sigh. "You didn't do anything wrong, Ava. That blame belongs with me, and I'll have to live with it for the rest of my life. I want you to know I did get to talk to him. I wanted him to know all he had to do was come back and I knew you'd go with him. I tried, but he was so closed off. I couldn't get him to listen to me."

As he confesses that he was willing to watch me leave with his brother, I realize how much I love Matthias. Reaching out, I take his hand in mine and hold it, needing to feel him right now.

"I wouldn't have gone. Theo was right. I didn't tell him what happened between us because it meant something to me. If I had left with him, I'd have missed you. Even in the darkness of all my sadness these last couple months, I knew you were there for me. You have no idea how important that was because more than a few times, I felt myself slipping away. But then you'd come sit with me or I'd see you at dinner and I knew I had you. What I didn't think about was how you had nobody this whole time, Matthias, and I'm sorry for that."

He nods but doesn't say anything before he goes back to drawing me. After a while, out of the corner of my eye I see papers sticking out from under his pillow.

"Do you keep that picture you drew of me under your head when you sleep?" I ask, touched at such a small gesture.

But he shakes his head before glancing up at me. "No. It's right where it's always been in my sketchbook."

I reach over and pull out a small stack of papers from under his pillow. "Oh, I thought these were that sketch. What are they?"

Matthias gives me a tiny smile and returns to his drawing. "Letters."

Quickly, I stuff them back in their original place. "Oh, I'm sorry. I didn't mean to pry. I just thought..."

"You can look at them. They're letters to you."

"To me? What do you mean?"

He turns and slides them out from under the pillow before setting them in my lap. In his dark eyes, I see he wants me to read them.

"I wrote you letters these past few months. I was going to give them to you each time I wrote one, but then I decided to just keep them. They're yours, though, so you can read them if you want."

The memory of the last time he wrote to me and never having the chance to read those letters makes sadness wash over me. I don't want anything between us this time, so whatever he said, no matter how hard it is for me to read, I have to face up to what I've done to him.

"Okay," I say quietly as fear begins to creep into me.

I unfold the first piece of paper and see only a few words on it. As my gaze slowly slides over them, I can't help feeling like Matthias has suffered so much more than I ever thought.

Ava,

I wish you were there with me today when we said goodbye to Theo. I kept reaching for your hand as I stood by the gravesite with my brothers, but there was no hand to hold. I know you're grieving like I am, but I miss you.

I love you.

M.

. . .

He doesn't look at me as he focuses on drawing my hair, so I touch his leg with my hand while I try to think of what to say. How will I ever make up for leaving him alone when he needed me most?

I move to the next letter, wishing it would be easier but knowing I have to understand nothing's been easy for him these past few months. Guilt fills me, but it's more than that. It's heartbreak at how lonely he was that he felt like he had to write me letters to try to reach me.

Ava,

I stood outside Theo's bedroom door for nearly half an hour wishing I knew the right words to say to make you feel better tonight. It's been a week since the funeral, and I feel you slipping away with every minute you stay in there. I want to carry you out and back to my bed, but the doctor says it's better for you to stay there. When I finally opened the door, you were in the same spot as you were this afternoon holding that picture of the two of you.

I don't want to feel guilty, but I do because even as I mourn the loss of Theo, I can't help but be so jealous I hate him sometimes. It's wrong. I know that, but I can't help it.

God, I love you.
M.

When I look up from the letter with tears in my eyes, I see Matthias staring at me. "I hope you don't think less of me now that you read that letter. That day was particularly hard."

"You don't have to explain anything to me. Like you said, everyone mourns in their own way."

He nods and returns to drawing as I set that letter aside and move on to the next one. That letter and three more after it break my heart as I read word after word he could tell no one so he wrote them down on these sheets of notebook paper.

When I get to the last letter, I don't know if I can keep reading. This is too hard. I wanted tonight to be a fresh start for us, and these are ruining that.

I cringe at my selfishness. Matthias needed me when he wrote these letters, and I wasn't there for him. The least I can do is read them to understand the pain he was going through.

With my mind filling with trepidation at what I'll find in this last one, I unfold the sheet of paper and feel my chest contract like someone's got my heart in a vice. How could I have left him to deal with all of this pain by himself? I don't know how he found it in him to let me in tonight after all he's gone through.

Ava,

I just told you this as I watched you sleep and know you didn't hear me. It doesn't matter. I don't have any other words tonight but these.

Don't leave me to live this life alone. Please. I can't handle losing you both. Not you and Theo. Stay with me, Ava. I'll do whatever I need to if you'll stay with me.

I love you so much, but today was the hardest day of

them all because I'm afraid I've lost you for good. Come back to me. Please. I'll do whatever you want me to if you'll only come back to me.

M.

TEARS ROLL DOWN MY CHEEKS AS MY EMOTIONS GET the best of me. I never meant to hurt him like this. After all he went through, he had to watch me stay in his brother's room and believe he was losing me.

I take his hand in mine and gently squeeze it as he lifts his gaze from his sketchbook. "I'm so sorry, Matthias. You had to deal with losing your brother, and then you thought you were losing me. I didn't mean to do that to you. How can you ever forgive me?"

He smiles and pulls me to him to kiss me before wiping my tears away. "I'm just happy you're here with me tonight."

I look up into his eyes full of love for me and know I don't deserve it. "Why? I've done so many things to hurt you. I can say I didn't mean to, but that doesn't change the fact that I hurt you so much when I left and then when I was with Theo and these past two months."

"I missed you, Ava. I think this time was worse than when you left after the blizzard because you were right here in the house with me, so close but I couldn't reach you."

Pulling him to me, I softly kiss his lips and whisper against them, "I love you. Thank you for everything."

With a smile, he whispers, "Always."

"I promise I'll make it up to you, Matthias. I promise."

He returns to sketching me, and as I watch him, enthralled by how talented he truly is, he says in a low voice, "Ava, I've been seeing someone."

With only those five words, my blood runs cold. Tears instantly fill my eyes as I tell myself I deserve this. I wasn't there for him when he needed me the most, so how could I be angry he's turned to someone else? I spent the last two months mourning in his brother's room while he watched me cry over another man.

But even as I tell myself that, those five words crush me. After all the times I wasn't there for him, he finally found someone else.

I swallow hard and repeat his words back to him. "Seeing someone?"

When he lifts his head, the look in his eyes is pure confusion. Then after a few moments, he reaches out to hold my hand and smiles. "I didn't mean a woman. I meant a therapist. I'm sorry. I didn't think you'd jump to that conclusion."

"Why wouldn't I? Every time we could have been happy together, I've done something to ruin it. I left for my aunt's. I got together with Theo. Then I spent two months hiding away grieving his death. All those times you needed me, and I wasn't there for you. So if you did find someone else to care for you, how could I blame you? I'd be the one to blame, Matthias."

Bringing my hand to his lips, he kisses my knuckles and closes his eyes like that simple gesture brings him real happiness. Against my skin, he whispers, "There's never been anyone but you after those days we spent here snowbound."

My heart soars at those words. After all that's happened, he still loves me.

Lifting his head from my hand, he smiles. "This therapist has been helping me deal with all that's happened. I seem to have some issues with abandonment to work through."

And just like that, my happiness is dashed because I know I've added to those issues. "I'm so sorry, Matthias. I never meant to hurt you. I know I keep saying that, but I am sorry."

"There's nothing to be sorry for. What I'm dealing with goes back to my mother dying. Losing you didn't help, but it isn't the cause of my issues, so don't blame yourself."

"But if I hadn't left, and if I only knew..."

I stop myself because I know those recriminations are a waste of time. Still, if only things had worked out differently, we could have been happy all this time.

Matthias sets his pencil down and tenderly cradles my face. Staring into my eyes, he says, "I would go through all of it again—all the pain, all the hurt—if I knew in the end you'd be mine, Ava."

Closing my eyes, I revel in the feel of his strong hands against my cheeks. "I've always been yours, Matthias. Even when I was too foolish to realize it, I was yours."

His lips softly brush against mine in a kiss that makes my heart flutter. "And I've always been yours."

He seems to sense I need him tonight and eases me back onto the bed. Looking down into my eyes, Matthias says nothing, but I know what he's feeling because I'm feeling it too. We lost the last two months as I mourned.

Alone in his sadness, he waited for me, for this night. I want him to know and never doubt I love him with all my heart and soul.

I tug his T-shirt over his head, and he gently lifts my dress off. Both movements are slow, but it's okay. We have all the time in the world now that we're back together.

Our lovemaking is quiet and gentle because I think that's what we both need tonight. Other times desire has nearly overwhelmed us, making our time together more passionate than I've ever experienced with anyone else. This time it's something deeper we share because of all we've been through.

I cling to him as he slowly shows me how much he's missed me, and I revel in every deliberate movement his body makes. He's as beautiful to me at this moment as he was that first time we gave in to our feelings for one another all those years ago. The depth of his emotions comes through loud and clear as it always has with Matthias. He's that intense man he's always been, and all I want to show him tonight is how much I love who he is.

The man who stole my heart during those snowy December days. The man who loved me when I was with his brother. The man who patiently waited for me while I mourned Theo's death.

His kiss leaves me breathless like always, and when I come, it's as if a wall is being torn down that kept us apart. I'm his completely, and nothing could make me happier.

Matthias smiles down at me and sighs. "I missed you so much, Ava. I'm so happy you've come back to me."

I kiss him softly on the lips and whisper against them,

"I never want to be without you again. I love you, Matthias."

Wrapped in his strong arms, I rest my head on his chest and close my eyes. Many men wouldn't have waited for me to find my way back. As I settle close to his body, I smile because I know I'm so lucky to have him by my side.

After the months of darkness, I'm back where I belong.

CHAPTER FORTY-THREE

Matthias

I FIND AVA IN THE KITCHEN WITH ELEANOR AND MORE cookies than I've ever seen in my life. Trays stacked five and six high fill the countertops, the top of the stove, and the kitchen table. For a second, I look around, unsure if I should just turn around and leave.

"We're almost done and ready for the party. We've got all kinds of cookies. Want to try some?" Ava asks, and for the first time, I notice she's got flour on the tip of her nose and a smudge of chocolate on her cheek.

When she stops in front of me, I smile at how cute she looks. "Decided to wear some of the batter?"

For a moment, she stares up at me in confusion before I touch her nose and show her the flour on my fingertip. Quickly, she pulls up her apron covered in everything they've put into the cookies and wipes her face.

"I like to get into my baking. You need to try the sugar cookies. They're delicious! Everyone is going to love them."

"Any chance you can tear yourself away for a little while? I have something I want to talk to you about before our families descend on us later today."

"Sure, yeah! We're just about done."

Turning around to face Eleanor, she says, "I'll be back in a few minutes to help you get everything set up and clean this kitchen. Now that I'm looking around, it looks like a bomb went off in here."

She waves her off with a smile. "No hurry. I've got this. I'm sure you have a million things to do before everyone gets here."

Ava slips her dirty apron over her head and sets it on a pile of dish cloths that need to be washed. "I had fun today. We made some great cookies, Eleanor."

"We did! I bet everyone is going to love them. Now go take care of whatever you need to do. I'll have this all cleaned up and ready for guests in no time."

With that assurance, I gently begin guiding Ava down the hallway toward the living room. The lights on the tree glow a warm white against the silver ornaments that are traditional for the King family Christmas decorations, and a fire roars in the fireplace making the room perfect for what I have in mind.

"What are we doing? I should go change, Matthias. That apron didn't help much, so I'm covered in cookie dough and flour," she says as I take her by the hand and lead her to the couch directly looking at the fourteen-foot Christmas tree.

"You're fine. Please, sit and relax. You've been slaving away in that kitchen all day."

She does as I command and sits, but I see in her expression she's uneasy. "Okay, but it wasn't anything like work, you know. I like baking, and Eleanor makes it so much fun. Wait until you try this recipe she and I found for these lacy cookies I saw in one of her cookbooks. She's never made them before, but they're so pretty, I wanted to try. They came out so good."

"I'll have to look for them," I say, my mind on what I have planned more than on some cookies.

The two of us fall silent as I try to remember everything I rehearsed to say. Unfortunately, there's not a single word anywhere in my head at this moment. Damnit! I wanted this to be perfect.

"Matthias, is something wrong? You're still dressed in your suit, even though you quit working hours ago for the holiday."

She abruptly stops and bolts up from the sofa. "Did something happen? Is someone not coming? Who? Why?"

This plan is quickly falling apart. My hands on her shoulders, I gently sit her down again so I can do what I've been waiting to do for days.

"Everyone's coming, and if I don't get through this, they're going to be here before I get done."

As she breathes a sigh of relief, she says, "If everything's okay, what are we doing then?"

I take that as my cue from the universe it's time to start and bend down on one knee in front of her. Sliding the black velvet box out of my suit coat pocket, I set it in the palm of my hand and slowly open the lid.

"Ava, I've loved you for so long I can't remember a time when you weren't the woman I'm absolutely crazy about. You make me smile when no one else can. You make me want to be the kind of man who deserves you. I want to spend the rest of my life showing you how much I adore you. Will you marry me?"

Her eyes grow wide, and she covers her face with her hands as she begins to cry. From behind them, I hear her say, "Oh, my God! Of course I'll marry you."

I slip the three-carat round diamond engagement ring onto her finger and watch as she looks at her hand in awe. "Matthias, this is gorgeous. I've never seen a more beautiful ring in my life."

"You like it?" I ask as I study it on her hand and have to admit the jeweler was right. It's perfect for Ava.

"Like it? I love it!" she squeals before throwing her arms around me. "I love you."

I hold her to me and sigh in relief. She said yes.

"I love you. Now tomorrow when everyone's here, they'll get to see we're engaged."

Ava leans back away from me and smiles as she holds her left hand up to admire her ring. "I guess we won't have to announce it. Wait until Eden sees this. She's going to go crazy!"

Seeing the woman I love so happy fills my heart with joy. It's been a long road we've traveled together, and finally, I'll soon be able to say Ava is my wife.

"I love you, Ava. Thank you for making me the happiest man in the world."

She leans forward and kisses me softly on the lips.

"And thank you for making me the happiest woman in the world. I love you, Matthias. More than you can ever know, I love you."

Once again, the King house is full of people laughing and enjoying themselves. It's been far too long since the last time it was like this, and I'm happier than I thought possible that our families have come to spend the holidays with us. We've had far too much sadness this past year. I want this to be the start of far happier times.

As Eleanor sets the last dish on the table, everyone prepares to eat, but I want to tell all the people we love about Ava and me. Standing from my spot at the head of the formal dining table, I wave Ava down to me and take her hand in mine.

"We have something to announce. Yesterday, I asked Ava to marry me, and she said yes."

Beside me, she lifts her left hand to show off the engagement ring, and more than a few people let out audible gasps. My youngest brother chuckles and asks, "So did you leave any diamonds at the mine, or did you just decide to buy the mine for that ring, Matthias?"

Ava giggles at his teasing as I pull her close. "No, I didn't buy the mine, Ronan."

From the other end of the table, her friend Eden says, "So when is the big day?"

I turn to look at Ava because we never got to discuss that after I proposed since we spent the rest of the day and all night in bed. The two of us shrug, and she answers, "We don't know yet, but you're all invited. It wouldn't be right not to have you all there on our most important day."

Lifting my glass in the air, I make a toast. "To family."

The entire table raises their glasses and answers, "To family!"

AFTER DINNER, ANDREW, HIS WIFE, AND THEIR GIRLS leave to go to their hotel in town with Ava's father while she and Eden huddle together with Eleanor looking through wedding dress pictures on their phones. Kellen and Ronan head upstairs to shoot pool, so Marius and I relax with a drink.

"So marriage, huh? I don't know why I never thought about you getting married, but this is your second one. If you're thinking the rest of us need to catch up, you can forget it," my brother says before taking a gulp of his whiskey.

I can't help but laugh. He's still so jaded. "Nobody's suggesting that. Ronan and Kellen still have a lot of life to lead before they settle down, and I doubt you'll ever get married. You hate love too much."

Marius smiles because he knows I'm right. "Love never got me anything but misery."

Since there's no way I'm going to dissuade him from his dislike of love, I drop the conversation, happy to know I've found it with the woman of my dreams. Maybe he'll change his mind someday.

When Ava, Eden, and Eleanor move their wedding dress search into the kitchen to enjoy more of those cookies everyone loved, I sense something change with Marius. Curious, I pour him more whiskey and sit back to look out the window at the snow beginning to fall, wondering if he's planning to tell me he's actually found someone and won't remain alone forever.

Instead, he looks at me and says, "You know, I talked to Theo the week of the crash. We were making plans to get together when I went to Paris for a shoot." He stops for a long moment before he continues. "He didn't hate you, Matthias."

I try to smile, but it never really happens. "I hope you're right."

"He seemed okay. At one point, he joked that one day he was going to drop in here and act like nothing happened just to see how you guys reacted."

That makes me chuckle. "I can see him walking through the front door and giving me one of his Theo smiles and asking, 'What the hell is new, Matthias?' I like to think it would be like we always were with each other."

"I think it would have been. He missed you. I could tell."

Hearing that makes me choke up, and I look away as tears fill my eyes. "I miss him. More than I know how to handle some days, Marius."

"Ava seems okay now. I wasn't sure she would be when I was here for the funeral."

I nod, relieved we're past those terrible weeks when she wouldn't leave Theo's room. "She struggled for a long time. He was her best friend for her whole life."

"He loved her to the end, Matthias. He never said those words, but he told me if you ever hurt her, he was going to come back here and kick your ass."

If only he was still here to say that to me in person.

"I'm happy he didn't hate us after what happened."

Never one to spend too much time on serious talks, Marius rolls his eyes and says, "And this is exactly why love is nothing I ever want. It tears brothers apart and makes everyone unhappy. No thanks."

I shake my head as I lift my glass to toast his happiness at being single. "To you and your life of being single and loving it."

With a grin that reminds me so much of Theo, he lifts his glass and says, "To you and Ava and the happiness you've found."

This first holiday without our brother has been bittersweet, but knowing he didn't hate us for what happened is the best Christmas gift I could get. Well, the second best. The best would be having Theo here with all of us.

CHAPTER FORTY-FOUR

va

SIX YEARS LATER

The sound of a little boy making a mess downstairs travels up to where I sit on the edge of the bed trying to dress a very squirmy one-year-old who doesn't want to wear clothes today. Actually, it's every day lately. It must be a faze.

"Elizabeth, Mommy needs to get this dress over your head, honey. We're going to miss all the fun at the carnival if we don't hurry."

My daughter stops for a few seconds, as if to decide if she cares about our outing we've planned for today, and then sticks her arms up in the air, finally willing to cooperate. "Carnmal," she says with a smile.

"Yes, we're going to the carnival. We need to get everyone together first, though."

Now that she's actually wearing clothes, I sit her up on the bed and slip her shoes on. Oddly enough, she doesn't fight me with those at all. She must love shoes like Eden.

"Carnmal!" she screams before jutting her arms out in front of her. "Up, mama."

I do as she demands and pick her up before heading downstairs to find the rest of my family. When I reach the kitchen, I see Eleanor entertaining my four-year-old son Matty as he shovels a bowl of cereal into his mouth using what looks like a serving spoon.

When I notice, she sheepishly says, "He insisted that he needed a big spoon so he could get finished quicker. I think someone is excited about the outing today."

I wave off her concern and then turn my attention back to him to see milk and half-chewed pieces of cereal down the front of his shirt he just put on less than half an hour ago. "Matthias Joseph King! You need to get back up to your room and change your shirt. It's covered in food."

He looks up at me with innocence in his dark eyes like he can't understand why I'm upset. With a mouth full of food, he says, "Mommy, we're going to the carnival!"

"Not dressed like that. Now get back upstairs and change your shirt, or we won't go anywhere. I'll have your father take your brother, and that will be that for you."

The threat of his older brother getting something he won't is enough to make him take off like a shot out of the kitchen, and a few seconds later, I hear him running up the stairs to do as I said. Eleanor smiles at me as she begins to clean up where Matty had been sitting, wiping the table and the floor underneath of milk and cereal.

"He reminds me so much of Theo when he was that age. You know that?" she says as she walks over to the closet to get the mop.

I nod, remembering how he always made a mess when he ate when we were very young. "It's odd. He's named after his father, but he's nothing like him."

"Second child syndrome," she says definitively. "Always in such a hurry to prove themselves. That's why your threat of his brother going today and not him worked."

I'm not sure if this is a real syndrome or just something Eleanor has decided is what my middle child has, but now that I think of it, his uncle always had a way of having to compete about him. My son is like him in other ways too, strangely enough. Always wearing a smile, Matty loves to play jokes on people. And if he's awake, he's more than likely laughing.

So much like his uncle.

Matty reappears before us wearing a clean shirt and a huge smile. "Ready for the carnival!"

He takes my hand to pull me toward the door, so I say to Eleanor, "I guess I'm leaving now."

"Have a good time!"

"Mommy, come on," Matty whines. "We have to go, or we'll miss the carnival."

In my arms, my daughter offers her opinion too. "Carnmal!"

"We need to make one stop before we can go. Who can get to the art house first?" I ask, a challenge to my son to race me down to the carriage house.

He takes off out the kitchen door with me following behind carrying his sister, running full speed toward my old house that's now my husband's art studio. Once I formally moved into the main house with Matthias, the house sat empty since he never wanted to hire an estate manager like his father had. One day, he walked down to the carriage house and started sketching. A week later, he announced that it would be the art house from then on.

Now whenever work gets too much for him or he can carve out some time for himself, he walks down there and enjoys his art. He's never been happier since he finally has a dedicated place to draw, and it warms my heart to know he spends time in the home I grew up in.

Since my legs are much longer than a four-year-old boy's, I quickly catch up to Matty on the lawn. Giggling the entire way, he squeals, "I'm going to get there first!"

His sister bounces in my hold, as excited as her brother to reach the art house. Neither of them is ever allowed there alone, so whenever we visit, it's a real treat.

Matty reaches the front steps of the carriage house first and jumps for joy at being the winner of our little race. "I won again! You need to be faster, Mommy!"

I smile and nod, happy to let him win every race we have. "You're so fast. I bet you're going to be a runner when you grow up."

He beams happiness at that comment since I've told him many times about how I used to play soccer. "Just like you, right?"

"Just like me," I say before bending down to kiss his flushed cheek.

"Now what are the rules for the art house, honey?" I

ask, knowing that if I don't remind him not to run around like a madman that as soon as we walk through the front door, he's going to do his human tornado act and tear up the place. I love my son, but he's got enough concentrated enthusiasm to power an entire city.

Staring up at me with sincerity, he says, "No running. No jumping. Be calm. If Daddy is working, no yelling."

I smile at his ability to remember all the rules, even if he doesn't always follow them. "Actually, no yelling is good no matter if Daddy is drawing or not. Remember to use your indoor voice, right?"

Like they taught him at preschool, he puts his finger to his lips and whispers, "Use my indoor voice."

"Very good. Let me see if your father's ready before we walk in, okay?"

He nods, and I open the front door of the carriage house a tiny crack before saying, "Matthias, is it okay if we all come in?"

From inside, he yells back, "Come on in! We're almost finished."

I push the door open, and Matty runs inside, completely forgetting everything he just promised me he'd remember. Seated on a stool in front of the fireplace, his brother grins when we join them.

"Daddy's doing my picture!"

That makes his brother pout and ask, "When is he going to do my picture? Daddy, I want mine done."

Matthias smiles and takes the pencil from between his teeth. "I'm almost finished. Just putting the final touches on it. Theo's been a very good boy for me this whole time."

He leans down to kiss me and the baby before

whispering, "As opposed to his brother, who is never a good boy when we try to do this with him."

"Shhhh. You'll hurt his feelings."

Our five-year-old son who's named after his uncle Theo is nothing like him and everything like Matthias. Far calmer than Matty, he's always been easier to handle. I guess our blessing was to have an angelic first child. I've been told each mother gets one, and Theo Maximilian King is mine.

"Isn't it amazing how different they are?" I ask Matthias as Matty runs out the front door and his brother waits for us.

"I think Theo just hides his hellion side better." As he puts his pencils away, he says, "Well, I guess that's it for art time today, unless you're interested in sitting for me this morning."

I shake my head to that suggestion. "Oh, no. I'm not feeling up to modeling for you right now. Maybe next week. Anyway, today is carnival day."

"Carnmal!" our daughter squeals.

With a smile, she reaches her arms out for her father to take her as he says, "Someone's learned a new word, I see."

"She's very excited about it. I think that's the only reason she let me dress her."

As we walk toward the front door, Matthias asks, "Are you worried our daughter is going to be a nudist?"

I shake my head and chuckle. "Not really. I think I might have gone through a stage like that when I was around her age."

Theo runs out of the house ahead of us, and I hear the boys screaming as they race up to the main house.

When we reach the porch, I see them heading around the back of the house.

Matthias winces like he's in pain and shakes his head as he hands me the baby once more. "I think I hear the boys playing with the hose again, so I'll be right back after I rescue the groundskeeper."

As I watch him sprint off to stop our sons from drenching poor Mick for the third time this week, I press a kiss onto our daughter's cheek and whisper against her soft skin, "Boys. I'll never understand them as long as I live."

She smiles like she understands, and the two of us slowly walk back toward the house to all pile into the car. We have a carnival to enjoy today, and nobody—not a soul from King Industries and not a single person from the hospital where I work—is going to spoil our time.

I never dreamed our life together would be like this, but we made it. After all we went through, Matthias and I found our happily ever after.

ABOUT THE AUTHOR

K.M. Scott writes contemporary romance stories of sexy, intense, and unforgettable love. A New York Times and USA Today bestselling author, she's been in love with romance since reading her first romance novel in junior high (she was a very curious girl!). Under her Gabrielle Bisset name, she writes paranormal and historical romance. She lives in Pennsylvania with a herd of animals and when she's not writing can be found reading or feeding her TV addiction.

Be sure to visit K.M.'s Facebook page at **https://www.-facebook.com/kmscottauthor** for all the latest on her books, along with giveaways and other goodies! And to hear all the news on K.M. Scott books first, sign up for her newsletter today and be sure to visit her website at **http://www.kmscottbooks.com**

BOOKS BY K.M. SCOTT

HEART OF STONE SERIES

Crash Into Me (Heart of Stone #1)

Fall Into Me (Heart of Stone #2)

Give In To Me (Heart of Stone #3)

Heart of Stone Volume One

Ever After (Heart of Stone #4)

A Heart of Stone Christmas (Heart of Stone #5)

Return To Me (Heart of Stone #6)

Forever With Me (Heart of Stone #7)

Heart of Stone Volume Two

Hard As Stone (Heart of Stone #8)

Set In Stone (Heart of Stone #9)

Silent As A Stone (Heart of Stone #10)

Heart of Stone Volume Three

All of Me (Heart of Stone #11)

CLUB X SERIES

Temptation (Club X #1)

Surrender (Club X #2)

Possession (Club X #3)

Satisfaction (Club X #4)

Acceptance (Club X #5)

Complete Club X Series Box Set

NeXt SERIES

Notorious (NeXt #1)

Infamous (NeXt #2)

Ravenous (NeXt #3)

Ambitious (NeXt #4)

Flirtatious (NeXt #5)

Mysterious (NeXt #6)

Sensuous (NeXt #7)

Desirous (NeXt #8)

CORRUPTED LOVE TRILOGY

If I Dream (Corrupted Love #1)

If You Fight (Corrupted Love #2)

If We Fall (Corrupted Love #3)

Corrupted Love Trilogy Box Set

ADDICTED TO YOU SERIES

Crave (Addicted To You #1)

Adore (Addicted To You #2)

Shatter (Addicted To You #3)

Claim (Addicted To You #4)

Addicted To You Series Box Set

PROJECT ARTEMIS SERIES

In The Darkness (Project Artemis #1)

After The Storm (Project Artemis #2)

Behind The Scenes (Project Artemis #3)

Project Artemis Box Set

FINDING THE ONE SERIES

Hard Work (Finding The One #1)

Big Love (Finding The One #2)

DIRTY BOSS SERIES

Sweet Things (Dirty Boss #1)

Private Secretary (Dirty Boss #2)

Play Date (Dirty Boss #3)

Dirty Boss Volume One

K.M.'S BOOKS ARE IN AUDIOBOOK TOO! AND
LOOK FOR THEM IN FRENCH AND GERMAN ALSO!

BOOKS BY K.M. SCOTT WRITING AS GABRIELLE BISSET

SONS OF NAVARUS SERIES

Vampire Dreams Revamped (A Sons of Navarus Prequel)

Blood Avenged (Sons of Navarus #1)

Blood Betrayed (Sons of Navarus #2)

Longing (A Sons of Navarus Short Story)

Blood Spirit (Sons of Navarus #3)

The Deepest Cut (A Sons of Navarus Short Story)

Blood Prophecy (Sons of Navarus #4)

Blood Craving (Sons of Navarus #5)

Blood Eclipse (Sons of Navarus #6)

Blood Ascendant (Sons of Navarus #7)

The Sons of Navarus Box Set #1

The Sons of Navarus Box Set #2

DESTINED ONES DUET

Stolen Destiny (Destined Ones Duet #1)

Destiny Redeemed (Destined Ones Duet #2)

VICTORIAN EROTIC ROMANCES

Love's Master

Masquerade

The Victorian Erotic Romance Trilogy